fire

Also by
Molly McAdams

The Brewed Series

Fix

Whiskey

Glow

The Rebel Series

Lyric

Lock

Limit

The Redemption Series

Blackbird

Firefly

Nightshade

The Thatch Series

Letting Go

To The Stars

Show Me How

The Sharing You Series

Capturing Peace (novella)

Sharing You

The Forgiving Lies Series

fire

Molly McAdams

New York Times Bestselling Author

Molly McAdams
www.mollysmcadams.com
Cover Design by RBA Designs
Photo by © Samantha Weaver Photography
Illustrations by © Oleksandr Babich
Editing by Unicorn Editing

Print ISBN: 9781950048977
eBook ISBN: 9781950048960

For the Coles.
Your Plantation House is magical, and we are so blessed to have been married there.

prologue

BEAU
TWO WEEKS AGO

I leaned forward and bit at Wyatt's afternoon snack, pretending like I was gonna snatch it out of his hand mid-air.

"Dad!" he called out again through his laughter and playfully pushed at my face. "That's mine."

"Mine," I argued and pointed to the rest of his snack on the plate in front of him. "Says my name right there."

Quinn giggled softly from my other side as another belly laugh left my oldest son.

"It doesn't say nothin'," he drawled.

"Anything," I corrected gently. "Doesn't say *anything*."

Wyatt just smiled like the little cheeser he was and took a big bite.

I ruffled his hair as I stood from the large, round table in the kitchen and leaned down to kiss the top of Quinn's head before heading over to where Savannah was standing at one of the islands. Her tiny body moving to the soft music filling the kitchen. A subtle smile on her face as she rolled out dough for whatever she planned on baking next, even though there was a cake cooling on the other island.

"Wife," I murmured as I brought her into my arms and dipped down to capture her mouth—all sugar with hints of lemon.

"Missed you," she whispered when I pulled away, her golden eyes bright as they searched my face. "How was work?"

"Work," I responded with my typical answer.

I liked my job. I really did.

Coaching the sports teams at the high school was good for me, and it was financially necessary for my family. With Amber as small as it was, we barely had enough people coming through, staying at our bed and breakfast, to cover the bills. But my other job meant leaving Savannah to run Blossom alone for half the day. Not being there to help her? That shit weighed heavily on me.

So, it didn't matter how much I enjoyed it. It was only, ever, *just* work.

"How was it here?" I asked as my attention shifted to where our baby, Levi, was sleeping on an activity blanket.

"Pretty quiet actu—"

My head snapped to the side when loud banging sounded at the front door. A quick glance at Savannah's furrowed brow had me releasing her and heading that way, making another sweep around the kitchen to make sure my kids were where I'd left them as I did.

If we were expecting a new guest, Savannah would've told me.

If one had called last minute, she wouldn't have looked surprised.

If it were Sawyer? Guy would've walked in without knocking.

And something about the knock set me on edge—like it'd been filled with anger. Anger that called out to me because it filled me too.

My steps quickened when I heard the front door open. That familiar, red haze slowly drifting in until I rounded the corner from the kitchen into the entryway and felt like I ran into a brick-fucking-wall.

Because halfway through the entryway was Hunter.

My brother.

A man I hadn't seen in nearly ten years because of too many sins to list.

"The fuck—" The shock at seeing him standing there abruptly faded when I realized who was beside him.

Madison Black.

My stare darted back to Hunter, finally noticing the wrath and betrayal pouring from him as he stared me down, and my stomach dropped. Straight to the fucking floor.

Because there was only one reason for Hunter to look at me the way he was, and it had everything to do with the woman beside him. With the woman beside him and *me*.

And my wife was a room away.

Jesus Christ, Savannah . . .

The outright fear for what they were about to do—what they were about to say—mixed with my hatred for Madison. For everything she'd done. Everything she'd gotten me to agree to, only to go back on it all. To try and uproot my life now.

But I couldn't let her.

I couldn't let *this* happen.

A harsh breath left Hunter as if my reaction had confirmed everything. "Yeah."

I hadn't realized he'd moved until my head snapped back from the force of his hit. Before I had a chance to react, he was there. Grabbing the front of my shirt and pulling me closer as his fist connected with my jaw.

Then all I saw was red. All I felt was that rage burning through my veins.

And for the first time in my life, I took it.

Welcomed that sickening darkness and let it use me.

But everything still happened the way it always had. Nothing more than bits and pieces made up into a blur. That thick haze messing with my mind as I unleashed all of my fear and anger on him.

Ramming him into the far wall across the room.

Punching him once . . . twice.

His head cracking against the wall.

Hunter was fast. I'd forgotten that. But once I started going, he couldn't stop me. Almost nothing could.

Not even my own horror when the next thing I knew, I had my hands on a *woman*. Madison was pinned against the wall, and I was holding her so damn tight. Fucking shaking as I kept her arm twisted between us and gripped her jaw.

But all I could think in that moment was this was on *her*. She'd put everything at risk the moment she'd thrown away our agreement and set foot in my town. And now, she was actively threatening my marriage. "What'd you do, Madison?" I demanded through clenched teeth. "The fuck did—"

A pained breath burst from me when I landed on the floor with Hunter on top of me. Swinging and connecting with my cheek as he seethed, "That's for fucking my girl."

No!

Fear and rage exploded from me as he struck again. Yelling more accusations as I used Hunter's weight to throw him onto the floor—twisting and shoving my foot into his chest. Sending him back a couple feet as I scrambled to my knees and swung as he did the same. Connecting with his nose and feeling the crunch beneath my knuckles. Knowing it wasn't enough.

It never would be.

That rage and that haze blinding me to everything except the threat in front of me.

"Beau."

That voice . . . that *girl* . . . stopped everything.

My name couldn't have been louder than a breath, but it stripped me. Cooled that fire and filled me with the deepest shame in an instant.

My world, my world, my world.

Oh God.

Fear slipped back into my veins like poison as I stared at the floor I knelt on. Unable to meet her eyes for the first time in my life because I knew—I *knew* she'd heard.

It was in the way she'd said my name.

In the betrayal I could feel crawling toward me, reaching out and gripping me.

In the shock hanging in the air, making the silence we were surrounded in seem so damn loud.

Silence . . . it was silent.

Shit.

"Where are the kids?" I asked through the knot in my throat.

"What'd you say?" Savannah asked, the cold demand clearly not meant for me.

Still, I repeated, "Savannah, where are the kids?"

Her voice hitched around the words as she ignored my plea. "Hunter, what did you say?"

"Savannah." Her name wrenched from me as I sat back to finally look at her. The world trembled beneath me seeing the pain she was trying so hard to conceal. "Where are my kids?"

"I am not talking to you," she shouted, whirling on me. Betrayal and accusation bleeding from her. "You know—you *promised*. And . . ." Her head moved in rough shakes as she looked away, her eyes darting between the three of us. "Someone tell me what Hunter said and *why*."

Piercing silence once again filled the entryway as she waited. As my life with her flashed before my eyes. As I struggled to hold onto it when I knew I couldn't.

The ice-cold fear gripping my heart told me as much.

Hunter stood, wiping at the blood on his face as he said, "It's their story."

Savannah's eyes met mine again. Anguish churning in their depths and a plea for me to tell her this was all a mistake. That she'd heard wrong.

"Savannah—"

"Madison," I said in warning, stopping whatever she'd been about to say.

She'd done enough. She'd said more than enough.

Savannah blinked quickly when her eyes glazed over with tears, refusing to let them fall. Her voice soft and cutting straight to my heart when she said, "I know what I think I heard, and I *need* to be wrong. Do not make me ask you, Beau."

My lungs ached and begged for air as I watched her.

Studied her.

Took her in like I had every day for most of my life and prayed it wouldn't be the last.

"I—" I lifted one of my arms, gesturing toward Madison before my hand fell roughly to my chest. To the excruciating pain there.

How do you tell your wife that you betrayed her, even unknowingly? How do you tell the woman you would rip out your heart for that you've hurt her in unforgivable ways? How do you destroy her?

"Did you have sex with Madison, yes or no?" she asked when I didn't go on, holding my stare and trying to keep her voice firm.

"Savannah, you don't—"

"Yes or no?" she demanded, the force of her anger slamming into me.

My hand gripped at my chest in a vain attempt to relieve the pain there as my gaze drifted toward Madison. Hatred and rage building in the split second I met her stare before I met Savannah's eyes again.

The pain there. The knowing. The plea for this not to be true . . .

I would've died to take it all away.

"Beau," she whispered. *Begged*.

"Yes." The admission came out on a breath, but I hurried to add, "But it wasn't—"

"Get out."

No.

I stumbled as I pushed to standing, feeling like those two words had me bleeding out on the floor. "It wasn't what you think." She needed to know what happened. That I'd never knowingly betray her.

Savannah slashed a hand through the air as she took steps back that I matched. "Get out!"

"Savannah, you have to let me explain."

"Get out of my fucking house," she screamed as the tears finally fell, fast and heavy. The gut-wrenching combination bringing me to a halt.

She stared at me with a mixture of unfamiliarity and hatred, the look enough to bring me to my knees again if I'd been able to move.

I'd done that . . . I'd put that look on her face. Put that pain in her eyes.

Madison had done that.

Think I'd known ever since I came home to find Madison sitting in our kitchen a few weeks ago that this moment was coming. There'd been no stopping it, but I would've given the world to.

I would give literally anything to take Savannah's pain away.

Her stare dragged away from me, her expression twisting with betrayal as she locked on Madison and watched her leave.

"Sava—"

"Get out of my sight," she bit out, leveling me with an ice-cold glare.

I wavered for a moment before staggering back a step. Only finding the strength to move because it was Savannah and it was what she needed. And I would always do whatever she needed.

I cut a warning look at Hunter as I turned. At his hardened expression and the smeared blood. The red mark on his jaw and the bruising already beginning under his eyes.

The dark part inside me roared to life, craving more. Aching to sink my fist into his face again. Aching to make him—*anyone*—feel a fraction of the pain slowly tearing me apart as I forced myself out of my house and away from my family. To make someone pay for what—

Fucking Madison.

The reaction to seeing her was instant. The red haze. The way my body began trembling from the rage pounding through my veins.

I was across the porch and clearing the last step less than a second after her. Gripping her arm and yanking her back. Watching as the surprise and pain that flashed across her face quickly gave way to fear.

"Beau—"

"What'd you do?" I demanded, voice twisting with my own pain and hatred.

Hatred for her.

Me.

What we'd done.

Her lips parted but nothing left them. Her head shook faintly, quickly, as she stared up at me.

But I wanted to hear her say it. I wanted her to acknowledge what she'd done—what she'd ruined. Everything she'd demanded of me so long ago only to carelessly toss it away at the cost of my life and Savannah's happiness.

"You came back to town and everything started falling apart," I ground out. "If you just ripped my kids away from me? My *wife*?"

My heart dropped as the words I'd just said had a cold realization settling in.

"Beau," Hunter said as he stepped up beside us, tone laced with warning. Fingers curling around my wrist and digging into the pressure point there in an attempt to get me to release Madison.

I tightened instinctively.

Not to hold on to Madison. I didn't give a shit about her.

But because of that realization—that fear gripping my spine and stealing my breath. Because what just happened might not end in something as difficult as having to fight for Savannah's heart and her trust again. It was possible I'd just lost her in a forever kind of way.

And losing Savannah?

That wasn't something I'd survive. Ever.

"Get your fucking hand off her." Hunter's words were pure threat and shook me out of my internal torment.

I blinked.

Focused on the girl in front of me.

Her fear and sorrow. Her lies.

Why couldn't you have stayed away, Madison?

"Go back to wherever the hell you were before you can do any more damage." I released my hold on her and shrugged out of Hunter's grasp as I turned and headed for my truck on the far side of the house.

With each step, my body begged me to go inside. To do whatever it took until Savannah knew the truth. To beg for forgiveness.

With each weak, pained beat of my heart, my blood seemed to call out to her.

My world, my world, my world.

I'm sorry. I'm sorry.

I'm so fucking sorry.

One

BEAU

I stared at the house I'd grown up in as rain fell relentlessly around me. Wondering how long it had been since I'd stood in front of it.

Almost exactly ten years? Would've been longer if the people inside hadn't destroyed my life. Taken everything I loved and ripped it away from me without a goddamn care in the world. Just to go on with their lives as if nothing had happened, if all the cars parked in front of the house were any indication.

I made my way across the rest of the drive and up the porch steps. My breaths coming a little rougher with each step. My fingers curling into fists and relaxing over and over again. My blood racing and heart pumping this unforgiving beat the closer I came to the door . . . just as it opened.

Leaving only the glass storm door between Hunter and me.

But not just Hunter.

He was holding the hand of Madison's little girl and

pushing her behind him. *Hiding* her. And at his other side was Madison.

Fucking *Madison*. The reason behind all my anguish.

Looking like a little family when they'd stolen mine.

I reached for the storm door, and Madison reacted. Staggering back and grabbing the girl from Hunter before rushing her away—in the direction of my other brothers and their girlfriends.

"Beau."

"Fifteen days," I said in a cold, grave tone as my attention dragged back to Hunter. "I haven't seen my wife or my kids in fifteen days because of you."

"I'm sorry," he said, trying to be all placating and shit. "I'm sorry. But whatever you're about to do isn't gonna change that. You know that better than anyone."

"Fix it," I ground out.

"Beau—"

"Fucking *fix it*," I snapped just as Madison returned alone. Slipping up to Hunter's side and glaring at me like she would refuse to back down even though she was trembling. Even though Hunter was trying to push her back the same way he'd done to her daughter.

But she stood her ground and grabbed Hunter's arm. Whether to help keep her stance or silently tell him she wasn't leaving, I wasn't sure.

It didn't matter.

Just seeing them together had an all-too-familiar red haze threatening to slip over my vision as everything I'd just lost mixed with her words from so long ago.

"You don't understand what you'll be doing to all of us!" Madison *had cried out. "Risking your relationship by not telling Savannah? Beau, all of our relationships are going to be ruined when you do."*

"Ruin everyone?" I ground out, throwing her words back at her as my head moved in rough shakes. "Just Savannah. Just me."

"Beau, I'm sorry," Madison whispered, trying to sound sincere when everything falling from her lips sounded like bullshit. When nothing she said now would make a difference.

My wife had kicked me out. She'd kept my kids from me.

All because of the woman in front of me. Because she liked to make demands and then go back on them when it was convenient for her.

"It wasn't just y'all," Hunter said quickly, seeming to sense where my thoughts were—my growing anger—but that's when I saw it.

Madison's hand where it was still clinging to Hunter. Her finger. The band covered in diamonds.

I clenched my teeth. Sucked in shallow breaths as my blood pumped faster and faster. My stare flashed to Hunter when I asked, "Sure about that?"

Our younger brothers, Sawyer and Cayson, came up on either side of them then. Looking like they were prepared to stand up for Hunter. Stand united against *me*.

The possibilities of why they would need to made my heart beat faster when I was struggling to calm it. The demons I'd battled lately of that exact scene—my brothers standing against me—tore through me. Had that fear building and shifting into barely restrained rage in an instant when I was already so weighed down by it.

My jaw ached from the pressure I was putting on it as I willed that red haze back.

As I fought against the anger and the darkness that was so quick to fill my veins.

But then Sawyer leaned against the open door where he stood next to Madison and said, "Beau, you have to take fault in this."

And I lost it.

That frail grasp on my control.

On reason.

I don't remember moving. Only knew that I was trying to get to Sawyer as Hunter held me back. All while I shouted, "I've tried!"

I *had* tried. I'd been ready to confess everything so damn long ago, and I'd kept my mouth shut for Madison. *Because* of her. Then she'd come back into all our lives about a month ago and destroyed everything exactly the way she'd begged me not to over a dozen years ago.

All of this came down to Madison.

I gripped one of Hunter's arms where he struggled to keep me back and turned my glare on him. "Why the fuck do you think Madison left? Because I tried to come clean."

Hunter's tone was that same, soft calm when he said, "I already know."

"I mean *now*," Sawyer sighed and gave me a look like he was already over the confrontation. "This. What y'all did is only part of it for Savannah."

A shock. Right to my fucking heart.

That's what hearing her name did to me.

"What you're doing now?" Sawyer continued. "That's—"

"You talked to her?" I asked, chest heaving as I thought of anyone talking to my wife. Of anyone seeing her.

My world.

The answer to every fucked-up part of me.

As if finally realizing what this was doing to me, Sawyer

shifted. Straightened. The annoyance slipped away from his expression as he gave a slight dip of a nod. "Yeah. We all have," he said. "We'll be there for her the same as we'll be here for you. But, man, you're not hearing me. This, what you're doing right now, is a huge part of it for her. Your anger. Your fighting . . ."

When he didn't continue, Cayson spoke up from Hunter's other side. "That's why you aren't seeing them."

The rage and need for revenge fled from me on a jagged breath and were replaced with the deepest kind of pain.

The kind that ripped through you. Slow and brutal.

Both Sawyer and Cayson had spoken softly. Gently. As if trying to soften a critical blow. But there's no lessening the knowledge that you're being kept from your family because of *you*. Because of something so deep inside you that is nearly impossible to control.

Something dark and sickening and toxic.

I staggered away from Hunter, my head moving in slow shakes as my life with Savannah and our kids flashed through my mind.

I had a problem with my anger—had since I was a kid. But Savannah had always been my calm. The ice to my fire.

One look at her. One touch. Even just hearing her voice, and my rage cooled. Disappeared.

But that constant, simmering rage was a lot to deal with. I knew that. And she'd told me long ago that if I got in one more fight, she was done.

I'd never been more afraid of anything than losing her. Then, when we had our kids, losing them as well.

I'd never fought as hard against anything as I had to keep myself in check, every day, until Hunter and Madison threatened to hurt my marriage.

"Savannah—my kids—I've never hurt them," I said through the grief choking me.

"I know. She knows you wouldn't," Hunter said just as softly as our other brothers had spoken. The smallest spark of hope flared in my chest until he added, "But you got to a point . . ."

I forced my stare to him. To where he seemed to waver with what he was about to tell me.

And it fucking terrified me.

"Beau," Hunter began hesitantly, "she's afraid she can't stop you anymore."

The air rushed from my lungs on a pained breath as his words stripped me bare. Confirmed what I'd been agonizing over these past months—those demons I'd been battling. The reason my brothers would all take up against me. The same reason I'd stayed away when they'd begun reconciling.

Because I didn't want to see the look in their eyes when they realized I was like our dad—the worry that I would become him someday. A man who physically and verbally abused his own kid for years.

Worse than all that . . . that my own wife would realize I wasn't any better than him. That she was truly afraid of me.

My knees hit the wooden porch.

My fingers dug into my chest. Trying to tear at it. To relieve the fierce pain. To take my heart and offer it up to Savannah because I didn't want it if I didn't have her.

I had *nothing* if I didn't have her or our kids.

It'd been one thing when I'd thought she'd been keeping them from me because of Hunter and Madison. Because of the betrayal and lies. I would've gone to the ends of the earth to fix that. To make it right.

But taking our kids to protect them *from* me?

Saying she knew I wouldn't hurt them only to say she was afraid she couldn't stop me?

There was no fixing that.

Savannah had known me most of my life. She knew the way I worked better than anyone. Better than *me*. And she'd been witness to the past ten years of keeping that anger leashed.

If she was scared, she had every reason to be.

And I'd put that fear there.

"Why are you sad?"

"*Avalee.*"

I forced my head up to see Madison holding her daughter to her. Protecting her. Stopping her from coming closer to me.

"Avalee, go back to the kitchen," Madison continued, voice a hushed plea.

But her daughter just tilted her head as she studied me. "I saw you that one time when I was with my friends, Quinn and Wyatt, and you were mad. But right now, you're sad. Like, *so*, so sad. *This* sad," she said, spreading her arms wide.

My heart wrenched at the names of two of my children, the shock of the pain stealing my breath.

"I'm sorry," Madison whispered as she stepped backward with her daughter in tow.

"Beau," Hunter began after they'd left, voice uncertain, but I spoke over him.

"Am I Dad?" I met each of my brother's blank stares when there wasn't a response, my chest pitching with my uneven breaths the rougher they came. "Am I Dad?" I demanded harshly.

Hunter's stare flashed Cayson's way for a moment before

meeting me again. "Come inside, man. Dry off. We'll talk." He reached for my shoulder, and I jerked back.

Staggered to standing and continued backward as he followed.

"Beau—"

"*Answer me*," I shouted as I reached the lip of the top step.

"Let's go inside and talk," he said calmly as he neared me.

One of my hands shot out to shove him back, but he grabbed my forearm and twisted it to the side before I could touch him. In the next second, I had the collar of his shirt clenched tight in my other hand and was pulling him closer.

My jaw aching in protest as I seethed, "Be a fucking man and answer me."

His nostrils flared as he watched me slowly give over to that haze of anger. "You want a real answer? Then you need to talk to all of us," he ground out. "Sawyer's been there nearly every day—he sees you with your kids. Cayson lived through the bullshit with Dad—he's the only one who saw that side of him. I was your best friend before you destroyed my life." His grip on my arm tightened as I struggled to escape the anger surrounding me. "But it's been ten years since we've seen each other, Beau. I can't answer that."

"You can. You won't." I shoved him back and raked my trembling hands through my hair as that pain continued to tear through me like a dull, jagged blade.

I turned. Moving down the porch steps instinctively as Hunter called out my name.

His voice getting closer and closer as I walked through the rain even though my feet were moving faster as I reached the cluster of cars and trucks.

"Beau, *stop*," he shouted. Grabbing my arm and jerking me to a stop.

I had a hand around Hunter's throat and had him slammed up against the side of a truck in the next second.

My entire body trembling with the rage that always stayed just beneath the surface. Ready to explode. Racing through my veins and consuming me.

His brows were drawn close and his eyes were narrowed. One of his hands was on my chest to keep me back, the other was wrapped around my rain-soaked wrist and was squeezing in an attempt to make me loosen my hold on him.

I gripped tighter.

"You got what you wanted," I seethed. "You got your life back at the cost of mine."

"Beau, that isn't—" His jaw flexed when I shoved him harder against the window.

"We're done," I said slowly, making sure he heard me. "Forever. Understood?"

"Yeah."

I pushed away from him and stalked across the gravel driveway, never stopping even as I passed my truck. Fighting to see through the red haze and pouring rain. Struggling to breathe as the agony and fear and self-hatred built so high, it felt like I was suffocating.

By the time I stepped onto the main road just off the property, I was running.

Running from my demons.

Running from the nightmare I was living in.

Trying to outrun the man I'd become—the man who had destroyed everything good and pure in my life—knowing I never could.

Two

BEAU
NINE YEARS OLD

"I'm gonna kill you!"

Cayson took off, letting the bucket he'd used to dump mud over my head and down my back drop behind him.

Jerk was fast.

But when I was like this? When that gross feeling began in my chest and went all the way to my fingers and toes, making it so I was like someone else? There was no getting away from me.

But I kinda wished he *could*.

Because I didn't like it. I didn't like feeling like I couldn't stop. Like there was something wrong with me or the way it always felt like I was gonna be sick once it was finally over.

Hated everything about it.

About me.

Hearing my parents when they thought they were alone. My momma crying, saying she didn't know what to do with me anymore. That I was getting worse.

Calling me things like *uncontrollable* and *violent*. Saying I was *hopeless*.

I wanted to be better. Show them I wasn't those things.

I tried. I really did.

But I couldn't stop it.

Cayson cried out when I caught up to him and tackled him to the ground. Called out for help when I rolled him over and sank my fist into his stomach.

"Get off me!" he yelled as he tried to fight back.

But it never mattered if he fought back—if anyone did. It couldn't slow me down.

I saw when he started crying. I heard his grunts and shouts with each hit. And it made me fight harder. Faster.

I yelled out when I was ripped away from him and slammed onto my back. My thrashing arms and legs pinned down. My dad's face coming into view.

Talking and talking.

Saying things I couldn't hear because I needed to move. I needed to fight. And he was stopping me.

I wrestled against my dad's hold. My fingers clenched tight into fists as I tried to move him off me, a frustrated cry bursting free when I barely lifted my arms off the ground.

"Why are you so angry?"

I flinched and looked up and to the side. My chest shaking with deep, deep breaths as I searched for the voice that broke through everything. For the girl who'd washed away the anger and that sick feeling as soon as she'd spoken, in a way nothing ever had.

Staring down at me, eyebrows pinched together. Looking at me like she was worried for me instead of afraid of me.

"I'm sorry," my dad was saying, sounding all kinds of embarrassed. "You probably shouldn't be here."

No.

"Who're you?" I asked before my dad could send her away.

"Savannah, honey," someone called out from farther away.

The girl looked behind her before skipping off in that direction, and I tried to go after her. Stop her. But I couldn't move because my dad was still holding me in place.

"She can't go. Dad, she can't—who is she?"

When he didn't say anything, I looked up. Heart racing like a stampede of wild horses because I needed to stop that girl before she disappeared.

But he was just staring at me. Eyes and mouth wide like he couldn't believe what he was seeing.

"I'm so sorry," that same, distant voice called out, and we both looked in that direction, but I couldn't see anything from where I was. "We wanted to come introduce ourselves, but we'll come back another time."

"Oh no," Momma began, and Dad huffed out a soft laugh as he waved and said, "Just another day around here, ma'am. Sorry for the wild welcome wagon, but don't feel like y'all have to run off. It was just clearin' up here."

Silence followed for a few seconds before that same voice said, "If you're sure. We won't take up much of your time."

"'Course we're sure," Dad said, then gave me a look. Like he was making sure I wasn't gonna go for Cayson again as soon as he let me up.

I didn't say a thing. I just waited, needing to see that girl. To know I hadn't imagined her.

As soon as he stood, I scrambled to follow. My eyes searching and landing on where she stood next to a real pretty lady.

Both were looking at me. Something about their stares

had my stomach twisting up. But not like it did when I felt sick. This was different. Like I was embarrassed for something I had no control over.

The woman reached into the car they were next to and pulled out something covered up that looked like it might've been a cake, but it didn't matter. I wasn't sure anything mattered anymore other than the girl beside her because she'd *stopped* it.

"Well, I'm Christi Riley, and this is my daughter, Savannah," the woman said as they came closer.

"Riley!" my momma said, sounding all kinds of excited like she knew who these people were. "Y'all bought the land next to ours."

"That's right," Mrs. Riley said, a smile stretching over her face.

"Oh, and what an impression we've made," Momma said as she walked up to hug her like they were friends or something. "I'm Wendy, and this is my husband, Mike. These are just two of our boys, Cayson and . . . well, you heard our Beau." Momma laughed, but the way she looked at me was the same way she always did after I got mad.

Like she was tired. Like *I* made her tired.

"Well, it's great meeting you," Mrs. Riley said. "My husband would've joined us, but he got a call from the company he's separating from as we were headed out, and these calls have lasted hours lately."

"We'll meet him soon," Momma said with a wave of her hand. "Why don't y'all come in? I just made some tea."

Mrs. Riley looked from me to my dad and then my momma. "We don't want to impose . . ."

"Nonsense," Momma said.

Dad gave another one of those soft laughs. "What you see

is what you get with us. Gets a little loud and crazy around here sometimes, but that happens when you have four boys close in age. Might as well just dive on in with this rowdy crew seeing as we're now each other's only neighbors for miles."

At that, Mrs. Riley laughed and started for the house. "I guess we can stay for a few minutes."

I watched her daughter follow after her, her head turning to continue looking at me. But Dad had a hand on my shoulder, keeping me in place until they were up the stairs and inside.

Then he was turning me to face him and bending down to my eye level, looking at me like he was real concerned. "You good, son?"

My head bobbed.

"You were hurtin' your brother."

"I know, sir," I said quietly as the fight with Cayson flashed through my mind the way it always did. Dizzying me up because it was blurry and confusing. Bits and pieces that only told parts of what happened.

He let out a slow, long breath. "Gotta be more careful. Gotta control it," he said and tapped his fingers against my chest.

I went still.

Too still.

And then I started shaking from deep in my bones. A warning that the anger would come if I was pushed a little more . . . and all because he'd tapped me.

"We'll talk more later," he said firmly as he straightened. "Hose yourself off."

I don't know how long I stayed there, trying to do what he'd said—control it. But by the time I finally started moving toward the side of the house where the hose was, she was there.

"Why are you so angry?"

My head snapped up and my eyes found her instantly. Standing on the porch, leaning over the railing and looking at me the way she had earlier . . . like she was worried.

Eyes like honey full of concern instead of fear. Long black hair twisted in a braid and falling over her shoulder. Face so dang pretty it was hard to look at her, but I also wasn't sure I could look away.

"I don't know," I answered.

Her head tilted like she was thinking real hard. "You get in a fight with your brother?"

"I always get in fights with my brothers."

"But is that why you're mad?"

My head was shaking before she finished asking the question. "No, ma'am. I get in fights with them because I'm mad."

A bright smile crossed her face, her giggle following soon after. "Ma'am? I'm nine years old!"

"Me too." I shrugged. "But my momma taught us to respect women of all ages, and I'm pretty sure you're an angel."

She threw her head back as another laugh left her. When she looked at me again, her eyes were narrowed curiously. "What's your name?"

"Beau Dixon."

"Well, why do you say that, Beau Dixon?"

I dropped my stare to the grass for a moment as that feeling from earlier formed in my stomach—like I was embarrassed. With another shrug, I looked at her and said, "Because you made it stop."

Her smile disappeared. "Made what stop?"

"Everything."

She watched me for a while, her eyebrows pulling together again. "What's that mean?"

I thought about the way her voice had broken through the anger and need to hurt someone. Thought about the way my anger could take over in an instant . . .

I didn't understand it. I couldn't control it. How was I supposed to explain it to some girl?

"Can't explain it," I mumbled. "Any of it."

"Well, can you tell me why you're covered in mud?"

The corner of my mouth pulled into a frown. "My brother."

She nodded before turning and walking away.

I wanted to go after her. Chase her. Ask her not to turn away from me the way everyone else did. But I had a feeling chasing after her would change her worry to fear real fast, so I trudged off to the hose and had just gotten it turned on when she appeared beside me.

"Can I ask you something?" When I nodded, she said, "When I got out of the car, your dad was holding you down, and your brother was crying." She took a step closer and looked right into my eyes. "Why?"

And the truth just came out of me. "Because I was hitting him."

She didn't move. Not sure the girl even blinked. "But *why*?"

"Because I was mad."

"I know." Another step closer, and I was pretty sure she was trying to get inside my head with the way she was looking at me. Dizzying me up in a different way than my anger did with how she smelled—like sugar with a hint of lemon. "But I've never seen anyone mad the way you were mad, Beau Dixon, and I wanna understand it."

"Why?"

Her mouth lifted in a smile that kinda made her look like her momma. "The way you looked at me. It made me sad."

"You musta messed up real bad," Hunter interrupted as he rounded the corner. "Who're you?"

"Who're you?" Savannah echoed, lifting her chin.

"I live here," Hunter answered as he moved closer.

"Her name's Savannah," I said before it could continue. "She moved onto the property next to ours."

Hunter's mouth formed an O as he hooked a thumb toward our house. "Momma and Dad are telling some lady all about you."

"Saying you *Hulks-out!*" Sawyer yelled as he and Emberly came running from the same direction Hunter had come from.

"Yeah," Hunter added, "and lots of other bad stuff."

My teeth clenched tight. My jaw hurting real bad as that embarrassment grew and grew until I felt sick with it.

"We got sents outside," Sawyer said as he smiled at the girl next to me. "You're real pretty, but I'm marrying my Leightons. Sorry."

Savannah giggled behind her hand before waving at Emberly. "Are you Leighton?"

"*Ew!*" Sawyer and Emberly said at the same time before shoving at each other and taking off running toward the barn.

"That's Emberly," I said softly, trying to breathe through my embarrassment and the anger that came with it. "She's basically our sister."

"Oops," Savannah whispered.

I finally brought the hose up over my head and started

scrubbing at my hair and neck. Trying to drown out Hunter's voice when he said, "Saw Cays . . . you really got him, Beau. And Momma's tellin' that lady about all the things they've tried with you. How nothin' helps or stops you. How you're gettin' wor—"

I had him shoved up against the side of the house before he could finish what he was saying. Arms shaking so bad, I was pretty sure I was shaking my brother too.

He didn't say anything. Just watched me.

He knew . . . he knew when he'd pushed me too far.

Every part of my body felt like I'd been shocked—like lightning had struck me—when Savannah placed her hand on my arm.

"You should let him go," she said softly, her golden eyes on me.

Just like before, it was gone. Disappearing as fast as it had taken over me.

My arms fell to my sides, and Hunter took off running, but I didn't look away from the girl next to me. Just tried to figure out who she was and *how* she could do that.

And then that shame rose again until it was too much.

I'd been angry with myself and whatever was wrong with me. But I'd never been embarrassed until this girl had shown up. And I hated the feeling.

My head shook as I pulled away from her and stormed off until I was hidden under the trees at the back of the house. But not long after I sat against one of them, she sat down next to me.

"I turned off the hose," she said softly.

"Thanks."

"You're still dirty."

I knew that. I could feel it on my skin. That dirty feeling kinda like when I lost control, except I wasn't angry. "Yup."

"My mom told me to stay away from you," she said like she was telling me a secret as she played with the grass. "You know . . . when she was sending me outside."

I glanced at her and then quickly looked away when I found her watching me. "Lotta folks tell their kids to stay away from me."

"That's sad."

I shrugged. I hadn't ever thought so. Not until then. Not until her.

I stared at the tall, swaying grass covering up the part of our land we could see from where we sat for a while before asking, "Can I tell you something?"

Instead of answering, she scooted closer so she was in front of me and looking directly at me.

"I get real angry, and I can't stop it. I dunno how. And everyone says it isn't normal."

I didn't tell her that my parents had taken me to see people for it. That I'd just stopped going to the last doctor because I was getting worse, not better. Didn't tell her the words my momma used when she talked about me. I was too embarrassed to.

"Hulk," she said, her eyes getting big and round. "That's what your brother said. Like the big, green guy."

I shook my head, my shoulders jerking up to my ears. "I dunno. I've heard her say it, but I dunno what it means."

"He's this guy who explodes into a super huge, green guy when he gets mad. He smashes and destroys things, and it's hard for him to get back to not being so mad."

Oh.

My stare fell to my lap as my stomach twisted and turned.

That would be why I didn't know who he was. My parents tried to stop me from seeing anything with violence, worried it would make me worse. One of my doctors had said so.

"Yeah, guess that sounds like me." I looked at her and nodded off to the side. "You should maybe listen to your momma."

She didn't say anything for a real long time, but when she did, she sounded all kinds of crazy. "Are you gonna stay away from me because of my freckles?"

"What? Why in the heck would I stay away from you 'cause you have freckles?"

"I don't like them," she said sadly, then touched her face before forcing her hands under her legs. "I don't think they belong on my face."

I looked at her tan skin and bright eyes and the dots on her cheeks and nose that were so light, I hadn't noticed them until then. "Well, I like 'em. And they aren't gonna make me stay away from you."

"Then, okay."

"I don't think we're talking 'bout the same kinds of things."

"Sure we are." She reached to the side to pick a dandelion and then looked back at me. "There was a boy at my old school, and he was so, so mean. But he liked being mean, you could tell. He laughed at people when he hurt them or made them cry. I don't think you're like that at all, Beau Dixon." She slowly blew the white, puffy seeds off the stem before saying, "You don't wanna be angry. I think it bothers you—makes you sad."

"You don't know that. You don't even know me."

"But I told you, I felt sad when you looked at me because *you* felt sad."

"That makes no sense."

"Sure it does," she said as she picked another dandelion and held it out to me.

I didn't take it.

"My freckles make me sad, and I don't like them. You getting angry makes you sad, and you don't want to be that way. So, why on earth would I stay away from you?"

This girl really was crazy. "Not the same things."

"They are to me."

"They're freckles," I said as I leaned forward to tug on her long braid. "Just a part of you like this is."

"You get angry. It's just a part of you."

A heavy breath left me when I fell back against the tree and watched her, staring at me like she really believed what she said.

This girl I didn't know at all.

This angel who had fallen into my life.

Saying things no one else ever had. Looking at me like there wasn't something wrong with me. Like I was just Beau.

Not *the violent Dixon boy*. Not *the angry one*.

Just Beau.

"Are you real?"

Another one of those giggles left her, head tilted back and everything. "Of course I am," she said when she faced me again. "Better question! Do you like lemon?"

Crazy girl.

Crazy, angel girl, that's what Savannah was.

"Uh . . ." My shoulders bunched up. "I dunno. Sure?"

"Me and my mom made lemon pound cake for your family, and it's so way good. You should try it." She stood and held a hand out for me to take, reaching for me like she wasn't afraid of me at all.

I took it.

Letting her help me up as I tried to understand how she could say and think the things she did . . .

We hadn't made it out of the trees when I figured it out.

She saw me push Hunter against the house. She saw me being held down when my anger was already fading. Which meant she hadn't seen a whole lot of anything. Nothing close to the worst I'd done.

"You'll see somethin'," I said quietly. "Somethin' that'll change your mind about me. About, you know, what's wrong with me. Just so you know . . . it's okay. I'll understand."

She grabbed my arm and turned me toward her. "I don't think there's anything wrong with you."

"You're wrong."

"Because you turn into the Hulk?"

I looked away as my teeth clenched tight. As my chest burned in a funny way that was cold and hot all at once. "I don't like that name."

"Okay then," she said like it was as simple as that. "Because you turn into a bear?"

A laugh broke past my shame, and I glanced at her. "What?"

She shrugged. "You were kinda roaring like a bear when I found you."

"I—sure. 'Cause of that."

"Well, I happen to like bears," she said and held out the same dandelion from earlier to me.

I watched her for a while before taking the dandelion and starting for the house again with her by my side.

"You sure you're not an angel?"

She shrugged. "I don't think so. My dad calls me 'Pumpkin' . . . maybe I'm one of those."

I laughed and knocked my shoulder against hers.

She skipped away, laughing as she did and looking at me over her shoulder. "Come get me, Beau Dixon!"

I watched her dart away, too stunned to move for a few seconds, before taking off after her.

Running after someone without that sickly feeling covering me. Without anger pushing me faster and faster.

Chasing that crazy, angel girl because she wanted me to. Because *I* wanted to.

Had a feeling when I finally caught up to her that I wanted to spend every day chasing Savannah Riley.

Three

SAVANNAH

"That sounds perfect, then we'll be ready for you at noon on the twenty-ninth," I said as I scrawled down the last of the details. "Please let me know if you have any questions before then."

After a quick goodbye, I ended the call, my expression falling when I set the bed and breakfast's phone on the counter. "Next weekend's full too," I said to the kitchen lamely, hating that the excitement of that moment was missing. That I couldn't share it with Beau . . .

Hating that he wouldn't be there for the graduation weekend or the full weekend we had just ahead. That he wouldn't be there to say *let's live that dream* before the first guest arrived, as he had since we'd first opened up Blossom Bed and Breakfast.

Hating that he wasn't there at all.

I rubbed at the burning ache in my chest that hadn't seemed to dull these past weeks. The stabbing betrayal that lingered and twisted in the moments when I had too much time to think. Like *now*.

Pushing my calendar away, I turned from the kitchen, refusing to give my thoughts the chance to form. I had a to-do list that would keep my hands and mind busy for days if I was lucky.

But just as I was stepping into our large supply closet to grab cleaning supplies, the front door opened.

Hope bloomed so fast and so deep that my next exhale sounded like I was in pain as I turned and raced for the entryway . . . only to come crashing down around me when it was Sawyer heading toward the kitchen instead of his oldest brother.

"Oh," I said thickly, throat working feverishly to swallow past the knot there. "Hey, Sawyer, hi." My head bobbed all kinds of awkwardly as I stepped closer to where he was watching me curiously. "Did y'all forget something last night?"

"No, just coming to check on you."

"Oh. Well, I—" I waved toward the kitchen and living room just beyond it, trying to shrug as I did. "Everything's fine today. Nothing needs to be fixed. I don't need help with anything."

He stepped back to lean against the kitchen archway, folding his arms across his chest as he did. "Yeah, that isn't what I meant. Where are the kids?"

"School," I answered a little uncertainly, even though I was sure of that, and Sawyer would've known the answer to that too.

"Levi?"

"Napping. Why do I feel like you're interrogating me?"

"Do you have guests checking in?"

I straightened my back and tried to stare him down.

"Sawyer Dixon, I am not playing twenty questions with you. Why are you here?"

He gestured to my kitchen. "I'm trying to figure out why you have enough desserts to feed all of Amber sitting in your kitchen when none of that shit was here last night. I wanna know if you're okay. I need to get a feel on where you're at after what we told you last night."

"Stop looking at me like that. I couldn't sleep," I ground out, refusing to let him make me feel worse than I already did. "You already know I'm not okay, and as for last night?"

"BEAU SHOWED up at the ranch yesterday morning," my mother-in-law had informed me after dinner had ended.

A ragged breath had ripped from my lungs as I'd looked around to make sure my kids weren't within hearing distance of her.

Both Sawyer and his girlfriend, Rae, looked at her as if they couldn't believe she'd mentioned it at all.

"That's, um . . . yeah, good."

"Oh, I wouldn't say that," she'd said thoughtfully, then looked to Sawyer.

After a long sigh, he'd met my stare. "He isn't doing well, Savannah. He's a mess without you and the kids."

"And I'm doing much better?" I'd challenged, voice trembling.

"You need to talk to him," Sawyer had gently pleaded. "It's been more than two weeks. You can't keep him from his kids like this."

I knew that.

I'd known that.

But I was afraid of what would happen when I saw Beau again.

Would I fall apart and say something I could never take back? Would I fall into his arms and forgive everything simply because that man held my heart and soul in his hands? Would I ever be able to look

*at him and not see him and the girl who had been my best friend?
Because every time I'd thought of him since the day I'd found out, all I
could see was him and Madison.*

Worse yet? The vow he'd broken.

"SAWYER, HE MADE ME A PROMISE," I said shakily. "He promised no more fighting."

"I know," he began placatingly.

"And I promised that I would be done," I hurried over him, voice a pained cry. "I made a promise to myself that I wouldn't watch him destroy our future, and I don't know—" My chin trembled as I fought the quick-to-build tears. My steps were hurried as I pushed past him and moved through the kitchen to sit at the large table.

Once I sank into a chair, Sawyer was there, sitting next to me and waiting patiently.

"I never wanted to change Beau," I said when my breathing had returned to normal and those jagged pieces in my throat had disappeared. "But his anger had changed . . . heightened. And I just had this terrible, crushing feeling in my gut each time he lost control that I wouldn't get the chance to have a future with him because he wouldn't be there for it. So, as much as it killed me, I knew if there was going to be any hope of a life with him, I had to stand up for myself and mean it."

"What if he hadn't been able to stop fighting back then?" Sawyer asked after nearly a minute had passed in silence.

"Then we wouldn't be here at all," I answered and swiped at a tear that slipped free. "And now . . . I don't know how I'm supposed to go back on my word when a broken promise is why we're here. And I don't know how to keep my word when that means losing him."

"Don't do either. Don't think of it that way," Sawyer urged as he leaned forward. "It was bad, yeah, I know. He promised you he wouldn't anymore. I get it, Savannah, I do—but this was different. You have to see that. His world was getting ripped out beneath his feet, and he snapped because he was trying to stop it from happening. And from what I've been told, he stopped as soon as you said his name."

"I know, but—"

"This was different," he repeated, trying to make me see something I couldn't. When my head just shook, he said, "Savannah, he asked us if we think he's like our dad."

My shoulders caved as a muted sob pulled from deep within me, my eyes shutting at the grief that wove through me.

"Which means *Beau* thinks he's just like our dad," Sawyer finished carefully.

But I already knew all that. "I know," I wheezed through my pain for my husband. "I know. Ever since Cayson revealed everything, he's been . . . different. Absolutely terrified that he'll turn into your dad one day. Do to one of our kids what your dad did to Cayson."

"Fuck," Sawyer mumbled.

"It's been breaking my heart," I said in agreement.

"Everything that's happening, and you keeping him from the kids," Sawyer began, voice uncertain, "I think it's confirming all those fears for Beau. Savannah, he isn't okay without you."

"I'm not okay without him, but I don't know how to do this. I don't know how to navigate through all this pain and the broken trust and promises. I'm so afraid I'll say something that ends us before I give him a chance, and what if—" I pressed my lips close together, the thought that had been plaguing me for weeks trying to crawl free. "What if that isn't it?"

"What do you mean?"

"He kept all that from me for so long. What if I find out there's more?"

"Savannah," Sawyer began, doubt weaving through my name, but he clamped his mouth shut when I cut him with a look. Nodding subtly because he knew just as I did that we couldn't *know*. "Talk to him. Let him see the kids at least. He needs that, and so do your kids."

"I know," I said on a breath, my stare drifting toward the windows. "I know."

Sawyer stood and turned to go, squeezing my shoulder as he went. But when he reached the kitchen entrance, he called my name, drawing my attention to him. "Beau? You've been there for so much of it. You've seen him at his worst. His anger and the impulse to fight is second nature, but he's fought it all this time for you and those kids. He's only losing control now because he's afraid of losing you."

All I could offer him was a hesitant nod.

Beau should've never done anything for that fear to be real, and I hated that he had. His betrayal and this entire situation made me feel sick. Made my body heavy with unease and unknowns.

Still, I knew I couldn't continue on the way I had. Knew Sawyer was right.

I pushed from my chair and wove through the kitchen in search of my phone once Sawyer was gone, my stare catching on my inner wrist as I brought the screen to life. On the quarter-sized outline of angel wings that brought dozens of memories bursting to mind and had thousands more tied to it.

My phone clattered to the tiled floor just before I fell heavily to my knees. A sob wrenched from deep inside my soul and poured into the empty room. Filling the space with my grief and anger and confusion until it surrounded me.

Four

BEAU
THIRTEEN YEARS OLD

Golden eyes.

Savannah.

Right in front of me with destruction surrounding me.

God.

She didn't say anything. She didn't have to. Just stared at me with that same look she always gave me—like she understood. Like she *saw* me in a way no one else did.

And I wanted to die.

My stomach twisted and lurched, but I sucked in shallow breaths, forcing it to calm as I held her gaze. Clung to it so that sickening haze wouldn't cover my eyes and that need to hurt someone wouldn't take over again.

"Mr. Dixon."

I worked my jaw but didn't look away from Savannah.

"*Mr. Dixon*, my office *now*."

I ripped my stare away from her and turned, scanning the circle of our classmates that had gathered around.

Some of them whispering.

Some of them pointing.

Nearly all of them looking at me like they were afraid of what my next step would be.

I looked at the three boys being helped up by their friends and led to where the gym teacher and vice principal were waiting, then met Hunter's disappointed gaze. His head shook slowly where he stood with his girlfriend, Madison, in the crowd.

Before I could make it to where everyone had parted for our principal, he called out, "Grab your bag, Mr. Dixon."

Damn it.

I turned, not even sure where it had ended up, and found Savannah holding it close to her chest.

"I'll see you after school," she said firmly as she handed it over.

I didn't respond. I never did when these things happened. I was always waiting for her to realize what she should've years ago.

That I was bad news. Dangerous. That she should get far from me and never look back—everything her parents told her on a near-daily basis.

But that girl hadn't left my side since the day she'd fallen into my life. Truthfully? I didn't know what I would do if she did. But if it was better for Savannah, I would find a way to deal.

I would do anything for her.

"Mr. Dixon," the principal said, sighing heavily when I followed him into the office. "Why was I not surprised to see you in the middle of that fight? Wait, no!" he said quickly like I'd been about to answer.

I hadn't been.

"Not in the middle of it. You'd already taken out three

students and were looking for someone else to fight. Anyone else. Isn't that right?"

I wasn't sure about that part. Didn't mean he was wrong.

I couldn't remember anything that happened between turning for the third guy and the moment I found Savannah directly in front of me.

"Got anything to say for yourself?" He leaned toward me from where he was sitting on the edge of his desk. "Be thankful those boys were getting up, or we'd be having a different conversation."

Another heavy sigh left him when I didn't respond.

"Mr. Dixon, I want to be able to help you. I do—we all do here. But you make it hard when you don't talk to us and you terrorize the hallways and my students."

My jaw ached when I met his stare.

His head slanted like he was expecting something from me. "If there's anything you want to say before I call your parents, now's the time."

"You should be calling their parents," I murmured.

"What's that?"

"Call *their* parents," I snapped. "I'm not the one terrorizing your precious hallways."

"Check the way you're speaking to me, Mr. Dixon."

"I'm not the one terrorizing other kids," I continued, voice getting low with my rising anger. "Those assholes are there every day, calling out shit to everyone."

"Okay, language," the principal said in a calming tone.

It had the opposite effect on me.

"Making fun of kids. Talking about girls in ways they shouldn't. *Touching* them."

"Let's sit down."

"Don't fucking touch me," I bit out and jerked away from his hand.

I hadn't realized I'd stood. But I was there. Right in front of him. Hands clenched into tight fists and body trembling with the anger that was always waiting to be set free.

"Sit down," he shouted.

The edges of my vision went red in response.

I turned and shoved the door to his office open, storming through it and down the hall with him right behind me.

"Get back here, Mr. Dixon."

"I got it, I'm suspended," I called out as I continued away from him.

By the time I made it out of the main office, I was running.

Running to get away before I could make it worse. Trying to outrun the anger and humiliation fighting for dominance in my veins.

By the time I made it home, Mom was waiting outside, and Dad was pulling up from the orchard.

Mom just looked at me, hands slapping against her thighs as a soft sob left her. "Beau—"

"Let's take a second," Dad said, trying to remain the calm one. "Let's take a breath and get inside, then we'll talk."

"It's the third time," she cried out to him before looking back at me. "Third time *this year*, Beau. What if those boys are seriously injured? What if—"

"Wendy," Dad said, disapproval filling his tone.

She let out another cry and wiped at her face. "Beau, I just . . ." A breath left her, heavy and weighed down, looking like it dragged her shoulders down with it. She didn't need to finish the thought, I already knew what she was thinking.

She didn't know what to do with me anymore.

She'd been saying that for a long, long time.

I nodded and started walking for the house, already knowing they were gonna send me to my room, but stopped when she asked, "What could possibly have happened this time to make you do this?"

A jagged breath left me as the echo of their taunts played in my mind.

"Damn, Riley, been hiding those girls under sweatshirts all winter?"

"It's a crime to keep those from the rest of us."

"Give us a little peek."

Things those idiots said to girls all the time.

Shit that should've been stopped long ago. But that hadn't been what set me off—Savannah had kept a firm hand on me as we'd passed them. Keeping me moving. Grounded. Making sure I wouldn't react when I'd tried to.

It had been the high five Savannah received when she'd come into one of the classes we shared later. The gossip that followed.

Two of the guys had blocked her path to class while the third had grabbed her ass. She'd turned and slapped him.

Philip Rowe.

I hated that guy.

What's worse? His family was close to Savannah's. Their dads had been in the same fraternity in college, and Philip's dad was the whole reason Mr. Riley took a job near Amber, prompting their move here.

And I got to listen to Mrs. Riley talk about how *perfect* it would be if Savannah and Philip got married when they grew up. How *great* of a kid Philip was—so polite and proper and *that young boy's going places . . . just you watch.*

Bullshit.

If she only knew.

Savannah had tried to get my attention all throughout class. She'd tried to stop me when the bell rang. But I was already so far gone, racing out of class and down the halls.

No one touched Savannah. Ever.

Especially not perfect, fucking Philip.

"They did something," I finally answered with a quick shrug before continuing to the house.

Mom let out a sound that shouted all her frustration and sadness.

Dad tried to calm her.

I went inside and climbed the stairs, then hid behind the hallway wall. Waiting for when they would enter the house.

"What do we do?" Mom said through her tears. "What are we gonna do with him, Mike?"

"Wendy, just breathe."

"I am breathing," she cried out. "You don't understand what it's like having to deal with the calls from parents. What it's like having to listen to them describe what Beau did to them. Having to apologize and try to explain something I *don't know how* to explain."

"Then I'll take the calls," he said calmly.

"And what happens when he puts someone in the hospital?" The last words were said so softly, they almost didn't make it up the stairs.

But I heard them.

And they cut right into my chest.

When Mom continued, her voice was trembling about as bad as I was. "What happens then, Mike?"

"He won't."

"You can't know that! The principal said he took down

three boys before Savannah managed to stop him. *Three*. It's getting worse, you know it is."

There was a long silence before Dad said, "We don't know that. We don't know what happened."

"Mike—"

"He ain't any worse with his brothers than he's always been. He's just stronger."

"And he'll get stronger," Mom argued. "And nothing makes a difference to him. The therapists and doctors only aggravated the situation. Discipline did the same. He accepts groundings and-and-and suspensions quietly. But it *doesn't make a difference*."

"I know, honey. That's why we gotta respond differently with him. Be open and calm."

"He doesn't need open and calm. He needs to go to—"

"No," Dad snapped.

"Mike—"

"I said no, Wendy. I ain't changin' my mind on that."

I looked toward the stairs when my dad's heavy steps moved through the house, wondering what Mom had been about to say.

When her soft cries followed after him, I turned and slipped down the hall and into my room. Falling onto my bed and dragging my hands over my face as the jumbled blur of a fight played out in my mind until sleep claimed me.

"Shit," I hissed when something heavy landed on my stomach and launched the object away from me as I scrambled to sitting on my bed.

My backpack hit the wall next to where Hunter stood inside my room with his arms folded over his chest.

"What's your problem?"

"You left that in the principal's office," he said softly. "I got to hear all about why."

My chest shook as I thought about what our principal might've said to him—how his older brother was a problem. A bad influence. Not someone to look up to.

It wouldn't be the first time.

"Couldn't stay there," I said instead of explaining myself.

"Yeah. Got that."

"How long am I suspended for?"

A smirk stretched across his face. "You don't know?"

"Think I'd be asking if I did?"

"Three days." He started for the open door and shrugged. "Same goes for the trio of ass wipes."

Surprise swirled in my chest, but before I could ask, Savannah was slipping past him and into my room.

My heart and stomach dropped as I staggered off my bed. Shame building so great that it nearly took me to my knees.

As soon as Hunter shut the door behind him, I was stepping close enough to Savannah that I was nearly touching her. "I'm sorry."

Disappointment poured from her as she studied me. "*Why?*"

I blinked slowly as I absorbed that one word that seemed to pack a punch.

In the four years of knowing Savannah, she'd ended up near most of the fights I'd found myself in.

Her family spent holidays with ours, and she spent all her free time with me, trying to get lost on the property when my brothers refused to let that happen. Then there was school. Whatever it was, she was usually there, by my side.

Lighting up my life and making my days better. Pulling me out of that sick darkness and waiting until we were alone again to show anything other than her support.

But she hadn't questioned my apologies until then.

"Because I'm proving everyone right," I said softly. "Because I can't stop."

Because I can't be better for you.

"No, why did you do it?"

Wasn't sure I'd ever felt as low as I did then. Not when I'd thought she was the only person who understood.

I took an unsteady step toward my bed.

Savannah followed, her eyebrows pulled close together like she was begging to understand. "Beau, I tried to stop you."

My eyelids closed and my head slanted when it felt like her words had a pit of ice and fire opening up in my stomach. I sank to the bed and dropped my head in my hands when she continued.

"You ignored me and *ran* from me."

"Savannah, he touched you."

"I handled myself."

"Savannah, he touched you!" I ground out and met her golden-eyed stare again. But the disappointment was fading away into surprise. "I'm sorry. I'm sorry for losing it. For not stopping. For being like this."

"No," she said quickly and sat beside me. "Beau, no."

"When are you gonna realize your parents are right? That you need to stay away from me?"

"They're wrong."

My head shook. "You're the only one who thinks that."

"You think I need to stay away from you too?"

"Yeah." When her shoulders sagged and sorrow creased her beautiful face, I gestured toward my door. "Ask Hunter or even Madison, they'll say the same thing. Jesus, Savannah. You walk right into the middle of fights for me. You're gonna get hit."

"You wouldn't hit me," she said confidently.

"Not me, Savannah. Someone else is gonna hit you one of these times because they're not gonna realize you're there." I pressed a hand to my chest. "You think I'll be able to handle knowing you got hurt because of me?"

Her gaze fell to her lap for a while before she asked, "Okay, but is that what you want?"

I clenched my teeth and slowly exhaled because I knew what she was asking, just as she knew I wouldn't lie to her. "I want you to be safe," I said carefully.

"That isn't what I'm asking."

"No," I answered quickly. "You know that isn't what I want. But it's what *you* should want."

"That might be difficult." She played with her fingers as she wavered and then shifted to face me again. "Because I really like bears, and my favorite person just so happens to be a bear."

The corners of my mouth lifted in a grin, and I was met with one of her bright smiles.

"You can't get rid of me that easily. You don't scare me, Beau Dixon."

I should.

We jolted away from each other when my door swung open, even though we hadn't been doing anything.

My mom gave me a frustrated look, her head shaking. "Grounded," she said, pointing at me, then shifted her finger to Savannah. "Your momma just called, looking for you. Said you gotta leave for dance soon."

"Oh, shoot," Savannah whispered, hopping up off the bed.

With a hard look directed at both of us, my mom said, "No girls allowed in bedrooms. You know this. Add two days onto your grounding."

"We were just talking," I argued, gesturing to where Savannah was staring wide-eyed at me.

"There's a girl in your room," Mom said. "The door was closed. Don't talk back to me. I have half a mind to add another week, Beau."

"I'm sorry," Savannah whispered when Mom's voice trailed off down the hall. "We knew you'd be grounded, so Hunter snuck me in."

I waved off her worried expression and stood to follow her. "Before you go," I said, stopping at my dresser and digging under the stack of shirts. "It's looking like I won't see you tomorrow." My face creased with apology as I palmed the unwrapped present and shut the drawer. "So, happy birthday, Savannah."

Her mouth popped open as I handed over the bracelet I'd made. Dark, braided leather with a hollowed-out charm of angel wings woven in.

The smile that crossed her face made me want to do anything to be better for her. Be someone she shouldn't have to stay away from.

"Did you make this?"

I dipped my head as I watched her turn it around, her smile somehow growing when she found the wings.

"Why?"

My brow furrowed. "Your birthday."

A soft laugh left her as she slipped it on and turned it to

continue looking at the charm. "Right, but . . . you didn't have to get me anything. And you *made* me something?"

"I wanted to. You're my best friend."

Everything . . . you're everything. You're my entire world.

Savannah's smile changed. Dimmed, so it no longer reached her eyes.

I'd done that. Taken away her excitement because I was afraid *for* her.

Because about the same time I'd realized that Savannah Riley was more than just the angel who fell into my life and took away my anger, I'd realized that I needed to protect her from me. And that meant keeping my feelings for her to myself. Telling myself it was best for her.

But I hadn't been prepared to hurt her in doing that.

"I love it," she whispered. "I love it so much. Thank you, Beau." She turned for the door and then turned back to me. "I have to go."

My chest felt like it was burning and crumbling all at once as I nodded and followed her. "Right."

She stopped just inside the doorway and asked, "What if I'd wanted him to touch me?"

Everything went still. So, scarily still. "What?"

She studied the door for a moment before looking at me. "This morning . . . what if I'd wanted Philip to touch me?"

I would've killed him.

The thought was instant and continued to shout out in my mind.

I swallowed.

Tried . . . tried to. Because I couldn't anymore.

The thought of seeing Savannah around town or in the halls at school next to someone else . . . holding their hand or with their arm around her . . . it made me sick.

But I couldn't stop her.

I wouldn't.

So, I forced myself to nod and watched her try to hide the deep disappointment in her eyes as she returned the gesture and slipped out of my room.

I softly closed the door behind her and tried to slowly count backward from ten.

But by the time I got to three, I exploded.

Lashing out and punching the wall as everything went red. Yelling out a curse as my knuckles split.

Not more than a few seconds later, my door flung open, and Hunter came rushing in. Eyes wide as he looked around the room before landing on the dent in my wall.

He sounded all kinds of annoyed when he asked, "Again?"

"*Out,*" I snapped.

He lifted his hands and started backing out. "Where's Savannah?"

My eyes narrowed as I stalked toward him, cradling my bleeding hand in the bottom of my shirt.

"It's a question," he said louder, trying to get my attention. "She was just here, and now you're punching a wall."

"I'm right," I said through clenched teeth.

"What?"

"Tell me I'm right!" I yelled. "That she needs to stay away from me. That I'm bad for her—that I'm too dangerous."

"Savannah?" Hunter asked slowly and lowered his hands. "That girl can handle herself against all four of us even better than Emberly can, and Em was raised with us. And, dude, don't hit me, but you can't decide what Savannah wants."

"Move."

"What?"

"*Move,*" I snapped when he just stood in front of the door, my chest pitching with ragged breaths and my arms trembling as I struggled so hard not to let that haze take control.

As soon as Hunter stepped back, I pushed past him and ran across the top floor and down the stairs. Our mom yelled after me when she saw me, but I raced out the front door and off the porch, running faster when I saw Savannah nearing the end of our property.

"Savannah!" I called out when she started moving around our fence.

She whirled around, her eyes going wide when she saw me. "What are you doing?"

"Stopping you," I said through my uneven breaths, slowing as I neared her.

"I have . . ." She looked off to the side, then back to me. "I have dance."

My head bobbed as I came to a stop a couple feet away. "I know. But I had to tell you that I can't. I can't do that," I said roughly and gestured to her.

Her breath caught when she saw my blood-stained hand, but I continued.

"I can't watch Philip touch you—I can't watch anyone touch you. I'll kill them because I wanna be the one touching you."

Shock covered her face and a soft blush crept up her cheeks.

"I think your parents are right," I said, nodding before quickly shaking my head. "I think you're better off away from me, but I don't know how to let you go because I think I started falling in love with you the first day you called me a bear."

A breath of a laugh fell from her lips only to end in a

sharp inhale when I stepped closer so I was nearly pressed to her.

Her golden eyes so wide. Her tongue darting out to wet her lips. Filling my head with everything that was Savannah —all sugar with a hint of cinnamon that day.

"You're not just my best friend, Savannah. You're everything."

She pushed up on her toes and pressed her lips to mine, and I'm pretty sure the world went still.

I wrapped my arms around her, holding her closer as I moved my mouth against hers in what had to be the best moment of my life. A moment I knew I wanted to relive again and again.

Savannah was all unrestrained smiles and dancing eyes when the kiss ended, her cheeks red with heat. She started pulling away, but at the last second, lifted up to press another quick kiss to my mouth.

"About time, Beau Dixon."

Five

SAVANNAH

I was a mess.

I'd changed my outfit five times—maybe seven—before realizing with absolute horror that I was dressed for a fancy dinner rather than a day in my home. After forcing myself back into my regular leggings and shirt combo, I'd reached for my favorite necklaces before panicking over the way they would look.

I never panicked over jewelry.

I never panicked over what I wore, *period*.

I'd turned my curling iron on for the first time in years before forcing myself to shut it off and twisting my hair up in a messy knot on my head . . . and then I'd turned the curling iron back on.

My makeup was usually minimal—mascara if I felt like it. But I'd just finished putting on a slightly tinted lip gloss to complete my fully done face before fluffing the curls in my hair.

All because my husband was coming over.

To our home.

I tried telling myself that I was channeling my inner Rae, wanting to look good to feel good, but I knew it was a lie. I wanted to look good for him. And a part of me wanted to show him that I was fine when I was the furthest thing from it.

Once I'd gotten a handle on myself the day before, I'd picked up my phone. Cursing myself for dropping it while inspecting the shattered screen that was beyond repair as I stood to find the bed and breakfast's phone.

Beau had answered on the first ring.

"SAVANNAH." My name was agony and relief and had new tears forming. "God, Savannah, talk to me," he'd begged when I hadn't been able to respond. "I need to see you. The kids."

I'd nodded shakily, sucking in an audible breath. "Yeah, um, you can. The kids, I mean."

The following silence didn't need words. I felt his gratitude and absolute fear leaking through the phone. When he'd spoken, his voice was strained. "Okay. Okay, I'll be there as soon as work's over."

"No."

His exhale was pure pain and had ripped through me, shredding the remaining pieces of me.

"No, um, not today," I'd said quickly, stumbling over the words as I'd looked around the kitchen that was a testament to how horribly I was handling everything. "Tomorrow."

"Tomorrow," he'd repeated. "Savannah—"

"Tomorrow, Beau." I'd hung up before he could say anything else, sharp cries tearing from my chest and threatening to send me to my knees all over again.

. . .

I'D GOTTEN rid of as many desserts as I could by giving them to friends and family and anyone in town who would take them. I'd frozen what I could and hid the rest. Then I'd spent the rest of the afternoon and late into the night cleaning when I wasn't playing with the kids.

Today had been slow and torturous, watching the hours crawl by as I waited for this moment. But now that it was here, I wished it wasn't.

I wished I had let him come the day before, so I would've already been done with it. Or that I'd held off for a couple more days, so we would have guests, and I'd have them as a distraction because I wasn't sure I could handle seeing Beau and not fall apart. Wasn't sure I could stop myself from begging him to make our lives go back to the way they'd been before my heart had been destroyed.

I reached for my phone to check the time, forgetting that I didn't have it on me because it was useless with only a small portion of the screen working. The only good thing to come from that was I hadn't been able to spend hours going through pictures and listening to Beau's voicemails once I'd gotten in bed the night before, just to hear his voice and see him.

"Oh, you look real pretty, Mommy," Quinn said when I poked my head into their playroom.

"Yeah, real pretty," Wyatt echoed.

A shaky smile tugged at my mouth. "Thank you. I need y'all to finish cleaning up and then come out to the kitchen please." I hefted Levi higher up on my hip, then continued through the halls, stare darting everywhere to make sure nothing was out of place or needed to be cleaned.

I wasn't sure the house had ever looked this good—even when my parents came. But I was restless over it. As if the way the kids, the house, and I looked directly reflected how I was dealing. And it was so important to me that Beau thought I was handling this well.

Even if it had taken me over two weeks to call him back.

Just as I was walking toward the living room to set Levi down with some toys, the front door opened, and my heart leaped into my throat.

Hard, thunderous steps echoed through the entryway, my spirit going all kinds of crazy because I knew the man those steps belonged to. I'd been loved by him most of my life. Worshipped. Cherished.

Lied to.

I tried to steel my jaw as I turned just as he came into the room, his body seeming to cave when he saw me standing there. Face twisting in pain and relief and some indescribable emotion that made my chest *ache*.

"Dadda!" Levi cried out, reaching for him, and Beau stumbled.

A choked sob breaking free as his eyes filled with tears. "Fuck," he whispered as he closed the distance, grabbing Levi from me and pulling him close. "I'm sorry. I'm sorry. I'm so sorry."

Levi grabbed at Beau's hair and pressed their heads together, babbling *Dadda* over and over.

Beau's smile was joy and pain and regret as he nodded against Levi. "Missed you, buddy." Just as his glassy eyes slid my way, Quinn and Wyatt's shouts had him turning in time for them to barrel into his side.

"Daddy, you're here!" Quinn shouted as she tried to hug all the way around his waist.

"We missed you, where'd you go?" Wyatt called out as he tried to climb up his side.

"Are you *back*, back? All the time back?" Quinn asked. "Don't leave again. Okay, Daddy?"

Beau's head dropped back to face the ceiling, his jaw trembling for those long moments before he looked at our kids again, trying desperately to hold all three of them. "I missed y'all so much."

"And Momma too?" Wyatt asked, all unreserved excitement. "You missed Momma too, right? Doesn't she look real pretty today?"

Midnight eyes found me, piercing me and tearing me apart from the pain and sadness etched there. "Every day," Beau said, voice thick as his gaze slowly dragged over me. "She's beautiful every day."

"Are you getting divorces?" Quinn asked unexpectedly, shocking me.

"What?" I asked, the word a breath as I met her sad stare.

"Avalee said when she didn't see her daddy for a long time, it was because her mommy and daddy were getting divorces, and they weren't gonna be married anymore. Are you getting divorces because we haven't seen Daddy for a long time?"

I grabbed the back of the couch to keep me grounded. To hold me up.

"N-no," I finally said, head moving in small, fast shakes. "Of course we're not getting a divorce."

We've already been through so much. We can make it through this too. We have to.

But even as that thought entered my mind, I wondered how we were supposed to.

And Beau . . . he looked terrified. Sick. The dark circles under his eyes seemed even more pronounced than they had a minute before, as if he'd heard every thought.

"Things have just been . . ." I struggled to swallow past the grief gripping my throat, my head shaking as I thought of anything to say. "Busy," I said, going with the excuse that had pacified them these past two weeks. "He's been busy."

"We're *always* busy," Wyatt groaned. "Why can't Daddy be busy here?"

"Sometimes things are hard," Beau began, voice soft but edged with that steel I'd known since I was nine years old, "and sometimes we can't understand them, but we find a way through them. Together." His pleading stare met mine at the last word.

I jolted at the high-pitched shriek from Levi and automatically reached for him, mumbling, "He's hungry."

"I know," Beau responded just as softly, a hint of offense weaving through the two small words. "I've got it." He moved past my awaiting hands, keeping Levi close to his chest with the older kids trailing close behind.

And I stood frozen in my grief.

At the paralyzing unfamiliarity and coldness that stretched between us for the first time in our lives. It felt wrong, so wrong. But I was helpless to stop it when the thought of him, let alone the sight of him, had me spiraling down a dark hole of everything he'd done.

Every way he'd betrayed me.

My eyelids slipped shut when the kids' laughter rang free behind me, mixing with Beau's low, gravelly voice as he spoke to them and fixed snacks. As he and Levi babbled nonsense to each other, and whatever our youngest did had one of those rare, rough laughs scraping up Beau's throat.

Unable to stand there any longer without falling into that precious time that I missed and craved—or, worse, falling into my husband's arms—I forced myself to walk away.

Hurrying through the house until I ended up in the supply closet again. Staring vacantly at towels and linens and supplies until they blurred from view.

My shoulders jerked when Beau was suddenly there. Gently gripping at my wrist to move my hand away from my mouth.

"I wasn't biting it."

"I know," he murmured as he stepped into my line of sight. "Savannah—"

"I can't," I said before he could continue, head shaking furiously. "I can't do this in front of the kids."

His stare shifted to the doorway and lingered when he said, "They're playing. Levi's in his sit-and-play."

I wondered for only a second how long I'd been in there if the kids were all playing but shook off the thought and took a step back until I was pressed to the shelving. "I *won't* do this in front of the kids, Beau. Not while they're here."

"Savannah, we have to talk—"

"I said *no*," I cried out.

The muscle in his jaw feathered before he gave a harsh nod and left the closet, leaving a trail of his anguish and fear. Mixed with my grief and betrayal, it felt lethal.

THE BOOK in my lap was unopened, but I didn't care.

I wasn't sure if I'd even grabbed the book I'd recently been reading, I'd just reached out and grabbed *a* book on my way to sit in one of the living room chairs that evening. Waiting, waiting, waiting for when Beau would come downstairs.

For when he would leave.

My soul was screaming for him to stay. To make this hellish nightmare go away. But my heart needed him to leave because if this day had shown me anything, it was that I wasn't ready.

He'd played with the kids for hours, and when Quinn had begun crying at the thought of him not being there for another dinner, he'd assured her he would be there.

And I'd nearly crumpled.

Wondering what kind of mom I was to put her children through that. I'd been so consumed by my own pain that I'd neglected their own confusion and hurt.

I'd choked back tears all through making dinner and hadn't been able to eat once we were sitting, my stomach in knots from being pulled in so many directions. My body trembling from the overwhelming emotions I'd been drowning under for so long.

When I'd dropped a plate I was washing afterward, Beau had gently eased me aside and told me to go sit down, that he had it.

"Don't touch me and don't tell me what to do," I'd quietly seethed, picking the pieces of the plate out of the sink.

He hadn't responded or said a word to me since.

But he'd been there.

Tall and commanding and somber. Looking better than any man should in his signature Converse and dark jeans with his white tee stretched perfectly over his muscled build. Drawing me closer while my mind screamed to turn away. Making my soul sing and my chest wrench open. Stealing my heart repeatedly just to crush it.

I'd never been so conflicted or tormented. My entire being was so utterly exhausted after the hours near him. And I was sure if I would've had to watch him interact with our kids for another five minutes, I would've forgotten why I'd told him to leave in the first place.

The man was dangerous to my heart. He always had been.

I stilled when his steps sounded on the stairs, mentally counting each one so I knew where he was. But instead of turning for the front door, he turned toward me.

A trembling breath broke free when he entered the living room, my eyes focusing on the unopened book as he came closer and closer.

"They're all in bed."

I nodded when he stepped in front of me, squeezing my eyes tight when I had the strongest urge to look up at him. "Thank you."

"Thank *you* for letting me see them," he said, sounding like I'd given him the greatest gift in the world.

"I shouldn't have kept you from them like that." My head shook subtly as I lost the fight and looked into his eyes. Studying the emotions there and the sleepless nights defined beneath them and the way his black hair was all kinds of messed up from running his hands through it. "You can do this—what you did today. You know, come after work and stay until they go to bed. If you want."

"If I *want*?" His tongue darted out to wet his lips as a huff left him. "Where else would I want to be? It's killing me not being here with them every day—not being with *you*. We need to talk about what happened."

"No, we don't. I said not when the kids are here."

"Then *when*?" he demanded. When my head only continued moving in rapid shakes, he rocked back a step, his fingers curling into fists before he flexed them and drove them through his hair. And then he was crouching down in front of me, hands on the arms of the chair. "You won't talk to me when they're home, but that's the only time I can be here. How the hell are we—"

"I'm not ready, Beau," I cried softly. "I can barely navigate my thoughts, let alone get through a day. I'm not ready."

"Together," he said, rough and firm. "We get through things together. Remember?"

"Not this," I breathed, my soul crying out as our combined agony surged through the room. "Please go."

Beau stood, body slightly swaying as he looked at me with open fear. "Savannah . . ."

"Do you have any idea what you've done?"

His chest pitched, pain and regret twisting his features as he gestured to me before gesturing in the direction he'd just come from. "Yeah." His head hung and one of his hands came up to grip at his chest. "I—fuck." He started away, steps slow and staggered before they stopped altogether at the edge of the living room. "Every last breath."

And then he was gone.

As soon as the front door shut, I broke. A sob ripping from deep within the hollow of my chest as I crumpled in on myself. Body shuddering. Heart shattering. Soul grieving in a way I wasn't sure I'd ever come back from.

Six

SAVANNAH
FIFTEEN YEARS OLD

"*What?*"

I grabbed Madi's hand and hurried her farther away from the boys, hushing her as I did.

Her eyes were round, her face lit up with surprise and excitement for new dirty deets. "When did this happen?" she whisper-yelled.

"It hasn't."

"But y'all are *ready*," she said meaningfully. "When did *that* happen?"

"Well, why do you think I'm tellin' you?"

She glanced behind her, a mixture of a snort and a giggle leaving her as she grasped my hand even tighter and danced forward with me like we weren't already being suspicious. Like we weren't talking about the two Dixon boys behind us.

Hunter and Madison were officially done with middle school and would be joining Beau and me at the high school next year, and I couldn't wait to have my best friend at school with me again. But to celebrate the last day of this school year, we'd met up at the diner for milkshakes and fries the same as we had the last couple of years.

And I'd just told her what I'd been dying to tell her for days: I was ready.

You know . . . to go *there* with Beau.

Come end of summer, Beau and I were gonna be connected in an even deeper way, and I would no longer be a virgin.

Oh. My. God.

She stopped mid-pirouette and pulled me to a jarring halt with her. "Wait, have you told Beau?"

My mouth parted but nothing came out for a moment. "I mean, he knows. I didn't *tell him*, tell him. But he knows because we, you know, do stuff, and it's going that direction."

She smacked at my arm. "You told me before telling Beau?"

"Shh!" I skipped forward, dragging her with me, and jumped onto a storefront bench. Hurrying across it and leaping off in a grand jeté that was nowhere near as good as Madison's.

"Gorgeous," she said when she linked her arm through mine.

I bumped her hip. "Liar."

"It was!"

I just rolled my eyes, knowing we would go back and forth on this all day.

We'd both been dancing since we could walk and taking lessons since we were three. I'd met her the week we moved to Amber when my mom had taken me to check out the tiny studio in town.

But while I was good at ballet, it wasn't my strength like

it was Madison's. Probably because everything we danced to in ballet kinda made me wanna fall asleep, and I craved music that I felt in my bones. The kind of music that *made* me move.

Hip-hop, on the other hand? That's where I thrived.

But taking classes with Madison was only one of the reasons we were so close. The other had everything to do with the boys trailing behind us.

"So, when are you gonna tell him? Because you have to actually tell him . . . right?" she asked, sounding a little unsure. "I'm telling Hunter."

I shoved her away before pulling her super close, a gasp ripping through me as the conversation turned around to her. "You're *what?*"

Shock and confusion covered her face before it fell dramatically. "No! Not that—not yet." Her cheeks blazed red as a soft laugh left her. "Oh my word, we haven't even—" She glanced over her shoulder before dipping her head closer to me, her voice dropping to a whisper. "He hasn't even touched my *that*. You know this. He just touched my *these*"—she subtly gestured to her boobs—"for the first time, like, a month ago!"

"You said you were telling him. I thought—"

"I meant when I'm ready, I'm gonna tell him." She lifted her hands to her cheeks. "Oh my gosh, I feel like I'm gonna pass out."

My head tilted back as a laugh tumbled free, and then I was linking our arms again and continuing on the trek toward the Dixons' house and mine.

"Well, I don't know how to tell him," I said, finally answering. "It feels weird, trying to think of a way to say to him, 'Hey, I want to have sex.'" The last was said so softly, it almost got lost in the late spring breeze. "Like, I just want it to happen and be perfect and beautiful."

When Madi didn't respond, I glanced over to find her looking at me like she was trying so hard not to laugh.

"Don't make fun of me, you brat!"

The laugh broke free. So hard and loud, she immediately began wheezing. Head slowly shaking as she tried to speak and catch her breath. By the time she finally did, tears were slipping out of the corners of her eyes.

"I'm sorry, friend, it's just the thought of anything *Beau* and *beautiful* is funny." Another sharp laugh left her when I smacked her shoulder. "Maybe *brutal*."

"You're so hateful," I chastised as I turned to face Beau and Hunter while walking backward.

Beau was watching me, taking in my every move in that intense way that always made my heart race and my stomach dance. His signature tight-white-shirt-and-jeans combo making him look like something right out of the fifties and doing crazy things to me. The hint of a smirk on his gorgeous face telling me he most definitely knew we were talking about them.

"You know he's different with me," I said softly.

"I know, I know," Madison admitted. "But since you're the only one who sees that side of him, it *is* funny for the rest of us—even someone like me who sees teeny, tiny glimpses of your private moments—to think of Beau Dixon being *beautiful*."

"His heart's beautiful," I confessed.

She exhaled slowly before shrugging. "If you say it is, then it is." A worried noise left her when she turned to face the boys just as Beau shoved Hunter a few feet away.

But Beau's powerful stare never left me, and Hunter's laugh crossed the distance between us.

"He's fine," I murmured and tried to ignore Madison's silence that seemed to shout what she was clearly thinking.

This time.

A bomb set to explode—that's how everyone else saw Beau, including his parents and especially mine. They just didn't understand him. They didn't see underneath all the anger to the pain and frustration he held *for* that anger.

Then again . . . it wasn't exactly their faults. He didn't let anyone in except me.

But I saw him differently. I saw how he struggled to control what he felt controlled him. Saw how much it wrecked him when he hurt the people he cared about.

Beau's anger was big. So big. But so were the rest of his emotions.

The way he cared. The way he hurt. The way he loved and cherished me. All so intense in that Beau way . . . he just hid those amazing parts of himself from the rest of the world.

I stopped walking when Hunter started jogging our way, never slowing down when he wrapped Madison up in his arms, her laugh trailing behind them just as Beau reached me.

Pulling me close and resting his forehead on mine as he slowly walked me backward. One hand pressed firmly to the small of my back, the other around my cheek and teasing my hair as his mouth brushed across mine.

"What were y'all talking about?"

My lips twisted into a coy smirk before pressing against his again. "Wouldn't you like to know?"

A rumble sounded deep in his chest before he effortlessly

turned me so I was facing forward and tucked against his side.

"Why'd you push Hunter?"

Beau glanced down at me, his deep, deep dimples flashing a rare *hello* to match his even rarer smile. "Wouldn't you like to know?"

My lips parted on a huff because that was *so* not fair, but he wouldn't get me to talk that easily. I could fight my curiosity.

"Nope," I lied, popping the *p* and earning a rough, whispered laugh from him.

"So, what do you wanna do this summer?"

You.

I felt my cheeks and neck get hot at the thought and hurried to look at the road slowly passing beneath our feet.

"You have cheer camp and dance," he said softly when I didn't answer. "I'll be in the orchard a lot. But we have nights."

Oh my God, am I sweating?

I'm definitely sweating.

"And the party out by our lake in a couple nights." He cleared his throat. "And you're still not talking . . ."

"Yes, I am."

He pulled us to a stop and made sure I wasn't standing on the road before looking around us, running a hand nervously through his jet-black hair. "Savannah, I asked what you wanted to do this summer about five minutes ago."

"No, you—" I glanced behind us, surprised to see we were nowhere near where I remembered us just being.

How long had I been freaking out over Beau figuring out my super-embarrassing thoughts?

His dark blue eyes studied me when I faced him again,

looking worried and curious. "If you want to do something else, you just gotta say it, Savannah."

"I wanna be with you this summer," I said quickly, the words falling from my lips like I was confessing something bad.

Beau nodded and took a step to the side to continue home.

"I'm ready. I want it. With you—us," I rambled. "I wanna do that. Be with you—sex. I want sex."

That was *as awkward as I thought it'd be!*

Beau had come to a stop as soon as the word *sex* left me, his head whipping back around to look at me and eyes wider than I'd ever seen them.

For long seconds or maybe minutes or hours, he just stood there staring at me.

"That's what Madison and I were talking about. That's why I wasn't talking just now . . . because *that's* what I want. I just didn't know how to tell you, and I didn't really wanna tell you because I wanted it to happen like in the movies, you know? Where they don't have to say anything, it just hap—"

He stopped me with his mouth to mine. The kiss was firm until I melted against him, and then he was teasing my lips with his tongue and slipping it inside my mouth when I opened for him.

Soft.

Inviting.

Easy.

"Got it, angel."

And then he was pulling back from me and walking away, leaving me in a daze in a way only Beau Dixon and his lips could.

"Wait," I said, snapping out of it and hurrying after him.

"That's it? You aren't gonna say anything? You don't have any thoughts like maybe I'm crazy or you want that too or-or-or *anything*?"

"We're not talking about it."

My feet became one with the road beneath me.

My heart sank and humiliation rushed through me for the half-second that he left me hanging there.

"We're not talking about it because you want it to happen like in the movies. No saying anything, just letting it happen when it's meant to," he said in that soft, rough tone. Glancing over his shoulder and studying me with that fierce, adoring passion that had a way of knocking me off my feet. "And that's exactly what I'm gonna give you."

I was sure if I could've moved, I would've run up and kissed him. But I was too stunned as I tried to process the way he'd let me know he wanted it too. He wanted *that* with me.

Beau reached out for me, the corner of his mouth lifting in that way he had of smirking. The tilt of his lips so subtle, and yet it changed his expression so completely. Did the most amazing things to my heart and body.

I slipped my hand into his and let him pull me close, tucking me against his side as my pulse raced wildly for this boy.

"Crazy girl," he murmured against the top of my head before placing a kiss there.

I pushed against his stomach as a smile stole across my face. "Bear."

Hunter came jogging toward us with Madison bouncing on his back and giggling like crazy. "Y'all are slow as hell," he called out as he neared us.

"And?" Beau challenged.

"And it's hot," Hunter fired back. "Let's go so we can get in the lake."

"I gotta go home—"

"No," Madison said before I could finish talking, drawing out the word. "I thought we were gonna hang out all day and night."

"We are. Just gotta grab my bag for your place tonight and check in with my mom. Show her I haven't joined a cult or shaved my head. You know . . . the usual."

Beau squeezed me a little closer, the apology practically screaming from him even though he remained silent.

Even though our families had become so close that we spent all our free time and holidays with the Dixons, my parents had serious issues with Beau, and he knew it. It was impossible for him not to.

They didn't exactly hold back their thoughts in front of him.

And even though our families had a deep bond that I was thankful for, my parents didn't want me with Beau for long unless they were around too. So, if I was hanging out with him, I had to check in every so often to assure them he hadn't gone and done something crazy—like hit me.

I'd already swung by my house after school, and I'd probably have to check in again before going to Madison's tonight.

"Well, then we're getting in the AC until then," Hunter said as he turned and started down the last stretch toward our driveways.

"See you soon!" Madison called out, already laughing again as Hunter's jogging started up her bouncing all over again.

"Your dad's home," Beau said suddenly.

"What?" I looked toward my house and down the long drive, my chest getting cold and hot all at once when I saw his car. "Guess he got off early," I whispered, but something about his car in the driveway that early in the afternoon had me worried.

And I wasn't even sure *why*.

I'd gotten a near-perfect GPA my first year of high school, and that was all while maintaining dance and cheer. I hadn't gotten in trouble lately—well, Beau had, and I'd been there. But they already knew about that.

Still, there was a twisting in my stomach like I was about to get caught with my hand in the cookie jar. Except I had no jar. There were no cookies.

I hadn't even realized I'd starting biting at my thumb nail until Beau moved my hand away and curled his fingers around mine.

"I wasn't biting it," I said automatically.

"I know."

I knew he knew that.

I didn't bite my nails. I kinda-sorta tapped on them with my teeth. My parents were the ones who couldn't see the difference. But at the moment, I was freaking out over why my dad would be home so early. I mean, it wasn't like he never came home early . . . just . . . *almost* never.

"I'll come with you," Beau offered when we stopped in front of my driveway, his dark eyes searching mine like he could feel the ridiculous spiral my mind was going down.

I wanted to say *yes*.

Beau was everything to me . . . my comfort and safety and happiness. If I could, I would cling to him and never let go. But he and I both knew it would be so, so much worse if he walked into that house with me.

My mom was afraid of Beau even though he'd never so much as said an unkind word to her or my dad. So, if my dad wasn't around, she tried to bite her tongue around Beau and sometimes succeeded. But when my parents were together, the verbal gloves came off.

Watching Beau take their words like he deserved them before he stormed out because he couldn't handle anymore . . . trying to run after him only to be stopped by my parents . . . the screaming that followed that always led to me being grounded from very few things because they knew all I wanted was to see him . . .

It just wasn't worth it.

"No, it's fine," I said softly as my stare drifted to my dad's car again. My stomach clenching tighter and tighter.

Beau's hands cradled my cheeks, forcing me to look up at him. "You sure?"

"Positive." I pushed up on my toes to kiss him. "I'll be over soon."

He studied me for a while before nodding. "I'll be waiting for you."

"You better be," I teased, a soft laugh sounding in my throat when he pulled me back for another kiss. This one slower. Longer. Making my knees weak and my head spin and drowning out my worries by the time he released me.

A wicked grin crossed his face as if he knew exactly what he did to me as he turned and continued down the road toward his house.

I was smiling like crazy as I walked down my driveway in a Beau-daze. By the time I was walking through my front door, I'd forgotten why I'd been freaking out in the first place.

"Savannah."

I turned for the living room instead of the kitchen, my smile slipping when I found my parents standing there like they'd been waiting for me. Looking super disappointed. Super angry.

And sitting open on the coffee table in front of them . . . my diary.

BEAU

FIFTEEN YEARS OLD

We hadn't gone out to the lake that sat on the back part of our property, near the orchard. We'd gotten *ready*. But we hadn't gone.

Because Savannah still hadn't come over . . . four hours later.

We'd all talked about going to see what she was doing—what was taking so long, but my mom had put a stop to that. Saying Savannah's parents probably just wanted some time with her.

I'd told Hunter and Madison to go to the lake without me, especially once Sawyer, Leighton, and Emberly decided they were going too, but they'd stayed put. Turning on a movie instead while I paced.

"Mom." I glanced meaningfully at the clock once the dinner table was cleared and Leighton had gone home.

"Beau, she probably just couldn't come back over," she said gently. "Y'all can go a few hours without seeing each other, you know."

But Savannah said she'd be there, and she wasn't.

And it had me feeling all kinds of anxious and restless. Had that dark, steady thrum under my skin waking up to a nauseating rumble.

I hated it.

"Mrs. Dixon," Madison began, "Savannah's actually supposed to be spending the night with me tonight, and my parents should be on their way soon."

"Oh." Mom looked to the clock the same as I did even though the time hadn't changed. "Well, that doesn't sound like them. She would've at least called if something had changed," she mumbled to herself, then faced us again. "Okay, fine. Y'all can go."

I was already rushing for the door by the time she said *fine*. Flinging it open and bounding off the porch.

"You gonna wait?" Hunter called after me.

I didn't respond. I didn't slow.

I pushed faster.

There had been a ton of times that Savannah hadn't shown when she was supposed to, but like Mom said, she'd called. Or, at least, her parents had with some bullshit excuse for why they were trying to keep her from me that day.

I hated the times I was expecting her and the phone rang.

The more time had passed that afternoon, the more I'd expected that call. Except it hadn't come. And as I raced to her house, all I could think about was how worried Savannah had been over her dad being home early.

Wondering what the reason was behind it—if something had happened to her mom or someone else in her family. If something had happened to her dad's job. If—*fuck*—if they were moving again.

I knocked quickly on the Rileys' door, my chest pitching

as I waited and silently prayed that the latter wasn't something we would ever have to deal with.

Savannah's mom opened the door and immediately stepped back when she saw me—putting distance between us the way she had since the day she met me.

"Good evening, ma'am."

"Jason," she called out as she took another step back.

My stare darted into the house before focusing on her. "Can I talk to Savannah please?"

"Jason," she yelled again, this time with a hint of fear I'd learned well throughout my life. It pissed me off almost as much as it made me want to dig a hole for myself.

Mr. Riley came into the doorway and put himself half a step in front of his wife.

"Sir—"

"Savannah isn't here."

I jerked back, my stare swinging in the direction of my house before I turned around to look at the end of their driveway. "Uh, she—uh . . ." My head shook as I faced them again. "She never came over."

"I'm aware." He folded his arms over his chest and loosed a slow sigh. "Beau, we love your family, you know we do. They've become part of our family over the years. But I'm going to tell you right now that if you lose your temper, I have no problem being the next person to call the sheriff on you."

I went still.

The threat alone had that red haze creeping in.

The reminder of being cuffed and put in the back of a deputy's car just weeks ago had my hands curling into fists.

"Do we understand each other?"

I nodded, unable to speak with how tightly I was clenching my teeth.

"We have tried," he began, unfolding one of his arms to gesture to me. "We have tried *many* times to put an end to this. Beneath all your anger, you're a fine boy, I'm sure of it. But not for our Savannah. She shouldn't be around all that hostility."

My body ached from how still I was trying to hold myself. How fiercely I was shaking from all that *hostility* he'd just mentioned.

"It's time you let her go," he said, pointing at me to emphasize each drawn-out word.

"I can't. I love her."

His nostrils flared. "You will. She deserves a life where she isn't continually cleaning up after a rage-fueled disaster."

I felt his words like a strike to my chest. The air fleeing from my lungs on a pained wheeze as the truth of them rang in my soul.

"By the way, my daughter is fifteen." He stepped back and reached for the door, his face turning red as he glared down at me, seething. "If I ever find out that you've been *touching* her again . . ."

Even as my stomach dropped and my mind raced, trying to figure out *how* they knew what Savannah and I did, my anger rose in response to his. A reaction I had no control over. Hot and sickening and consuming.

"The next time she goes, it won't just be for the summer," he finished slowly, his lip curling. "I will not let you ruin my daughter any more than you already have."

"Summer—wait, where's Savannah?" I demanded in a tone sharper than I'd ever used with them.

Mrs. Riley stepped back even farther at the sound of it,

and I forced myself to do the same, my entire body trembling as I struggled to calm.

"Where's Savannah?" I nearly begged when Mr. Riley started shutting the door without answering.

"Better cool it, Beau."

"I'm calm. Just tell me where Savannah is," I snapped, driving my hands into my hair as I fought every urge coursing through my veins.

Mr. Riley released a sharp, disapproving huff, his stare and tone full of warning when he said, "On a train to her grandparents' for the summer."

I bent slightly, feeling like I'd taken a hit to the gut. "What?"

"If a couple months apart doesn't get you out of her system, I trust you'll come to your senses and do what's right for her."

I staggered back and nearly tripped down the stairs when he shut the door.

My feet were like lead when I slowly started back to my house. Staring straight ahead but not really seeing anything as I battled the threat of red lining my vision. As his words replayed again and again and made me feel worthless. Made me feel exactly like what Mr. Riley had called me . . .

A rage-fueled disaster.

I didn't notice Hunter and Madison making out against the fence in the spot where you couldn't be seen by either house until I was walking past them. And then they were stumbling after me and trying to stop me.

"Where's Savannah?" Madison asked quickly. "Is she not coming to my house?"

My eyelids slowly shut as my fingers curled tight.

"Beau, what happened?" Hunter asked, reaching for my shoulder when I still didn't respond. "You good?"

I swung.

I didn't think about it. Didn't even realize I was doing it until it was already done and I was staring at the two of them. My fist having just missed Hunter's face because the asshole was fast.

"Don't touch me."

He slowly raised his hands but followed after me as soon as I began walking again. "Talk to us—where's Savannah?"

"She's fucking gone, Hunter," I snapped. "Her parents sent her away."

"But . . . why?" Madison asked softly, almost as if she was talking to herself.

I turned on them, my brows raised as I stared her down. "Really. You *really* can't think of any reason why they would send her away?"

"That's enough," Hunter said in soft warning.

"That isn't what I—"

"*Me*, Madison," I ground out, cutting her off. "To get her away from me. Hoping a summer apart will be enough for her to be done with me."

"I didn't mean why *literally*," she yelled. "I just can't believe they would do this to her."

I opened my mouth to fire back, but Hunter was suddenly there, hand against my chest and glare full of warning.

"Get away from me," I said, low and threatening. "Now."

"You need to take a breath and walk away before this gets worse." He held my stare, knowing I was already on the edge of worse, and lowered his voice. "Beau, *walk*."

I shoved him back and stalked off toward our house, dragging my fingers through my hair and over my face as I fought against the growing anger.

Savannah's gone.

I hadn't gone more than a couple days without her since I'd met her. Even then, it had only been if one of us was grounded—usually me. An entire summer, all while knowing it was because of me? Because they wanted us apart that badly?

"Mom," I said through clenched teeth when I stormed through the front door, narrowed eyes searching for her as I headed for the living room where she was watching shows with my youngest brothers and Emberly. "Mom, did you know?"

"Know wh—" Her eyes widened when she saw me, her stare darting behind me like she was looking for Savannah. "What's wrong, honey?"

"What's happened?" Dad asked, following me into the living room.

"Tell me if you knew," I demanded and then curled my hands tighter as I tried to rein it in.

Mom stood and placed her hands up in front of her stomach as she spoke in a calming tone. "Beau, sweetie, I don't even know what you're talking about."

"Savannah. Her parents sent her away for the summer. To get her away from me—hoping she'll wanna break up with me. And if she doesn't, they want me to break up with her."

Mom's mouth fell open. "They wouldn't ever want—"

"They just told me that," I yelled and then clenched my hands until they ached. "Mom, you know how they feel about me—you *know*."

"No, honey, they adore you."

A sharp laugh ripped from me, filled with pain and frustration.

"But you're in love with their baby girl. That's gotta be hard for any parents. And then . . ."

"And then *what?*" I asked when she didn't continue. "And then add in the fact that I'm like this?" I gestured to where I was shaking uncontrollably. "A rage-fueled disaster?"

"You are *not.*"

"That's what Mr. Riley just called me," I shouted, my voice booming in the room. I jerked away from my dad when he came up beside me, chest heaving from my ragged breaths. "Don't touch me."

"Don't give me a reason to," he said in warning.

A tone that had me on edge worse than I'd already been.

Mom's stare bounced between us for a moment, her head moving faintly before she said, "Then your father and I are just gonna have to have a talk with them. But, right now, you need to calm down."

"No, I don't—*no*. I don't need y'all to talk with them," I bit out. "I already know what they're saying is true."

"Now you know it ain't," my dad murmured, but I continued.

"What I need is Savannah back." My jaw trembled with a lethal combination of rage and devastation. "I need—I need . . . to not be like this." I reeled back a few steps, my hand clawing at my chest as that poisonous need thrummed beneath my skin. "Why am I—what's wrong with me?" I gritted out.

"Honey, no," Mom began as Dad said, "Not a damn thing."

Cayson stood from the couch and scoffed. "Yeah, okay."

Screaming . . .

That was the next thing I registered as everything came into focus for one brief moment. I was on top of Cayson, and my arm was cocked back. Blood was pooling from his nose.

Blood as red as the rest of my world.

I swung at someone else. I know that.

But that's all I remembered before my back met the hardwood floor.

"Get the fuck off me," I roared and fought to remove the people pinning me down.

"Enough," Dad yelled just as loudly from where he held one side of me down.

"Calm down, Beau, calm down," Hunter wheezed from where he struggled to help keep me in place. He grunted and slammed my arm back down when I managed to lift him. "Jesus, Beau, *stop*."

"Let go," I seethed.

He glanced at me, head shaking in refusal. Blood was trickling out of the corner of his mouth.

Shit.

My head hit the hardwood as I squeezed my eyes tight and tried like hell to calm myself. But that feeling was in my veins and on my skin. Telling me to keep going.

"I can't," Mom sobbed. "I can't—we can't do this anymore. It has to be done."

"Wendy," Dad said, voice sharp.

"He needs help!" she yelled, her voice fading from the room but still managing to pierce my chest. When she continued, her words steadily grew louder as she returned. "He needs what we can't give him. He needs people who can control him, Mike, and we can't do that."

"The answer is *no*," he said firmly. "We'll talk later."

"We're talking now," she argued. "I am his mother, and I

need to do what's best for him."

"What's best is his family," Dad shouted louder than I'd ever heard. "Stability. Not that bullshit you're trying to put on him. That'll only make him worse."

"You're wrong. I've talked with them. They've had plenty of boys like Beau, and they've helped them. I know they'll— know they'll—" She burst into tears and sagged to the arm of a chair. "They'll help."

I'd gone still long before.

My heart so, so slow as I listened. Watched. Felt every word cut through me.

That sickness inside lingering.

Waiting.

Ready to ignite.

"We ain't doin' this in front of the kids," Dad said firmly.

"I already sent in an application."

Dad pushed off me, turning to look fully at Mom at her confession.

Another sob broke free from her. "It has to be done." Her eyes drifted to me. "I'm so sorry. I'm sorry, I love you. I love you so much, but I don't know what else to do."

Hunter's grip slowly tightened on my shoulder. As if he could feel the shift in me. Like he was holding onto a bomb that was about to explode.

My stare went to Cayson's blood-smeared face and then over to where Sawyer was cradling his arm. Knowing whatever happened to him had been my fault even though I couldn't remember it. Just past them, Madison stood, holding Emberly close to her side.

All of them were watching my mom, waiting to find out what was going on.

But as much as I was dreading whatever had my parents

fighting in a way I'd never seen and had my mom looking the way she did, I was more afraid to find out when the room was full.

If I lost control when no one was around, I lashed out against the closest thing to me—like a wall.

I wouldn't take my family down with me . . . again.

"I should be alone when I find out," I choked out.

"Nothin' to find out because it ain't happenin'," Dad said decisively.

"It has—"

"Wendy—"

"I sent in an application to a military academy," she yelled over him, fat tears falling down her cheeks as she looked at me.

I couldn't move.

I couldn't breathe.

That feeling building inside me? It terrified me.

"Down in Harlingen," she explained. "If you get in, we'll see how things are for you at the end of next school year."

What the fuck?

She shrugged as her cries prevented her from continuing for a while. "But this has to be done. They can help you."

What the fuck? What the fuck?

"Nothin' to help," Dad ground out. "He's not goin'—you ain't goin', Beau."

My voice was low and ragged when I said, "Get away from me."

"Take a breath, man," Hunter said quickly. "Think of Savannah—what she would say right now." From his hushed curse, he realized his mistake as soon as he mentioned her.

My heart twisted. Splintered. Shattered.

And everything went so, so red.

BEAU

I tossed my keys to the side, not bothering to pick them up when they slid off the table and hit the hardwood floor. Each step feeling like it took all my strength as I struggled to make it somewhere I could lay down.

But just as I was nearing the couch, a key sounded in the lock. After a longing look at the couch, I turned to stare at the door, brows drawn close together. No one had come to the condo in the two and a half weeks I'd been staying there, but I didn't have the energy to care about who it might be.

And then my brother walked in.

Stare sweeping the place until catching on me, body going still as the door closed behind him. "Beau."

"Cayson." I nodded toward the table my keys hadn't landed on. "Here for your stuff?"

Hesitation crept through the space between us for a moment before he reacted. Body rocking to the side and head slanting. "No. Uh . . ." He cleared his throat and gestured around. "We're keeping it like this. Emberly wants to rent it out."

I dipped my head, gaze darting around to the few things I had there. "I'll leave."

"No, no. Stay however long you need. Just something we were talking about for later," he explained as he moved deeper into the condo, toward me. Stopping when he was a handful of feet away, watching me like he didn't know where to begin.

Knew the look because I felt the same.

I'd only seen Cayson a handful of times in the six-or-so months since he'd come back to Amber. The first two had gone about how I'd always thought they would—all hostile sneers ripping from me as I'd tried dragging him from my home.

Then again, I'd hated him for a damn long time.

Blamed him for the painful domino effect that had destroyed our family.

The next time he'd shown up, explaining all the fucked-up shit our dad had done to him and the family business, I'd once again wished Cayson had never come back. Because in his revelation, he'd torn apart a man I'd looked up to, revealing his true, abusive nature. And I'd been slammed with the horrifying realization that Dad and I were the same. Consumed with the crippling fear that, one day, I would turn on one of my kids the way he'd done to Cayson. Verbally, mentally, and physically beating them down because I was no better than he was.

"You busy?" Cayson finally asked, trying to break through the awkward tension sitting between us.

I lifted a hand as if to show I wasn't. "Just got back from Blossom."

His brows lifted. "Yeah?"

A lifeless laugh tumbled past my lips. "Yeah." I stepped

back to the couch and sank heavily onto it, running my hands over my face and through my hair before letting them hang between my knees. "Savannah finally let me back yesterday to see the kids."

My jaw worked as I thought through the hours with them. Hours that went by too quickly in the middle of days that were so damn long.

"She's letting me go over after work until they go to bed. I'll take what I can get."

"Damn," he breathed as he sat in a large chair opposite me. "Have y'all talked about it?"

My narrowed stare shifted to where he was messing with his phone. "She won't. The hell is that shit?" I asked when a song started playing through his phone.

"Dixie Chicks."

"No."

A wry smile slowly crossed his face as he turned the volume down a little and set his phone aside. "Emberly said I had to." He lifted his hands as if to say there was nothing he could do about it. "Said they help everything."

"Emberly isn't here. Turn it off."

He shrugged but didn't reach for his phone. When he spoke, his amusement faded into genuine sorrow. "I'm sorry about Savannah. She . . . you know how we've talked to her?" At my hard nod, he said, "Hunter told her everything, hoping to help y'all so she would understand that night better. But *that* mixed with the fight the other day and you being behind Madison leaving—"

"She knows that?" My chest seared with white-hot pain as I realized they'd told her *everything*.

Madison's side of everything.

"You don't want her to?"

"If someone's gonna tell her, I want it to be me," I ground out. "Not Madison's side of how all that shit went down."

"Are they different?"

"Of course they are," I snapped. Pushing back into the couch, I forced myself to take shuddering breaths before continuing. "Overall, no. They're not. But the details? I haven't heard Madison's side, but I know damn well they're different because Madison wasn't fucking here. She doesn't know that, after she left, I was the one who told Savannah that Hunter needed to know where Madison was. That he needed to go after her. Madison doesn't know that, when Hunter drained his savings, I paid for his last flight out there. All so he could get her back, so he would *bring her back*. Madison *can't* know about the dozens of calls I made to her because she ditched her number when she left. When Hunter couldn't bring her back, I got desperate enough to grab the new number from Savannah's phone, except Madison had already ditched that number too. She doesn't know any of the bullshit Savannah and I went through—stuff Savannah still might not realize was because of my guilt over what happened."

Cayson waited until I was done, head moving in a slow, faint nod as he listened. "So, tell her."

A harsh breath burst from me, all pain and defeat. "She won't even let me talk to her."

"Find a way."

My narrowed gaze cut to him before shifting to the floor.

"When's the last time you slept, man?"

My shoulders shifted from the force of my muted laugh. "No idea."

"Maybe try doing that first," he suggested as he pushed from the chair.

"I should've known," I said when he scooped up his phone. After a moment, I met his questioning stare. "About you . . . about Dad. I should've known."

His jaw tensed but he forced a shrug. "It is what it is."

"Had no idea how alike we were until you told us everything," I went on, regret pooling in my gut as I remembered his words.

"You and me?" he asked doubtfully, a hint of a laugh leaving him.

A grunt of affirmation rumbled in my chest. "There were so many times I got arrested or in trouble at school, and I hadn't done anything," I said, flashes of the past rushing up to taunt me. "But it was easy to put the blame on me. The angry one. The violent one. And I'd just take it because . . ." I lifted a shoulder and met his hardened stare. "They already thought it about me anyway, and I *was* violent, right?"

Cayson watched me, some unknown emotion streaking across his face before he gave a hesitant nod.

"I never stopped to think maybe people were putting shit on you just because they could. Because you were always causing trouble. Because it was easy to pin stuff on us. And Dad . . . I didn't know, but I should've. He was just always more patient with me than I deserved, so I thought he was doing the same with you when you got off the hook again and again."

"You're not him," Cayson said suddenly, then jerked his chin at me. "You asked Hunter that the other day . . . there's your answer."

"You don't know me anymore."

A scoff of a laugh left him as he took his seat in the chair again, setting his phone back down as the music continued playing. "Yeah, I'm aware. But I've talked to Sawyer a lot, and I did grow up with you. And I can see you now."

"I saw Dad nearly every day of my life, and I didn't know that about him, Cays. I couldn't see that he had the same darkness that courses through me."

"That's it," he said quickly. "Right there. Dad hid who he was and hid his anger, pretending to be someone else for our family and the entire town. But I think a part of him loved that angry side. He'd push me until he thought I was gonna fight him. And then he'd encourage it and get mad when I wouldn't." He gestured to me, his hand falling heavily to his legs. "I don't think you know how to hide your anger even though Savannah said you'd been controlling it. Because even though it isn't *who* you are, it's a part of you, and you know that. Understand that. And from the look on your face the other day, I'm pretty damn sure you don't love it. That you might even be afraid of it."

I had been afraid of it.

It had controlled me for so long. Blocking out moments of my life while I took down everything in my path. It had threatened to destroy my marriage and my family for so long before it finally *did*.

"You said you think we're alike," Cayson murmured, head bobbing quickly. "Then remember that I hid everything about who I really was from everyone, only letting them see the troublemaker. The asshole. Same goes for you. I think you hide who you really are and only let people see your anger. But I know Savannah sees who you really are. I know she always has because that girl has stood up for you forever, even when you didn't deserve it. And I'd bet your kids get the real you. Just as I'd bet my life that you'd do anything to keep your anger away from them."

My chin wavered as I gave a hard nod.

"That isn't Dad," he said simply.

My fingers curled and relaxed. Forming fists over and over as the fear that had plagued me for months scraped up my throat and settled heavily on my tongue.

Meeting Cayson's confident stare, I asked, "But what if that changes?"

MY EYELIDS SLOWLY OPENED, feeling like they weighed a ton as I glanced around the living room of the condo. Lights still on from when I'd come in the night before, but that wasn't why the place was so bright.

I glanced at the windows where sunlight was filtering in from the partially opened curtains and tried to figure out how it could be morning when I'd just gotten back. When Cayson had just stopped by, and we'd been talking . . .

Looking to the side at the thought, I saw my brother squished into the same chair he'd been in the night before. Legs hanging over one of the arms of the chair and completely passed out.

Unfolding my tightly crossed arms, I sat up and rubbed at the back of my neck. Searching for my phone and wondering at what point in our conversation we'd fallen asleep. Grabbing my phone when I found it on the couch, I looked at the time and mumbled a curse.

"Cayson," I murmured as I pushed to my feet. Taking the few steps over to him, I smacked his arm. "Wake up."

His hands shot out, curling into fists like he was prepared for anything, even in sleep. "The hell?"

"I gotta get to work."

When he saw me there, his eyes widened and he glanced around, trying to figure out where he was the same way I'd done. "Shit."

"Yeah. Go home."

Disbelief colored his expression as he slowly straightened from the position he'd been in. "Emberly was right. Freaking Dixie Chicks, man."

A scoff left me, my eyes rolling as I walked away. "Idiot."

"I enjoyed our heart-to-heart too," he called out, all playful amusement.

"Go home, Cayson."

"Hey." At the change in his tone, I turned to face where he was standing a couple feet from the chair. "Be patient with her," he said, repeating words he'd said to me the night before.

"The longest I've ever gone without her was the summer her parents sent her away. Since we've been married?" My shoulders lifted in a hint of a shrug. "It's been her and me, every night . . . until now. And she wants nothing to do with me."

Sympathy washed over his face, his head shaking as he took a step back. "I know that isn't true, but maybe you should talk to Sawyer. He sees her almost every day."

Something twisted in my chest.

Not that I was surprised. Sawyer had always been at our house, helping out with renovations or fixing whatever went wrong. Or just to be there. But knowing my wife was confiding in my youngest brother when she wouldn't talk to me? It *hurt*.

"Or maybe you should talk to Hunter since he's been on her side of it."

My eyes narrowed in warning. "You know where I stand with him."

"Maybe you should talk to Hunter," he repeated firmly, brows lifting knowingly as he turned and walked out the door.

Yeah, that wasn't gonna happen.

Nine

SAVANNAH

My gaze moved to where the small, rectangular box sat on the side counter for the umpteenth time since I'd started baking. My hand paused with the icing-covered spoon mid-air before I was able to push the box from my mind and focus on what I was doing: Drizzling icing over the Danish pastries for the guests that would be arriving throughout the day.

A full bed and breakfast that weekend and a full bed and breakfast the weekend after.

All while my world was crumbling.

I can do this.

I have this handled.

I watched my oldest kids dash through the kitchen, laughs bouncing off the walls as Quinn tried to catch her younger brother. Warming my soul and making me confident that I could do this. Until my stare shifted to the side counter once again . . .

A sound of frustration burst from me when I finally

moved around the island so my back was to that counter. Helping me focus on the task at hand.

At least for a little while.

I somehow made it through dishes and cleaning the islands while the icing dried on the Danishes. But once they were in their display case and off to the side, next to my momma's favorite lemon pound cake and the peach hand pies —because I had no control when I was an emotional wreck— I found myself standing at the counter I'd been struggling to avoid. Staring at the box like it could destroy me.

I knew what was in there—a new phone. The box was familiar enough, and the picture on the outside told me as much. But it was that Beau had done this . . . without a word. Without a question as to what happened to my original one. He'd just taken care of it.

When he'd shown up again the day before, it had been different. More painful. I'd desperately wanted to fall into that place beside him as I listened to the familiar sounds of his deep, gravelly voice mixing with the animated tones of our kids' voices as they had conversations and played. As I'd watched him care for them the way he always had.

But I'd stayed off to the side, letting them have that time together.

And even when his stare had drifted to me, all that intense passion capturing me up and weakening my anger and my resolve, he hadn't tried closing that distance between us the way he had the first night. He also hadn't said anything to me until he was leaving, and then it was just two words.

The only ones that mattered when it came to us.

"Every breath."

Once he was gone, I'd headed to the kitchen to stress-bake. And that's when the box had first caught my eye—sitting in the exact spot where I'd left my phone after accidentally shattering the screen a couple days before. I'd stood there staring at it much the same way I was then before going to the freezer and grabbing a pint of ice cream instead.

"This is stupid. He's your husband, he's allowed to replace your broken phone," I muttered to myself, snatching up the box and carefully opening the lid.

I don't know what I'd been expecting, considering I knew what the box held, but my shoulders sagged when I found a phone. Already set up to look exactly like my old one with every picture and message still there.

Maybe it was because I'd immediately gone through all the missed calls and messages, looking for anything from Beau . . . and finding nothing. Since I'd first told him to leave, he'd called a couple times a day and messaged dozens more. But there hadn't been one call or text from him since he'd first come over.

I wasn't sure why it hurt so badly, why it made my chest ache with dread, even though I'd told him I wasn't ready.

Maybe because it felt like a step down a path we couldn't come back from. Maybe because our distance and silence terrified me as much as it felt necessary.

I hurried to grab up the box when I heard Levi waking from his nap, babbling and cooing to himself, my movements coming to an abrupt stop when I saw it.

Setting the phone on the counter, I pulled away the slip of paper stuck to the inside of the box, my heart racing this unforgiving beat when I turned it around and saw Beau's scrawl.

. . .

I LOVE YOU.

CRADLING the paper in my palm, I took the box upstairs and set the paper on my nightstand, letting my gaze linger on it for a moment longer before I hurried off to see one of my favorite guys.

"Handsome boy," I whispered, expression bright when I snuck into Levi's room and found him staring at me through the slats of his crib. A cheesy grin spreading wide across his face and showcasing his dimples. "How was your nap?"

He babbled endlessly as I changed his diaper and put him in a new outfit.

"Tell me about it," I teased as I lifted him into my arms and started for the door. "Your life sounds so rough."

"Dadda?" he asked, pointing at the doorway and twisting my heart.

"Mmhm," I forced out, nodding and keeping my smile in place. "Daddy will be here soon. So will lots of other people, including Grandma and Grandpa. Isn't that fun?"

"Dadda," he said again, continuing to lead the way with his finger.

"Yeah." I took a fortifying breath as I started down the stairs. Trying to ignore the fierce ache in my chest and the way it felt like I would fall to the floor and never get up again if I stopped for just one second. "I know, buddy."

Following the sounds of my older kids down the stairs and into their tucked-away playroom, I let my stare dance over them as they colored side by side. Their lightsabers still lit up and lying forgotten beside them after what I was sure was an epic battle.

"Qin."

A soft gasp left me as I looked to where Levi was pointing at them, excitement bursting from me as I bounced him, slowly dancing with him. "That's right! Is that your sister, Quinn?"

"Qin," he repeated before giving a big belly laugh as if he'd just said the funniest thing in the world.

The older two scrambled to their feet and ran over at hearing his laugh, having just noticed us there. Cooing over their little brother the way they always did, as if he were a newborn and not nine months old.

"He's trying to say your name," I told Quinn, my throat tightening because Beau wasn't there.

But that was silly.

He wouldn't have been there anyway. He would've still been at work.

When they tried and failed to get him to say it again, and Levi just leaned his head on my shoulder and smiled at them like they were being funny, I cleared my throat. "Okay, guests are gonna start arriving soon, and we'll have a completely full house this weekend."

"Like Grandma and Grandpa?" Quinn asked excitedly.

"Yes," I answered as Wyatt did some sort of karate chop to show his excitement. "But they're coming in later tonight. Other people are coming before them. Do you remember the rules when guests are here?"

"No running through the house," Quinn recited, her excitement still beaming through and making her all kinds of squirmy.

"No killing Quinn with lightsabers."

A snort left me, my chest shaking with the laughter I was trying so hard to suppress. "Yeah, uh . . . no killing your sister ever. But definitely not when guests are here." I studied them, love and adoration pulling at my chest. "If you need to be all wild and crazy, be crazy in here or your rooms, right?"

"Right," they said in unison.

"But I think one last lap through the house might be needed," I said slowly, pretending to think it over. Stepping back, I nodded toward the open door. "Ready, set, go."

They were gone before I finished talking, screaming like mad and declaring who would win when they'd only just begun.

"They're so silly," I whispered to Levi when he giggled and reached after them.

But before they could return, the sound of the doorbell filled the house.

"Oh, someone's early," I mumbled mostly to myself as I hurried out of the playroom, silently cursing myself for not being more prepared.

Not for the guests, everything was ready for them. But for the first arrival. I'd wanted to get the kids at least settled with a snack before anyone showed. Then again, I hadn't been expecting anyone until after Beau was supposed to be there.

Hitching Levi higher up on my hip when I made it into the entryway, I high-fived Quinn and Wyatt when I found them hurrying back to the playroom, covering their giggling faces with one of their hands because they knew the time for screaming was over.

"Who was winning?" I asked as they passed.

Wyatt huffed. "C'mon, Momma. You know I'm so super-fast."

"Of course." I playfully rolled my eyes. "How could I forget?"

Quinn spun around, mischievous expression falling. "Daddy's coming, right?"

Her tone and the worry on her face was enough to make me miss a step before stopping altogether. The fear that had been plaguing her ever since Beau came over a couple days before had only grown.

As if she understood far more than she should. As if she saw these hours with her dad for what they were.

Hours.

Not him truly coming *home* for the night.

"Of course," I said, head bobbing frantically. "He should be home soon. I'll get you when he is."

At my assurance, she took off for the playroom, features as bright and excited as ever.

If it weren't for the second ring of the doorbell that sounded, I would've crumpled right there. For what we were going through, for what he had done, for how I was hurting my family and lying to my children.

Forcing myself to keep going, I took a deep, steeling breath and reached for the handle of the door as Beau's voice drifted through my thoughts.

Let's live that dream.

Forcing the fakest smile of my life, I pulled open the door, already talking as I did. "Hi, I'm so sorry about—" Shock filled me and stole the rest of my words as I stared at the man in front of me.

At once familiar and like looking at a stranger.

A sound of disbelief fled from me, my head shaking absentmindedly as I tried to wrap my head around the fact that he was *there*. "Peter?"

That familiar, wry grin stole across his face. "Hey, Anna-Hannah."

"Oh my God!" I nearly shouted as I rushed forward to crush myself to him while carefully holding Levi away.

Amusement left him on a soft laugh as he hugged me. "Missed you too."

A huff tumbled past my lips, all wavering emotion because crying was all I seemed capable of anymore. "I can't believe you're here. What are you doing here? I mean, I know what you're doing—I just didn't know you would be here. I missed you." I shoved his shoulder when I pulled away, a sob of a laugh bursting free. "And it's *Savannah*, you ass."

His head tipped back on a barking laugh, his eyes all familiar mischief when he met my stare again. "Better watch that mouth, Riley, you have little ears around now."

I waved him off as I stepped back to let him inside.

"Excuse me—*Dixon*." He gave me a look that was all kinds of amused and not at all surprised as I shut the door behind him. "Sorry I missed the wedding."

"My wedding?" I asked, disbelief coating my words. "Peter, I thought you weren't even gonna be here for your *brother's* wedding."

His eyes dragged to the side, rolling as they did. "Would you blame me?"

A noncommittal hum sounded in my throat as I shifted Levi around, giving myself something to do so I wouldn't have to answer that. "But you're here," I said, happiness pouring free as I eyed the bag in his hand. "All our rooms are taken—your parents rented out most of them. But I'll move some things around and get a bed ready for you."

"Actually . . ." He gave me one of those looks that was so utterly the Peter I'd known growing up. All humor even though he was trying to look hesitant. "I kinda talked my grandma into giving up her room here. She's staying at my parents' now."

A sharp huff left me. "Peter Rowe . . ."

"Again, do you blame me?" Something dark and heavy passed over his face as he shrugged. "Hadn't been here more than a minute before my mom started in on all the ways I ruined my marriage."

"What?" It was nothing more than a breath as his pain echoed my own and made the soul-deep ache flare. "Oh, I hadn't . . . I hadn't heard."

"Surprising in this town." He glanced away, head shaking subtly as he did. "Then again, I think my mom's in denial and embarrassed for anyone to find out—especially with Philip getting married." His voice softened to an irritated murmur. "And then I went and thought I'd be able to handle my family for Philip's three-day wedding weekend."

I cleared my throat, nodding to the side as I did. "You wanna talk about it over coffee?"

"Well, damn, Anna-Hannah," he muttered, some of that amusement coming back to his tone. "Been in this place for about a minute. It's about time you start showing some hospitality."

A laugh left me as I pushed him away. "Such a jerk."

He followed me into the kitchen, a low whistle coming from him as he took everything in.

"I'll give you a tour later when I show you to your room," I offered as I went over to the coffee maker to get a pot going. "Or did you want to go relax now? Sorry, I didn't even think. I'm still in shock that you're here."

"No, I'm good." He set his bag down near the archway, something like awe in his voice as he looked around. "Can't believe y'all did it—got the house and made your dream."

After a moment, he huffed, his tone all wicked teasing. "Can't believe your parents let you marry Beau Dixon."

My face fell, and I was thankful my back was to Peter. This man I'd grown up with and spent nearly as much time with as the Dixon boys. Who had been like an older brother to me before he'd left for college and then the Navy, where he'd stayed. He would've seen right through it, down to the root of my pain.

"Yeah." I tried to laugh, tried to joke, but it fell flat. "Actually, they really love him now."

"No shit?"

Another one of those noncommittal hums built in my throat. "Yeah, it took a long time, but things started changing the night—well, the last night I saw you, I guess. Before you left for the Navy."

"You good?" he asked suddenly, voice much closer than it had been and dripping with concern.

"Yeah." I shrugged, barely making eye contact with him as I turned to grab a banana and an avocado for Levi's snack.

But I saw his furrowed brow. The worry and the wonder. And if Peter was anything like he used to be, I knew he wouldn't let it go.

"So, tell me what happened," I asked as I moved through the kitchen to put Levi in his high chair, trying to get the focus off me. "I'd heard about you getting married from my parents, but not the rest." When I faced him again, I let my expression fall with my apology. "To be honest, I try not to keep up with your family all that much."

He waved a hand lazily through the air. "I don't keep up with them much either." With an exhausted sigh, he said, "There isn't a whole lot to say. She didn't like how much I was gone with my job, so she left."

I paused in cutting open the avocado, my voice hesitant when I asked, "Your job . . . in the Navy? You're a SEAL, right?"

His eyes narrowed playfully at me. "Thought you didn't keep up with my family."

"You should've heard the girls in this town when it got loose that you were a Navy SEAL." An exaggerated groan left me that faded into a laugh. "There are probably still some who have been desperately waiting for you to come back. Your being in Amber is probably making their entire life."

"Yay me," he said dryly. "But, yeah. Going overseas. Missions. She didn't like it. I told her I'd get out. I would've done anything for her. But she still left, even after I got the paperwork started."

"Oh my God," I whispered, sorrow pulling at my chest. "I'm so sorry." When he just shrugged, trying to feign indifference, I asked. "So, are you still getting out?"

"Already am. Have been for over a month. But if my mom asks, I just got out this week."

At the mischievous grin on his face, a soft laugh bled from me. "I see. And what are you gonna do? Come back here?"

A huff left him, his expression saying I should've known better. "Not everyone loves Amber the way you do, Savannah," he said, repeating words he'd told me so, so long ago.

"You do have a problem with returning," I mumbled meaningfully.

His brows lifted in agreement. "A couple guys from my Team live in South Carolina now. When everything happened and I got out, I went there to get my mind off everything. Be pissed at the world, I dunno." His shoulders lifted in a quick shrug. "And that place . . . there's just something about it."

"You like it there," I said when he didn't continue.

His head dipped in a slow nod, stare unfocused for a while before one of those grins lit up his entire face. "Small as hell, but it's nothing like Amber. And the gossip there? They think they have it on lockdown, and it cracks me up because they can't touch the Amber networking system."

"Nothing can," I said in agreement as I put Levi's snack in front of him, making babbling noises back at him for a moment before turning to clean up as Peter poured coffee, making himself at home.

"A lot of people know a lot of people, but there's still some sense of privacy. Place is adorable as hell. But . . . it doesn't have my parents *and* we have more than one traffic light."

I drew in a shallow gasp as if he'd told me something scandalous. "What kind of sacrilegious place has more than one traffic light?"

One of those big, contagious laughs burst from him as he slid a mug my way. "The kind that . . ." His words trailed off when my laugh immediately died as my heart took off in a frantic, painful race toward the man who'd just entered the kitchen.

Midnight-blue eyes locked on me for long moments, holding me prisoner with all that love and pain before they slid toward Peter and narrowed.

"Oh, hey," Peter said, quickly recovering when he saw Beau. "Damn, man, it's been a long time."

"Peter," Beau said gruffly, then turned to leave the kitchen, his stare catching on me as he did.

My hand shot out to the counter as my knees weakened. Because that fierce look had said it all.

He was hurting, I knew. But this encounter hurt him

more. The betrayal that ripped through his eyes said as much.

Except I hadn't been doing anything. I wasn't the one who had betrayed the other. And this was *Peter*. It was no different than having a conversation with one of Beau's brothers. And I hated that he'd left me feeling like I'd done something wrong, like I needed to fix things, when everything had been on him.

When I finally looked away from the archway Beau had left through, Peter was studying me. Expression solemn and knowing. Lifting the entire pot of coffee, he asked, "Got anything stronger?"

A soggy laugh broke free as tears filled my eyes, but I quickly shook my head, stepping back and holding up a hand when he stepped forward. "No, no. Don't. I'm fine." Sucking in a broken breath, I blinked quickly until the threat of tears was gone, then gave him a shaky smile. "See? Fine."

One of his eyebrows lifted as he said, "Yeah, and my brother's a saint." All sarcasm and dripping with doubt as he silently prompted me to explain what that had been about.

"Peter, please?" I softly begged as the sound of my kids coming down the hall with Beau filtered into the kitchen.

His head had slanted that way, listening to the same soul-warming voices, before shifting back to me. With a slight dip of his chin, he murmured, "But we're drinking more than coffee later."

My voice was all a hesitant breath and did nothing to mask the lie when I said, "Yeah, sure."

Ten

SAVANNAH
SIXTEEN YEARS OLD

Beau curled his arm around me as we followed Hunter and Madison, laughing and teasing each other on their way into the Dixons' house. Dancing around him the way she always did while his eyes tracked her because they were never anywhere else.

A smile tugged at my lips when Hunter's hand shot out, grabbing Madison and pulling her close before she could get away. Her laugh pouring free as he tickled her side.

Beau's fingers flexed against my waist as if he was craving that kind of freedom with me.

Not that we were in any way like Madison and Hunter. Hunter was all lighthearted teases, where Beau was broody passion that set my soul on fire. Still, there was a softness to Beau when it was just the two of us. There was a playfulness mixed in with all that intensity. There was a guy no one else ever got to see, even though he was much more open with Hunter and Madison than the rest of Amber.

But on nights like tonight?

Beau was quiet and careful. That moody boy I loved so

much radiating all that intensity behind midnight eyes and a clenched jaw.

Because my parents were here.

Ever since I'd come home from my grandparents' a year ago, he'd been that way. Afraid to say or do the wrong thing in front of them even though just being with me was the wrong thing in their eyes.

Not that it had stopped us.

Not that they hadn't *truly* tried last summer.

My mom's parents had been given strict instructions to not let me have access to their phone or computer. They'd gone so far as to unplug the phone and take it to their room every night so I wouldn't be able to contact Beau. They'd also found the letter I'd tried to sneak in with their outgoing mail and torn it in front of me.

But not talking with him for those months had only been part of my punishment.

My parents weren't exactly religious . . . but my grandparents were.

I'd spent my days doing endless house and yardwork while my grandmother prayed for my sinful ways. My nights consisted of being forced to read the pages of my diary *out loud* while being whacked on my knuckles with a wooden spoon every time I mentioned that Beau and I kissed or touched. With every scandalous sentence read and every spoon brought down upon my hands, she'd bless the air as if I'd breathed evil into it. Before I was sent to bed, my grandfather tried to prove with scripture that Beau's type of anger meant he had the devil inside him.

My grandmother had slapped me across the face when, after a month of listening to it all, I'd said, "Well, one thing we do know is the devil sure can kiss."

When I'd still gone running straight for the Dixons' house when I'd arrived back in Amber and been swept into Beau's arms, my parents had lost it. It had been the first time mine and Beau's parents had gotten into an argument . . . *screaming match* might be more accurate. And it had lasted hours.

My parents still didn't approve of our relationship, but they were no longer horrifically mean to his face. They saved those thoughts until it was only me they were unleashing their fears and frustrations on. Everything else was just a snide comment here and there.

"It won't hurt you to go more than a minute without being connected to each other," my mom said with a sigh when we walked into the Dixons' kitchen.

Like that.

Beau's hand slipped from my waist, but I curled my fingers around his, refusing to lose that connection.

Hunter looked from my parents to me, clearly biting back a laugh from where he was now carrying Madison on his back.

"Leave 'em alone," Mrs. Dixon said, slapping playfully at my mom's arm before going back to the food she was prepping.

"What's your problem?" Hunter asked suddenly, stare just past me.

I turned to see Cayson halfway between the kitchen and entryway, expression strangely withdrawn.

He shrugged. "Trying to get away from the trio. Everywhere I go, they're there, laughing and being loud as all get-out."

Hunter released Madison's legs and turned to face his

mom, gesturing toward the ceiling. "Em and Leighton are upstairs again?"

"I'm perfectly aware."

A laugh that bordered on frustrated burst from him. "Why is it that the no-girls-upstairs rule has never *once* applied to Saw?"

Their mom released an amused breath before waving toward the ceiling. "Because that's different. Y'all know it is."

"Except it isn't," Hunter argued.

She gave him a warning look but still explained, "For one, it's Emberly. Two, there's nothing Sawyer and Leighton are gonna get into trouble doing when she's there with them."

Cayson huffed and mumbled, "Yeah, okay," before heading for the front door.

"And three—and most importantly might I add—I am your mother. I make the rules. Now, if you still wanna go out tonight and don't wanna lose certain privileges right before school starts, I would maybe just say 'yes, ma'am' and get that back-talking behind out of my kitchen until dinner's ready."

"Yes, ma'am," Hunter said softly and reached for Madison. "But the girls wanted to say *bye*."

Mrs. Dixon's face fell. "Oh, what? Y'all are leaving already? Both of y'all?"

"Yeah, my momma's expecting us for dinner," Madison explained.

"And we have to be up early for all-day cheer practice, so I'm staying at her place tonight," I added.

"Well, we'll miss you girls around the table." She looked pointedly at Beau and Hunter and teased, "Some of us much more than others, I'm sure."

Beau simply ran his thumb along my knuckles in agreement.

The action alone had chills erupting all over my body and my breath catching.

Madison eagerly accepted one of Mrs. Dixon's hugs, but my mom caught my eye and sharply signaled me to her.

I went. My feet moving automatically and my body tensing when my dad's suspicious glare shifted from Beau to me just as I passed him.

Mom looked around, either to make sure no one could hear us or no one was watching, and harshly whispered, "Where is he going?"

I blinked slowly and started turning to see who she was talking about, but she grabbed my hand in a silent command to stop.

"Wendy said Hunter was going somewhere tonight." One of her eyebrows lifted meaningfully. "I know that boy, Savannah. If he's going somewhere, that means Madison is going too."

My stomach clenched and a cool, crippling sensation stole through my body.

"If she's going, that means you aren't going to be where you said you were. Now, tell me. Where is he going?"

"To a party," I said honestly. My tongue darted out to wet my lips that always seemed to dry out when I had these interrogation-type talks with my parents. "Beau too. It's a last-weekend-before-school thing for all the sports teams."

She stepped even closer. "And where will you be tonight?"

"At Madison's." I started pointing to where I could hear Madison talking behind me, but my mom pushed my hand down. "That party is for the sports teams only. But even if it wasn't, we have to be at the school at six, and we're there all day. We need to sleep."

"If you need to sleep tonight, then it would be best for you and Madison to be apart."

"Mom—"

She held up a hand. "I won't do that only because Madison's parents are expecting you for dinner and to give Madison a ride tonight and tomorrow. But *Madison's* is where you better be with Madison *only*."

I nodded as I stepped away, having heard the warning in her words.

They would be checking to make sure.

"I know, Mom."

I turned without saying goodbye and found Mrs. Dixon waiting for me, understanding pouring from her. She spread her arms, and I fell into one of her warm hugs.

"Love you, sweet girl," she said softly.

"Love you too."

"It'll be okay." She rubbed at my back. "They just want what's best for you, so they're trying to protect their girl."

I nodded as I pulled back. "Thank you for letting us come over."

She scoffed. "Anytime. You know that."

I gave her a grateful smile, then turned, immediately finding narrowed blue eyes watching me. Studying me. Saying so many things and blaming himself for a dozen others.

I went to him, wanting to crush all that blame and feeling beyond ready for some space from everyone else so we could talk. So I could have *my* Beau.

But the moment my hand slipped into his, and he began

leading me away, my dad said, "I think you can say goodbye right here."

I smacked into Beau's side when he immediately stopped, my head turning to look at my dad as disbelief swam through me.

Mr. Dixon clicked his tongue. "Don't y'all think that's pushin' it a little far?"

"Christi," Mrs. Dixon whispered in disapproval. "Let the kids at least say goodbye."

"Our daughter, our decision on her privacy with boys," my dad said, tone firm. "Besides, what do they need to say goodbye for? They say goodbye for five . . . ten minutes each time like they don't see each other every day. There's no reason for it. They can say goodnight here."

When Beau turned around, his jaw was clenched so, so tight. The muscle there feathering under the pressure he was putting on it.

His hardened stare drifted over my parents before meeting me, looking at me like an animal trapped.

And I didn't know how to help him. Not when we had four sets of eyes on us. Two of which belonged to *my* parents.

"I'm sorry," I said under my breath.

His head shook so faintly I wouldn't have noticed it if I hadn't been as close as I was.

He reached for me, his fingers grazing my cheeks and his forehead falling to mine just before my dad snapped, "If I were you, I would think very carefully about how close you are to my daughter."

"Jason," Mr. Dixon said on a rough sigh, but it didn't matter . . .

Beau had already stepped back. Arms falling heavily to his

sides. Hands curled into tight fists. Looking like a mixture of anger and sorrow as he stared down at me.

All I wanted was to be held by him. To let the world around us fade away. But I was afraid to move, knowing if I so much as touched him, he would beat himself up even more than he already was.

"Now, just wait a second," my dad began. "You have your views on what's appropriate, we have ours. Respect that. As for the two of you . . ."

I slowly turned to face my parents, my own anger and humiliation rising as he continued.

"You're too close. As your mom pointed out, you're always touching in some way. It's gone on too long and escalated too far. No more kissing. No more hugging and holding onto each other. Anything more than holding hands is unacceptable. Period."

By the time he finished, I wanted to curl into a ball and hide. My jaw was trembling in response to the anger in my dad's eyes as he pointedly stared at the boy standing tall behind me. Tears of frustration and mortification were filling my eyes, and I had no chance of stopping them.

Mrs. Dixon placed the tips of her fingers over her mouth like she was keeping herself from responding.

Mr. Dixon dragged a hand through his hair, then gestured to my dad as he spoke to Beau. "You heard him. Your momma and I gotta respect our friends' wishes. You gotta respect your girlfriend's parents. Understood?"

"Yes, sir," Beau rumbled.

I turned to leave just as the first tear slipped free.

Beau's expression fell, and he reached for me before quickly pulling his hand back, his fingers clenched tight and a harsh breath rushing from him.

"I love you," I whispered, too soft for anyone else to hear.

"Love *you*," he responded in that low, rough voice that always shot straight to my heart.

I wiped furiously at my cheeks as I left the house and hurried off the porch, Madison and Hunter barely separating to see who had come outside before Madison jerked back.

"Oh my gosh, what's wrong?"

"I'll tell you in the car."

"Where's Beau?" Hunter asked as he pushed off my car with Madison's hips still firmly in his grip.

"Inside, following my parents' newest attempt at keeping us as far apart as possible."

"Aw, friend," Madison whispered and reached for my hand.

Hunter sighed and looked to the house.

"Yeah, you should probably get in there," I said as I headed for my car door. "There's a lot of tension in there, and he's surrounded in it."

"Yeah," he mumbled, then asked, "We still on for tonight?"

I gave a hard nod as I opened my door. "Absolutely."

"IT'S STILL SO crazy to me that your parents do this," Madison began later that night. "I mean, I'm not surprised because it's *them*, you know? But still . . ."

A dull laugh tumbled from my lips when she sank next to where I sat on her bed, waiting.

Because I knew it was coming. Correction . . . *they* were coming.

With Beau and Hunter out, we all knew my parents would

follow. Giving enough time for me to sneak off somewhere I wasn't supposed be at—like a party I had no intention of going to—before checking on me.

And it was only a matter of time now, because Hunter had called Madison about an hour before, letting us know they'd left for the party. Starting the check-in countdown.

"Yeah, well, not everyone has super awesome parents like y'all do."

Madison's head slanted, her eyebrows pulling together with sympathy. "Mine can be strict too," she said slowly, knowing it was a weak addition.

"You can tell your parents things," I argued gently. "If you wanted to go to a party, you wouldn't have to sneak out. If you wanted to spend all your time with Hunter, they would be okay with that." I gestured toward the window. "Okay, so I feel bad for Leighton because her parents are *always* gone. But, like, Emberly is either in a bar or with Leighton and the Dixons because she literally has the coolest mom ever. And the Dixon house is basically perfection. They have rules, but they're still extremely casual. I mean, I'm pretty sure Mrs. Dixon got choked up the first time she saw Beau and me kiss. What mom does that?"

A soft laugh escaped Madison. "Right? She probably wouldn't be like that if she had four girls though. Like, my mom is totally cool about a lot of things, but if she saw Hunter kiss me?" The last was said on a whisper, her eyes widening as she leaned back, head shaking. "She'd freak. One hundred percent."

"Yeah, but would she send you away?" I asked, my voice softening with a year-long bitterness. "Would they forbid you from even hugging Hunter?"

"No," she responded after a minute. "Can't—" Her lips thinned into a tight line.

"What?"

She hesitated before releasing a rough breath. "Can't Beau talk to them? Be like, 'Hey, y'all aren't being fair,' or something?"

A stunned laugh left me. "No. No, he can't. They would . . ." My head shook quickly. "Madi, he's so afraid, that he doesn't even really talk around them."

"I know," she said, her face creasing like she was trying to figure out how to explain what she was thinking. "But it just doesn't make sense. Beau . . . *Beau Dixon* . . . afraid of anyone or anything."

"He isn't afraid of *them*, he's afraid of what they can do. You saw how fast I was gone last summer. He's terrified that if he so much as says the wrong thing in front of them—let alone loses control—they'll send me back to my grandparents' until I graduate."

Worry danced across her face as she nodded.

"You remember how bad it was when he told them he wasn't gonna break up with me," I said. "That fight between my parents and his."

"Yeah. Yeah, you're right." She glanced to the side. "I guess it must be really hard for him between *that* and trying to prove to his mom that he doesn't need to go to the military academy."

"Yeah," I whispered.

That.

Coming home last summer only to find out I'd almost returned to Beau being eight hours away at the Marine Military Academy had shaken me to my core. It had put everything about Beau and our relationship on a delicate, razor-sharp edge.

One that we struggled every day to remain balanced on because the threat of either of us being sent away still lingered overhead.

Thankfully, his dad was very much on the side of not sending Beau away for now. But just loving Beau was reason enough for my parents to want me away from him. One wrong move, and I would be back in Utah.

I loosed a long sigh when my cell phone rang. "Surprise, surprise." Flipping it open, I pressed the answer button and held it to my ear, "Hi, Mom."

"Savannah, where are you?"

"At Madison's," I said slowly. "Remember, I'm spending—"

"Okay, we're outside. Come here please."

I should've probably tried to seem shocked or something, but I just stood from the bed and said, "Be right down."

After ending the call and tossing my phone next to Madison, I gave her an exaggerated eye roll and headed for her bedroom door as Madison's giggle sounded behind me.

I resisted the urge to fold my arms as I left Madison's house and headed for the idling car, knowing it would only make them angry. But my irritation had to be written all over my face.

My dad rolled down the driver's side window when I rounded the car, and my mom leaned over him, looking closely at me. Analyzing my pajamas, messy bun, and makeup-free face.

"What are the two of you doing in there?" she asked.

"Talking."

"Who else is here?"

I slowly dragged in a breath before releasing it. "Her parents."

"And?" she urged.

"I dunno. Maybe some ghosts."

She scoffed and sat back in her seat, waving off my sarcasm. "Your sass isn't appreciated, Savannah."

"Yes, ma'am, I'm sorry."

"Where's your phone?" my dad asked.

"Up in Madison's room."

He glanced at the second story, looking like he was debating on making me get it before asking, "Has Beau called you tonight?"

"No. Why? Did something happen after we left?"

He raised a hand to try to comfort me. "The boys left for that party, and we want to make sure the two of you aren't planning on going there with them."

I gestured to my outfit. "I'm clearly not going to a party. I already told mom it was only for the sports teams anyway." At least that part was all true.

My dad nodded after a moment before putting the car in reverse. But instead of backing up, he pointed at me. "No party. No leaving. No Dixon boys."

My lips parted to accept their rules, but a question I'd wondered for so long slipped free instead. "And if it wasn't a Dixon?"

Dad's head snapped to me, surprise written all over his face when he didn't receive immediate obedience. "Excuse me?"

"You said 'no Dixon boys.' If I was dating *Philip*,"—I sneered his name, hating that my parents loved Philip Rowe so much and always brought him up like he might ever be an option—"would y'all still be like this? With these rules and checking on me multiple times a day? Making it so I couldn't even *hug* him? Always reminding me that I could be back in Utah at a moment's notice?"

Shock and irritation fled from my mom, but it was my dad who spoke up. "Why don't you do everyone a favor and find out?" The words a pure challenge.

My mouth formed a hard line as my head slowly shook.

"If not?" he continued. "Well, what happens is up to you. No party. No leaving. No Dixon boys," he repeated slowly.

"I know." It was a whispered acceptance, but it was enough for them.

With another nod from my dad, they reversed out of the driveway, and I made my way back into the house and up to Madison's room.

In the time I'd been gone, she'd already cleaned it up and was fixing her hair at her vanity.

She gave me a wide-eyed look. "Do they need me to come out there too?"

"No, they left."

Her eyes darted over my face, studying me. "I'm sorry, friend."

I shrugged and headed for my bag. "I wonder if they'll ever realize that if they weren't like this, I wouldn't sneak out or go behind their backs."

At that, Madi snorted. "Um . . . you do realize that *I* do all this sneaking out and sneaking people in with you?"

I paused from pulling out my clothes, my lips stretching into a grin. "Valid point."

"What do you think?" she asked, gesturing to the skimpy little outfit she'd laid out on the bed.

"Super cute and super sexy." I turned to face her, my voice

dropping to a whisper. "But how long are you actually going to be wearing it?"

Her cheeks reddened, but she just shrugged. "It deserves to be worn, even if only for a few minutes. And don't think I didn't notice which way you decided to go tonight."

My grin turned mischievous as I finished pulling one of Beau's older football jerseys over my head.

"His favorite," Madison said bluntly.

"His favorite," I agreed as I stepped into my little dance shorts. Once I was dressed, I pulled my hair out of the bun and searched for my brush. "When are we gonna call them?"

"Already did as soon as you left," she said, looking all kinds of excited. "Hunter said they'd be here in a bit."

I sucked in a deep breath when hummingbirds took flight in my stomach. "Can't wait."

I needed this. Beau and I hadn't had any alone time since the beginning of summer. With our junior year starting next week, and everything that came along with it, alone time was going to be even harder to find.

Once we were both ready, and Madison had a robe covering her surprise outfit, I sank to her bed, my stomach clenching in a terrible way as my thoughts spun. "Madi . . . what would you do to be with Hunter?" At her impish look, I tossed a pillow at her, a huff dancing across my lips. "I mean *be* with him. Like, in a relationship. Always."

"Anything," she said immediately, not even taking time to breathe or blink. "I'm marrying him someday."

"I know." The corners of my mouth lifted, but the action took effort. "You've been telling me that since the week we met."

"Pretty sure I've been telling Hunter since the day we

met," she added, trying to sound amused but coming up short. "Why do you look so . . . not Savannah?"

"I have this feeling,"—I gestured to my stomach—"and I know it sounds super ridiculous and typical teenage drama, whatever. But I mean, I have a *really* strong feeling my parents will try to stop me from being with Beau. More than they already have."

Madi worried her bottom lip as she studied me, looking all kinds of concerned and apologetic. "I might just think you're crazy if I didn't know your parents. But . . ."

"Yeah. *But*," I said with a pathetic laugh. "After last summer and then how quickly they set all those rules tonight. And when they showed up here, I asked them if they would be doing all this if it was Philip Rowe I was dating instead of Beau. My dad said, 'Do everyone a favor and find out.'"

Madison's eyes went wide. "He didn't."

I just lifted my brows in response.

"What did you—but you aren't going to, right?"

"What? No. Of course not," I said quickly, shocked that she would even ask. "But then he said if not, what happens is up to me. And I had this feeling when he said it that he was threatening me. Not with more restrictions than they're already trying to put on us, but—"

"With sending you away again," Madison finished for me.

"Right."

She looked to the side, her fingers twisting together in worry. After a while, she asked, "What are you gonna do?"

I don't know, I don't know.

"I—" A shocked breath ripped from me when knocking sounded on the window behind me, my heart taking off in a painful sprint as I turned and saw Hunter's face. "*Jesus.*"

Madison giggled and rushed to the window, opening it soundlessly to let him in. Their mouths already fused together before he was fully in the room.

"Okay, okay," I said softly as I hurried over to them in case their kissing led to something worse—like Hunter falling. "Let him get in first and let me get out."

A low laugh left Hunter as he pressed another firm kiss to Madison before finishing climbing over the windowsill.

Madison grabbed my hand as I passed her. "See you soon?" But the squeeze of her hand and the way her eyebrows drew together in sympathy told me so much more.

She was sorry about my parents.

It would be okay.

Love you, I mouthed.

"Love you back," she whispered.

Hunter glanced from her to me, then hurried to stop me before I could climb onto the large oak tree's branches that were perfectly positioned outside the window. "Hey, I need to warn you . . ."

My stomach bottomed out.

My heart ached and twisted and reached for the boy I knew was waiting for me down below.

"What happened?" I asked, voice shallow.

"Beau's in a bad way tonight."

Eleven

SAVANNAH
SIXTEEN YEARS OLD

Hunter dragged the hand that wasn't holding on to Madison through his hair, his face creasing apologetically. "When I got inside after y'all left, our parents were getting into it. Yours said that ours were trying to undermine their parenting—their rules and wishes for you."

Embarrassment from the events of that night swirled through me so intensely that I felt sick from it.

"They got on Beau for dragging you into things he shouldn't, for putting you in positions and situations you shouldn't be in. Said he had you trapped in a toxic relationship. Told him if he cared about you at all, he'd let you go."

My stare shifted to Madison, to the sorrow there that only scratched the surface of what I felt for Beau. With everything they said about him, with every horrible word said *to* him, it opened another wound, slowly bleeding me out.

I reached for the windowsill, but Hunter stopped me again. "Savannah, he punched a wall as he was leaving the kitchen. Your parents saw him do it."

"Oh," I breathed, my hand coming up to clench at my stomach as my soul begged to get to Beau.

"He hasn't said a word all night."

As soon as Hunter released my arm, I carefully swung my leg out onto the branch that rested just outside Madison's window, then looked back at him. "What did your parents say?"

Hunter gave me a helpless look. "They were arguing, Savannah, they said a lot."

"When mine told Beau to let me go."

"They about lost it," he said, the corner of his mouth lifting with pride. "Mom started yelling then, asking why Beau wasn't good enough for you. Dad told them they should probably leave for the night if they were 'gonna be spoutin' that shit in his house.'"

A soft smile tugged at my lips. "Thanks, Hunt."

He nodded and helped me out the rest of the way. "Be careful."

I snorted my amusement as I deftly descended the thick branches that we'd been using for the past couple of years to sneak in and out of Madison's room. For years before that, we'd climbed it just to prove our fearlessness. I could get down that tree in my sleep.

Especially when Beau Dixon was waiting for me at the bottom.

I jumped from the last branch to the ground and was immediately swept into a pair of warm, muscled arms. His hands curling tight against me and holding me close as he buried his face into my neck, breathing me in.

I wove my fingers through his hair and let my eyelids close as I felt his anger and pain clash with his relief. "I love you."

"Why?"

My spirit wrenched at the self-loathing pouring from him and wrapping around that simple, terrible word. Leaning back to look into his darkened stare, I said, "Because you're good and—"

A harsh breath fled from him as he looked away, his jaw straining.

"You *are*."

"Savannah, the last thing I am is good."

I pushed against his chest. "That is not true. I know your heart, and I see beneath that bear of a surface you show everyone else. You're kind and patient and gentle." I gripped his shirt in my hands to keep him as close as possible. "And the way you love me? The way you treat me? Beau, you are *good*."

Disbelief rolled from him, his brows pulling low over his anguished stare. "You deserve the world," he said, voice thick, then hurried to amend, "Everything. You deserve everything."

His tone had acid rolling in my stomach and my arms falling heavily to my sides.

"And everyone knows I can't give you that. That I'll drag you down."

"They're wrong."

"They aren't," he maintained. "And I can't be the reason you don't succeed. Thrive. Get everything you want out of life. I won't."

"What are you saying?" It was a breath. A denial. Because my heart was screaming that he wasn't about to say what my mind knew was coming next.

His lips parted before forming a thin line. That jaw

straining and his body trembling as one of his hands lifted to his chest before cradling my head in his big palm.

"Beau, what are you saying?" I begged when no words left him.

His eyes searched my face for a long while before he spoke. The words forced and pained. "Savannah, I gotta let you go."

"No."

"Savannah," he pleaded when I smacked his hands away and staggered back.

"*No*," I choked out. "This is because of my parents? Hunter told me what they said—what they told you to do."

Beau's stare flashed up to the thick, full branches of the tree before meeting me again, frustration wavering on his expression before it was replaced with a broken mixture of devastation and determination.

"They can't do this."

"They're right," Beau said, the admission leaving him on a pained wheeze.

"No, they aren't. Why can't you see you the way I do?" I cried out. "Why can't you see how much I love you?"

"I do," he said quickly, reaching for me again as if he couldn't help it. Needing me as badly as I needed him. "Fuck, I do. But, Savannah, you *shouldn't*. From the day I met you, your mom's been telling you to stay away from me. You need to listen to her."

"Like hell I do."

He curled his hands around my cheeks, pulling me close as all that agony and self-hatred bled from him. "Staying with me will only ruin you, why can't *you* see *that*?"

I gripped his wrists, my chest rising and falling unevenly as I struggled to catch my breath. "You . . . having you—

being loved by you—is everything I want for my life." His forehead lowered to mine as I continued. "But if you tell me right now that you don't love me, that you want this to be over, then I will try to accept that."

His fingers curled tighter, tangling in my hair.

I knew he would do this—do what my parents were demanding—because he believed them. Because he believed everyone. But he wouldn't lie to me, even for the sake of giving me what *he* thought was a better life.

"I love you with every last breath in my body, and I will love you long after I die." The declaration was soft but filled with an intensity I felt in my bones.

My heart took off, trying desperately to reach the boy it belonged to. But I forced myself to remain still. To repeat the question he hadn't answered.

"You want this to be over?" I asked, my tongue darting out to wet my lips. "Us?"

"I want you to have—"

"You know that isn't what I'm asking."

His eyelids closed and he exhaled slowly. "Savannah, I want you for the rest of my life."

I nodded, my nose brushing along his. "Then ask me what *I* want."

His stare met mine, tense and pleading. "What do you want, angel?"

"I want you to understand that life without you doesn't make sense—it hasn't since the day I met an angry bear of a boy covered in mud. And I want you exactly the way you are." I released one of his wrists to place my hand over his fiercely beating heart. "I've always loved *you*. Not some idea of what you might be if you were different. Just you."

I let my other hand drift to his knuckles, rough and

already scabbing over from where he must've split them open again that evening, and watched as shame flickered across his face.

"I want you to understand that my parents are wrong about you. They're wrong for saying the things they do, and I'm so sorry that you've had to endure it for even a second. I want you to know I'm not going anywhere. That I'll be here, with you, by your side, forever." I lifted a shoulder in a weak shrug. "Or until you decide otherwise."

"That won't happen," he said gravely.

"Then you're stuck with me, Beau Dixon."

"Lucky," he corrected. "Fucking *lucky* to be with you." He brushed his mouth across mine, the action so light, so sweet, it stole my breath and left my lips tingling. A ragged breath left him, all acceptance and worry and relief, and released some of the weight on his shoulders. "Then can I take you somewhere?"

"I was hoping you would." A slight tease danced on my tongue when I said, "I got all dressed up for you and everything."

A soft groan rolled up his throat as he pressed his mouth to mine, stealing the giggle that had begun slipping free. "Saw that," he growled against the kiss. "You wearing my last name will always be my favorite."

"I know."

"Come on." He nipped at my bottom lip. "I have a surprise for you."

My eyes widened when he began pulling me away from the tree. "You do?"

His stare flashed my way when he tucked me against his side, a secretive smirk hinting at the corner of his mouth.

"What is it?"

"A surprise."

I pushed against his stomach. *"Beau."*

"Few minutes," he assured me. "Just gotta wait a few minutes."

I let my head fall back dramatically, then tried to pull him toward his Explorer faster, but he kept his steady pace. "A few minutes is an hour too long. Let's go."

A dark, rumble of a laugh left him, his dimples flashing. "Crazy girl."

"Bear."

He drew me closer when we neared his car and leaned down to press his lips to my ear. "You really wanna know?" he asked, disbelief coating the words.

I blew out a slow sigh. "No."

"Didn't think so." Reaching forward, he opened the passenger door, his eyes dancing with veiled excitement as he watched me climb in. Amusement lighting some of the darkness that clung to him when he reached out to trail the tips of his fingers along my jaw. "Been waiting all week for this, and it's fucking worth it. Waiting years would be worth it."

Confusion pulsed through me, but he just stepped back and closed the door.

I watched as he walked around the front of the car, trying to figure out what he could possibly be up to. What he could've kept from me for a week—what could be worth waiting years for.

Beau.

Beau was worth waiting years for.

But I had him.

"You haven't figured it out?" he asked as he started the car and pulled onto the street.

"I mean, if we were eighteen and it wasn't so late, I would

think you were taking me to the courthouse. Or Vegas, but that isn't minutes away."

His head snapped to the side. His stare locked on mine in a way that made my stomach curl with heat and my heart go all kinds of crazy, even long after he'd looked back at the road.

"Savannah, the day I marry you, we aren't gonna be in a courthouse or in front of a fake Elvis." His head shook faintly. "Small. Simple. Sunset. Peonies. At the plantation house."

My lips slowly parted as surprise wove through my love for this boy. "You remember that?"

His gaze drifted to me for a second. "You say something, I'm listening. You say something about our future? Babe, I'm never forgetting it."

"Beau . . ."

"And that'll be worth waiting for. Just like that house will be worth waiting for because it's gonna be ours."

One of those rare, breathtaking smiles crossed his face, shifting his expression entirely. Chasing away any darkness and anger that lingered under the surface, making him look so light and free for that brief moment.

"That's why I think tonight is worth any wait too."

I managed to tear my attention away when the car dipped as Beau turned into a driveway, a smile of my own breaking free when I saw the plantation house sprawled out before us.

Sleeping peacefully, waiting for the day when Beau and I would make it ours.

The giant house sat on five acres and sang comfort and hospitality. From the sweeping porch to the grand doors and the rest of the stunning architecture, it was pure southern charm.

I'd fallen in love with it the first time I saw it.

The same year I'd moved here, the family who had owned it for generations had left it to the town of Amber. I'd taken it as a sign. Over the years, Beau and I had made big plans for the place. One of which was getting married on the back of the property.

We might have snuck onto it a time or two.

"This is a great surprise," I murmured, my smile still impossibly wide as Beau pulled around to the far side of the house so his Explorer wouldn't be seen.

"What do you mean?"

"Our place," I said, voice wistful as I reached for the handle of my door. But he grabbed my arm to stop me.

Excitement and mischief tugged at his mouth as he studied me. "You think this is your surprise?"

My stare darted out the windshield before meeting his again. "What—yeah. We haven't been here in months."

"Yeah," he said as he leaned forward to capture my lips with his. "But we've never been inside."

I sucked in a sharp breath as he pulled away and got out of the small SUV, a wicked smirk on his handsome face.

I scrambled out of the passenger side and met him around the back just as he was pulling blankets out. "Wait, what do you mean? You can't—we can't . . ." I looked to the house, words failing me.

"I found a window that wasn't locked," he said softly, hesitantly, his brow creasing when he looked at me. "Say the word, and we'll stay in the back instead."

"I wanna go in." I reached for the arm that wasn't cradling the blankets, awe swirling through me before what he said finally registered. "What do you mean you found a window? You just went around looking? You could've—"

"Gotten arrested?" His arrests had been such a sensitive

subject since they'd both been linked to his anger—his fighting. He'd been so ashamed of them. Embarrassed for *me*. But the way he'd just tossed the words out there, it was as if the thought didn't bother him at all. "Putting this look on your face? Getting you in that house? It would've been worth it."

My pulse went all kinds of crazy with affection and excitement. "You're crazy."

One side of his face scrunched up in an adorable, teasing expression. "That title belongs to you."

I pushed at him, feigning offense even though I couldn't stop smiling. "Have you been in?"

His head shook, just a slight shift, but it still made such a big statement. Then again, everything Beau did seemed to be that way. Subtle looks or movements that had a massive impact. "Not setting foot in there without you."

"Then let's go."

He reached for me with his free hand, not saying a word as he led me around the large house to where we normally spent hours getting lost in each other and dreams for our future.

But instead of continuing through the overgrown flowers to the gazebo, he took me up to the back porch. The faded wood creaking beneath our feet as he pulled me past the bay windows I knew looked into the kitchen and over to the opposite edge of the porch where another unkempt flowerbed began. A knowing look on his face when I glanced from the large windows overhead to him.

"One of those?" I assumed. At his faint nod, I asked, "How did you find this . . . *why?*" A hushed laugh made up of excitement and nervousness and awe bubbled past my lips. "What made you decide to go looking?"

He shifted the bundle of blankets to my arms and headed

into the mess of wildflowers growing up and tangling with the dormant spring plants. Talking as he stopped below the second window in and began working on it. "Last week, after one of your fights with your parents, you said you'd give anything to be just you and me, in this place, living out our future." The window opened with a groan, and Beau just stared at the open space for a moment before looking to me, hand stretched out in invitation. "I can't speed up time, but I can give you the rest."

I went to him, my soul dancing from the overwhelming love I felt for this boy. "Beau—"

"It isn't too late," he said quickly, softly. "We don't have to go in."

"Why wouldn't I wanna go in?"

"The worst thing you've ever done is sneak out to be with me. This—going into the house—that's . . . Savannah, that's big."

I lifted my chin to stare him down and watched as the corners of his mouth kept tilting up as if he was fighting a grin. "Excuse me, but I'm gonna own this house one day. And as the future owner, I'm simply checking on it because I'm concerned for its current state."

"Uh-huh," he rumbled, all kinds of amused. "Sheriff's gonna love that one."

"I'm sure he will. Now, help me up."

"Yes, ma'am."

Beau easily hoisted me up, the same way he'd done so many times when helping me get to that first big branch at Madison's tree, and I hurried to dump the blankets through the window before carefully climbing in and dropping down.

My mouth parting as the size of the house hit me anew.

Seconds later, Beau's loud thud as he landed behind me

echoed through the empty great room, chasing away the silence for a fleeting moment before we were surrounded in it again.

And then he was beside me.

Quiet.

Fingers weaving through mine and gripping tight.

Trying to take in this dream we'd shared for so long—and it was just one room. Darkened except for the moon shining in through the many windows. Haunting and beautiful and more than I ever could've imagined.

Perfect.

The day I'd met Beau, my heart had felt full in an inexplicable way. Like it was too big for my chest. Like it might escape me at any given moment.

At nine years old, I hadn't understood.

It'd taken time to realize what that feeling meant.

That he was special to me, and me alone. That he was mine, and I was his. That he was my home.

Standing in that house, I had the same feeling. My heart was too full—too big. And with each breath, it was threatening to escape.

Without a doubt, this was home.

"Beau . . ."

"I know." He stepped forward, glancing back over his shoulder when I just stood there in wonder, a small smile lighting up his features. "Come on."

A GIGGLE WRAPPED up in a moan slipped free when Beau placed soft, open-mouthed kisses on my stomach hours later.

The action tickling and making me ache for him all over again.

I laced my fingers through his dark hair, my eyelids slipping shut as a peace settled over me in a way I'd never known.

We'd explored the entirety of the house, falling more and more in love with it with each room we stumbled upon. Expanding on the dream we'd had for so long now that we were finally *seeing* it.

The plantation house turned into our bed and breakfast.

Beau had been saving everything he made working for his dad in their orchard. I'd just started teaching three- four- and five-year-olds at the dance studio—it wasn't much with taking my own classes, cheer, and going to school, but it was something.

We'd find a way to make it work. We had to. This was our future—I could see it.

"You really wanna double the size of the kitchen?" Beau asked, resting his chin on my stomach so he could look at me. "Thing's already big."

I lifted an eyebrow in defiance and felt his hushed laugh.

He raced his hands up my thighs to grip my bare hips, making my stomach curl with heat even though I was still trembling from the bliss he'd just given me. Slow. Reverent. Easy.

"It's big enough for how much I like baking *now*. Baking and cooking for other people?" I tugged playfully at his short hair. "Double the size. And I want two islands in there."

"Two," he said dully.

"Mmhm. Need them, actually."

He studied me for a moment before those dimples graced me with a *hello*. "Yes, ma'am." When he continued, there was a hint of humor behind his words. "Blossom Bed and Breakfast."

"It's a great name," I said defensively.

"I know it is," he agreed immediately.

"You're making fun of it."

"Babe," he murmured, giving me a look that said he clearly hadn't been. "I was thinking about tiny you in a massive kitchen with two islands."

I gave his hair another tug. "Watch me dominate that kitchen one day."

"I plan to." He shifted his head to sweep his mouth along my stomach before meeting my stare again. "I'm gonna get you this house, Savannah," he continued, voice softer than before. "I'll do whatever it takes to make that dream come true, I swear to you."

"I know." I let my fingers drift through his hair to lightly scratch along his neck and back. "What do you want?" One of his brows ticked up in question. "I've been talking about all the things I wanna do to the house . . . what do you want?"

"You," he said without hesitation. "I just want you."

Instead of getting lost in Beau's undeniable love for me, my dad's words echoed in my mind, hushed and ominous, like a wraith in the abandoned home. I let my head fall back against the cushion of blankets as I struggled with worry over the unknown. "Beau, no matter what happens, I'll always come back to you."

He went still.

His fingers gripping me like he could keep me there. The air in the great room filling with suffocating dread in an instant.

"What?" he asked, voice soft, dark.

"Please don't let your mind go there," I begged, heart wrenching because I could feel the way he was at once terrified that I was leaving him and accepting it because he thought it was best for me. "You know I would never willingly leave you."

He didn't respond.

Just stayed there, partially laying on me, still as stone.

"My dad said something tonight when they came to check on me, and I—" My throat tightened as that deep worry rose and bloomed in my chest. "What he said, I just know—I could feel it—they're going to do something."

A slow sigh sounded from him before he rolled away, his deep voice echoing in the room. "Your grandparents'?"

"I don't know. Maybe."

His hand slowly curled around mine in response.

"I'll always come back to you, no matter what happens," I repeated. When the responding silence got to be too much, I said, "I need to know where your head's at."

"Trying to figure out what to do," he said softly. "If following their rules around them will be enough, or if . . ." Beau cleared his throat, his voice twisting with sorrow when he continued. "If I really do need to let you go for—"

"No."

"Savannah—"

"No," I said quickly and scrambled to sitting, grabbing at the closest thing to me to cover my bare chest. "Just *no*."

He sat up with me, anguish and denial ripping across his fierce expression. "Savannah, if I need to let you go for the next year and a half so I can at least have you *near* me? I'll do it."

"I can't," I said, choking over the emotion tightening my throat.

"So, you'd rather spend the next year and a half with states between us?"

"*No*, I just—" My chest shook from my trembling breaths. "I can't pretend that I don't love you. That I don't need you."

"I wouldn't be pretending shit," he ground out. "I'd make sure the entire town, including your parents, knew what we were sacrificing to keep the peace. Knew that every day was a day closer to when we got to be together again."

My head shook wildly as he spoke. "I can't, I won't. Beau, I'm not going to let them push us apart just to keep them happy for any length of time. I just needed you to know that I think it might be coming, and if it does, I will do whatever it takes to get back to you."

He dragged his palm across his jaw, dipping his head in acceptance as he did.

"And I think . . . I think maybe we should consider some of those things we were talking about earlier." I curled my fingers into what I was clutching to my chest—Beau's jersey. My heart racing with anticipation and maybe breaking a little at the same time as I erased a seven-year dream. "I can't tell you what it does to me that you remember the things I say and that you want to make them all come true. But I just want a life with you. And with our situation—with my parents—we have to take control of it so it can't be taken from us. We have to do whatever we can."

Beau's dark brows slowly pulled together as I rambled.

Watching. Studying. Listening.

"And that fake Elvis or the courthouse is what I want. With you. The day I turn eighteen, or the day after. I don't care. Whatever it takes because they won't be able to do anything once we're married, and then it'll just be us the way it's supposed to be."

Long, torturous seconds passed before he uttered a single word: "No."

My shoulders shook with the force of my exhale. "What?"

Beau's eyes drifted down, lingering on my chest for a while before he reached out. His fingers grazing my arm before touching the jersey. "That name on you, Savannah . . . it's right, and it'll be right one day. But not like that." His darkened stare flashed back up to mine, intense and somber. "Your dream for how we get married changes, then it changes for me too. Whatever it is, I'm there. But we're not sneaking off to try to end this war with your parents. It'll just make everything worse."

"Any added time of having to live with them doing this, of them treating you the way they do, will be worse than the fallout from us getting married."

Beau's head slanted in disagreement as I spoke. "If you wanna keep going like we always have and just prepare for whatever might happen in the next year and a half, then that's what we'll do. When we're both eighteen, we'll test new boundaries and take it from there. But I'm not gonna marry you for a solution."

My spirit trembled with remorse at the whisper of offense in his voice. "Beau, I—" My eyelids slipped shut, and I lowered my head into one of my hands. Shame gathered in my throat, thick and hot. "I would do anything to be with you, to make sure they can't take me from you. But you're right."

A heavy sigh left him as he pulled me into the comfort of his arms and gently lowered us onto the blankets again. His fingers trailing up and down my spine as he spoke against the top of my head, soft and low. "Physical distance can be reclaimed. In the end, only thing that can take you from me is you. Understood?"

I nodded, my eyelids squeezing tight as I brushed my fingers across his bare chest.

"Crazy girl," he murmured, all adoration wrapped up in that deep, gravelly voice.

"I love you."

"Every last breath, Savannah."

Twelve

BEAU
SIXTEEN YEARS OLD

I knocked on the Rileys' door a few evenings later, teeth clenched tight as I tried to breathe. To calm myself when nothing was wrong.

It was just that house. The anticipation of what I was about to be met with acted like a match to gasoline and had me all kinds of twisted up. Had that anger simmering and that haze creeping in before I ever lowered my fist to my side. Seven years of fear and hatred from the people within that house would do that to someone.

My eyelids slid shut and I forced out a breath, trying to relax.

Then another.

By the time the lock sounded, I was just as bad as when I'd set foot on their porch.

I opened my eyes just as Savannah's mom opened the door.

Her expression fell into a careful mask to cover her fear as she took a step away, keeping her hand on the door like she might want to shut it in my face.

"Jason," she called out the way she always did, then said softer, "Savannah isn't here." Tone almost a warning. A threat.

I tried really damn hard not to let it affect me.

A harsh breath left me, my head nodding sharply as my stare darted past her to watch her husband approach, irritation practically pouring from him when he saw me.

"Savannah's at dance, Beau," he said as he continued toward us. "Why don't you go on home."

"I know she is," I said, voice a little on edge. "I wanted to talk to y'all."

Mr. Riley let out a slow sigh before ushering me in with his fingers. "All right, come on in."

His wife flinched away from me where she was trapped between him and the door when I stepped inside. I pretended not to notice, running a hand through my hair and counting down from ten as I did.

She'd always kept plenty of distance between us, but that was a first, and I had a feeling it had a lot to do with the other night. Couldn't imagine what she'd do if she saw me actually hit someone rather than a wall.

I followed them into the living room and watched as they moved to stand in front of the couch.

Mr. Riley held his arm out toward one of the chairs. "Sit down."

"I need to stand," I said in automatic response, then hurried to add, "Thank you though."

They shared a look before eyeing me curiously, more so than usual. But I stood firm near the chair he'd indicated, waiting for them to decide if they were going to sit or stand with me.

"It helps me," I finally explained when their indecision

seemed to lean toward suspicion. "I get restless when I'm sitting."

"All right," Mr. Riley said as they both sank down to the couch. "What is it you want to talk about, Beau?"

My head bobbed nervously for a moment, my throat getting all kinds of dry before I said, "I would like y'alls permission to date Savannah. Please."

Silence fell over the room, heavy and tense and so damn loud. At the same time, I was sure they could hear how fiercely my heart was beating.

After what felt like an eternity, a huff of a laugh left Mr. Riley. "Uh . . . I'd say it's a little late to be asking permission seeing as you've been dating her for, God, I don't know. How many years now?"

"It's never too late to ask your permission."

He glanced at his wife, studying her for a few seconds before he looked my way again. His head slowly shaking as his shoulders lifted. "You already know what our answer is."

I did.

I hadn't expected anything less from them.

Still, knowing your girlfriend's parents didn't want her with you hit hard. It was damaging because I knew they had valid reasons, just as I knew no one would ever love Savannah the way I did.

I dipped my head and started to respond, but he continued. "You know how we feel about your family. We've never had friends like your parents—people we've come to care for as if they're our own family. And we love you kids—we love *you*. But not for Savannah. Beau . . . listen to me."

I was.

I was taking in every word he said while also making sure

I had myself under control in case he said something that pushed me over my crumbling edge.

"We love you," he said slowly, emphasizing the words. "That doesn't change what you are capable of. Your parents are just as aware of it, that doesn't diminish their love for you. However, *we* need to protect our daughter from that."

"What I'm capable of," I murmured, my head shaking faintly as a huff of bemused frustration tumbled free. "I *know* what I'm capable of, but I've never touched Savannah. I've never so much as gotten angry with her. I would do anything to protect her, I'm not capable of hurting her. My parents are aware of that." My tone was low as I twisted his words back around on him.

From the slight tick of Mr. Riley's eyebrow, he didn't appreciate it.

"Y'all are the ones who've never been able to see that," I continued. "Instead, y'all always tell me to keep calm before I ever have the chance to get mad, or back away like I might do something. Your wife just *cowered* from me, but I've never given her a reason to. This is the most I've ever even talked to y'all."

At the thick, uncomfortable tension that settled between us and had me feeling like I was about to crawl out of my skin, I started for the door.

"I love your daughter," I said softly, my steps slowing to a stop. "I know she deserves someone better than me—I've tried to get her to realize that. But I'll always try to be the guy she deserves."

God, I'd tried. From before I ever told her how I felt about her up until just a few nights ago, I'd given Savannah so many opportunities to have a life better than one I could offer her, all while being terrified she would take it. Because a life without Savannah was . . . well, I couldn't imagine one.

She was my entire world. Had been since the day she'd dropped out of the sky with her freckles and captivating laugh and her endearing view on everything.

"I'm coming back," I said firmly. "I'll come back until I get your approval because as long as she wants me, I'm keeping that girl. And one day, I'm marrying your daughter."

Mr. Riley blew out a harsh breath from his nose as he twisted to face me better. "If you didn't intend on respecting our wishes anyway, why ask? Why the show?"

"It's no show, sir. It's a hard situation when, like you said, I'm already dating her, and I already knew full well what your response would be. But that's how much Savannah means to me. I *want* your approval, and I plan on being here, asking you until you change your mind."

"We won't." The answer was simple, but he almost sounded saddened by it, as if he was the one receiving the answer.

My head lowered in the beginnings of a nod and my weight shifted to continue toward the door again, but I stilled. "You know the old plantation house?"

Their eyes darted from me to each other and back again, clearly taken aback by the change in direction.

Mr. Riley cleared his throat. "Uh, yes. Yes, of course."

"Savannah's dream is to get married there. Did y'all know that?"

Her mom seemed to melt at that for a moment before she controlled her expression, the way she always did around me. Her dad's face just creased as he studied me as if he was trying to figure out where this was headed.

"No," he finally answered. "We didn't."

"For years, we've been talking about that place," I said, voice soft as I gave them this.

Not that it was a secret. My family knew because Savannah and I talked about it all the time. But I'd never outright told someone because it was *ours*.

"About a future there. About owning it one day—turning it into a bed and breakfast. Getting married there."

Twin looks of amusement crept across their faces, and Mr. Riley scoffed, as if they thought our dreams were farfetched.

"I will make it happen," I said confidently and tried to ignore the way my blood simmered in reaction to their disbelief. The way my entire being tried to lash out in response. I took a couple deep breaths and forced my jaw to unclench as I continued. "Like I said, we've talked about this for years. Savannah's told me for years about the wedding she wants there, in detail. But she wants to give up that dream wedding for a *courthouse*."

Their amusement faded in an instant.

"Or Vegas." I felt their anger and fear slam into me. Felt it fuel what was already inside me. "As soon as she turns eighteen—"

"Out of the question," Mr. Riley barked before I could finish.

"Absolutely not," his wife said, voice subdued.

"I told her no." I hated that I wasn't able to unclench my fists. But I could feel their hostility. Could feel their blame as Mr. Riley rose to his feet, narrowed eyes on me. "I told her no," I repeated. "I'm giving her that dream wedding one day. I'm not sneaking off to a courthouse or Vegas just so we can be together. So y'all can't keep us apart."

At that, Mr. Riley jerked back, and his wife slowly lifted her hand to her chest.

"But that's where Savannah's head is at. Your constant trying to force us apart makes her want to give up her dream and go to extremes. Thought y'all should know."

"Thought you should try telling us how to parent," Mr. Riley shot back, frustration wrapping around every low word in a way that made everything go so still.

I slowly counted backward and rolled my neck before meeting his hardened stare. "Didn't say that."

"Better cool it, Beau."

"You know, that doesn't actually help," I ground out, teeth clenching tight and a fine layer of red coating my world at his response.

His reaction.

All it ever did was fuel what I tried so hard to suppress.

Disapproval poured from him as he gave me a look that shouted I was proving why they wanted me away from their daughter. "Think it's time you left."

I slanted my head in assent and started turning for the door again when Mrs. Riley spoke up.

"You think you wouldn't hurt Savannah," she said, voice soft and hesitant, almost shaky. "You tell yourself that, and I'm sure you want to believe it. But we've experienced differently. We've seen it." Her head moved absentmindedly as her stare remained fixed on the floor, looking in a way I'd never seen Savannah's mom.

Then again, she was usually either backing away from me or mad at Savannah because of me.

When she didn't go on, her husband released a slow sigh and gestured to her. "One of Christi's good friends in college went through an abusive relationship. Everything started out fine until it wasn't. She swore up and down he was a great guy, that nothing was happening, but everyone knew. You could see it in him."

"And then we were almost too late," Savannah's mom said, voice wavering. "She wouldn't come around anywhere we were, claiming it was because of the things we said about him, but we had a feeling. So, we went to her." My eyes followed when she abruptly stood from the couch, her terrified stare snapping to me. "And I will not watch my daughter go through the same."

Mr. Riley watched her leave the room, looking conflicted when he turned back to me. "Christi and another friend found her. They thought she was dead at first. Body completely beaten and broken from repeated abuse." He cleared his throat, head bobbing. "*His* family and friends couldn't believe it. They kept saying he was the greatest guy. Had a little bit of an anger problem growing up and got in fights in school, but he would've never hurt her." He gave me a knowing look.

Of everything they had ever told me, tried to make me believe, it was the one thing that didn't hit me right in the gut with the truth of it.

"I'm sorry," I said after a moment. "I'm sorry for what happened to her. But . . ." I lifted my arms before letting them fall. "For so many reasons including my anger, I know I'm not good enough for Savannah. And I know I have a problem, I'm aware of that. But I know down to my soul that I'm not that guy."

"That's just it," he said sadly. "You don't."

"No, you *want* me to be him, and you won't give me a chance to prove you wrong."

"I won't give you a chance to prove me right."

A disbelieving huff scraped up my throat. "Okay," I

mumbled as I once again headed for the door. A few feet away from it, I turned back to find him following a good, *safe*, distance away from me. "Does Savannah know?" I jerked my chin toward the living room. "About her mom's friend? About where y'alls fear of me comes from?"

"It also comes from what you've done," he said pointedly.

"Does she?"

He studied me for long, tension-filled seconds before answering, "There isn't a need for her to know right now."

I nodded at his veiled warning even though I didn't agree with it. "I'll be back," I said again as I took the last steps toward the door and reached for the handle, refusing to waver. "I won't stop coming back until I get your approval."

It wasn't until I was already off the porch that he stopped me. "We know Savannah helps with your anger. Chases it away, or whatever your parents said. You can't cling to our daughter for that reason."

"I'm not—"

"At some point, you need to stand on your own and face whatever you've got going on inside. Your anger isn't our daughter's problem to worry about and fix and get mixed up in. It's time you learned that. Time you stopped relying on others—relying on her."

My body slowly locked up until it felt like I might shatter. "I don't."

The words were nothing more than a rumbled warning, and from the way Mr. Riley raised his hand and listed his head as if he was about to reprimand me, he heard it.

The actions didn't help. My jaw clenched impossibly tighter in response. My knuckles ached in protest. Every muscle in my arms twitched as if preparing for something I couldn't let happen.

It felt like something inside me was screaming. Clawing at me. Trying to force its way out.

Every part of me knew it would be so easy to let go. To give in. That standing there, holding myself so damn still, was physically draining. But I'd lived with this feeling for as long as I could remember. I'd fought against it daily—until I couldn't. And after years of these demeaning conversations with the Rileys, I knew when to get out.

The other night, I'd lingered too long.

Right then, I was dangerously close to that line again.

"Same as you have your reasons for clinging to Savannah," he went on as I took that first, rigid step back, "she's only clung so hard to you because we've told her to stay away from you all these years. And one of these days, that rebellion will end for her. *You* will end for her."

I managed to dip my head as I forced myself to back away. "You're wrong."

Thirteen

SAVANNAH

I stepped back that evening, hands raised as my stare darted over the kitchen. Making sure everything was ready and it all looked exactly the way I wanted it. Decaf coffee was ready to start brewing, the kettle had water ready to heat for tea, and the lemon pound cake honestly looked perfect.

"Plates, forks, napkins . . ." I murmured, face creasing as I looked at the island where the dessert rested. "What am I forgetting?"

I didn't normally have dessert and drinks ready for guests who stayed at Blossom. I made breakfast and I set out a treat sometime mid-afternoon if they were around and not out exploring Amber or spending time with whoever they were visiting. But this weekend was different. Everyone in the house was there for Philip Rowe's wedding, which meant I'd grown up with those people. A second family of sorts.

I turned at the sound of ceramic clinking together, my heart stopping painfully before racing toward the man who was pulling down mugs.

"I forgot those," I mumbled lamely.

He set out enough for the guests, leaving them on the edge of the island because he knew I would rearrange them anyway, then turned to look at me. Expression tense and arms folded tightly over his chest.

Once the mugs were set up how I wanted them, he said, "Levi said Quinn's name."

"I know."

Frustration and pain flashed through his eyes before they shifted away, his head shaking subtly. "Were you gonna tell me?"

"It happened right before you came over today."

His chest pitched but his stare remained on the floor when he said, "In the five hours I've been here, you couldn't find a second to tell me?"

"You're just telling me," I shot back, tone all kinds of defensive and sharp. "What if I hadn't known?"

At that, his hardened stare drifted back to me, but there was a deep sadness lingering in his eyes and weaving through his words. "It just happened when I was putting him down."

"Oh, well . . ." I swallowed, trying to push back the lump forming in my throat, and jerked up one of my shoulders. Feigning indifference so I wouldn't turn into an emotional mess again. "That happened today. Thank you for the phone. I'll see you tomorrow."

"Savannah—"

"No, I need you to go," I said, trying desperately to channel the harsh tone that came so naturally to Beau. "I have a full house, and the guests—"

"*We* have a full house," he said firmly.

"No, right now, *I* do," I argued and tried not to react to the way my words had a physical effect on him.

Arms falling to his sides and his body seeming to sag even though he was still standing so tall. The absolute fear and panic that played out on his face before every emotion slipped away.

"My guests will be back any minute," I said, struggling to maintain the same callousness. "I don't have time for you or this."

"You don't have time for your husband," he said gravely. "You don't have time to fix our marriage."

"Not right now, no."

A huff left him, all pain and defeat. "Savannah, we are more important than the guests, than this house—"

"No. No," I bit out, head shaking furiously. "If we were more important, you wouldn't have fucked my best friend. You wouldn't have helped her *leave*. You wouldn't have watched me *grieve* her and pretended to know *nothing* about it. You wouldn't have built our entire life together on a lie."

By the time I finished, I was screaming at him.

By the time I finished, he looked like he was dying under the grief he was carrying. Gripping at his chest that was roughly pitching and falling. Face creased like he was in agony.

It was a terrible feeling, looking at him and wanting to continue screaming. Wanting to throw something and rage at him for everything he'd done—every hurt and humiliation he'd caused. Yet, at the same time, my chest felt like it was on fire and encased in ice because the man I loved was in pain, and it made me *ache* for him. Made me want to comfort him.

But we were in this pain because of what he'd done, and I needed to remember that. Needed to remember that if I gave in, if I fell into his arms so we could try to forget for a little while, my own hurts and betrayals would still be there in the morning.

"That isn't—"

"I don't care," I said over him, stopping him. "I don't care. Right now, I want you to go. I need you to go," I repeated, knowing deep down, Beau would always give me what I needed.

"We *have* to talk," he said, voice pleading.

"We really don't."

Irritation bled from him. "What, but you'll talk to my brothers? You'll talk to Peter Rowe? Someone you haven't seen in—God, I don't fucking know."

"Peter's like family. Of course I'm gonna talk to him."

"About *us?*" he ground out meaningfully. "I'm your husband. You need to be talking to me so we can start working through this. So we can fix this."

"I'm not ready, you need to be okay with that."

"Savannah, I'm losing my fucking wife. How am I supposed to be okay with that?"

"No, this is losing your wife," I said as I closed the distance between us, pulling my rings off my finger and putting them and my shattered heart in one of his hands.

Beau went still in a terrifying sort of way.

The air seemed to be sucked from the room as his fingers slowly curled around my engagement ring and wedding band before his agony and denial burst from him. Filling the room and amplifying my own anguish. After an eternity in our suffering, his stare lifted to meet mine, eyes glassy with tears just as a couple fell, slipping down his horrified face.

"Who let me come back to Amber?" Peter called out on a groan, making me jerk back.

I hadn't even heard the front door open.

His eyes widened when he stepped fully into the tension-filled kitchen, a low whistle leaving him. "Your parents are right behind me," he warned softly as he turned back around and left.

I stepped away from Beau and glanced around, wiping at my cheeks and surprised to find them wet. Feeling frantic and out of sorts and sure the kitchen must have looked the same. But it was just as I'd left it.

Once I had the coffee pot and kettle started, I turned to go greet everyone and found Beau standing under the archway that led out to the entryway. Hand pressed to his chest again and head slowly shaking as he glanced back at me.

Letting his hand fall, a mixture of a hushed laugh and a cry that was pure pain escaped him. "Every last breath," he whispered, the words strained. "And then long after."

I watched him go, trembling from the sobs moving through my body and tearing at my soul.

Oh God.

What have I done?

What have I done?

Fourteen

BEAU

"Beau."

I stopped at my father-in-law's voice, rocking back when my body desperately wanted to get farther than the dozen-or-so feet I'd made it past the porch of my house. To get to my truck and get out of there before the night could get worse.

If it *could* get worse.

Lifting my head, I glanced over to where he was saying something to my mother-in-law as she headed into the house, waving at me with a saddened expression as she did.

I offered a halfhearted wave back, then watched my father-in-law start my way.

"You going?" he asked as he neared, keeping his voice soft so it wouldn't carry.

I nodded, unable to respond when this time seemed so much more final.

Because Savannah had tried separating us in so many ways in one conversation. From claiming I had nothing to do with what was happening in our business to putting her wedding and engagement rings in my hand and saying I was, in fact, losing her.

He clicked his tongue and inhaled slowly. "We didn't talk much after we arrived because the kids were awake. Savannah told Christi and me that they don't know anything's going on."

"Right," I choked out and wanted to dig a hole for myself when I realized he knew what happened.

At least, he knew Savannah's side . . . *Madison's* side.

He turned and glanced at the house before walking away from it, nodding for me to follow. "You should know, Savannah called us after that first day. Told us about the fight with your brother and what was said."

My head slanted. "Jason—"

He held up a hand. "She called us again after Hunter told her what really happened between you and Madison." He stopped walking once we were halfway down the driveway and turned to look at me, heaving a slow sigh. "Beau, I misjudged you greatly when you were younger. Christi and I both did, and we're sorry for that."

"I know, sir." They'd apologized to me for years; he didn't need to continue. I was the one who needed to be apologizing.

But the person who deserved every apology and explanation wouldn't talk to me.

"We've watched you grow up, caring for our daughter along the way. We've seen you at your best and worst, and even at your worst, we're damn lucky to have you as our son-in-law."

Fuck.

My jaw ached from the strain I put on it to hold back the

emotions that were already at the front of everything else from what had just gone down with Savannah.

"We were deeply saddened when we got that first call, but Christi and I knew something wasn't right." His shoulders lifted. "Cheating happens . . . however sad it is, it's true. Think it says a lot about your character that we knew you wouldn't have."

"Jason, I—" I began, choking over my words, my head shaking. "I appreciate that, but I don't know what to do. There's so much she doesn't know, and I can't . . . I can't lose her."

"You won't," he said confidently, but the rings in my hand felt like they were burning me. "You made some mistakes, I won't tell you that you didn't. But everyone makes mistakes, and couples work through them. Come out stronger for them."

"What if we can't?"

He gave me a sad smile. "I don't believe that. Not the two of you."

"What if she *won't*?"

For a long time, Jason just stood there, seeming to think over my question and analyzing the desperation in my tone. After a while, he carefully reached out and put a hand on my shoulder, encouragement and a hint of amusement on his face when not one damn thing about my life was amusing.

"At one point, long, long ago, I would've given anything for my daughter to give up on you. Because she didn't, I was shown just how wrong I was and how wrong people can be about a person. I also lucked out in the son-in-law department and got some damn cute grandkids out of it."

My chin trembled and I dropped my head, my eyes closing tight against the burning there.

"Now, I'm not much of a prayer, but I'll be praying that my daughter will be able to see through the hurt this has caused and find forgiveness so she *won't* give up on you."

I nodded, the movement sharp and rigid as I struggled to thank him—to say anything—but the rock lodged in my throat prevented it.

"It's gonna be okay," he said, letting his hand fall from my shoulder. "Speed bumps are hard to get over in marriages. Mountains are harder."

"I never wanted to hurt her," I finally managed to say, words strangled.

"Oh." He tapped his hand on his chest a few times, just above his heart. "I know, son." Taking a step away, he gestured toward the house. "When will you be back?"

"After work tomorrow."

He offered a small smile. "Looking forward to it. I'll watch after our girl until then."

"Jason, thank you." My mouth parted as words failed me for a moment. "I don't deserve your kindness after what I did."

A stunned breath left him and, after a second, he reclaimed his step. "I remember a very determined, very confident boy who remained unnervingly polite, despite the horrible things we said to him for years." He lifted his brows meaningfully. "You made an honest mistake, Beau. You made a worse one by trying to cover it, but from what I gather, you weren't the only party in on it. As for the fight with your brother, well . . ." He slid his hands into his pockets and shrugged. "You know how I've always felt about your fighting. However, when it's manifested from an instinct to protect your family from any kind of hurt?" He took a few steps back, shrugging again as he said, "I think I might just understand that."

I nodded, grateful for his thoughts. But it didn't matter when Savannah didn't see it the same way.

"Get somewhere safe," he called out as he turned.

"Goodnight, sir," I said, stare drawn to the house. To where my wife and kids were.

My entire world.

With a jagged exhale, I started back up the drive and over to where my truck was hidden on the side of the house. Each night I'd left had torn a part of my soul, but this was different.

Putting Savannah's rings in my pocket, I pulled out my phone and climbed into my truck. Movements slow as I brought up the messages and ignored the impulse to go to Savannah's text thread.

Going to Sawyer's instead, I scrolled through to where he'd sent Cayson's number a few weeks back, then saved it to my phone before tapping out a message.

Each word seeming to take forever. My hands shaking. Body vibrating with all that pain and anger storming through me.

ME: *Cays, it's Beau.*
   Me: *How much to buy the condo from y'all?*

MY HAND CLENCHED tight around the phone when I sent the last message. My heart wrenching from my chest and leaving a void.

"*Fuck,*" I shouted, throwing my phone against the door

and letting my head fall back against the seat as everything crumbled around me.

Tears falling relentlessly because I was losing her.

My wife.

My wife.

My entire world.

"God damnit," I said through clenched teeth as I cranked the engine and quickly slammed my truck into reverse. Needing to get out of there before I made things worse by going back into the house and demanding Savannah talk to me.

Trying to force her to talk tonight had led to her giving me her rings.

I was terrified she'd ask for a divorce the next time.

I already didn't know how to survive this grief that seemed to be pulling me down into a hollow of torment. I wasn't sure there was any surviving what came next.

But when I pulled up in front of the condo, everything hit me all over again.

I'd spent half of my life saving to buy the plantation house, sure it would one day be mine and Savannah's. Knowing I would do anything to make that dream come true —that it would be the only house I would ever buy.

But our house and business was apparently only *Savannah's* now, and I was staring at the place I'd been crashing at for weeks and was about to make permanent because of a thirteen-year-old mistake.

Because I was losing my wife.

My family.

I gripped at the fierce ache in my chest as I opened up my door and got out of the truck, snatching my phone off the floorboard as I did. There wasn't a response from Cayson but there was a small crack in the corner of the screen from where I'd thrown it. And I wondered again what Savannah must've done to absolutely shatter hers.

Regardless, between that and her refusing to talk to me in person, I'd understood: Stop calling. Stop texting.

So, I had.

And then I'd pushed her too far.

I made it up the walkway and into the condo, each step taking all my energy when I felt so weighed down and hollow at the same time. My body sagging against the door for long minutes as that harrowing moment played out in my mind, over and over like an unbidden nightmare.

Pushing forward, I trudged over to the dining room table and fell heavily into one of the chairs before pulling Savannah's rings out and setting them down. The sound of them hitting the wood clawed at my soul and tore me open as I wondered how I was supposed to fix it.

She'd ignored me completely for two weeks. Then a few days near her, hardly saying a word, had resulted in this new hell. Trying to talk to her felt like a death sentence to our marriage. Giving her space seemed like I was accepting what she wanted—what she'd *said*.

"No, this is losing your wife."

I glanced up when a key sounded in the lock for the second night in a row, struggling to control the desperation and fear and suffering I could feel pouring from me as the door opened and the lights flipped on.

"Beau," Sawyer called out, but Cayson was the first one to come into my line of sight, head shifting my way and shoulders sagging with a heavy sigh.

"This isn't the time for Dixie Chicks," I said, the words scraping up my throat and showing every ounce of my pain.

"Yeah, well, that was some S-O-S text," Cayson said as he and Sawyer started my way just as the door shut.

My stare drifted past them in time to see Hunter come into view. Expression all kinds of guarded as he studied me as if waiting for me to go off on him.

"Forever," he muttered. "I heard you. But we told you we'd be there for you."

"And that means telling you that you can't buy the condo," Cayson said as he took a seat at the table. "You and Savannah are gonna figure this out. I told you, just be patient."

My head moved in fast, tight jerks as I slid my hand forward on the table, the metal and diamonds scraping against the wood. "We're not," I confessed, lifting my hand and closing my eyes to block out the way their faces fell in unison. "She's done."

Fifteen

SAVANNAH
SEVENTEEN YEARS OLD

"I was thinking we could meet up with the boys tomorrow for Amber Fest," Madison went on, never stopping from her ramble even though she'd changed the subject three times, "and then after, maybe we could *spend the night* at each other's houses because I may have heard the Dixon house is going to be parent-free tomorrow." She gave me a bright smile, looking all kinds of proud of herself.

I sucked in a small breath as I glanced up at Beau from where I was tucked into his side, pressing my hand to his stomach as I spoke to get his attention from Hunter. "Your parents are gonna be gone tomorrow night?"

Beau just looked down at me, a slow, wicked smirk tugging at his mouth as his dark blue eyes held mine. "Got plans?"

I bit at my bottom lip to hide the ridiculous smile on my face as hummingbirds took flight in my stomach. "Guess we'll see."

A rumble of disbelief rolled up his throat. "Uh-huh."

I gripped at his football jersey as pure excitement swept

through me, then focused on Madison as I began the process of responding to her. "One, you're not gonna change my mind. Coffee is meant to have creamer or something else in it. Two, you're absolutely insane, you have that routine *nailed*. Madi, you're one of the best on the squad. And I say *one of* because I'm out there," I said jokingly, complete with a dramatic flip of my long ponytail.

She pushed at my shoulder, a wild laugh tumbling free. "Brat."

"Three—I forgot what three was," I mumbled as I tried to think back to her long-winded, totally Madi-esque ramble.

"I asked if you've seen my that."

"Oh right, your *that*," I said with a roll of my eyes. "Except, I don't know what *that* you're talking about."

"Her cheer jacket," Hunter said from Beau's other side.

My mouth popped open, but the answer stalled in my throat. "How does he do that?" I asked on a whisper instead.

"Friend, I have no idea," she said just as softly. "But it makes my life a whole lot easier."

"With all your *this* and *thats*?" I teased, dancing away when she playfully swatted at me. Once I was back by Beau's side, I said, "I dunno where your jacket is. Have you checked Hunter's bedroom?"

Her stare drifted to the side as if she hadn't thought to before a giddy, little smile crossed her face.

"Gross. Gross. Whatever you're thinking, *gross*."

She gave me a dry look. "You're one to talk."

"And *four*," I began, ignoring that because she was absolutely right, "I am totally down for Amber Fest and spending the night."

"Oh, Miss Riley."

The four of us stopped, and I turned, looking back at

where the slightly frenzied voice had come from. My expression shifting into something more adult appropriate—and totally fake—when I saw the guidance counselor coming our way.

"Good morning, Mrs. Warin. How are you today?"

"Oh, I'm really good. You know, it's Friday," she said, voice softening as she closed in on us, travel mug in her grasp and large purse falling from her shoulder. Her eyes darted from me to Beau and then back again. "I was wondering if I could speak with you?"

That fake smile became a lot more fixed as I tried to figure out why the guidance counselor would want to speak to me for the first time in all the years that I'd been at the school, but I just nodded. "Sure. After school?"

"I was thinking now, actually." When I just stood there, she hurried to add, "I'll give you a pass to first period if we chat too long. I know y'all are busy, and you have the pep rally for tonight's game." She lifted her hands in forced excitement. "Go Eagles."

"Yay," Madi said from beside me, almost as unenthusiastically as Mrs. Warin had, and a breath of a laugh punched from my chest.

"Uh, yeah. Yes," I said, head bobbing all kinds of awkwardly. "Of course. I'd love to talk." I tried to avoid the curious look from my best friend but couldn't escape Beau's when I turned in his hold to grab my bag that he always insisted on carrying.

Fierce.

Passionate.

Silently letting me know he was there for me and would be there when it was done. Whatever *it* was.

He trailed the tips of his fingers over my forearm, then

stepped back. But even as he walked backward with Hunter and Madison—who were speaking quietly and stealing glances my way—he didn't look away from me, holding me in all that captivating intensity.

"You ready?"

I looked to Mrs. Warin, fixing that smile back on my face as I turned to follow her. "Yes, ma'am."

"Sorry to catch you in the halls so early, and *today*," she said as she quickly maneuvered to the cluster of offices at the front of the school. "As I said, I know you have the pep rally." She waved her mug in the air. "I don't keep up with sports much, but I see the signs around school. Undefeated, huh?"

"Yes, ma'am, and this is the final game before playoffs."

She nodded, trying to look enthusiastic. "Exciting. And how's Beau handling the pressure? That must be hard on him, I imagine. On all the players," she added as an afterthought.

I missed a step at the unexpected question. "Um, he, uh —" I shook away the confusion and warning bells that rose up because it was ridiculous to get suspicious of her line of questioning.

She was a guidance counselor. She was supposed to be invested in our lives.

"He's great, actually. He loves playing. It helps him with . . . it just helps him," I finished quickly.

She sucked in a deep breath when we reached her door, then gave me a comical look. "That's about the extent of my sports questions. I'm probably the only Texan who *really* doesn't care for football." She lifted her travel mug over her mouth and whispered, "Don't tell anyone."

"Your secret's safe with me," I assured her.

She pretended to sag in relief as she opened the door and ushered me in. "Thank goodness. Have a seat, get comfy."

I placed my bag down and sat on the little couch she had in her office as she hurried around, setting things down and turning things on, murmuring to herself and to me as she did.

Asking how the school year was starting off, if I was excited for my final year, and what colleges I was applying to.

But with the way she'd stop and ask before scurrying around again while I answered, I had a feeling none of those questions were why I was there. Questions I would think *would* be why I was there. And it had those warning bells ringing in the back of my head again.

"Okay," she said with an exhale when she finally sat, her seat pulled around her desk so she was near me. "Well, I've looked at your transcripts, Savannah, and I have to say . . . you're a fantastic student. Your GPA has remained solid and, honestly, terrific. Your SAT and ACT results were also pretty wonderful. I think we should talk about you considering something more along the lines of a private university than what you mentioned. *However*, that can maybe wait for another meeting."

I didn't tell her I wasn't interested in those things. That I already knew what I was going to college for, and I was firm on going somewhere close by so I could continue living in Amber to save as much as possible for the plantation house.

I just sat there, waiting for the real reason why I'd been brought in there. My stomach getting all tangled up with nerves and my heart beating like crazy as if I'd done something wrong.

She offered me a kind smile as she leaned forward, elbows

on her legs and hands clasped together. "I was kind of hoping we could just talk, Savannah."

"About?" I asked when she didn't elaborate, voice thick with worry.

"Just talk. I just wanted to see how you're doing with school, cheer, life . . ."

"Oh," I said awkwardly and shifted on the couch as I tried to orient my thoughts while wondering if she was pulling all the students for chats like this. "Well, I'm . . . I'm good. I'm really good. I also dance outside of school, so I'm busy."

"Oh, wow."

"Yeah," I said, a breath of a laugh bubbling up my throat. "But I like being busy. I like moving. If I don't have anything to do, I bake."

"Do you feel restless if you aren't moving?" she asked, a crease forming between her eyebrows.

"No." I lifted a shoulder, trying to think of anything I might feel when I'm not moving. "No, I just really like being busy. I mean, I read. But only in bed because it's the only time that I'm still."

"You don't think there's a reason for you wanting to be busy?"

"Like . . ." My eyes darted around the office as those warning bells sounded again, louder than before. "Like what?"

"Nothing," she said, waving a hand through the air before clasping them again. "I was just curious. So, what do you like to bake? I'm a terrible baker. Then again, I'm a terrible cook. I can stir the heck out of some boxed potatoes though."

A startled laugh burst from me before I relented and told her about my favorite desserts, which led to me explaining all about the bed and breakfast Beau and I wanted to have one day.

By the time I finished, she was leaning back in her chair, travel mug in hand and excitement dancing in her eyes. "That's some dream, Savannah. And I'll tell you, Amber could sure use something like that."

"We think so too," I agreed.

Her smile dimmed a little as she nodded toward me with her chin. "I keep wondering if there's a particular reason you're wearing your jacket today."

I glanced down at my bare legs and cheer skirt before self-consciously touching my cheer jacket. "Well, it's . . . it's almost the end of October."

"Oh, I know. But this is Texas after all, and a little warm front blew in." She lifted her mug placatingly. "I like being comfy, so I'm with you on wanting jacket weather to get here."

I played with the bottom of my skirt before placing my hands on my legs. "I feel like there's something you want to ask me, so you should probably just ask."

"I'm just wondering if you decided to wear your jacket on a day that isn't exactly cool because you're maybe trying to hide something."

"Like wha—" My hands went to my stomach a split second before my gaze followed. Something close to horror washed over me as I wondered if I was getting fat, and my focus snapped back to her. "I'm not pregnant."

"No, no," she said quickly. "Never thought that, and you don't look it one bit, I promise."

"Okay. Well, then, what would I be hiding?" I demanded, voice frantic and offended.

"It's—" She blew out a harsh breath through her nose and

set her mug down before leaning forward in her chair. "I want you to know, I'm here," she continued. "I'm a safe space. You can talk to me without worrying about what will happen, and I'm going to do everything I can to help you."

Unease moved through me, slow and thick. "I . . . I don't—help me with what?"

She took a moment as if she needed to collect herself. When she began, her voice was soft and gentle. "Savannah, it has been brought to my attention that you've been seen with bruises this week. And that this isn't the first time."

Long seconds came and went as I waited for her to realize she was talking to the wrong person. But when her tone and declaration added up with all those previous warning bells, a disbelieving scoff burst from me. Because I knew exactly what she was insinuating.

Except she was wrong.

I got bruises all the time, sure. I was one of the smallest girls on the squad next to Madison, so I got tossed in the air a lot. If stunts didn't go right—which, let's face it, they didn't always—I was caught in any way the girls were able to catch me. Sometimes, I fell flat on my butt. Not to mention, dance.

Bruises just happened in my life. Not once before then had I thought anything about them, though. Also, I was pretty positive I didn't have any concerning bruises at that moment.

But I could see on Mrs. Warin's face that this was a big deal to her in a Beau-Dixon kinda way, and it made me want to cry for him and scream at the people who didn't understand him.

Instead, I pulled my bag close to my side and tried to keep my voice polite when I said, "I'm sorry, I think you've been misinformed."

"Savannah, Beau has a history—"

"I'm aware," I said tightly, that politeness replaced with ice in an instant.

She gave me a look as if to remind me that she was *there* for me. "The school has been informed that your relationship is abusive."

"The *school*?" I asked, choking over the word. "As in, *multiple people*? More than just you?"

"This is very serious," she confirmed calmly.

"Who? *Who* is saying this?" I bit out, my anger making my throat thick and my eyes burn with tears I refused to shed because I was too busy being pissed. "Because not once in the years that I've known Beau has he ever done anything but love and protect me."

"Okay, let's maybe just take a second and take a breath," Mrs. Warin said. "I'm not your enemy, Savannah. I'm here for you. Remember, you can tell me anything."

"If you're waiting for my answer to change about him, it won't."

"Okay." She lifted her hands in a calming motion. "There's something else we need to address."

"Fantastic," I said through clenched teeth. "Let's do that."

A sigh left her before she said, "Within the information we received about your relationship, it was said that this abuse—"

"Which isn't happening," I said bitterly.

She paused for a moment before continuing. "This abuse might also be sexual in nature."

I was so caught off guard that I sat there, too stunned to fully process what she was saying. I wasn't sure I *could* process what she was saying.

My mind raced as I thought of the times when Beau and I were together.

His breath fanned my lips as he demanded, "Rough or easy?"

"I don't care. I just want you."

The slight sting of pain as he bit down on my lip had heat unfurling in my stomach and was enough to let me know what he needed before he said, "Rough then."

BUT THAT . . . that was different. That wasn't anything like what Mrs. Warin was hinting at. It was always my choice, and *rough* only meant he wasn't gentle with me. That it wasn't slow and tender. But it was still full of love. It was just passion and need and, well, *rough.*

It was Beau.

It was *us.*

"This is ridiculous," I muttered. "Who even said this, and why is my relationship any of their business?"

"People who are very concerned about you."

"Bullshit," I snapped, then rolled my eyes when hers widened in surprise. "Sorry for cursing."

Mrs. Warin just waved a hand through the air again. "Safe space."

"Beau would destroy anyone who hurt me," I said bluntly. Angrily. "He would destroy himself before hurting me . . . emotionally, physically, in any form. This is just someone being an asshole because they got bored . . . one . . . day." My words slowed and softened, and my stomach bottomed out as a very real possibility came to mind. When I continued, my voice was nothing more than a distracted mumble. "Or maybe they're trying to get a rise out of Beau for one reason or another. And when he hears this, that's exactly what they'll get. Did you ever consider the timing of when you were told all this? Right before a game against our biggest rival when we're undefeated? What if someone is trying to make sure Beau doesn't play because they know he'll get himself kicked out of school before the game?"

"Savannah, these are very serious accusations against—"

"And they're bullshit," I repeated. "I don't even have any bruises that I'm aware of. Look." I grabbed the zipper of my jacket and roughly yanked it down, shrugging my arms free and shoving them out for Mrs. Warin to inspect since my legs were already mostly bared to her. "Let's be real, my parents would love a solid reason to have Beau and me separated because of that history you mentioned, but even they know he would never touch me."

She gave a slow sigh, her voice the same unnerving calm it had been since we'd begun that part of our discussion. "That only gives me a small relief, Savannah. Bruises fade—"

"Oh my God," I groaned, standing and shrugging back into my jacket.

"There is the other side of the accusations," she continued as she stood with me, understanding practically pouring from her as her eyes begged me to come clean to something that wasn't happening. "Abuse can be emotional. I've seen the way he keeps you close."

"There is no abuse, Mrs. Warin," I nearly shouted, unable to take anymore. "God, if this town would just give him a chance. He is . . . he is . . ." A sound of aggravation rose in my throat as I tried and failed to explain that boy.

No one had ever understood Beau except me. Even still, I

couldn't begin to figure out how to make someone truly see him. Because for me, it'd been immediate. The sense that he was important. The feeling that flowed through my veins and whispered to my soul everything I needed to know about Beau Dixon.

I knew how he raged and lost all control. Knew how he hated himself and broke for those he hurt. I saw it. I felt it all the same as I felt how deeply he loved me.

"Beau is good and beautiful and cares more passionately than anyone I know," I finally said. "But no one else has ever seen him as anything other than destructive, so he's grown up thinking they're right." My head shook as I snatched my bag off the couch. "Give him a chance."

She called my name when I headed for the door, but I continued out into the hall without slowing. Eyes catching on the stares of the front office ladies as I hurried through. Their gazes concerned and discerning, as if they were trying to find whatever Mrs. Warin had expected to see.

I tossed a saccharine smile their way as I pressed my back to the door leading to the school's main hall, my voice like honey. "Don't you know it's rude to stare?"

Their heads fell in sync. Their shamed eyes shifting, looking anywhere else as their lips moved, whispering words to each other that were far too low for me to hear as the door slowly fell open behind me.

I whirled around into the empty hall, my expression slipping and jaw wavering as I fought back the tears that threatened to spill over. As I wondered why this was happening to us—to *him*.

As I wondered if it would ever stop . . .

"It has to," I mumbled under my breath as I headed to class. "There has to be a day where this stops for us."

I nodded resolutely and forced an extra bounce in my step as if my positivity alone might make it so. But that positive outlook came crashing down around me when I rounded the corner to the long hall that held mine and Beau's first-period class and the seniors' lockers. Mainly, *Beau's* locker.

I knew it as well as my own because I decorated it before games and left little treats in there for him. I'd decorated it late yesterday afternoon—every football player had his locker decorated.

But I hadn't done *that* . . .

At least a dozen strips of red barricade tape were spilling to the floor from the slots on his locker, displaying one word over and over again.

DANGER.

I passed one of the other classrooms as I slowly moved to his locker, my heart cracking with each step closer as my eyes darted over the addition. I tried to take comfort in knowing Beau hadn't seen it—that he *wouldn't* see it. Because it had to have been done after class began. Otherwise, someone would've torn it down.

A teacher, at least.

But like everything else that morning, that comfort died, and the tears I'd been fighting broke free as I carefully tore strip after strip away, revealing the large words scrawled in permanent ink across his locker.

SAVAGE.

DANGEROUS.

HEARTLESS.

All written throughout one, repeated word: **ABUSER**.

I let the barricade tape fall to my feet, my fingers trembling as I lifted them to touch Beau's locker. As if the words, the tape, Mrs. Warin . . . *everything* . . . might disappear once I did.

But it was real.

And the sob that burst from me echoed down the hall like a siren.

My blurry stare went everywhere as I tried to figure out what to do. As my heart *broke* for the boy I loved.

The sound of my bag hitting the floor was lost beneath the reverberating sound of my pounding feet as I tore through the empty hallways of the school. My heart beating faster and my tears falling harder with each second that passed. As if my soul was mentally counting down the minutes and knew there wasn't enough time.

Relief barreled through me when I found the large storage closet where we kept our decorating supplies unlocked. Grabbing a paintbrush and the small can of Eagle-blue paint I'd used the night before, I ran out of the closet and back the way I came. The entire time, whispering prayers that the bell wouldn't ring anytime soon.

That I would have time.

A cry of sorrow and disappointment scraped up my throat when I rounded the last corner and saw him there.

Leaning up against his locker. Arms folded. My backpack hanging from his fingers.

His head shifted my way, the look on his handsome face slaying me until I was sure I would do anything to take this moment and this pain from Beau.

Give my life.

Sell my soul.

Beg God until He agreed to turn back time.

Anything.

Because that pain and shame radiating from Beau were

real and soul deep. That question in his eyes was the most dangerous thing about him because he was wondering if they were right—just as he always did. He agonized over their words until he *feared* what he was capable of. Until he exploded with it.

And that apology creasing his forehead? I wanted to erase it. I wanted to kiss it away. He had absolutely nothing to apologize to me for—not when it came to who he was.

Not now.

Not ever.

"I'm sorry." The words were a whisper when I reached him, wrapped in regret and my tears.

His head slanted and his face twisted with humiliation and lightly concealed rage. "Savannah, I—"

"Don't," I said quickly as I set down the paint. "Don't go there." Placing my hands on his face, I felt the way his strained jaw tensed and twitched beneath my fingers for a moment before softly continuing. "You don't deserve this. None of this is you."

Doubt rumbled deep in his chest.

"It *isn't*," I maintained. "This is someone trying to get in your head. This is someone trying to make you do something —like with what they said to Mrs. Warin."

"What?"

Ice-cold fingers tore at my chest and gripped my throat as soon as I realized what I'd done.

Oh God.

No. No, no, no . . .

He needed to know, but not right then. Not in the middle of a school hallway next to a locker full of cruelties.

"Savannah." Beau's tone was low and careful as he pressed his fingers below my chin to lift my head. Eyes searching and studying mine, looking ready for whatever else I might throw at him. "What did Mrs. Warin say?"

I swallowed thickly, my eyelids slowly closing as I sucked in a deep breath. "Beau, the school was *informed* that our relationship is abusive."

His body went still against mine.

His jaw tightened so forcefully it felt like granite beneath my fingertips.

"They were also told that it . . ." When my eyes opened, I was staring at Beau's jersey. Unable to continue. Still struggling to fully digest what Mrs. Warin had said—what it meant.

"What?" he demanded, the question like whispered poison.

My head moved in small, harsh shakes as I repeated what the counselor had said like a dirty confession. "They were told the abuse was also sexual." I tried to swallow, but my throat was suddenly too dry. Too thick. "I think . . ." I met Beau's blank stare and wanted to curl into a ball and die. "I think someone's saying you're raping me."

Seconds passed before Beau reacted. Head bobbing as he carefully moved out from between me and the locker.

"Beau—"

He held up a hand as he backed away, a silent plea for a minute alone.

Except he never needed minutes when he was with me. I calmed him. Always.

His steps were slow and unsteady as he turned and started down the hall, his trembling hands moving to rake through his jet-black hair and forming into fists.

Not more than a dozen feet away, he stopped. Body subtly moving with all that aggression rolling off him and filling the narrow hall before he turned and headed back to me.

Steps hard and fast.

Expression fierce and terrified.

Eyes glassy and shattering my soul.

He stopped a foot away, making sure not to touch me. As if any closer, and what was said about him would be true.

"Beau, don't let it get in your head. It's someone being horrible to hurt you."

"Answer something for me," he begged in that deep, gravelly tone.

"Anything," I cried softly.

"Have I ever—"

"No," I said before he could finish, already knowing where he was going with the question.

The muscles in his jaw shifted as he studied me, and after a shuddering breath, he asked, "Have I ever forced myself on you? Have I ever hurt you?"

"No," I repeated, my voice cracking with my own grief.

At that, he stepped closer and dipped down to press his forehead to mine. "Savannah, I love you."

And then he was gone.

Ripping himself away from me and stalking down the hall.

I hurried after him, the ringing bell drowning me out when I asked, "Where are you going?" Grabbing his hand, I tried pulling him to a stop as kids poured out of classes. "Beau, *please*."

"Savannah, I need to get out of here."

"Then I'm coming with you."

He squeezed my hand tighter before slipping his fingers from mine. "Not this time, angel."

I watched him walk away through the tears filling my eyes until he was out of sight. But throughout covering up the words on his locker, the pep rally, and the next couple of classes, all I could focus on was his pain and self-hatred and humiliation. All I could think of was who would've done this to us.

All I could feel was the hurt of Beau needing time alone.

Time without me.

"Hey, Riley."

I jerked away from the too-close voice and smacked the fingers teasing the bottom of my skirt. "Feel like a trip to the hospital?" I sneered as I slammed my locker shut and sent an icy glare Philip Rowe's way. "Or how about the morgue?"

He smirked as he leaned a shoulder against the locker next to mine, his stare darting over my body as if the thought didn't bother him.

As if the entire school didn't know exactly how afraid Philip was of Beau.

Once his eyes met mine again, he shrugged, then looked around at the other kids passing by, heading to lunch. "Look at that . . . no Beau." He leaned closer, continuing to move with me even when I stepped back. "No threat to the students here. No threat to little Savannah Riley."

"He isn't a threat to me," I snapped.

"No? I heard a rumor that he hurts you."

I shoved his shoulder back with as much force as my body was capable of the moment I felt him trailing something up my arm, then felt anger burn in my veins when I saw the big Sharpie in his hand. A tiny piece of red barricade tape was attached to the cap, proudly flaunting what he'd done.

"You bastard." It was barely a breath, but I felt the words and the hatred for him down to my soul.

Philip took a step closer, a victorious grin crossing his face. "I heard a rumor that he beats you. Uses you. Rapes you."

He dodged my fist, that smile growing with my rising anger.

"With that swing, you probably don't stand a chan—" His grunt of pain was quickly met by shocked *ohs* from surrounding students when my knee met his groin.

As he bent, I moved with him to speak in his ear. "*I* heard a rumor you made up lies about him and our relationship because you'll never be as good as Beau at anything in your life, and that kills you. School. Football. Girls . . . you'll never satisfy anyone the way he satisfies me."

Philip shifted back so his eyes met mine. All hard steel.

"You'll never make anyone scream your name the way I scream his when he fucks me."

His nostrils flared as possession ripped across his pained features. "Remember those words when I have you screaming *my* name, Riley."

Disgust rolled up my throat, but I managed to choke it down. "And when Beau finds out all this was *you*?" I let that linger in the small space between us for a moment. Let the possibilities of what Beau would do swirl in his mind until that hint of fear flashed in his eyes. "I heard a rumor he's gonna destroy you."

Sixteen

SAVANNAH
SEVENTEEN YEARS OLD

"Wait, wait, wait," I said breathlessly, stopping my hips' movements to look for my phone beneath the pile of mine and Beau's clothes.

A giggle broke free when I leaned over and Beau took the opportunity to switch our positions, rolling us so I was on my back and he was settled between my legs. The sound bouncing around the great room of the plantation house.

Just as empty and haunting and beautiful as it always was when we snuck in. But the cold, dreary days of winter seemed to magnify it all.

My moan cut short when I finally found my cell phone and flipped it open to see my mom's name on the screen. "Oh God, shh," I said, slightly frantic as I covered Beau's mouth with one hand and answered the call with the other. "Mom?"

"Where are you?" It was all a suspicious demand, and although I knew I needed to be convincing, it was really hard when I was there. Beneath Beau Dixon and in his arms. His teeth nipping at my palm and moving down to my wrist as his hips started a slow, steady rhythm that made my eyes roll back.

"I'm—" I swallowed a moan and curled my legs around Beau's back. "I'm with Madison."

"And where should you be?" she asked impatiently.

Here.

Right here.

Always.

"Um . . ."

"Are you out of breath?" she asked suddenly. "Why are you out of breath? *Why* are you breathing so hard, Savannah?"

I squeezed my legs tighter against Beau to stop his movements and tried like hell to think clearly.

"I'm—we're . . . dancing." I met Beau's dark eyes—the wicked amusement there—and fumbled to continue. "We're rehearsing our numbers for the winter performance."

My heart pounded in the seconds before my mom responded, an intense mixture of worry and need to continue being loved by Beau.

"Isn't there a clock where you are?" she finally asked. "The Rowes are already here. Dinner will be ready soon."

My lips parted and eyes went wide at the reminder.

"Right," I said, trying to sound apologetic and probably totally failing since I really didn't want to be present for that dinner. "Sorry. I'm on my way." I snapped the phone shut without saying goodbye and faced an irritated Beau.

"I hate Philip Rowe," Beau said as soon as the phone left my hands, having heard my mom.

"I know."

"I fucking hate him," he repeated, voice soft and lethal.

Just the mention of the Rowes was enough to change

Beau. Tremors rolled through his body as that anger he always fought back tried to push through to the surface.

I slid my fingers into his hair and pulled his face close enough to brush a feather-soft kiss across his lips. "I know."

"Need to get you home." When he started moving away, I locked my ankles around his back and pulled him closer, relishing in the heat that flared in his eyes as they darted over my face.

"I need you more right now."

His large body curled back over mine, his head dipping down but staying just out of reach. "You have people waiting for you."

"I'm where I'm supposed to be."

Those eyes locked on mine, saying so much with just a look.

He felt the same. He never wanted to leave. He loved me.

"I can't be easy with you right now."

A scoff sounded in the back of my throat at his familiar warning. "All I want is you, however you are. You always ask what I want . . . *how* I want it. Every time, all I want is you. Easy. Rough. It doesn't matter. But when you *need* it rough, you warn me against it. Like I might suddenly change my mind—like I should. But I'm here, and I want you. I want this every way you or I need it or want it," I said, ending on a whisper. "Understand?"

From the way his eyebrows had slowly drawn together as I spoke, he didn't agree. "Right. You know where that side is coming from. What happens the one time you're not expecting it the way I *need* it, and I end up hurting you physically? Emotionally? Any fucking way? I can't do that, Savannah."

"I see you in a way no one else does," I reminded him. "I

know when you're struggling. I see the change in you as soon as it happens." Sitting up, I pressed my mouth to his.

The kiss was hard.

Slow.

And full of everything I felt for him.

The rumble that built in his chest when I bit his lower lip had my belly flooding with heat and my body buzzing with need. And then he was laying me down and taking control of the kiss. His fingers tight on my wrists as he brought my arms over my head and dipped down to make a trail of bites down my neck.

Once he was settled between my thighs again and staring down at me, driving me crazy as he teased me with what was about to come, I said, "Understand? However you need it or want it, I'm already there with you."

His mouth shifted. Just the smallest twitch of acknowledgment, but the carnal way he was looking at me had my heart pounding out a wild, beautiful rhythm. "Rough then."

"I'M HERE!" I called out as I burst through our front door sometime later, still breathless from all things Beau Dixon and then rushing to dress and sneak back out of the plantation house.

It felt like I'd run all the way home instead of racing through town in my car.

My mom's voice preceded her from where she and Mrs. Rowe were coming out of the kitchen area. "What took so long? I was getting ready to call you again."

"Sorry," I said quickly as I nervously smoothed down my

hair and inched toward the living room. "Sorry, Mrs. Rowe. I couldn't find my keys and then Nicole showed up."

Mom's eyes narrowed enough to let me know she was on the line of not believing me. "To where you and Madison were dancing?" She forced a smile that I knew was for Mrs. Rowe's benefit and said, "I thought Nicole only cheered with you. When did she start dancing?"

"She doesn't, but she still has a project due with Madison." I shrugged like it wasn't a big deal.

Like I wasn't about to pass out with fear that my mom would see straight through everything I was feeding her. At least the last part was one hundred percent truth and *actually* what Madison and Nicole were doing at that moment.

"I'm gonna go change," I said before she could ask anything else. I gave Mrs. Rowe an apologetic wave as I started for the living room again, my feet getting all tangled up beneath me and a gasp ripping free when another Rowe stepped into the room behind them.

"Peter!"

He'd barely gotten a greeting out before I barreled into Philip's older brother, hugging him tight as he struggled to keep us upright. His voice all a familiar tease as he said, "Hey there, Anna."

I took a step back and feigned annoyance at the back-and-forth we'd done since long before I'd ever moved to Texas. "It's Savannah."

"Hannah?"

I scrunched my face up and stuck my tongue out for good measure before a soft laugh broke free. "Can't believe you're here. It's been so long."

His brows lifted in an *I know* kind of look as he glanced over his shoulder to make sure our moms had left. When he continued, his voice was just loud enough to be heard. "And I can't believe you think anyone's gonna buy that." At my confusion, he said, "Dancing, my ass." He glanced down for just a second, his mouth forming a tight line as he struggled not to laugh. "Your shirt is inside out and backward. You smell like a guy. And your hair is a wreck."

"Don't be rude," I hissed even as another laugh left me.

"I'm not the one who tried to ditch out on dinner to get laid."

I murmured a curse and looked behind him to make sure no one was close enough to hear him. "I'm here, aren't I? Besides, you know I'd ditch out on anything for him."

"I know." He playfully rolled his eyes, then jerked his chin to the side. "Go change before someone else notices."

"So bossy," I muttered even as I turned, but I abruptly stopped when I found Philip there, smirking like he was in on some secret that I didn't want to know.

"Savannah."

I hated the way he said my name. Intimate. Passionate. Like he knew me in ways he never would.

"Go fuck yourself," I mumbled as I wove around him.

Peter's loud laugh was the only response as I finally darted into the living room and up the stairs to my room.

And *oh my God*, Peter was right.

My shirt *was* inside out and backward, and I did look like I'd just finished having sex.

Either my mom was going to start screaming at me the instant the Rowes left, or she was refusing to acknowledge what was happening in my world. Because we all knew I didn't look like this after dancing.

Once I was changed and looked a little more Savannah-like again, I hurried down the stairs and came face to face with the younger Rowe.

"I hate you."

He smiled in response. "You keep saying that, but you wanna know what I think?"

I snorted and started around him. "No."

"I think you're afraid to admit that you want me."

I pretended to gag. "We're supposed to eat soon. If you could stop, I'd appreciate it."

"You know—"

I stopped but didn't face him. "Beau's right next door, and he's just itchin' for a reason to come over since he knows you're here." When Philip didn't respond, I felt a smile cross my face. "That's what I thought."

But I'd only made it a couple feet before he grabbed my arm and turned me toward him. "One of these days—"

"Let go," I demanded and tried to yank my arm free, but he tightened his grip.

"One of these days," he repeated, getting in my face, "you're not gonna have that psycho to hide behind. One of these days, you're gonna have to face the world without unleashing that disaster on anyone you don't wanna have to deal with."

"If you don't let go of me, I'll gladly remind you that I have no problem dealing with cowards like you on my own."

"What?" he goaded as his fingers curled even tighter. "I thought you liked guys who take what they want and give a little pain while they do it."

"Beau would never touch me without my permission," I said through gritted teeth. "And he would never grab me like an insecure little shit who isn't getting his way." I shoved my free palm into his chest and snatched my arm from his grasp just as my mom's voice rang through the house.

"Dinner's just about ready!"

I rolled my shoulder back to shift away from Philip when he fell into step beside me and hissed under my breath, "Touch me again, the next time you eat will be when I shove your balls down your throat."

"You're so passionate, Savannah," he murmured. "I love it."

"I hate you," I snapped back as I veered away when we entered the kitchen and took solace near Peter. "I hate your brother."

He scoffed as he set his drink on the counter behind him. "What else is new?"

"I missed you?" I teased, making it sound like a question and choking back a laugh when he elbowed my side.

"Brat."

I sighed as some of the anger started easing from my body just being near Peter. He'd always been one of my favorite people, the brother I never had until I met the Dixon boys and became surrounded by them.

"Seriously, though. You've been gone, what . . . two and a half years now?" I thought for a second, making sure I had my dates correct. "I thought you would've come back for the holidays—or at least summers."

A soft grunt sounded from him as he picked up his drink again. But he didn't respond or take a sip.

When I finally looked at him, he was just staring at the contents of his glass. "Peter?"

He shrugged and forced a smile. "Not everyone loves Amber the way you do, Savannah."

I felt the corners of my mouth tug down at the weight he

seemed to be holding on his shoulders. So different from just seconds before, even. "But you must be liking school then, right?"

"About that . . ." His stare darted around the kitchen to where our moms were finishing putting everything out, his voice dropping low when he continued. "I'm dropping out."

Shock punched from me. "What?"

"I just enlisted in the Navy."

Words failed me. Instead of responding in any way, I stood there, unable to figure out if he was joking.

Peter was at Columbia, studying to be an architect.

His parents told everyone in town pretty much every day —followed closely by the news that Philip was going to Yale for pre-law. Their pride in their children was widely known, just as Peter's dream of being an architect had always been known. At least by us.

"Game face, Anna-Hannah," Peter whispered.

I tried to school my features and kept my voice as soft as his. "I don't understand."

"I'm miserable," he explained. "Honest to God, miserable. Here . . . there. I hate everything about what I'm doing. I wanna do something that means something to me."

I nodded, the action probably going on longer than necessary as I absorbed what he was saying. "Well, then, you should."

"Yeah?"

"Absolutely," I said more assuredly. "Why should you be miserable?"

He gave a grateful smile and reached out to ruffle my hair, softly laughing when I smacked his hand away. "I knew you'd be the only one on my side."

"One, of course I'm on your side. Two, I *just* fixed my hair."

"It still looked terrible."

"You're such a jerk," I said half-heartedly, but the words trailed off as I caught the tail end of what Mrs. Rowe was saying to my mom.

". . . everything that Beau has done to our Philip."

"Dana," my mom said with a shake of her head. "I know, but you have to remember the Dixons are like family to us."

"And what about us?" Mrs. Rowe gently argued, looking offended that my mom would defend the Dixons. "After all we've been through, I would think our friendship would mean more."

My mom gave her a look as she set a stack of plates down. "Don't say that. You know what your friendship means to me —what your family means to mine."

"Then you shouldn't condone any type of relationship between y'alls families. And especially between *Savannah*"— she said my name on a whisper as though I hadn't inched closer to hear every word—"and that beast of a boy when, just last week, Philip needed stitches on his head because of what Beau did to him."

"Excuse me?" I demanded, causing Mrs. Rowe to flinch as she turned to meet my enraged stare.

"Savannah, why don't you kids start getting your plates ready?" my mom suggested.

"No, I wanna know what Mrs. Rowe was talking about." I sought out Philip, sulking in a corner and looking like he'd just seen a ghost.

Good.

"Can we not do this right now?" Mom quietly begged.

"It has to be done at some point," Mrs. Rowe countered

without ever looking away from me. "The fact that you continue dating that *boy*"—she sneered the word—"is a slap in the face to Philip and our family."

"I clearly don't agree," I said, voice quivering as I fought my anger and sorrow for Beau. "But about last week. Those stitches—I wanna know about that."

"It's not a big deal," Philip mumbled.

"Of course it is," Mrs. Rowe nearly yelled as I snapped over her, "I'm sure you don't think so. Why don't you tell your mom what really happened?"

No one in the kitchen spoke.

Philip stared straight at the floor, looking like he wanted to crawl into a hole.

I wished he would.

"You said Beau was the reason Philip needed stitches?" I asked Mrs. Rowe as I faced her again. At her firm nod, I forced myself to take a breath so I wouldn't scream at Philip. "Last week, Philip ran up and sucker-punched the back of Beau's head, trying to goad him into a fight—the way he always does," I said loudly, sending a quick glare Philip's way. "I stopped Beau from going after him, but Philip was running backward, taunting Beau, and tripped and fell into the corner of the lockers. *That's* why he needed stitches."

"That's outrageous," Mrs. Rowe scoffed just as my dad and Mr. Rowe came in from the back door.

"What's outrageous?" Dad asked, still holding the tray of meat they'd been grilling.

"Philip told his parents that Beau was the reason he needed stitches when *Philip* had been trying to get Beau to fight him and tripped into some lockers. I can give you a list of students that were in the hall at that time. I'm pretty sure a teacher even saw it happen!"

Mr. Rowe cleared his throat and looked to his youngest son. "Philip?"

When he didn't respond, I turned on him. "*I* do not hide behind Beau Dixon. I can stand up for myself. I can defend myself. Out of respect for your family, I refrain from doing that most times. *You* are the one who hides behind Beau and what he has done, and you are even more disgusting for it."

"Savannah," my mom whispered, disapproving.

"No!" I cried out. "I'm always letting him get away with things because of his parents and what they mean to y'all, but I've had enough." I took a step closer to Philip, loving and hating that he didn't have the guts to look at me. "I am so tired of the way you get possessive over me even though I've never been and will never be yours because I cannot stand you. I am tired of the way you talk to me and touch me like the disgusting creep you are."

"Wait, you *touched* her?" Peter asked, voice harsh.

"What are you talking about, Savannah?" Mom asked, concern now lining her words.

"Are you gonna tell them, or should I?" I asked Philip, voice soft enough that it felt like the words were only for him, but I knew everyone else could hear with how silent the room had gotten.

He glanced up at me from under his eyelashes, looking all kinds of pissed and promising a wrath that couldn't scare me.

I turned, my stare finding Mrs. Rowe. "Your *perfect son* harasses me on a near-daily basis. He has since middle school."

"That can't be—"

"It's true," I ground out, cutting her off. "He talks about how we're gonna be together. How I'm gonna be *screaming his name* one day."

"Oh God," my mom whispered as my dad slammed down the tray he'd been holding.

"All of this while grabbing me and refusing to let me leave. No matter what I tell him, he somehow twists it around so that it means I love him, or has some hidden, sexual meaning. And on that topic," I said, biting out each word as I glanced over my shoulder to cut a hard look at him, "Philip called the school *anonymously* and told them that mine and Beau's relationship is abusive. That he *rapes* me."

"Well, does he?" Mrs. Rowe asked without missing a beat.

"Are you kidding?" I yelled, not caring in the least bit about respect at that point.

"Dana," her husband said with an irritated sigh.

"I've been called into the guidance counselor's office twice a week since then because she still doesn't believe me," I informed them. "And Beau has been called in there a few times to talk with her *and the sheriff* about how to respect and treat women. Philip also wrote words like *abuser* and *dangerous* and *savage* all over Beau's locker with a big Sharpie on the same day that first began. But even when Beau found out it was him, he didn't do anything to Philip."

"That . . ." Mr. Rowe sighed, his head shaking. "That will be dealt with along with some other things. That doesn't change that Beau *has* hurt our son and others in the past."

"I'm aware of that," I conceded. "Clearly not as many times as Philip is making y'all believe, and he's probably not telling y'all *why*. Beau's only ever reacting to what Philip does to me . . . what Philip does to *him*. That day Philip punched him and tripped into the lockers? That isn't the first time Philip has done something like that. He's *always* trying to get Beau to fight because he knows Beau is the one who will get in trouble. Then there are the days Beau walks up on Philip holding me in place even though I'm trying to get away. Or when Philip grabs my butt or my boobs—"

"What?" multiple people shouted at once.

"—or runs up and tries to kiss me right in front of Beau. It kind of sets Beau off."

"What the hell is wrong with you?" Peter demanded.

"I've been asking him that for years," I said as I spared one last glance at the boy who was turning red with anger and embarrassment. Looking back at his mom, I tried to force back the emotion that sprang forward. "Y'all always have something bad to say about Beau. Now you're questioning my parents' friendship with the Dixons because of him? Because of what *he's* done? What about what *your son* has done? A vile, spoiled brat who doesn't understand when a girl says 'no,' thinks he can treat me like I'm a *thing*, and takes joy in ruining other peoples' lives."

She folded her arms, then lifted her hand to cover the tremor in her mouth.

"I know Beau has a problem with his anger. I've seen it, and I've seen how hard he tries to control it. But it's jerks like *your son* who make Beau think all he's capable of is anger, and it's people like you who make him afraid of his anger. Who make him try so hard to suppress it until he just-just-just . . . explodes. But he's—" I choked back a cry of frustration. "God, he is *good*. His heart is so kind and beautiful, and for the life of me, I can't understand why everyone else refuses to see that."

I hurried from the kitchen and through the house, ignoring the calls for me to stop.

By the time I reached the front door, I was running, long past caring about dinner or respecting the people that had always been like a second family to ours. Off the porch and down our long driveway that never seemed to end. Across the little stretch of road that separated our house from the Dixons' and up their graveled drive. My stare bouncing around the front of the property the closer I got.

Sawyer running to catch a football Hunter had thrown.

Cayson sitting across the porch steps, arms folded and back propped up against the railing.

No Beau.

Sawyer saw me first. His easy smile fell along with the football, bouncing awkwardly behind him as he raced over to meet me. "You already heard?" he asked, all worry and understanding.

And it made my heart stop. Had ice splintering in my veins.

"Heard what?"

Seventeen

SAVANNAH
SEVENTEEN YEARS OLD

Sawyer's light eyes went wide before he tried to cover his reaction by glancing away. He forced out a cough as he faced me again, all hints of his slip gone. "What's going on?"

"Where's Beau?"

"It's uh, you know, not really a good time."

"You okay?" Hunter asked as he came up behind him with Cayson on his heels.

"No," I said tightly. "Where's Beau?"

Cayson scratched at his jaw before pointing absently behind him as Hunter started to speak, but Sawyer forced out another cough and roughly shook his head.

I looked from him to Hunter and demanded, "What is going on?"

Hunter studied the ground for a moment before meeting my stare, his face creased with apology when he said, "Probably not the best time, yeah? What can we do? You look mad, are you okay?"

"What? I—no, I need to see Beau."

"Want me to call Mads?" he offered.

I took a step back to look them each in the eye. "I want you to tell me what is going on and why I can't see him." When none of them offered anything, I folded my arms over my chest and lifted my chin. "Now."

Cayson slid his hands into his pockets and shrugged. "I wasn't there."

"Yeah, where were you?" Sawyer demanded.

A sly smirk stole across Cayson's face. "I had things to set up."

"Idiot," Sawyer murmured.

"Beau," I snapped. "Tell me about *Beau*."

Silence.

Just when I was about to scream from the unknown and the aggravation whipping through me from the past few minutes, Hunter sighed.

"Y'all were out . . . yeah?"

I nodded, my head bobbing shakily. "Yeah. Why?"

"Two . . . maybe three minutes before he got back, this guy shows up with the sheriff right behind him, asking for Beau."

My stomach clenched as I thought about our spot at the plantation house—all the times we'd snuck into the back and inside.

I gripped at my stomach and prayed the churning would ease, my voice light and breathless when I asked, "Why?"

Hunter's mouth formed a tight line as he studied me, his hand reaching out to gently grip my upper arm as he said, "Why don't you sit."

"No, just tell me!" I shouted.

"Savannah—"

"Hunter, I swear to God, if you don't tell me, I'm going inside and finding out—"

"He isn't here," he said softly, bringing me up short.

I blinked quickly, causing tears to fall as I looked from him to the house and back again. Dread bloomed in my chest as I asked the question I feared I already knew the answer to. "Where is he?"

"County," he finally answered, the word nothing more than a shamed apology.

As if it were Hunter's fault his brother had been arrested.

A strangled sob climbed up my throat before I was able to force it all back. The tears. The devastation. The sorrow for Beau.

I'd let it out later.

Right then, I needed to be strong for him.

With a steadying breath, I asked, "Why? He hasn't done anything."

"I dunno. I came in as the sheriff was putting him in cuffs. All I heard was the other guy say the family had decided to press charges and file a civil suit against Beau for what he had done."

Oh God.

"But he hasn't done anything," I maintained.

Hunter shrugged, and we all looked when a car turned into the drive, the headlights softly glowing in the early evening sky.

Hope swirled in my chest as I watched Mrs. Dixon's car get closer and closer, only to shatter when I realized Beau wasn't with his parents.

I took thin, shallow breaths. Refusing to break down. Refusing to be anything but strong right then.

"Oh, Savannah, honey," Mrs. Dixon said as she exited the passenger side, face a mess and voice thick from tears. "Now isn't a good time. I'm sorry, sweet girl."

"Please, I want to know what happened."

"Bullshit is what happened," Mr. Dixon snapped as he slammed the driver's door shut behind him.

"Mike," Mrs. Dixon said, sounding too exhausted to argue.

"It is," he continued. "You know damn well Beau wouldn't do that shit."

"We can't—" Mrs. Dixon's glassy gaze met mine and her lips formed a thin line before lifting into a pained smile. "We'll let Beau know you stopped by."

"He hasn't done anything," I said confidently. "He's been trying so hard to keep calm. He *is* keeping himself calm."

"Yeah, well," Mr. Dixon said with an irritated huff, "that ain't what your little friend is sayin', and Beau ain't sayin' a damn thing to defend himself."

Of course he wasn't.

"Wait . . . what friend?"

"Mike, please," Mrs. Dixon whispered.

"No, she deserves to know what's goin' on," he said, then jerked his head in the direction of town. "That Rowe kid. The younger one."

Disbelief and anger consumed me so quickly that it stole my breath. "Excuse me?"

"Wait, *Philip*?" Hunter asked, sounding nearly as pissed as I was. "Are you fucking kidding me?"

"Language," Mrs. Dixon chastised.

Hunter scoffed. "Anything Beau did to him, that jackass deserved."

"Well, apparently your brother put him in the hospital last week—the poor boy only needed stitches, thank God," his mom went on.

I rocked back a step, my hands balling into fists as I struggled to say anything and only managed something that resembled an enraged scream.

"Bullshit," Hunter barked.

"Exactly," Mr. Dixon said, waving a hand in Hunter's direction.

"Again," Mrs. Dixon seethed, *"language."*

"Philip tripped into the lockers last week—Beau wasn't even near him," Hunter said, explaining what I had just minutes before. "We were all there."

"I'm gonna kill him," I whispered, sounding all kinds of hysterical.

"Didn't he hit Beau?" Hunter asked.

"He did," I confirmed as I started backing away. "Then he took off, trying to antagonize Beau into going after him. But Beau never left my side."

"See?" Hunter said, then looked to where I was leaving. "Where are you going?"

"Taking care of it," was all I said as I hurried back the way I'd come, the run home seeming to take a fraction of the time.

I was both relieved and pissed off as I ran up my driveway and passed the Rowes' car. Because I didn't have to go to them, but it meant they were *there*.

"You're still here?" I yelled as I shut the front door behind me, my eyes locked on where the Rowes and my parents were standing halfway between the kitchen and entryway.

"Savannah," my mom reprimanded in a low tone. "I know you're upset, but you need to remember your manners."

My head shook fiercely. "No. No, no, no. You're still *here*," I repeated, my voice cracking as I pointed at the door behind me. "You know you were wrong—that Philip lied to you—

and you're here when my boyfriend is sitting in jail because of you."

Shock covered my parents' faces as they turned to Mr. and Mrs. Rowe, both wearing twin expressions of shame.

"Jesus," Peter sighed before making his way through everyone. He set his hands on my shoulders, eyebrows drawn together in apology. "I'm sorry for my family. Love you, Anna-Hannah."

"You too."

He gave my shoulders a squeeze and moved past me, the door opening and closing as my dad asked, "What's happening now?"

"Beau was arrested tonight. They're suing him and pressing charges for what he did to Philip—also known as what Philip did to himself," I answered for the Rowes before focusing on them. "And even after I told y'all what really happened, you stayed here. You *knew* what was happening to him tonight, and you didn't care to fix your mistakes. Mistakes that Beau *accepted* even though he knew he had no fault in them. He let them arrest him without saying a word." I looked at where Philip was trying to blend into a wall. "If you even make it that far, you are going to be the worst lawyer. How did you think this would end when there were dozens of witnesses?"

"Well," my dad murmured, then cleared his throat. Everything about his expression and tone dismissive when he continued. "I don't think there's anything else to say other than we'll follow you to the county jail to make sure you drop the charges and suit."

"Come on, Jason, don't be like that," Mr. Rowe said, trying to laugh. "We'll take care of this, and it can all be forgotten."

My dad grabbed the keys to his car off the hook in the entryway, his head bobbing slightly. "We have our reservations about Beau and Savannah as a couple, you know that. It's never been a secret. But he has never once treated her the way your son has apparently been treating our daughter for years." He held up a hand when Mr. Rowe started speaking. "*Years*. And that was only the few things she said. What about all the others she still hasn't told us? And you have the nerve to come in and question our friendship to that family all while you were having one of their kids arrested for something you weren't even positive happened?" A humorless laugh left him. "I'm questioning our friendship with you."

"Jason," both Mr. and Mrs. Rowe said, sounding horrified.

When he only continued toward me, curling his arm around my shoulders to lead me toward the front door, Mrs. Rowe said, "Christi, please."

"You heard my husband. We'll see you at county."

I wasn't sure I'd ever been so shocked by my parents in my life. I also wasn't sure if there would ever be another time where they were on Beau's side for any reason—even if only slightly.

But I would take it.

I would take it and be so grateful.

"Thank you," I whispered as my dad led me outside.

"You should've told us," he said in response. "Doesn't matter who the person or their family is. You tell us what's happening."

"Understood."

We watched the Rowes leave the house with my mom trailing behind, then started heading for our car.

"Anything you need to tell us about Beau?" my dad asked

as I reached for the handle of my door, sounding far too curious and expectant.

I rolled my eyes and released a deep sigh. "*Dad.*"

"Needed to check," he said unapologetically as he ducked into the car.

"Wendy must be a wreck," my mom muttered as she sank into the passenger seat and shut the door behind her.

"She is." I looked out the window as I bit at my thumb nail and tried not to think about how long it took to get to the county jail as I added, "Mr. Dixon's super mad. And that was before Hunter and I told them that Philip lied."

She sighed and released her seatbelt before it could click shut. "The two of you go on ahead. I'm gonna check on her." Glancing behind her, she pointed at me. "Stop."

I forced my hand into my lap. "I'm not biting it."

Her face softened. "I'm sorry about this. I really am, Savannah."

I watched as she got out of the car and began walking down the drive, then crawled across the center console to sit up front as my dad began reversing. "How fast can we get there?"

"It won't make a difference. He won't be released until they drop everything."

I nodded, already knowing that even though my heart couldn't understand it.

Getting there meant getting to *him*. Simple as that.

"I'm so mad," I whispered a few minutes later.

Dad released a slow breath. "I know."

"And I think I might be mad at Beau . . ."

He shifted in his seat. Knowing my dad the way I did, I had a feeling he was trying not to jump for joy at the idea of me being mad enough to want to break up with Beau.

As if that would ever happen.

"Yeah?"

"He just let them take him," I explained. "He didn't say anything. He never does. Beau figures if someone thinks something about him, then it either must be true, or he isn't going to change their mind about him anyway, so why try? And it hurts my heart because I want him to see himself the way I do." I gestured to my dad before letting my hand fall. "Just like I want you and mom and everyone else to see him the way I do. There's this guy apart from the anger that is so incredible—he just refuses to show anyone else because they already have their minds made up about him."

A hum sounded in my dad's throat. "But he shows you?"

"Yeah," I said as if that should've been obvious.

"And why do you think that is?"

"Because I looked at him that first day and saw him around all that anger he was trying to get away from."

My dad shrugged. "Or maybe it's because the boy loves you."

"It's because I saw him," I said resolutely. "It's because I always see *him*." Before he could argue, I said, "You know he fights with his brothers all the time. Physically. But Beau and Hunter are best friends despite that because Hunter sees him too. He knows."

He didn't respond, and for a long time, we drove in silence until Dad finally said, "I can't figure out why you want to be with someone like him."

"Dad—"

"Someone you always have to defend. Someone who is always putting you in dangerous situations because he can't control himself. Someone you have to beg people to give a chance to when he's had more than enough."

"He has not," I said quietly, angrily. "It's like with Philip
—he has always started fights with Beau, knowing Beau will
finish them. Knowing only *Beau* will get in trouble because
he's known for his anger. Because it's so easy for everyone to
believe that Beau snapped *just because*. How is that giving him
a chance?"

"He *has* snapped just because, Savannah."

"You're wrong." I started biting at my thumb nail but
forced my hand into my lap as I thought of how to explain
Beau to my dad in the first real conversation we'd ever had
about him.

Usually, my parents just yelled or tossed out the reminder
Utah, and that was the end of it.

"When he loses it, it's big—I know," I said carefully. "But
he just . . . *everything* is bigger to Beau. He hurts deeper.
Loves harder. Rages stronger. He feels everything on such a
massive level, and he spends nearly every minute of every day
trying to suppress *all of it*. So, when he's pushed, it explodes
from him."

"Tell me how that isn't dangerous for you," he said
gruffly, doubt weaving through his tone.

The corners of my mouth twitched into a ghost of a smile.
"Because he likes being pushed by me." I turned in my seat
to face my dad and reminded him, "And he shows me those
sides of him that he's usually trying to suppress. I'm good for
him."

"He isn't your responsibility to fix, Savannah."

I jerked against the door at the assumption. "I don't
wanna fix him," I said firmly. "He doesn't need to be fixed or
changed or-or-or . . . anything. He's fine. He's perfect, Dad."

He shot me a glance, some horrible mixture of disbelief
and an apology as I continued.

"And he's good for me too. But you wouldn't know that because you don't *want* to know. You and Mom don't care about the things he does for me or how he cares for me or how he loves me in a way that continues to steal my heart all over again."

"We care about you," Dad interjected over me.

"Instead, you want me with some horrible excuse for a guy who has assaulted and harassed me more times than I can remember just because he isn't known to have an anger problem. How does that make sense?"

My dad scrubbed his palm over his face before placing it on the steering wheel again but didn't respond otherwise, and I didn't say anything else.

I didn't want to push him further, not after everything he'd already done for Beau and me tonight.

When we pulled into the parking area for the county jail a few minutes later, I whispered, "Thank you again. I'm sure this must have been really hard for you and Mom."

My dad sighed as he put the car in park and faced me. "What's hard is what we missed. What's hard is what you went through and felt like you couldn't tell us. I'm sorry." His mouth fell into a shaky frown as he studied me for a moment longer before getting out of the car.

I followed, eager to get inside. Wanting to run into the small station and get to where my heart was calling me and feeling trapped when we had to wait.

And wait.

And wait.

"Dad," I groaned sometime later.

He grabbed my arm and pulled me into the seat beside him to stop my pacing. "He'll be out soon."

"You said that forever ago." My stare went to the clock,

and I dropped my head against the wall. "You said that over forty minutes ago."

And we'd arrived long before that.

The deputy on duty—who knew quite well who I was to Beau Dixon—wanted to make sure we weren't making the Rowes drop the charges by force or threat. Especially since the Dixons had been there not long before. And once the Rowes realized that admitting Beau hadn't actually done anything also meant that Philip had intentionally filed a false police report, they'd wanted their lawyer present before they went ahead with anything.

"He's been in there for hours for nothing," I whispered, my gaze narrowing on the corner the Rowes had remained huddled in with their lawyer ever since coming out of the back room where they'd discussed who-knew-what. "They already know they're dropping the charges against Beau. Why can't they just release him?"

"I don't know, pumpkin," he muttered, then released an exhausted sigh. "*Savannah*."

I ignored his hushed calls as I pushed from the chair and hurried over to the front desk, intent on at least finding out something.

The deputy took a breath when he saw me coming as if he was preparing for a verbal attack. "Yes, Miss Riley?"

"Has he said anything?"

The deputy's brows rose in surprise. "I'm sorry, what was that?"

"Beau. Has he said anything since the sheriff arrested him and brought him in?"

His head slanted to the side. "Not a word, ma'am."

I nodded as I glanced toward the hall I knew he would

come down when he was released. "Does he know we're here?"

"No, ma'am. There's no point in tellin' him about all this when nothin' might come from it."

Surprise and frustration slammed into me. I looked back at him and then over to the Rowes as I wondered what was holding them up. "Can I . . . can I go talk to him?"

Sympathy swept across the deputy's face when I met his stare again. "You know you can't."

"Yes, sir," I said softly, then turned and headed back to where my dad was talking to Peter. "Are your parents not dropping the charges?"

My dad gestured to Peter and then over to the cluster of Rowes as if in response.

"They are," Peter assured me on a sigh. "They are, this is just . . . stupid. This whole thing is stupid, and I'll say I'm sorry for all of it because I know they won't. They were trying to figure out a way to make a deal for Philip first, and it's just . . ." He dragged his hands over his face and gave me an apologetic look. "Fucked up." He held out a hand toward my dad. "Sorry."

"That isn't fair," I said probably a little too loudly. "It isn't Beau's fault that Philip made a false report. He shouldn't have to wait because of him."

"Trust me, I know." Peter lifted his hands in a way like he was trying to remind me he wasn't on their side. "You wonder why I've stayed gone as long as I have," he tried to tease, but it fell flat.

"I hate your brother."

"Savannah," my dad mumbled in disapproval.

Peter just smiled. "What else is new?" His stare shifted

over my head and his smile grew. "Hey, Anna-Hannah . . . you should look behind you."

Before he even finished speaking, I turned. A sound of joy and sorrow climbing up my throat when I saw Beau walking down the hall and shrugging into his jacket.

Face fiercely unreadable to anyone else, but I knew him.

I understood the set of his brows and the tenseness of his jaw. I saw the anger swirling within his apology and embarrassment as his eyes locked on me.

As if he had done something when we both knew he hadn't.

I waited until he passed the faded, red and white *Do Not Cross* line before taking off across the lobby to meet him. Crashing against him and reveling in the feel of his hard body against mine. In the way one of his arms automatically curled around my waist to hold me close as his other hand lifted to my face. His fingers trailing along my jaw as his eyes searched mine, saying all the things he wouldn't when others were near.

I love you. I love you. I'm sorry. Forgive me.

"Stop," I begged, curling my fingers into his shirt. "You didn't do anything."

"Look where we are," he said, his voice nothing more than a dejected breath.

"Because Philip's a prick. But I told them—I told both my parents and his everything. What happened last week, what's been happening all these years. They're dropping the charges and suit."

His head moved, the slightest shift of a nod before he said, "Savannah, your dad's here."

The unknown and worry and question in those few words had a smile breaking free because I still couldn't believe it myself. "He drove me." I stepped even closer and lowered my voice as I excitedly told him, "When my parents found out about Philip and what happened tonight, they told the Rowes they would follow them here to make sure the Rowes dropped everything against you. But my mom ended up going to check on your mom instead."

All the tension in Beau's face disappeared as his stare snapped behind me, conveying his shock.

"I know." I took a step back, tugging him with me before releasing my grip on his shirt. "Let's get you home," I murmured and easily fell into his side as we headed toward the doors where my dad and Peter waited.

"I'll let y'all get out of here," Peter said, looking at Beau, "I just wanted to apologize for my family."

Beau shrugged. "Not necessary."

"Seriously, Peter," I added, "stop apologizing for something they did."

He nodded. "Again . . . *they* won't. Someone has to." He grabbed the handle of the door and opened it up for us. "Y'all have a good Christmas."

We returned the sentiment, but I caught his eye before slipping out the door. "You stay safe."

He mock-saluted me. "Will do."

"Beau," my dad called out as we stepped into the winter air. Jerking his head to the side, he started that way without another word.

Beau tensed but followed without hesitation, quickly catching up to where my dad waited for him. Looking all kinds of terrifying as he listened to my dad speak when I knew he was actually terrified.

And after what had to be the longest thirty seconds of my life, my dad turned away from Beau and started for the car.

Another handful of seconds later, Beau finally moved from where he'd seemed to be carved out of stone and walked toward me.

Head down.

Hands in his jacket pockets.

Not giving me any clues as to what had just happened.

"What'd my dad say?" I begged when he neared me.

He lifted his head, his dark eyes dancing in the light from the station as he fought a smile. "He said he still has some reservations . . . but that I have his permission to date you."

A startled laugh bubbled free. "Doesn't he know we've been dating for almost four years?"

The smile broke free. Just a small flash of bright, white teeth and deep, Dixon dimples before it was gone, but it melted me all the same. "Yeah," he rumbled as he slid his hand into mine. "He knows."

Eighteen

SAVANNAH

My steps were slow as I moved through the large living area to one of the closets just off the entryway to put Levi's toys away, holding them awkwardly in my arms with my head slanted. Ear trained to the second floor to catch whispers of the kids' laughter as Beau put them to bed the next night.

The new routine tearing at my chest because everything about it was wrong.

I couldn't remember a night where we hadn't put the kids to bed together, and I missed that time. Even more, I hated that my older kids could feel what was happening between Beau and me.

That they knew something was wrong with their dad not being there in the mornings and him being the only one to put them to bed. With us not speaking to each other during the hours he was there.

Most of all, I hated that I couldn't talk to my best friend and the man who held my heart without wanting to scream at him. That he couldn't pull me into his arms, and I couldn't curl up against him in our bed. That every part of us felt like a lie.

I hated that I didn't know how to stop this destructive path we were on even though every part of my soul screamed at me to find a way. But our relationship felt like a runaway train, and we were nearing the end of the track.

I looked up at the sound of his heavy steps on the stairs, hummingbirds taking flight in my stomach at the sight of him even as my fraying heart wrenched. Turning back to the opened closet, I dropped Levi's toys into the designated basket and tried to pretend I wasn't listening as his steps sounded on the entryway floor . . . and stopped.

My chest rising and falling faster and faster as I silently prayed he would just go while every part of me was crying out for him to stay.

I closed the closet door, my breaths turning shallow as I faced where he was waiting.

Arms folded.

Head slanted.

Jaw straining and body twitching like he was getting restless.

And then he looked at me, and I thought I might crumple under all that captivating intensity and unreserved pain.

"Tomorrow's Saturday," he mumbled, voice pure gravel.

"I know."

"The kids know I don't work," he said meaningfully.

"Oh, um . . ." I blinked quickly, trying desperately to think through the emotions crashing through me at having to have this type of conversation with him. At the crushing pain that came from having him speaking to me and looking at me for the first time that day. "Right."

"I'll be here first thing."

I just nodded, unable to form words when it felt like my throat was being crushed under the weight of my grief and my anger.

I forced myself to turn when he started for the door, stopping when he asked, "When does the last guest leave?"

"My parents," I managed to say, the words coming out strained. "Monday morning."

There was a long pause before he spoke. Voice soft and full of regret. "After the kids go to bed that night, I'll start moving out."

My hand shot out in front of me, gripping the wall when it felt like the floor was ripped out from beneath me and the world went dark for a moment. The air rushing from my lungs so fast and so forcefully, I felt dizzy.

Before I could utter a word, the door was opening, and my mind was screaming to stop him. But the sound of multiple people coming up the porch broke through everything else just as I finally managed to turn around.

Beau was standing off to the side, head slanted in an attempt to hide his expression as one of the Rowes' cousins came in. That terrifying, silent rage, but I could see the anguish lingering in his eyes. I could see the weight he was bearing. The absolute fear.

"Welcome back," I managed to say, forcing the same smile I'd worn since the guests had arrived the day before.

But their cousin just gave me a wide-eyed look as she turned for the stairs, muttering, "Biggest understatement of my life."

"Great," Peter said, voice like steel when he came charging through, pointing at Beau, "you're still here. I need someone to drink with since that one won't." He waved irritably at me, never slowing as he headed for the kitchen.

Beau didn't move, and I just stood there, too stunned from trying to piece together my wrecked soul to ask Peter what was happening.

My parents followed, looking at once excited to see me and like they were saddened for whatever must've happened at the rehearsal and dinner. But the moment they saw Beau, their spirits brightened considerably.

"Oh, honey, hi," my mom said to Beau, reaching for him and patting his shoulder.

"Glad you're still here," my dad said, then blew out a strained breath as he looked between us, scratching at his temple. Focusing on Beau, he gestured toward the kitchen. "Drink? I could use a drink."

"Let's make it two," my mom said, words all an exhausted sigh.

"What?" The word came out a breath, all shock and confusion just as the Rowes' aunt and uncle came inside, shutting the door behind them and looking about as worn out as everyone else. "Hi," I said awkwardly, offering another forced smile.

Peter's uncle clapped his hands together and returned the smile. "Do you have any alcohol?"

My lips parted just as the sound of glass clinking on granite sounded from the kitchen. Pointing in that direction, I said, "I think your nephew might've just found it."

"Fantastic," he grumbled, towing his wife along with him.

"What is going on?" I asked once they'd disappeared into the next room.

Before my parents could respond, Beau headed for the door again, dipping his head in a nod when he passed them. "Goodnight."

"Beau, honey," Mom began, her shaking fingers lifting to

cover her mouth when he left without a backward glance. A sharp breath left her as she turned on me, disapproval radiating from her. "Savannah . . ."

"What? Mom, how can you possibly—" I lifted my hands before squeezing them into tight fists. "We are in the entryway," I said softly, reminding them of how that space carried noise throughout the house.

Without another word, I hurried across the entryway and down one of the halls with my parents close behind.

"How can you possibly be on his side?" I asked once we were far enough away, still keeping my voice low.

"Savannah," she said reproachfully. "I *am* on your side. I am on Beau's side, and I am on your kids' sides. But, right now, you are only on the side of hurt. You're taking what happened and holding on to it, and you can't."

"Yes, I can."

"If you want to ruin your life, sure." She held up a hand to stop me when I started arguing. "You're treating this situation and him as if what he did was purposeful and recent."

"He lied to me for thirteen years," I reminded her. "He helped her leave, and then was there for me when I grieved her. He was *mad at her*."

"We never said Beau didn't make mistakes, Savannah," Dad cut in. "He did, and he knows that."

"So, that makes it okay? That means I should just get over it?"

"Of course not," Mom said wearily. "But, Savannah, you're shutting him out and you're closing doors that should never be closed in marriages."

My stare fell to the side as shame and anguish ripped through me.

"Kicking him out of the house for weeks," she went on

softly. "Not letting him see you or the kids for most of that time. Taking off your wedding ring?" Shock filled her tone at that. "That's such a huge and damaging statement, and he has to know that."

"I gave them to him," I confessed, my shoulders caving as that grief became too much.

As my parents' deafening silence said more than words could.

"He's moving out next week," I whispered shakily. "He told me just before y'all got back."

After a while, my dad huffed. "I know damn well from talking with him that it isn't by choice."

My blurry stare snapped to him. "I didn't ask him to."

"Did you ask him to come back?" He lifted his hands in a pleading gesture. "You're hurting. I know it, we all know it. Your husband knows it, Savannah. But if you aren't even going to give your marriage the chance to survive this, you might as well have some papers drawn up now. Save him the heartache of wondering."

"Y'all are talking like everything that's happened is my fault," I cried out.

"We're not," my dad gently argued. "But after these kinds of shocks and betrayals, what happens moving forward is up to the person who's been hurt. And you've decided to throw away your entire life with him by not even trying."

"That isn't—" A whispered sob tumbled past my lips, my head shaking quickly. "I don't know how when everything feels like a lie. I look back, and I don't know how I'm supposed to know what was real and what wasn't because I never even knew something was wrong."

"You know, Savannah," Mom said, all strength and encouragement. "In your heart, you do. And if you look carefully, maybe you'll even see that there were signs during those times that you dismissed or took as something else."

I nodded, even though I wasn't sure she was right.

"Your mom and I have been thinking," Dad began, the hesitance in his voice capturing my attention, "and after this conversation, I'm pretty positive in our decision."

Mom made an agreeing sort of hum in her throat as he continued.

"We're going to take the kids back to Utah with us for a week or so."

"What?" It might've been a breath or a scream or a cry, I wasn't sure. All I knew was they were trying to take the rest of my heart.

All that was keeping me going.

"No," I said quickly. Harshly. "No, you can't."

"Savannah, take a second and just think, sweetheart," Mom said softly. "Right now, you need to focus on your marriage, and you can't do that when one thousand percent of your focus is on your kids and this business."

"Of course my focus is on them. That's my life. My kids are my life."

"If any part of you wants to save your marriage, then your focus needs to be on that. You need to spend time thinking about what's happened and what is happening without those constant distractions fighting for your attention. Also," she added with a shrug, "we want time with our grandbabies. Are you really going to deprive us of that?"

My body sagged at the unfair jab. "But they have school."

They shared an amused look before my mom met my pleading stare. "They'll miss, what, the last two . . . three days of school? It's kindergarten and first grade, it isn't a big deal."

"Mom, please don't," I begged, my chin wavering when she set her hands on my shoulders.

"I love you," she said softly. "Your dad and I love you. We are doing this for you." With an exaggerated sigh, she turned to my dad. "I could use that drink now."

I stood there, shaking and shaking as they started down the hallway, trying desperately to hold myself together until they turned into the kitchen. Staggering back to the wall and bending, my hands on my knees and my chest pitching with sharp, broken breaths. Struggling to pull myself together when I had a house full of people—when my world was breaking.

In the back of my mind, I knew my parents were right. Knew I needed that time to let myself truly be consumed in the pain of what happened so I could start healing from it. But I was afraid.

Any time I had to myself, my mind went wild with what I knew and thoughts of my life with Beau. Anytime that happened, I hurried to shut the memories and pain down, busying myself with my kids or baking or cleaning until all that was left was an echo of pain and anger.

And I couldn't do that forever.

"Anna-Hannah."

I straightened, wiping at my cheeks and trying to force a smile when I met Peter's knowing stare.

He gestured to follow him, drink in hand. "Let's go. Time to talk it out."

A stuttered breath escaped me as I tried to come up with another excuse to get out of talking about my misery, but I eventually pushed from the wall and followed after him.

"That's two nights in a row that your husband has left around eight-ish," he said when I caught up to his side. "He also wasn't here at breakfast." One of his shoulders jerked up. "That doesn't necessarily mean anything, except your mini-me said he's never here for breakfast anymore."

Pain sliced through me, stealing my breath and forcing my eyes to shut.

When I managed to open them again, Peter was holding a drink out to me.

"Uh . . . no. No thanks," I whispered, then reached for a coffee mug and headed over to the pot of decaf I'd brewed while Beau was putting the kids to bed, eyes lingering on where my parents and Peter's aunt and uncle were outside by the fire pit.

Once I had my coffee made, I bent to open one of my cupboards, pulling out my secret stash of goodies and setting them on the counter.

Peter's brows lifted. "What are those?"

"Death-by-brownies," I answered numbly as I pulled one out and held it out to him. "Want one?"

He snatched it like I might take it back, glancing around as I grabbed one for myself before closing them back up. "How many desserts do you have made right now?"

I shrugged. "These don't count. These are mine."

"Leave those out," he groaned around a mouthful. His eyes widening in warning when I started putting them away. "I know where they are now."

"I'll hide them somewhere else later," I said, unaffected as I shut the cupboard door again.

"What's in these?" he asked as he took another giant bite.

"A peanut butter cup is in the middle of the batter, but the batter has a little something special in there."

He stopped chewing, eyes narrowing on me.

"Not like that," I said with a scoff. "It's just my extra

something." When he continued watching me expectantly, I slanted my head. "I can't tell you. It's mine."

"Okay, four-year-old."

I stuck my tongue out at him like we were kids again, earning a soft chuckle. "So, what happened tonight?" When his stare drifted to the side, I went on, prodding, "Y'all were just going to the rehearsal and dinner, right? I was surprised when everyone came back the way they did."

After a while, he exhaled quickly and said, "My brother happened," before knocking back the rest of his drink.

A hum of acknowledgment climbed up my throat. "Funny how that explains so much."

A huff fled from Peter, and he reached across the island where we stood, making a grabby hand. "Brownie."

"Who's four now? Also, no. I made so much for y'all to eat."

He gave me a look that was at once pleading and conceding. "I'll tell you what happened if you bring the brownies back out."

I studied him for a moment before sighing in defeat. "If you eat them all, I'll have to kill you."

One of his full laughs burst from him, his eyes dancing when he met my stare again. "I'd like to see you try."

Grabbing the brownies and my coffee, I headed for the large kitchen table that overlooked the back of the property and had a perfect view of the people sitting around the fire pit. Laughing and drinking and looking so much happier than when they'd first come back.

"Philip gave a toast," Peter said as soon as he was in a chair and stealing the brownies from me. "Asshole."

"That bad?"

He gave me a look before glancing out the window. "He

thanked everyone for coming, for wanting to share in their weekend," he went on, rolling his eyes as he did. "Then he turned to me."

"Oh no."

The corner of his mouth ticked, all frustration and resentment. "Said something like, 'Glad you actually made it. Now pay attention. I'll show you what it takes to keep a woman around.'"

Shock ripped from me on an exhale even though I shouldn't have been surprised. This was Philip we were talking about. Still, you'd expect someone like him to grow up. "What a dick."

"What else is new?" Peter mumbled. With a heavy sigh, he leaned back in his seat and put his attention on me. "All right, your turn. The hell's going on with you and Beau? Because it sure as shit doesn't look good."

My shoulders jerked with a muted sob, and I reached for the brownies.

Peter whistled. "That bad, huh?"

———

I TOLD Peter everything exactly the way it happened.

That day Hunter and Madison came over—what was said. What I found out later and what was currently happening between Beau and me.

By the time I finished, we'd eaten half the brownies, and Peter had switched to coffee.

"Okay, I have a question," he asked a while after I'd finished, fingers tapping on his mug. "Do you *want* your marriage to end?"

Pain exploded from me. "Why would I want it to?"

He lifted his hand before resuming his tapping. "Because it's been . . . how many weeks did you say?"

"Three."

"Three weeks, and it seems like your anger with him is growing. Like you tried to go through these stages of processing what happened and got stuck in a cluster of all of them. And now you're sabotaging any chance of fixing this."

"Why is everyone saying that?"

His brows lifted in a way that screamed I should take a hint. "You finally let him come over to see the kids, then tell him he can't talk to you. He tries talking to you, and you basically tell him y'all are over and give him your goddamn ring," he said, whispering the last part. "He tells you he's moving out, and you let him go without telling him that's a bad fucking idea." He sat back in his chair, head shaking. "I think your parents are right. I think you've been so focused on your kids and this place that you haven't actually taken time process what happened the way you need to, and it's gonna ruin y'all."

I stared into my empty mug for a while before saying, "But what happens when I *do* process it, and I find that I can't forgive him?"

"You're not forgiving him now, and it could end up being a huge mistake," he said soberly. When I didn't respond, he smacked the table and sat up. "All right, answer this: Have you ever been so blackout drunk that you don't remember what happened?"

"Yes, that same week," I explained with a huff. "But they *knew* what they did. It seems convenient that they *didn't know* it was with each other."

"Or they legitimately could have pieced it together the

way they're saying happened," he offered dryly. "The way people tend to piece together those kinds of nights."

I pulled the brownies back to my side of the table. "You don't get any more."

A breath of a laugh left him. "Savannah, that guy has always been in love with you. He stood up to your parents and took everything they had to say about him because he loved you. There's no way he was doing all that and cheating on you."

"And what about the rest?" I asked, not wanting to go around and around with him on what might've happened that night.

Peter looked away, the corner of his mouth ticking up with indecision. "Okay, yeah," he finally relented. "The whole part about Madison leaving and him not telling you is fucked up."

"Exactly."

"But there has to be more to it," he quickly added. "You glossed over Madison's part in that and focused on the fact that Beau kept it from you for all those years—that he lied about it."

"Because *he* is my husband."

"*He* is the one who stayed," he said softly, but his words rang with meaning. "There has to be more to it."

"You don't know that."

"Don't I? Because my wife—" The same agony I'd been living under these weeks flashed across his features. "My *ex*," he corrected slowly, then cleared his throat, "told her family and friends that I neglected her and left her to fend for herself in what I found out she referred to as a prison." He waved a hand to the side as if what he was talking about was just outside my windows. "Except I was fucking *there*, loving her every day unless I was on a mission. She had friends on the base. And I did everything to save us even though they think I could hardly be bothered to sign the divorce papers."

Sorrow and sympathy bled from me as I watched him try to force back the emotions breaking free. "Peter . . ."

His stare darted to mine. "You don't know his side, and unless you're just done and this is your way of getting out of a marriage I *know* you don't want out of . . . then he deserves the chance to say it."

My head dipped after a beat of hesitation. "Yeah, okay."

Nineteen

BEAU
NINETEEN YEARS OLD

"The fuck?" I yelled and swung—and immediately regretted it when it felt like my head split open. "Oh fuck."

The last was a groan . . . and it was still too loud. Too painful.

My back was stinging from the slap Hunter delivered to wake me, the throbbing from the blood rushing to the site beat in time with my aching skull. I was going to kill my brother.

I sucked in a sharp breath through my teeth when I tried to push to my knees, feeling like I'd taken a knockout punch and was about to get laid out. Pass right the fuck back out where I was . . .

In the hallway, apparently. And—*what the hell? Why am I naked and holding a trash can?*

I used the small trash can to push myself to standing, then staggered down the hall to the room Savannah and I were staying in.

"Babe," I murmured when I stumbled in, but she wasn't there.

The sheets were messed up, but the bed was empty.

I wanted that bed. I wanted to fall into it and not move for a long, damn time. But if Savannah was already awake, then I needed to be awake with her.

I bit back another groan to save my fiercely pounding head and went to my bag. Once I had a pair of boxer briefs and shorts on, I grabbed a shirt and left the way I'd come.

My steps so unsteady that I wasn't sure if I was *that* hungover or still drunk.

Over a dozen of us had come out to Alex and Adrianna's parents' lake house for spring break. Their parents and a couple relatives had come too, but they'd only stayed for a night before looking to Alex, his girlfriend, Savannah, and me to keep the rest of the kids in line . . .

All with sly smiles on their faces as they'd stocked the house full of enough food and alcohol to keep a fraternity going for a month. Then they'd left for Oklahoma to gamble for a couple days, leaving a bunch of seventeen- to nineteen-year-olds to their own devices.

And from the punishing rhythm that had taken residence in my skull, I wondered if they'd thought they were doing us a favor or teaching us a lesson.

The world seemed to tilt as I lifted my shirt, and I decided right then it had been a lesson.

I caught sight of Hunter and Madison and mumbled, "I'm gonna fucking kill you," loud enough for Hunter to hear as I descended the stairs and succeeded in pulling my shirt over my head.

Hunter gave me an amused look as he gestured to Madison. "My girl had to see your ugly ass. You deserved it."

I huffed . . . and regretted it.

Jesus fucking Christ.

"Wait," Madison began, voice all kinds of confused as she looked at my brother. "Didn't you see him when you left the room?"

He looked pointedly toward the back door. "I woke up on the table."

I glanced that way, then followed the cluster of people still passed out on the floor as Madison hesitantly claimed, "No, you came to bed."

"I don't think so," Hunter said softly.

I looked around the rest of the main room and then back up the stairs when I didn't see Savannah, rubbing at my head as I settled on where my brother was grabbing a container of orange juice from the fridge.

"You did," Madison argued.

"Okay," Hunter said, trying to placate her. "But the last thing I remember was being outside with everyone. You said you needed to change clothes because pandas make you wanna cry. Then I woke up on the table."

"Pandas are cute," Madison whispered in defense.

My eyes rolled as I stepped closer to my brother, earning an irritated look from him.

Or that could've been because I took the juice from him.

I wasn't sure. At that moment, I really didn't care about anything other than hydrating, finding somewhere steady, and figuring out where my girl was.

I trudged over to the table and sat on top of it, letting my head fall into my free hand. Dragging my fingers through my hair over and over again as I tried to take calming breaths. As I tried to sort through the blur that was last night.

It wasn't the same as when I lost control of my anger.

When that happened, it was like I saw everything in bursts. Speeding through parts and pausing for one crucial second. Only to continue until it was over.

Or until Savannah snapped me out of it.

Last night was different. I'd already been well into being wasted when someone had the brilliant idea of starting the Beer Olympics. With Savannah championing the idea, I hadn't been able to tell her no. I also couldn't really remember much of it even though I somehow knew I'd taken part in it.

I remembered the cheerleader pyramid that had gone all kinds of wrong right at the beginning. I remembered pressing Savannah up against a tree, and her begging me to take her upstairs before we'd been pulled into another round of . . .

Fuck, I can't remember. Something.

And Savannah.

Dancing around the way she always did . . . I remembered that. I remembered kissing the hell out of her.

But all of it was a blur.

The music. Our friends. The bonfire. The games.

I couldn't even remember how I'd ended up on the floor, let alone naked.

As if on cue, Hunter asked, "And what the hell were you doing? What was with the trash can?"

A breath fled from me. "The fuck if I know."

I rubbed at my dry, aching eyes as I struggled to remember. As my head raged in protest.

"Come ge'me."

I'd buried my face in her neck, breathing her in. "Gonna hide from me?"

I felt more than heard her giggle. "Never."

I squeezed my eyes shut against the hammering as that

piece of the night faded as fast as it had appeared. Trashed. We'd been so fucking trashed then. I'd been struggling to hold her up, and she'd been falling out of my lap.

All of our words more slurred than not.

I was just about to stand up to go look for her when I remembered stumbling into our room last night. Falling onto the bed as I'd tripped out of my pants.

Laughing as she'd pulled me closer. As I'd settled between her legs and pushed inside her. The room and the bed spinning, and I'd been struggling. Struggling to stay there with her. Stay *awake*. Going in and out of it before I'd collapsed on top of her.

Laughing. Again. We'd been laughing before she'd—

"I'm gon'be sick."

"Oh shit, Savannah got sick," I said softly, my stomach sinking as everything started adding up.

Waking up buck-ass naked in the hall. Trash can in hand.

Savannah had probably passed out in the bathroom, and I hadn't been there for her.

Fuck.

Hunter breathed out a laugh. "Yeah, don't think you made it back to her, man."

"Shit," I bit out as I pushed off the table and started for the stairs.

But I'd just reached the second step when my entire world came walking into the kitchen . . . from the downstairs hall.

Hunter laughed again, louder and full of amusement. "You sure as hell didn't make it back to her."

"Voices," Savannah whispered as she stumbled to a stop. "Volume. So loud." Using both hands, she waved awkwardly at everyone and forced a pained smile. "Didn't make it back to who?"

You.

Because you got sick, and I'd been trying to get back to you. To our room. Where we'd been . . .

"Beau was passed out in the upstairs hall with your trash can," Hunter said matter-of-factly.

Savannah looked up at me, face scrunching adorably before her head fell into her hands. "What trash can?"

"When did you go downstairs?" I asked, voice rough and demanding as that little blur I'd been given replayed in my mind.

What little I remembered of the night before, I was positive happened. And Savannah had been upstairs. With me. In that bed.

She shuffled in my direction and gestured down the hall she'd just come from. "As soon as we came in. Bunch of us passed out in Adrianna's room."

I went still as I absorbed her words.

As that fucking blur played again.

My body jolted slightly when Savannah was suddenly there on the stairs with me, falling against my chest. My arms automatically went around her, holding her to me. Protecting her from the nightmare path my mind was racing down.

"Drinking is the worst," she said. "I vote no."

My head ached as the pieces I could remember burst through my mind like condemning flashes—all the way up to waking in the hall.

Naked. The sheets on our bed all messed up in a telling way. And Savannah, downstairs the entire—*Oh God.*

My stomach twisted. Bile rose so fast I had to choke it back as Hunter and Madison's words from just minutes before came rushing back.

"My girl had to see your ugly ass. You deserved it."

"Wait, didn't you see him when you left the room?"

"I woke up on the table."

"No, you came to bed."

Savannah and Madison had shared a room on our first night at the lake house. Yesterday, we'd switched. I'd moved upstairs to be with Savannah. Madison had moved downstairs to be with Hunter.

There was no reason for Madison to have seen me this morning because the room she was talking about wasn't upstairs. Unless . . .

Fuck.

No. No, no, no.

My gaze slowly shifted to find Madison watching me. Eyes wide and face pale, looking about as sick as I felt. Like she'd already come to the horrifying realization that I was now.

"Why are you so tense?" Savannah mumbled against my chest.

"Feel like I'm dying." The words came out before I could filter myself, but they were the truth.

I was dying. This couldn't be real.

I couldn't have—I *wouldn't* have touched someone who wasn't the girl in my arms.

I knew Savannah. I knew every inch of her body. I knew her heart. My soul responded to hers. I would've known the girl I was in bed with wasn't her.

Right?

I drew Savannah even closer when Madison started toward us. Wanting to keep her far from the destruction happening between us. The way the world was shaking. Crumbling.

Falling apart in my hands and—*oh God, what have I done?*

"Beau, you're shaking," Savannah whispered as she inched back to look up at me, brow furrowed with worry. "Come on, let's go sit down."

I let her lead me down the steps and across the kitchen, my stare catching on Madison as she slipped around us on her way to the stairs.

Head down and expression twisted with the agony I was drowning in.

What the hell did we do? What the hell did we do? Why the fuck were you in my bed?

I roughly fell to the bench seat of the table and dropped my head into my hands. A trembling breath ripping from me as I drove my hands through my hair before sitting back. Wrapping an arm around Savannah and trying to breathe. To focus.

But all I could see were those two, short pieces of last night.

Savannah telling me to come get her and what I was *sure* was Savannah underneath me.

It had been so dark in the room, and I'd been fading in and out, but it had been her. It had been the girl I'd known and loved most of my life. I was sure of it.

But the twisting in my gut and the ice-cold pain ripping through my chest said differently.

"Jesus, Beau."

My head snapped up. The pain there exploding from the sharp movement as I met Hunter's watchful stare.

My brother.

My best friend.

Fuck. Fuck. Fuck.

"You look . . ." He hesitated, his head shaking. "You look bad off."

"I'm gonna be sick."

His brows rose in surprise, and Savannah twisted next to me, worry pouring from her as her hand moved to rest on my back.

"Really?" she asked softly. "What can I do? What do you need?"

I needed to go back in time.

I needed to make last night a bad dream.

I wanted to die.

"I gotta go," I muttered as I stood.

"Beau," she said as she scrambled to follow. "Let me help. What do you need?"

I turned and wrapped her in my arms, body trembling so damn bad for those few seconds I let myself hold her. "I'm good," I whispered against the top of her head. "Gonna take a shower, and I'll be fine."

I left before she could respond.

Jaw clenched tight and heart aching as I headed up the stairs because, on top of everything else, I'd just lied to Savannah for the first time in my life.

As soon as I was upstairs, I hurried across the hall and into the room that was supposed to be mine and Savannah's —the room I could hear Madison moving around in. Shutting the door quietly behind me, I stalked over to where she stood on the far side.

"No, no, no, no," she said, the plea nothing more than a breath as I closed the distance between us.

"The hell were you doing in here?" I ground out.

"I—"

I was so lost in my guilt and my denial that I hadn't noticed the haze that had slipped in. The simmering in my blood. I hadn't known I'd even reacted until suddenly, she was there. Staring up at me with a mixture of fear and grief.

My hand was over her mouth, and we'd moved.

I'd moved her.

I had Madison pressed to the wall. Her body shaking and fueling my own tremors and feeding that rage. And I didn't know how to make myself let go.

Savannah. Savannah. God damnit . . .

"This is mine and Savannah's room," I ground out as I struggled to calm myself—to rein it in. "You and Hunter are in the other room."

Her head shook when I forced my hand down so it was clenching her jaw. Struggling to control what I *needed* to control. Mentally repeating Savannah's name and trying to hear her calming voice in my head, and dying a little more each time.

"I don't—I don't—" Madison's body lurched and her eyes filled with tears.

I held her glassy stare as that haze started pulling back. As that burning anger in my veins began receding. "Stay the fuck away from me," I muttered in a low warning before finally pushing away from her.

A hushed cry burst from her, but instead of leaving, she stepped closer. Like being near me right then wasn't one of the most dangerous things she'd ever done. "What do I do with this?" she asked, holding out her hand.

I glanced at the balled-up Kleenex in her hand, confusion weaving through the storm of destructive emotions. "The hell—" *Shit.*

I sucked in shallow breaths in a vain attempt to calm my twisting stomach when the thin tissue unfurled enough for the corner of a condom wrapper to be seen.

Making it real. As if there had been some sliver of possibility that last night *hadn't* happened.

"Beau, we didn't use it."

I looked at her. Hope trying desperately to build in my chest despite everything.

"No. No," Madison said quickly, her face creasing with sorrow and regret. "Beau, *we didn't use it.*"

I barely managed to lock my knees when they gave at her implication and dragged a hand over my face.

I wouldn't. I would—

Oh God, Savannah, I'm sorry.

My jaw clenched tight as my denial clashed with the absolute guilt and regret swirling inside me. Grabbing the partially crumpled tissue from Madison, I kept my stare on my tightly clenched hand as I warned, "Madison . . . get away from me. Now."

That time, she listened.

Hurrying for the door as I stood there, wondering how I was supposed to ask Savannah to forgive me when I knew I would never forgive myself. Wondering how this could've happened at all.

"Mads?"

At Hunter's muffled voice, my blood went ice-cold. My head snapped up to see Madison standing in front of the closed door, hand hovering over the doorknob and a look of utter horror on her face.

Frozen.

Fuck. Fuck.

I rushed for her. Grabbing her and shoving her past a large wardrobe, out of sight, as the sound of the door clicking filled my head. Just as the door began opening, I grabbed it and threw it open the rest of the way.

Hunter stood there, hand still extended and looking surprised at seeing me there and having had the door ripped away from him. "Hey . . ."

"What?" I snapped.

"I thought Madison came upstairs. Is she not in here?"

I lifted the arm that wasn't gripping the door. "Does it look like she's in here?"

He rubbed at his forehead before letting his hand fall to the outer wall. Tapping a soft rhythm on it as his eyes narrowed on me. After a second, he shook his head and huffed. "Try being something other than an asshole every now and then. Yeah?"

I didn't respond as he turned and left.

I couldn't.

It was hard enough looking him in the eye. And maybe if he was at least mad at me, it'd help get me through the next second. Minute. *Hour* of knowing what I'd done.

God knew I deserved his hatred, but I had a feeling even that wouldn't be enough.

I shut the door and moved quietly to where Madison was pressed to the wall and wardrobe, trying to mute her cries.

"Get out."

She nodded and pushed from the wall, but had only made it a step when I grabbed her arm and pulled her back to me. Her lips parted with a silent cry as she slammed into my side.

"If Savannah ever finds out . . ." I tried to swallow around the jagged rock in my throat. Tried to speak around it. But I could barely breathe.

Someone was gripping my heart in their hands and slowly crushing it, and I wasn't sure what would remain of it after this—if anything.

Madison looked up at me, her head bobbing before

shaking quickly. "I can't—I couldn't—never. It would wreck us—*him*."

If there was anything I was sure of from that morning, it was *that*. Her ridiculous ramble of an agreement. I felt her anguish deep in my bones. Felt her guilt in my gut. Madison was suffering as badly as I was, but that didn't change anything. It didn't lessen what we'd done. It didn't erase it.

If anything, it made this more dangerous.

Because there was only so long we could live with that kind of guilt before it destroyed us. Before we confessed everything.

I gave her a subtle nod and left the room without another look back at her. Heading for the bathroom to discard the condom and start the shower.

I turned the water almost as hot as it could go and waited for the steam to start pouring into the bathroom before stepping under the punishing spray. My body tensing and locking up tight as I stood there. As the overwhelming shame and hatred crashed down around me until I snapped.

Striking out and biting back a curse as pain exploded along my knuckles and through my wrist. Blood pouring free and dripping onto the tiled floor of the shower. The throbbing in my hand matching the pounding in my head, one emphasizing the other.

And neither were enough.

No pain would ever be enough for what I had done to the one good and pure thing in my world.

Twenty

BEAU

NINETEEN YEARS OLD

I stared at the floor of my bedroom, gripping at my hair as that night clawed at my mind. Jaw clenched tight and shoulders feeling like they each weighed a ton.

It'd been two months . . . more than that . . . and each day had been filled with the worst kind of guilt and paranoia. Leaving me constantly on the edge of losing control in a way I'd never been.

I had a problem—I knew that. I'd known that most of my life. But not like this.

Hunter and Cayson had had to tear me off of Sawyer because he'd laughed near me. I didn't even know what he'd been laughing *at*, I'd just snapped.

I'd been arrested. Again.

A guy looked at Savannah, and I'd lost it. He'd been our waiter, and he'd just been taking her order. I'd known that as I unleashed my unfounded rage on him, but I hadn't been able to stop. All reason seemed to fade away as that red haze took over, and it was only getting worse.

Lying to Savannah. Looking at her and knowing what I'd done. Seeing the confusion and disappointment as my anger became more irrepressible. Pretending like everything was fucking *okay* when I saw my brother or when Madison was around even though it felt like I was dying the slowest, most painful death.

I was breaking. Literally crumbling.

And I was taking Savannah with me.

The door to my room opened at the same time Savannah called out, "Beau?"

My head snapped up and I turned in time to see her peek into my room, her expectant expression falling when she found me.

"Hey."

Her mouth lifted in a smile that was filled with so much uncertainty, and it tore at my already shredded heart. "Hi." Her stare darted around, looking everywhere but at me as she shut the door behind her and pressed up against it.

Not looking at me. Not coming to me.

Everything about it was wrong. Everything about it was the opposite of us. And that was on me.

The pain and worry dancing across her face. The unfamiliar way she spoke to me. All of it was there because of me.

"You weren't down there," she said as her eyes finally met mine. "Thought I'd come looking for you. See if—" She lifted one of her shoulders and shook her head, never finishing what she'd been about to say.

I wanted to beg her to just say it. To say whatever was on her mind. To yell at me. To do anything. But I just nodded, knowing her hesitation was in response to the way I'd been the past couple of months.

"Needed to get away for a minute," I said, giving her the only portion of the truth I could.

There was a party currently happening in my parents' house. Dozens of people filling the inside and spilling out, celebrating the next graduating class. Hunter and Madison's class. Where I was supposed to *pretend* some more.

Pretend like everything was okay.

Like I hadn't betrayed my brother and the girl in front of me. Like watching Madison go around as if nothing had happened, as if she wasn't suffering under the same guilt I was, didn't infuriate me. Like Savannah and I weren't breaking.

"And that included getting away from me?" Savannah asked softly, her chest shuddering as she sucked in a calming breath.

Fuck. Fuck, no, no, no. "Savannah—"

"Things have been different." She steeled her jaw and continued holding my stare, trying to look strong when I knew she was so close to crumpling. "I can feel it. I can *see* it," she continued, voice wavering. "I don't know what's happening, or what happened—"

"Nothing," I lied, fear gripping at my throat and freezing me in place as I struggled to think of what to do to make this okay.

To make this right when nothing could.

Her head shook slowly. "Beau, you're distant. Not just emotionally, but physically." A weak huff tumbled from her as she gestured to me, as if proving her point. "You're distracted when we're together. You don't—" Her tongue darted out to wet her lips and her stare fell away. Blush creeping up her neck when she said, "You don't touch me."

At the pain in her voice, my entire being reacted. Rushing for her as my heart wrenched and spirit thrashed.

"That isn't what I mean," she said quickly, a sharp cry falling from her lips when I stopped a couple feet away. She blinked up at me, each tear slipping down her cheeks like a cut to my chest. "It's like you're trying to escape me. If you want out—"

"Out?" I choked on the word as it scraped up my throat. My heart sank and my veins filled with ice. "Savannah, you're my world. Why the hell would I want out?"

"I don't know, but I can feel that you don't want this anymore."

"You're wrong."

Her head moved in wide, wild shakes before nodding fiercely. "Then, maybe you just want *me*." Her voice was so soft, so broken, so defeated that it knocked me forward a step.

Body trembling.

Chest pitching with uneven breaths.

But that haze was nowhere to be found. This? This was pure fear and denial and loss.

I wanted Savannah. I wanted her every day of the rest of my life . . . but I knew from her tone that she meant something different.

"What are you saying, Savannah?" I asked hesitantly.

"I know what it's like to be your world, Beau," she whispered, jaw trembling as she continued. "I don't know what happened, I just know I'm not that anymore."

"You're wrong," I said again as the backs of my eyes burned.

"I think maybe you won't admit it because you need me. Because I take it away."

Ice shot across the hollow in my chest, stealing my next breaths as I stared at the woman I loved. As I wondered how I could've fucked up so badly with her when she'd been the only thing I'd ever gotten right.

I closed the last of the distance between us and pulled her away from the door. Her chest heaved with a muted cry when I curled my hands around either side of her neck and looked into her honey eyes. Jaw clenched tight when I repeated, "You're *wrong*."

Her eyelids shut and her face pinched with pain and unknowns.

"If you really think I've been with you, or that I wanna spend the rest of my life with you, because you *take it away* . . . then I've failed at loving you."

A sob fell from her lips, her head moving in quick shakes as she looked at me again. "No. No, I—God, I don't know. You didn't fail anything, Beau. It's just . . ."

"I failed you."

"Beau . . ."

This was a new level of suffering.

It was cold and dark, and I felt myself falling deeper and deeper into it. Drowning with no way to the surface. Not when I was the reason I was being dragged down. Not when this went so far past what I had done—the guilt I was trying to live with.

Finding out the woman I'd loved and worshipped for years didn't truly know that? Didn't *feel* that?

Fuck . . .

I took her in. Her eyes and lips. The angles of her face I'd studied thousands of times before and the way she felt in my hands. My body trembling as I prayed this wouldn't be the last time I held her.

"If you believe that," I began, voice rough and thick with worry, "I need you to walk away."

Her expression fell and her body swayed toward mine.

"You deserve to feel like you're someone's world."

"I do," she breathed quickly.

"You deserve to know that someone's day starts and ends with you. That their heart beats your name."

"I do," she choked out as new tears raced down her cheeks. "I do—Beau, I know that!"

"No questions. No doubts." I tried to swallow, but my throat was so damn tight. "If I'm not giving you that, I need you to—"

"Stop," she cried and reached up to grip my wrists. "Beau, *stop*. I've never questioned us or the way you felt about me until . . ." She blinked quickly, her stare drifting to the side as she thought. "I don't know, recently. I told you, it's like you're trying to escape me, but at the same time, it's like you're afraid to not have me near you. And I've been trying —" A sob ripped from deep within her, and she released one of my wrists to press a hand to her chest. "I've been trying so hard to figure out what's going on . . . what changed between us. What I did—"

"Nothing," I assured her. "You've done nothing."

Her head moved in quick shakes as she continued. "And I just kept going around and around, grasping for anything because you wouldn't talk to me. Then the fight a few days ago . . . when I stopped you, you looked at me in this plead-ing, shamed way that broke my heart. And everything sorta just clicked."

"I—fuck." I wiped away her tears, but new ones replaced them. "There's nothing you've done," I said slowly, making sure she heard and understood those words. "I'm dealing with my own shit, and I see it pulling you down with me, so I've been doing everything to prevent that. But wanting out? Wanting to be with you because you *take it away*? Jesus Christ, Savannah."

"Then talk to me. Let me be there for you," she begged. "Don't push me away."

I lowered my forehead to hers. "Never," I whispered. "Never meant to push you away. Just been trying to protect you."

"When have I ever needed protection from you? When have I ever *wanted* protection from you?"

Since what I did could destroy us . . .

But what did it matter when my guilt and worry that Savannah and Hunter would figure it out, or that Madison would end up saying something, was destroying us anyway?

"I'm sorry." It was all I could say, and I hated that it wasn't enough.

Hated that the truth was trapped on the tip of my tongue, begging to fall.

But even though part of me raged that I owed Madison nothing, I couldn't do that to her. Because if the roles were reversed? If she told Hunter without giving me any kind of warning? Recovering from that kind of hit would be nearly impossible. I'd never forgive her for that.

I brushed my mouth across hers before pressing a soft kiss there. "I love you."

"I love *you*."

I leaned back enough to search her stare. "My fucking world."

The corners of her lips lifted shakily, her head bouncing before she reached up on her toes to steal another kiss. Then she was pulling away from my hold and moving deeper into my room.

I watched as she stopped by my dresser and opened the top drawer. Reaching in for the shirt I always left on top for her. The shirt she liked to wear when she was in my bed and in my arms. Her favorite.

Pretty sure it was mine too.

I took a step toward her, voice like gravel when I asked, "Staying?"

She nodded, but the heat and the need that usually sparked between us when she grabbed that shirt was absent. In its place were relief and exhaustion, mixing with the lingering pain and questions. Reminding me of all the things I hadn't been giving her—everything she needed.

She needed that physical connection, but she needed me more. To just be there. To hold her. To talk to her.

Forcing myself back the step I'd just taken, I slanted my head in the direction of the door. "Want me to grab food and drinks so we can hide away?"

A gentle smile crossed her face and gripped at my chest. "Please."

"Then I'll be back," I assured her. With one last look at where she stood holding my shirt, I slipped out into the hall and headed for the stairs.

Roughing a hand over my face as my entire being ached to do those things. To be absolutely everything she needed. To go back to being the person I'd been just months ago—where every action and thought and word had been so fucking effortless when it came to Savannah.

But even as I *knew* I would go downstairs and do what I'd told her. Even as I *knew* I would go back to my room and try to be open with her the way she needed me to be, I was afraid I would shut down again. Unintentionally push her away as fears of her finding out my deepest regrets consumed me again.

I dragged my hand over my face again as I reached the bottom step and released a shuddering breath.

I can't keep living like this.

As if in answer to my thoughts and torment, I looked up to see Madison moving away from me, toward the kitchen.

In an instant, I knew what I had to do.

Just as quickly, the anger and resentment that went hand-in-hand with Madison Black the past two months rose to the surface when I finally noticed her. She wasn't just walking away. She was fucking *bouncing*.

Again, like there wasn't a goddamn care in her world. Like she wasn't suffering. Like she wasn't being crushed under this guilt.

I let my eyes sweep the area as I headed in that direction, making sure Hunter wasn't with her or following her. Making sure no one was paying either of us any attention at all. And rushed through the kitchen when I found it empty except for her—bent over one of the large, tin buckets filled with ice and bottles.

With one last glance behind me, confirming we were still alone for now, I grabbed her arm and took her with me. Never slowing as I continued through the kitchen and down the hall that led to the guest room and bathroom.

Once I pulled her into the guest room, she ripped away from me. "*Ow!*"

I slowly looked over at her. That resentment burning hotter and hotter as I reached for the bedroom door to close it.

"No, no, no," she said quickly as she lunged forward,

grabbing for the door and narrowing her eyes at me. "Are you insane?" she snapped, voice soft and low. "We can't be in a closed-off room! What if someone finds us?"

I raised my brows knowingly as the morning at the lake house swirled through my mind—when Hunter had almost done exactly that. "What if someone finds us?"

I took the moment of deep pain that flashed across her face, distracting her, to remove her hand and shut the door.

At the sound of it closing, Madison jolted and reached for the knob, turning it so the door was cracked open.

Jesus Christ.

"It's so much worse if it's shut," she said when I slammed it closed, keeping my hand flat on the door and slanting a cold glare at her. Daring her to open it again.

"It's bad enough," I argued as I pushed away and began pacing the room.

Hands racing through my hair and body trembling as that blur of a night and the next horrific morning swarmed my mind. As Madison's reaction to what we had done mixed with her indifference the past two months, fueling my dread and anger.

I can't keep living like this.

I knew what I needed to do. What *we* needed to do.

Didn't make saying it out loud, even to Madison, any easier.

"Beau—"

"I'm telling Savannah." The words spilled out of me like poison, bringing my pacing to an abrupt stop.

I stared at the wall ahead of me as the energy in the room shifted. As fear burst from the girl near me and coated my skin.

"What? N-no," she said, voice soft as a breath. "No. You

can't."

"The fuck I can't," I ground out as I looked back at her, all that resentment burning so damn hot until I was trembling for an entirely different reason. Until that red haze was threatening at the edges of my vision. "That's my world, my future, and every time I look at her, I know I'm keeping something from her."

"Hunter's *my* world!" she cried loudly, then hurried to cover her mouth. Her body shook as she stared at me, the shame that had been absent these past months pouring from her when she continued. "He's my future too. He's your brother, and Savannah's my best friend. We can't risk our relationships and friendships over an honest mistake."

"Exactly," I said as I turned to fully face her. "It was a mistake, Madison."

"One that will still matter to them. One that will absolutely hurt them. It will cause doubt and suspicion and-and-and put wedges between us all. Hunter can't know."

"*Will?*" Something like a laugh and a huff and *pain* tore from me as the conversation I'd just had with Savannah played in my mind.

That haze took over completely in an instant, and I was helpless to stop it. Because Madison was talking about what *could* happen like none of that shit was touching her world—her relationship. And it wasn't. Because she was fine. She and Hunter were *fine*. She could turn this remorseful act off and on, but this was fucking with my life.

"Those wedges are already there," I seethed. "It's already put a goddamn wedge between Savannah and me. My *world*. I've never kept anything from her before this." I gestured to her with a jerk of my chin. "You're fine with lying to my brother, that's more than fucking clear. But I actually love Savannah."

The sting of her palm across my cheek came fast and fanned the anger burning in my veins.

My hands clenched tighter where they were already formed into fists as that wrath raced through my veins. My jaw ached from the pressure I was putting on it. But I fought against every reactive instinct. Tried to see Savannah in my mind. Tried to hear her voice.

Tried to force that anger to subside enough to think clearly.

"Fuck you, Beau," she whispered, voice wavering. "You wanted this silence just as much as I did."

Sucking in a deep breath once I was sure I was in control of myself, I said, "Here's how I see it: One day, I'll put a ring on her finger. One day, I'll watch her walk down an aisle toward me. And I don't want a pit of guilt inside me when I do." I stepped closer to Madison, lowering my voice to hide the pain there. "I don't want her finding out in the future, feeling even more betrayed and hurt than she needs to because I kept what we did from her."

"She doesn't have to—"

"She does," I said, stopping Madison from putting that idea between us again. After tonight, I knew there was no way to continue without confessing everything to Savannah. "That girl is the answer to my fucked-up soul. She's my everything. And I'm not gonna risk that because you're a coward."

Madison's shoulders curved in as her head slowly shook. As all that fear and pain she'd been hiding bled from her until she was viciously shaking. "Beau, please. You don't understand—"

A huff punched from my lungs.

"You don't understand . . ." Her hands moved to her stomach before they were suddenly in her hair. Gripping at her head as she looked at me, pleading with me with that look alone. "You don't understand what you'll be doing to all of us! Risking your relationship by not telling Savannah? Beau, all of our relationships are going to be ruined when you *do*."

My stare fell to the floor as her words caused a moment of doubt. Of hesitation. Before I remembered that my relationships were already being ruined, and they would only continue going down that path until we fixed this. Until we could fight for forgiveness.

And I would fight.

For Savannah, I would fight to the ends of the earth to win her heart. To earn her trust again. I would do whatever it took.

Determination built inside me, drowning out the doubt. With a look at Madison that conveyed exactly what I planned to do, I started for the door.

"I think I'm pregnant."

Chains reached up and brought me to a jarring stop. The world tilted. The room spun. My stomach clenched.

No, no, no. Oh God, no.

"Hunter's," she added quickly. "If I even am."

"*If*," I seethed as I looked back at her. "You're just gonna throw that shit out there when you don't even know?"

"I'm two weeks late . . . more than."

I sucked in shallow breaths as I tried to remember when spring break had been and what month we were in now. How long it had been since that wreck of a night.

I'd been sure of the timeline just half an hour before. But at that moment, I couldn't be sure of anything.

"Shit," I hissed as I shook my head, trying to clear it.

She lifted her hands in a pleading motion. "See what you'll be doing. The chances of Hunter and Savannah understanding or forgiving us for what happened are—" She choked on her words, her face creasing with emotion. "Low. So low. But if I'm pregnant? They're not going to believe what really happened. They're not going to believe it was a one-time thing—a one-time *mistake*. Beau, you will be destroying *all of us*."

"We already destroyed us," I murmured. "We've already done that, Madison. Don't you get that?" When her body swayed like her legs might give out on her, I admitted, "I'm afraid when Savannah says she's going to hang out with you. I fucking *hold my breath* when she says she talked to you. I can barely look at my brother, and when he mentions you? I feel like I'm gonna snap. When we're all together? I'm *terrified* they're gonna notice something's wrong between us and figure it out. And if you're pregnant? Jesus, Madison." I roughed my hands over my face and sucked in a fortifying breath. "I can't keep going on like this. This is killing me and hurting my relationship with Savannah. I have to tell her."

"Then, I'll go!" she cried out. "I'll go, I'll leave. Just don't do this."

I stilled, confusion pulsing through my veins and giving way to suspicion as I tried to decode her offer. "What?"

One of her hands loosely gestured to herself before falling, her body shaking so fiercely she could barely speak. "Everything you just said . . . it kept coming back to me. Savannah with me. Talking to me. Hunter talking about me, or us near each other." Her head moved in a jerky nod as a sob tore from her throat. "I'll leave."

"What do you mean, you'll *leave*?"

"Leave," she nearly yelled. "Leave Amber. Leave so this stops, and you won't do what you're about to!"

Surprise raced through me before doubt crept in because Madison had been with my brother even longer than I'd been with Savannah. There was no way she'd just *leave*.

"And how does that not destroy you and my brother?"

She sagged against the wall and silently cried. Hands gripping her stomach and chest as her grief filled the room and mixed with my own.

I studied her tears and her pain. All that emotion I thought she hadn't been drowning in all this time, but I'd been wrong. She'd just been hiding her agony in a way I couldn't. Trying to spare my brother and Savannah the same way she was now.

"Hunter will still have you," she said weakly. "Savannah will have you. You'll have them. Otherwise? Beau, I can feel it . . . this is destructive. We'll all end up without each other."

"That wasn't an answer."

"Because you already know that it *will*. But I would do it for him. I would do it for her."

But could I?

Could I lie to them about this on top of everything else? Could I watch them break and pretend I wasn't the reason behind it? Pretend I didn't know that Madison gave up *everything* to protect them from something else?

"You're going to crush them," I said softly, part of my mind rebelling against the words that were a step into this fucked-up agreement.

A sob escaped her as she nodded, but a crease formed between her brows when she challenged, "Which of the two do you think they can recover from?"

Neither.

The answer rushed onto my tongue but was silenced by Madison's earlier words.

"If I'm pregnant? They're not going to believe what really happened."

That?

I believed that.

Coward . . . I'd called Madison that earlier. But as I dipped my head and started walking away, I knew the title belonged to me.

"Beau, if I—"

"I won't," I whispered. "You leave?" I tried to swallow past the knot of shame choking me and looked to the floor when I couldn't meet her eyes anymore. "I won't say a thing."

I slowly walked out of the room, feeling like each step took all my strength. Feeling like that weight on me had tripled. Telling myself to go back and say I couldn't agree, only for that scenario where Madison *was* pregnant, and we all lost everything anyway, to play out again.

I rubbed at the excruciating ache in my chest as a curse slipped free, then jerked back when a hand fell to my shoulder.

My heart raced a wild, punishing rhythm when I glanced up to see my dad looking at me curiously, hands raised in mock surrender.

Because I'd grabbed him . . . fucking shit, I'd grabbed my dad.

"Okay there, kid?" he asked when I released the collar of his shirt.

"Yeah, uh . . . yeah." I tried to clear my throat, but that shame and guilt were so damn thick.

"Getting a drink?"

I blinked slowly, trying to understand his question when my mind was so weighed down with enough secrets and lies to bury me. When he pointed behind me, I turned, taking in the platters of food and buckets of ice and drinks.

Shit, Savannah.

"Yeah," I said quickly and reached for a plate. "Gonna go hang out with Savannah somewhere quieter."

A soft huff left him as he grabbed a few bottles of water, setting two in front of me. "That *quieter* best be somewhere that ain't your room."

A grunt rumbled in my chest, earning a laugh from him.

"I'll be sure to tell myself y'all are off being good kids, somewhere far, far away from a bed."

"Far away," I echoed and forced a smirk when he clapped my shoulder.

Once I had the plate full, I grabbed the bottles and slipped up the stairs. Heart growing heavier the higher I climbed.

I wasn't ready for this.

I'd been prepared to come upstairs and tell Savannah everything, not come back with more secrets. And I couldn't hide when something was wrong—clearly.

Dragging in a ragged breath, I tried to force all that shame and guilt back and opened my door.

"Hey," Savannah said from where she was sitting on my bed, legs crossed and bare beneath my shirt. She set down her phone and looked at me in a way she had so often over the past two months, like she was worried about me. "That took a while."

"Ran into my dad," I said from where I'd paused just inside my door, wavering as everything shifted and came at me from a new angle.

Madison was giving up everything to protect them and us. But in that, she was condemning me to a life of *lying* to the woman I loved.

Shit, what have I done?

Twenty-One

BEAU

"You're here early."

I slanted a cold glare in Peter Rowe's direction as he entered the kitchen the next morning, watching as he moved through it like he owned the damn place.

Didn't matter that we always told our guests to make themselves at home. Didn't matter that Peter and Savannah had been as close as siblings at one point. That was a long damn time ago. And at the moment, it was pissing me off that he was there. That Savannah was confiding in him instead of me.

"You see too much," I said, words nothing less than a threat as I went back to watching the coffee brew.

He breathed a laugh as he entered my line of sight again, leaning up against the opposite counter and clutching a bottle of water. "If it makes you feel any better, I'm pushing for y'all to work through this."

I lifted my chin but kept my eyes on the pot of coffee. After a moment, I muttered, "I wanted to be here before my kids woke up."

For once.

"Makes sense," he said as he twisted the cap off his water and started pushing away from the counter. "I'll stay out of y'alls way today."

I reached for a mug and then grabbed the pot. "Don't you have a wedding to go to?"

A huff burst from him. "Yeah, I'm not going."

I looked over at him before focusing on what I was doing. "That's your brother."

"Don't you remember my brother?"

Of course I did. I'd hated every day I'd been forced to spend near him. He'd tried ruining my life before I'd gone and done that on my own.

Still . . .

I settled against the island again and said, "You should go."

He let out an exaggerated breath, head shaking like he was trying to figure out why we were talking about this. "Why?"

"Hunter wasn't at mine and Savannah's wedding," I explained. "Not that I wanted him there for certain reasons. But it's killed me all this time that he wasn't."

He studied me for a moment before turning to leave, his head dipping in acknowledgment as he did.

"She'll come around," Peter said suddenly. When my only response was the delay in bringing my mug to my mouth, he continued. "Everything that happened? All those emotions are basically just sitting on her, weighing her down and growing because she hasn't dealt with it yet. Now she's lashing out at you with all that shit."

I finally glanced his way, brows slowly drawing together at the confidence in his tone.

Looking like he was holding back whatever he really wanted to say, he waved at me with the bottle and repeated, "She'll come around."

I didn't let his words give me hope. I couldn't.

Hope was something I couldn't afford in the hell I was trapped in.

Besides, I didn't know how much he knew, but it couldn't have been everything. If it had, he wouldn't have said that.

Glancing at the clock, I pushed from the island and started the way he'd gone. Taking the stairs up to the second floor and turning to go to our side of the house—where the kids' and our rooms were. Bypassing where I'd meant to go and continuing to the door at the end of the hall like I was being pulled. Drawn.

The half of my destroyed soul trying to get to its mate.

I stopped just outside our door. Head down and eyes closed as all the pain and regret and guilt I'd been living in came up to consume me. Hand lifted instinctively, reaching for the handle.

For her.

My fingers curled into a fist as I forced my hand back to my side. A ragged exhale tumbling free as I stepped back.

"I'm sorry," I breathed as I turned and headed to Quinn's room. Quietly opening the door and moving across the space to where she was curled up in a little ball.

Setting my mug on her nightstand, I sat on the edge of her bed and brushed a knuckle across her cheek, the way I'd done since she was a baby. "Quinn."

She curled tighter, her face squishing up before relaxing and pulling a soft laugh from me.

After another brush across her cheek, she stretched and lazily opened her eyes. "Hi, Daddy." Her eyes went wide and she nearly shouted, "Daddy, you're here!" as she scrambled out of the covers to launch herself at me.

A rumbling laugh built in my chest as I caught her, but her words broke something inside me. The reason for her excitement making all that hurt flare because it was affecting our kids.

"Of course I'm here," I said through the shards of glass in my throat.

"I miss you in the mornings, but Mommy says you're real busy. But I think you shouldn't be busy anymore because Mommy isn't happy when you're real busy," she rambled as she climbed onto my back and wrapped her arms around my neck.

My head moved in a bouncing sort of nod, and I forced a smile that felt like it showed just how slow and excruciating this death was. "I don't like when I'm busy either."

Putting one of my hands around both of hers, I stood and relished the loud giggle that burst from her. "Let's wake your brothers," I said as I grabbed my coffee and started for the door.

"I wanna wake Wyatt," she said excitedly.

"Yeah?"

"Yeah, because he woke me up a long time ago."

My chest shook with a muted laugh. "Got it. Hold tight," I warned as I released her hands to open Wyatt's door and stepped inside.

The light coming in from behind the blinds showed Wyatt sitting up in bed, looking groggily around.

I sucked in air through my teeth. "Today isn't your day, kid."

"Nuts," she hissed. "Wyatt, go back to bed."

His head whipped around to face us as if he'd just realized

we were there, then started bobbing in understanding as he sluggishly pulled back his covers and stumbled out of bed. Walk all sorts of unsteady as he met us halfway into the room and smacked into my leg.

"Morning, little man."

"Morning," he said, the word muffled.

"Rough night?" I teased when he leaned back to look at me, face scrunched up.

"I miss my friend, Avalee."

Quinn gasped in my ear. "Me too, me too! I miss her too. Why doesn't she come over anymore?"

Because I hate her mom.

She destroyed everything.

I cleared my throat and struggled for an answer when every one coming to mind needed to be kept from my kids.

"All right, let's get ready for the day, yeah?" I said, dismissing the Avalee thing completely. Grabbing one of Quinn's hands, I lowered her to the floor, then nodded toward the door. "Y'all use the bathroom and get changed while I get your brother."

The last words came out softer and softer as the door pushed open more to reveal my wife and our youngest son, eyes wide like she couldn't believe she was seeing me there.

"Mommy, look," Quinn said as she bounced past me. "Daddy's here!"

Savannah blinked quickly and forced her attention to Quinn, a shaky smile crossing her face. "I know, I see that." Her eyes darted to me before shifting back to the kids. "Do what he said. I'm gonna get started on breakfast for everyone."

Wyatt followed after her, spinning and kicking and

pretending he was holding a lightsaber, but Quinn just turned to face me, looking so confused and so damn sad.

"What's wrong?" I asked as she slowly made her way over to me.

"I thought Mommy would be happy now that you're not busy anymore, but she isn't."

Fuck.

A dull knife tearing through my chest.

That's what her words and her sadness felt like.

I crouched down to get on her level and tried to keep my voice even. "There are a lot of guests in the house right now, and Momma's taking care of them and taking care of y'all. It's okay if she doesn't seem happy, she just has a lot going on."

"But she's never happy anymore," Quinn said, then leaned closer to whisper, "She's been making desserts and stuff without playing music. And she doesn't dance. And she doesn't ask if we want to bake with her anymore or if we want to lick the spoons from the desserts she makes."

My grip on the mug tightened to the point I thought it might shatter in my hand.

My body trembled as my daughter laid out a perfect picture of how hurt Savannah was.

I forced myself to look into Quinn's eyes to reassure her. "She isn't trying to exclude y'all, you know Momma would never do that. And everything else?" I clenched my teeth tightly when my jaw shook. With a slow breath out, I said, "Everything's gonna be fine."

"You promise?"

My head moved in a slow nod as I looked right into my daughter's eyes and lied. "Promise."

She beamed at me as she turned and darted out of the

room, and I fell to a sitting position, head hanging low and my body shaking uncontrollably as all that pain fueled something else inside me.

I forced myself to sit in it.

To feel the way it moved over me and consumed me. Everything tinted a familiar red as that sickening need coursed through my veins. Begging me to give in. To react. To lash out at something. Anything.

Accepting every second of that darkness until it was gone.

Pushing to my feet, I started out of Wyatt's room and had to sidestep him when he came running through like a little speed demon.

"I'm *so* fast!" he yelled as he went by, stopping on a dime and whirling around. "Can I see my Avalee friend now? I brushed-ed my teeth. See!" He tilted his head back and bared all his teeth.

"I do see." I ruffled his hair, carefully avoiding the question as I said, "Get changed."

But I hadn't made it more than a few steps down the hall before he popped up next to me and begged, "Can I see her *now?*"

I slowly lowered my mug and swallowed the sip I'd taken before looking down at him. "I'll see what I can do." Before he could finish the victory fist-pump, I hurried to add, "No promises."

He paused for only a second before continuing, never once looking like I'd said anything less than *yes* as he took off for his room.

By the time I made it downstairs, the sounds and smells of Savannah cooking were filling the house.

All of it so familiar and comforting and finding pieces of what was left of my heart to break.

That could've been the last time I walked down the stairs to that comfort, and it was tearing me up inside. I hated that I hadn't drawn it out. That I hadn't committed every part to memory.

But I was already in the kitchen and struggling not to look at the girl moving like a robot in front of the range when she was usually swaying and dancing.

I rinsed out my mug and put it in the dishwasher as my stare continued dragging back to her. My heart thumping painfully at the sight of her.

My world.

My world.

My world.

"Dadda, Dadda," Levi babbled before screeching impatiently and pulling my attention to where he was sitting in his high chair.

"Hey, buddy," I murmured as I went to him, lifting him up and hitching him on my waist. "Wanna go somewhere?"

He screeched again before falling into a fit of laughter.

"That sounded like a *yes.*" I lifted my hand. "High five." As soon as he smacked it, I grabbed his hand in mine and lifted it to blow a raspberry on his arm, earning another belly laugh.

Turning with him in my arm, I walked through the kitchen, pulling things out of cabinets and drawers that Savannah would need. Plates and bowls. Glasses and mugs. Silverware and serving utensils. Once everything was out and where she generally set them up, I walked over to her but forced myself to stop before I could get so close that I'd forget I couldn't pull her against me.

Couldn't hold her and kiss her.

"Do you need anything?"

Her head shook a few times before she muttered, "No."

I studied the rigid way she held herself and the strain on her beautiful face. As if she'd spent so much time crying and was fighting more tears then.

And all of it was on me.

"All right," I said, clearing my throat, "I'm taking the kids."

She looked up, her head snapping to the side and eyes going wide. "What—*no!*" Her head shook quickly. "You can't. No."

I rubbed at my jaw with my free hand as her shock and fear mixed with her refusal and slammed into me.

Taking the kids on a weekend like then wasn't uncommon. When there was a house full of guests, I usually took the kids out for a few hours when they started getting restless so they could go crazy without having to worry about disturbing people.

But her reaction?

Shit.

That was personal.

"I'm taking the kids for the morning," I said slowly as she continued shaking her head, her expression pleading.

"Please don't—"

"They need to get out."

"Don't take my kids," she softly begged. "Not right now. Not today. Not with—" Her throat shifted with her forced swallow, her stare darting around.

"I'm not taking *our* kids from you," I said, voice low and coated with ice.

Her eyelids squeezed tight before opening again, revealing honey eyes glassy with tears. "No, just—God, Beau, not today."

"Getting out of the house is something they need right now," I said firmly. "But this?" I forced out a trembling breath as the reality of the moment hit me like a sledgehammer. "Them leaving with me is something you'll have to get used to."

Her body caved, her mouth parting as she struggled to speak.

"Something sure smells good," someone called out.

Savannah quickly turned back to the range at the voice of one of the guests, hands hovering over the pans for a few seconds like she didn't know what to do with them before choking out, "Good morning," just as a couple stepped through the archway. "Breakfast will be done in a little while, but there's coffee."

I dipped my head in a nod when they waved in my direction, and quietly left the kitchen when they started asking Savannah about the fire pit out back. By the time I switched out my keys for Savannah's, Wyatt and Quinn were racing down the stairs, sounding like a herd of elephants.

"It's early," I said quietly since we were standing in the entryway, a hint of reprimand in my tone.

Quinn stood up straight, eyes wide, as if just realizing their mistake.

Wyatt covered his mouth to quiet his laughter.

I rolled my eyes and fought a smile, knowing it had to be hard on them to keep it down for that long. "Let's get out of here."

"Yeah!" Wyatt yelled, fist-pumping the air.

Quinn smacked his arm. "Shh!"

I flicked her shoulder. "Don't hit your brother."

She scoffed, her shoulders sagging dramatically for effect.

"But, Daddy, he's always, *always* killing me with his lightsaber."

"Kill him back." At the lift of her eyebrow that made her look so much like Savannah, I pointed a finger at her. "With lightsabers. Fake ones. Pretend killing. Only. Ever."

She gave an exaggerated eye roll as she walked outside. "Fine."

"She's gotta catch me first," Wyatt said, all childlike arrogance even though he'd just started outrunning her.

"Speed isn't everything," I muttered as I led them to the SUV.

"Yeah-huh. I'm so, super-fast, so nothing can catch me."

"My brother was *so, super-fast*, but I was stronger, so I always won," I told him, leaving out a crucial part of the story.

That I'd won because I was gone to something I hadn't learned to control. I'd won because nothing could stop me once my world had gone red. And I'd *won* at destroying whatever had been in my path.

"Uncle Saw?" Quinn asked, wiggling like crazy as she climbed into the car and got into her booster, like the idea of being able to best her brother the way I had mine excited her.

"No." My gaze fell and my hold on Levi tightened as if I could protect him from the flashes assaulting me.

Bits and pieces of the blur I could remember from that last fight with him just weeks before.

Clearing my throat, I looked at where Wyatt was finishing buckling himself into his own booster seat. "Your uncle Hunter," I finally answered as I began putting Levi into his car seat.

"I haven't met my uncle Hunter," Quinn said thoughtfully.

I nodded, knowing that all too well.

My kids had only known Sawyer until about six months before when Cayson had shown back up in town. But even then, they'd only seen Cayson a couple times, and it'd been brief. There'd been too much disconnect between my family before then. We'd shattered too fully for them to have known Hunter and Cayson.

Just as I was leaning back and grabbing for the door, I paused.

My stare drifted to where the ranch sat on the North side of town as I was hit with the overwhelming need to be surrounded by the people I'd spent so long avoiding. As the soul-gripping urge to give my kids the family I'd been denying them about dropped me to my knees.

Looking into the car again, I asked, "You want to?"

Twenty-Two

SAVANNAH

I pushed from my spot at the island and had to stop myself from rushing through the kitchen when I heard the front door open. Forcing my steps to slow, I hurried to look over myself, making sure I didn't have any miscellaneous ingredients on me and praying my face and hair didn't look like a wreck.

"Oh my goodness," someone called out who most definitely was not my husband. "What is that smell?"

"I love this house."

Emberly and Rae.

"I'm in here," I said loud enough for them to hear me, then went back over to the island I'd been stationed at nearly the entire morning.

Once I'd finished breakfast and dishes, I'd cleaned until everyone had left for their various activities before the wedding.

The guys were going golfing. The women were heading to some salon out of town.

And my kids weren't there, and I didn't have time to

break down and think over everything the way people said I needed to.

Not when my kids *would* be back. Not when I still had guests to take care of.

After beds had been made and towels were replaced, I'd started baking. Because that's what I did when I was emotional.

Or stressed.

Or happy.

Really, I just baked a lot.

I had cinnamon rolls in the fridge for the morning and blueberry muffins in the oven, and I'd been going out of my mind watching the clock until that door had opened.

"What smells so good?" Rae asked when she and her sister, Emberly, stepped into the kitchen.

"Muffins," I said, offering a smile when Emberly passed me a coffee from her coffee shop and bar: Brewed. "Thank you."

"Considering what's about to go down, I really would've preferred something a little harder. But this one doesn't drink," she said, pointing to Rae, "and most importantly . . ." She rubbed at her still-flat belly as Rae echoed, "Yes, most importantly."

I pressed my trembling lips together and forced a tight nod. "How far along are y'all?"

"Ten weeks," Rae said with a soft smile.

"Fourteen," Emberly added as she plopped into a chair at the large table.

I made some sound of acknowledgment and smiled.

Tried to.

"That's so exciting. I can't believe those boys are gonna be dads. And, Emberly . . ." I gestured to her. "God, I met you the same day I met those boys. I can't believe you're gonna be a mom."

She did an excited little dance before sitting back in the chair and grabbing her drink. "I'm mad at this one though," she said, using the cup to gesture to where Rae had sat.

Rae just continued smiling.

"This brat has felt amazing since day one, and I still throw up at random," Emberly continued.

"It's my gift for being abandoned by our mom," Rae said, all affectionate teasing.

A sharp laugh burst from Emberly's chest before her face crumpled and tears started falling down her cheeks.

"Oh God," Rae said, hurrying out of her seat and over to the one next to Emberly. "It was a joke."

"I know." Emberly's head bounced jerkily before shaking fiercely. "But I think about it, like, *all* the time now. How could she have done that? I don't—I just don't get it." Gesturing to her stomach with both hands, she let out a soft cry and said, "All I've seen is a squishy, fuzzy bear and heard a heartbeat, and I can't imagine ever being able to do what she did. Who leaves their child?"

"She was trying to save herself and you," Rae said softly as a tear slipped down her own cheek.

"Oh, shut up," Emberly mumbled, her shoulders jerking with her hitched breaths as she grabbed Rae's hand. "You're just being nice. I already know you don't like her."

"But I love you."

"Love you too." Emberly wiped at her cheeks with her free hand and focused on me. "Sorry, that's not why—great, we already made Savannah cry."

A startled breath fled from me when I realized she was

right. I brushed away the tear that was there, standing and muttering, "Hormones," when the timer sounded.

When I finished pulling the muffins out of the oven, the girls were there. Standing directly beside me. Cheeks still wet but looking at me with a mixture of surprise and expectation.

I jolted back at their unexpected nearness and hurried to put the muffin tin on the counter. "Hi."

Emberly's head tilted, brow lifting slightly. "Yeah, *hi*. How are you?"

"Um . . ."

"How are you feeling?"

I looked between the two of them, not knowing what to say when my world was falling apart, and they were already well aware—at least, they knew most of it. Not the recent parts.

"I wouldn't think that's something I really need to answer," I finally said.

Something like a laugh left Rae. "Maybe not before that little comment of yours."

I thought back to what I'd last said, confusion weaving through me. "What comment?"

"That's adorable," Emberly said as a wry grin crossed her face. "You know, this really is going to be a tough conversation. I'll make you a drink."

"You brought me a drink. And I don't think we need to have whatever conversation you're expecting," I added when she started around the island, heading right for where we kept the liquor.

She lifted a shoulder but didn't stop, grabbing a barstool on the way to stand on. "I brought you coffee. Would you like it with a kick?"

"No thanks."

"Mimosa?" she asked, then looked to Rae. "It's still early enough for mimosas, right?"

"Why not?" Rae said with a mischievous grin as she leaned on the counter, searching my face like she was trying to read me.

"I'm really fine, and I—" I pressed a hand to my chest before gesturing to them. "I love y'all, I really do. But this isn't a great time."

"The kids and Beau aren't here," Emberly said as she grabbed my vodka.

"Emberly, I'm really fine," I repeated firmly.

"Oh, you meant it's not a good time for liquor." Her head slanted. "When will be? Nine months?"

Shock stole across the kitchen, silencing everything for long moments.

After a while, Emberly put the vodka back and gently explained, "You said 'hormones.'"

"When you realized you were crying," Rae added when I continued standing there.

"What if I'm PMS-ing?" I asked, voice and body trembling.

"I think you would've taken that drink," Emberly said confidently as she climbed off the barstool.

Rae touched my arm and waited for my attention to shift back to her. "Are you just PMS-ing?"

She and the rest of the kitchen went blurry before I shook my head, my chest lurching as I fought the urge to cry over something that should be celebrated.

"Someone needs to tell these Dixon boys to wrap it up," Emberly said, forcing a stunned laugh from me as she and Rae pulled me into a hug. When they released me, she asked, "Does he know?"

I let out a swift breath and looked away. "No, I, uh . . ." I shrugged and moved past them, heading for the table. "I haven't figured out a way to tell him yet."

"How long have you known?" Rae asked when she took her earlier seat.

"A week," I admitted, shame coating the word. When I looked at the two, there was no judgment in their eyes, and I was so thankful for it. "We'd been trying before everything happened. The kids—Quinn and Wyatt are so close in age, and we wanted that for Levi too." A sad laugh tumbled past my lips. "We found out we were pregnant with Wyatt when Quinn was nine months too."

"You know you have to tell him," Emberly said after we'd sat in weighted silence for a while. "Even if you . . ." A crease formed between her eyebrows, sadness swirling in her eyes. "Even if you go through with this."

"What do you mean?"

She briefly glanced at Rae before looking at the table, the tips of her fingers swirling around the lid of her coffee for a moment before she met my stare again. "Beau asked to buy our old condo."

Her words felt like a crushing blow to the already fragile remains of my marriage.

I'd heard Beau when he'd said he was going to start moving out, and it had terrified me. Paralyzed me.

His moving out was something we couldn't come back from, I was sure of it. Just as I knew I would need to prevent it. But I hadn't expected him to already be going through a process as permanent as buying somewhere to live.

"Cayson went to tell him *no*, but when he came back . . ." She lifted her hand from the cup as if there was nothing she could do. "He said you'd given your wedding ring to Beau and told him he'd lost you."

My head shook roughly even as I said, "I mean, I did, but I—" I dropped my head into one of my hands as I struggled over this week with Beau and everything that had happened.

The hostility.

The coldness.

All of it from me because I couldn't seem to give him anything else even though my soul cried out for him.

"That isn't all," Rae said, voice soft and foreboding. "Beau showed up with the kids for Saturday breakfast at the ranch this morning."

Surprise swirled through me but was overshadowed by the dread weighing me down.

"And, um . . ." Her brows lifted and she looked to Emberly for help.

She hesitated for a minute before taking over. "The kids were very excited to see Avalee," she began. "But then Quinn announced, 'Guess what! I think my mommy and daddy are getting *divorces* just like your mommy and daddy.'" Emberly's stare darted over my face when the air rushed from my body. "Beau just stood there for a second before walking into the other room. He never said anything about it."

"I—" My chest pitched wildly as I struggled to take a breath. "Oh my God." I felt dizzy.

I couldn't breathe.

"I can't breathe," I managed to say, pushing from the chair because I needed to move.

I needed air.

"Savannah," they called out behind me, one of them rushing up and grabbing my arm when I stumbled, but I'd already caught myself on one of the counters.

I pulled away, body shaking until everything bottled up inside of me exploded.

"I don't want a divorce," I yelled, turning on them. "I don't want him to leave. I want him here, but I'm so—" I choked over a sob, my head shaking as tears flowed free. "I'm so fucking mad at him for so many things, and I can't —*God*."

I pressed the backs of my hands to my eyes, my entire body jerking with the force of my cries.

"I can't look at him without seeing *her*. I can't look at him without wondering what else he might've lied about. And I want him to hold me and make it go away, and I never want to see him again. And, *yes*, I gave him my rings because I have so many goddamn emotions right now,"—I gestured to my stomach—"and I would already feel like a hormonal mess *without* what he did on top of it all. But with that, I just feel— I feel like I'm going crazy, and I'm breaking, and I have no fucking clue what I'm doing other than trying to run this business and take care of my kids."

My face crumpled and my knees buckled.

I grabbed the counter and slowly lowered myself to the floor.

"Except, I'm not," I said weakly. "My kids see it. My kids are suffering because of it. I'm ruining everything while trying not to let my world implode."

"Let it." Rae's voice was soft and filled with under-standing as she sat beside me. When I met her stare, she said, "Let your world implode so it can be put back together."

"I can't," I admitted. "I'm afraid of what happens when I do."

"The two of you fix it," she said confidently. "It isn't

helping anyone to keep all your emotions inside. All it will do is cause you to push him further and further away."

"We would know," Emberly said dully, and Rae nodded.

"Everyone keeps saying that," I muttered. "I just . . . I've never had to do this. Beau and I have always been effortless because there was never anything between us. If I needed to talk to him, I did. This is different because there's something between us, and it's big and painful and full of so much deceit. And it's unsettling to know it's *been* between us, and I had no idea. I feel so stupid."

"Don't," Emberly hurried to say as she joined us on the floor at the same time Rae said, "You shouldn't."

"How could I have been so blind to what was happening?"

"Hunter didn't know," Emberly reminded me.

"Hunter's a guy, and Madison left a couple months after it happened. He wasn't living with her, creating a life with her." I waved off to the side. "And yet, as soon as she came back, everything came out. What if she hadn't come back?"

They shared a quick look before Rae sighed and said, "That's something you're going to have to ask Beau."

"And you *need* to ask him," Emberly added. "You have to take the time to talk to him. Somewhere safe where you can scream if you want. Or throw things."

Rae laughed.

"Somewhere not near the kids," Emberly continued, voice soft and full of meaning. "If you want, we can help with that. We can—"

"No," I said quickly, head shaking. "No, my parents are taking them." A dejected laugh tumbled past my lips at how utterly pathetic and hopeless my life felt that everyone was offering to take my kids so I could deal with something. "They're taking the kids to Utah for a week."

Rae gave me an encouraging smile. "That'll be good. I think that's exactly what you need for yourself, and also what you and Beau need."

A hum sounded in my throat, all kinds of unconvinced.

"Everything's going to work out," Rae said when Emberly stood and headed back to the table. "I haven't been around you or that family as long as Emberly, but I know how fiercely those guys fight for what they want. And I've seen and heard exactly how much that man loves you." She grabbed one of my hands in hers and gave a quick squeeze. "You guys can get through this. Just let your world implode. Okay?"

My head moved in a quick nod. "Okay."

Emberly placed our drinks on the floor before straightening, her expression all lit up like she was waiting to spill gossip. "Okay, but can we please talk about how all four Dixon men were in one house this morning?"

Somehow, even though they'd told me Beau had shown up for Saturday breakfast, *that* hadn't registered. "Oh my God," I whispered.

"I know," she said, emphasizing each word as she went back around the island we were sitting against. "*And* there was no fighting. No yelling. No declarations of lifelong loathing. Their mom couldn't stop crying though."

"Oh, seriously." Rae rolled her eyes, but she looked anything but annoyed. "Every time I managed to stop crying, I'd look at her and start all over again. I'm pretty sure Sawyer's going to lose his mind before this pregnancy's over. Every time I start crying, he panics because he thinks something terrible has happened."

"I dunno what you made these for, but they smell delicious, and we're eating them," Emberly said as she sat down with the tin of muffins, clapping eagerly. "And, hey! Can we take a second to be excited that we get to raise our kids together?"

"Yay!" Rae said enthusiastically as she held up her drink.

"Y'all can't tell Sawyer and Cayson," I said quickly before we could press our cups together. "I need to tell Beau in my own time."

Emberly groaned. "Knowing something Beau Dixon doesn't is the worst, but we'll manage."

"Someone should probably warn Madison," Rae added, then squeezed my free hand when she noticed the way my face creased uncomfortably. "It's in the water or something."

"It's the dimples," Emberly disagreed.

I gave a conceding sigh. "It's definitely the dimples."

Twenty-Three

BEAU
TWENTY-TWO YEARS OLD

I clenched my hand tighter around the packets of papers in my hand, my heart pounding out a fierce beat as I opened the door to the mayor's office and stepped inside.

His young secretary gave me a look, one I knew and didn't care for. Eyes wide with interest and fear and curiosity.

"Beau Dixon . . . to what do I owe this . . ."—she sucked in a breath and pushed out her chest as she released it—"*pleasure.*"

I glanced pointedly at the closed door behind her. "I have an appointment."

"And you just happened to come early?" she asked, innuendo dripping from her words.

I rolled my eyes and headed for the office behind her, not caring if the mayor was ready for me or not. "You need a new secretary," I said in way of announcing myself as I opened his door.

The mayor looked between his secretary and me as she stumbled in after me, flailing to introduce me.

"Sorry, sir, he just barged in."

A scoff left me as I stopped behind one of the chairs and held his irritated gaze.

After a moment, he sighed and lifted a dismissive hand. "Thank you. Take a break please." With a stern look, he added, "*Away* from the office."

Once she'd closed the door behind us, I repeated, "You need a new secretary."

He grunted some sort of disagreement as he gestured for me to take a seat. "She's just fine. It's *you*. You *Dixons*." He said our last name as if it left a bad taste in his mouth, then leaned back in his seat and looked toward the ceiling. "What was it my daughter said when she found out I had a meeting with you? Oh right . . . 'hot commodity.' Apparently, that's what you boys are."

At my lack of response, he continued, muttering, "Trouble, is what I think. Nothin' but trouble. Your brother stole my car and left a cow in its place, Mr. Dixon."

"I'm not Cayson," I said evenly.

He clicked his tongue and sat forward, placing his elbows on the desk that sat between us. "You might just be worse. But that is not the reason you are here, and to be quite frank, I'm surprised to see you here again. When you showed up, what . . . five? Six years ago?"

"Three."

"I was sure I wouldn't see you again. Sure you would realize your little fantasy was nothin' more than that. Then I hear you're wantin' to meet again." He held his hands out before clasping them and gave me a condescending grin. "I can't wait to hear this."

I was starting to understand why Cayson had played a

prank on the mayor. Kid was an idiot for all his pranks, but this guy deserved it.

He was pushing me in ways he shouldn't, and I was struggling so damn hard not to let it show.

After taking a few breaths, I said, "Last time we met, I told you what I wanted to do. What I *planned* to do so you would be prepared for when I came back today." I set one of the packets on his desk, never losing his amused stare. "I'm buying that house."

He gave a little nod, that smile of his growing. "As you said before." Without looking at the papers, he shrugged. "It belongs to the town, son."

"I'm not your son," I said in a low tone, then forced myself to count backward before continuing. "The house is just sitting there. The town needs someone to take care of it —give it life. They need something like what Savannah and I wanna do to it."

"A bed and breakfast," he said, nodding as if remembering our last conversation. "It's great in theory, and I have to agree a B&B would be great for the town. But as I said, the plantation house belongs to the town."

"For now," I said confidently. "Savannah and I have saved everything we've ever made for that house. We're both double majoring in business and hospitality management, and Savannah's minoring in marketing, so we'll know what we're doing. Our business plan is in those papers as is—"

"Again, all great in theory."

"As is the agreement from the family who used to own it," I continued and watched as the mayor's eyebrows drew close as he finally grabbed the packet and started thumbing through the pages. "I was looking through public records on the plantation house and found that. After the part about leaving the house to the town of Amber and its *residents*, it says an Amber resident may purchase the house with the intent of caring for the house as the family had for generations."

He finally found the page he was looking for and read, eyes darting across the page, devouring each word until he finally sat back in his chair with a sigh, taking the packet with him. "I see."

"I'm buying that house."

He flipped to the front of the packet and scanned mine and Savannah's business plan as he asked, "And why has it been so important for you to prove to me that you *could*?"

I set the other, smaller packet on his desk and flipped it open to the right page. "Because you're the current mayor. And since the house currently belongs to the town, you have to sign off on it so I can purchase it. You also have to approve our business plan."

"I'm aware of that one, Mr. Dixon," he grumbled. After an eternity of reading through the packets, he huffed to himself and reached for a pen. "Fine. I can't wait to watch this fail."

I curled my hands into fists and focused only on breathing as I watched him sign everywhere that was needed.

Once he was done, I asked, "Why would you want it to?"

He slid the packets my way and then went back to leaning over the desk, resting on his elbows. "I've never known any person to get arrested as many times as you or that one brother of yours. And every time, y'all get off scot-free. I don't understand it, and it really grinds my gears. So, I would love, just once, to watch you fail in something, Mr. Dixon."

Grabbing the packets, I stood, nodding as I went. "This won't be it," I assured him as I turned and left the office. Never slowing as I got in my Explorer and headed to the bank for the second time that week. Wishing for once that I lived in a place where I wouldn't be recognized. Where I could come and go without anyone caring.

Savannah had gone to the next city over to hang out with her friends—I wasn't worried about her seeing me. It was the rest of the town and their watchful eyes and obsessive need to know and share everyone's business at every hour of the day.

Going anywhere in town had people talking for one reason or another. Going to the bank twice in one week? By the time I left, people were either going to think I had severe financial problems or they would be closer to the mark. And they were gonna tell everyone, including Savannah.

"Mr. Dixon," Mr. Coty, the loan officer, said when I walked into his office, hopefulness in his expression. "Do we have news?"

I set the packet with the signatures on his desk and sank into a chair. "He signed everything."

He clapped his hands and pulled the packet closer. "All right then, let's get this going."

"Can we wait?"

Surprise crossed his face as he slowly removed his hands. "If that's what you want to do. Can I ask why the change?"

"I want Savannah to be a part of buying the house."

Mr. Coty gave a slow nod as a gentle smile tugged at his mouth. "Understood."

"I didn't know how long any of this would take, or if the mayor would ever sign," I said, then jerked my chin toward the packet. "But I wanted to have it all ready so it could be a wedding gift for Savannah."

A shock of a laugh left him as he tapped the packet. "This is some wedding gift, Mr. Dixon."

My head slanted in the beginnings of a shake. "You don't understand what that house means to us. But I, uh . . . I wanna know if I can use the house. Now."

He gave a look as if his hands were tied. "If you purchase it, yes. But with wanting to wait . . ."

"Since we were kids, Savannah has described our wedding. There," I explained. "So, I wanna fix up the back of the property, and I will do whatever it takes to make that happen because it's her dream, and there's no way I'm not giving us that. But if it's possible, I'd like it to remain a surprise for her that the mayor signed off on the business and the house until we're married."

He sat there for a while, tapping his fingers on his desk as he seemed to think. "So, the two of you purchase *after* the wedding, but you fix up the property *before* and *have* the wedding there even though it doesn't belong to you. Correct?"

I grunted in affirmation.

"Technically, the family left the house to the town and its residents, and you are an Amber resident just wanting to care for the property."

My jaw twitched as I fought a smile. As excitement moved through me.

"And, *technically*, the mayor has already signed over the house and signed off on a bed and breakfast to be at that location and run by the two of you. So, I don't see why you can't be on the property. Just . . . maybe not *inside* yet since this is all technicalities and you don't own anything yet."

"Yet," I agreed.

"Now, if county shows up at your wedding, I can't help you there."

A breath of a laugh bled free. "Understood."

"Well, you sure have been busy," Mr. Coty said as he stood and slid the packet back in my direction. "Getting this taken care of, preparing for a wedding, about to graduate, and I heard you had a meeting with my brother."

I stilled as I closed my hand around the packet, my jaw tightening as I struggled to find something to say.

"Said he's pretty confident this is gonna be great for the kids and you."

I looked up, my brows drawing together in wonder and doubt. "Yeah?"

"Don't sound so surprised," he said with a laugh. "You got the job, didn't you?"

Lowering my head in a nod, I wondered why he wasn't getting it because there was no doubt he'd already heard.

I'd gone to my old high school football coach, asking for a job since I was gonna need it. Something that paid more than the orchard and would provide for Savannah and me while we got the bed and breakfast up and going.

About shocked the hell out of me when he hadn't hesitated in giving me a coaching position, saying, "Gonna need someone like you, helping me and learning all you can so I know we'll be in good hands when I retire in a couple years."

What hadn't surprised me was the reaction of parents when word started spreading around town . . . and I didn't even start working until this summer.

No one wanted the volatile Dixon near their kids, let alone in charge of them. They didn't want someone who could come unhinged at any moment. Someone *destructive*.

"Yeah, but I dunno how long he's gonna let me stay on." I shrugged like it didn't matter. "Or how long the Boosters will let him keep me on."

"I wouldn't listen to the town chitchat," Mr. Coty said

with a wave of his hand. "My brother said when you were doing anything with the team and when you were playing, you were a different kid. He said you were a leader. He thinks you'll be a great leader for the school."

I tapped the packet against my palm and started backing toward the door. "Appreciate that."

He pointed at me. "Now, I'll see you and Savannah back here in . . . when's the wedding?"

"Three months."

He let out a low whistle. "Probably the hardest thing you'll ever do, keep something this big from her for that long," he said with a laugh, but his words had a pit of ice and guilt opening up in my stomach.

I forced something that might've resembled a smile and choked out a single word around the pain clawing at my throat. "Yeah."

I barely remember leaving the bank or getting in my car.

I don't remember driving toward the plantation house, but I was suddenly there. Parked around the side, hidden from view as always. Vacantly staring at the place that would soon be ours, drowning in the past that was destroying me, years later.

The morning after that last fight with Madison, I'd woken up knowing our agreement was a mistake. There was no making up for what we'd done, but I knew in the twisting of my soul that there would be no forgiveness if Madison left and Savannah or Hunter ever found out the truth behind it all.

But before I had the chance to act, my mom had busted open the door and started yelling about girls in bedrooms. Demanding Savannah wake up and leave, and for me to get downstairs and clean up from Hunter's party the night before.

Mom never left my sight. Standing behind me, scolding me and pointing out every spot that needed cleaning until it happened . . .

Hunter's twisted cry of agony had sent us running through the house and had me biting out a curse as ice crept through my veins because I'd known I was too late.

She was already gone, and I hadn't stopped it.

As soon as I saw Hunter on his knees in the middle of the driveway, I'd turned and run upstairs to my room, searching for my phone. I'd called Madison again and again, but there was no ringing or voicemail. The call didn't even go through.

That afternoon, I had to be the one to tell Savannah that her friend had *left*.

I would've gone through any pain, taken any of Savannah's anger, if it took away the consuming grief that burst from her and continued to slowly bleed from her for months after. If it brought back that extra light that was still missing from her.

Fuck, I would've done anything if I could've just taken back that goddamn night.

The guilt I felt every time Hunter came to me, needing a friend in the months after Madison left, was unbearable. I verbally lashed out at him and eventually lost control, fighting him until he stopped coming around. Until we stopped talking at all.

Then he was gone too—off in the military.

And I was there, trying like hell to forget something that was always in the back of my mind, reminding me I was the reason for everyone's pain. Trying to keep my fiancée together when I knew things—had done things—that were the cause of her sorrow. Trying to make mine and Savannah's dreams come true when my lies and anger were always there, haunting me.

By the time Savannah called a few hours later, I was deep on the property, trying to scrub away the suffocating guilt by noting everything that needed to be done in the next few months.

"Angel," I said in answer, the word a soft rumble as I turned and took in the back of the property and the plantation house in a new light.

All those years of dreaming and planning, and it was about to be ours.

"Hey," she said, sounding relaxed and all sorts of mischievous, a tell that she'd had a drink or two. "Okay, so, don't be mad."

"I'm not mad."

"You don't even know what I did," she hissed into the phone.

"Trust me," I murmured as that earlier pit opened wide again, reminding me that Savannah could never do anything that would come close to what I'd done to her. "You're not gonna make me mad."

A scoff of disbelieving amusement met my ear, and I pictured her rolling her eyes. "Okay, so, we *may* have gone shopping and gotten our nails done."

"All right."

There was a pause before she hesitantly added, "I *may* have spent, like, two hundred dollars. *Fifty*. Two hundred and fifty." She made a distraught noise. "Oh my God, I'm sorry. I'm gonna take it back. I have to take it back, right? I can't believe I did that. I don't know what came over me. Or maybe I—I dunno . . ."

I waited until her self-scolding, inebriated ramble trailed off, rubbing at my jaw and fighting a smile as I listened. "Babe, when's the last time you went shopping?"

"Um . . . I'm not . . . maybe for my high school graduation dress?"

"Four years ago," I said slowly. "You're fine."

"But we need to save money," she whispered.

"We do—we *are*. You also need to do things for yourself every once and a while."

"What about you?" she countered softly.

"I hate shopping."

Her scoffing laugh filled the phone. "But you don't do anything for you."

She had no idea how wrong she was.

"I keep a girl I don't deserve," I murmured as I took in different parts of the property—each that had a memory tied to it. Where we'd first dreamt up our lives. Where Savannah wanted to get married. Where we'd first explored each other's bodies under a night of stars.

"That isn't . . ." She sighed gently, wonder filling her voice when she continued. "That isn't the same thing."

"It is," I argued. "Maybe one of these days, you'll understand that my life with you is everything I want."

"I love you."

"Every breath," I vowed.

She exhaled slowly and said, "Well, are you gonna come see what I spent all that money on?"

My mouth twitched in the beginnings of a smile. "Tell me where."

"Well, I was thinking on me for now, and later tonight, maybe on your bedroom floor . . ."

"Where are you?" It was all a low demand as I stalked

across the property to my SUV.

A breath of a laugh sounded in my ear. "My favorite place."

I stopped short and looked around even though I could hear subdued holiday music and laughter through the phone. "The plantation house," I said, confident in the answer even though I knew she wasn't there.

"Whoops—nope. Second favorite place. I'm there."

"Got it."

"Come find me." Wicked excitement lit her voice before she ended the call, and then I was climbing into my car and cranking the engine.

Carefully reversing down the side of the property to the large U-shaped drive, as if I was still afraid of getting caught. It wasn't until I was pulling onto the street that I realized those days were behind us.

Almost.

And I couldn't wait to get to Savannah so I could tell her . . . at least part of the news. But her second favorite place was a hole-in-the-wall restaurant in the next city over that we'd been going to for years, and it wasn't exactly close. Then again, nothing was close to Amber, but I didn't wanna be anywhere else.

When I was little, I'd always thought I'd escape one day. Escape the people and kids who feared me—who saw me a certain way. Find a place where I could hide away in a crowd.

Or just get lost.

And then Savannah happened and everything changed.

She made me see the world differently. Made me want more for myself. Pushed me to go for what I wanted, even if I thought I didn't deserve it. Even if the people of Amber thought I didn't . . .

Most of them were judgmental assholes anyway.

I glanced at my phone when it started ringing and started to decline the call since I was about to turn into the restaurant but accepted it at the last second.

"Mom," I answered as I lifted the phone to my ear.

"Hey, sweetheart, hi. Have you, uh . . ." She cleared her throat. "Are you with Savannah, by chance?"

I pulled into a parking space and turned my car off, not wasting time getting out and starting across the lot. "I'm about to be, why?"

"Well, I was with her earlier—"

"You were?" That brought me to a stop. I glanced at the restaurant and then turned around to block out the distraction of lights and people through the glass windows. "When?"

"Oh, she didn't—well, never mind. Anyway, she just seemed . . . *off* might be a word? Very Savannah, but also very not."

The muscles in my jaw worked as flashes of Savannah over the past couple of years burst to mind. Her smile not as bright. Always seeming to be waiting for something— some*one*. Never dancing unless it was for teaching.

"I think she's having a hard time," Mom added. "Especially today."

"What's today?" I asked, mind racing to think of what I could've missed.

"Oh, nothing. Well, it's just not for me to tell you."

"*Mom.*"

"Son, I have no doubt you'll find out as soon as you see her."

I mumbled a curse. "All right, then I gotta go."

"Love on that sweet girl and be gentle with her."

I lifted a hand. "As opposed to?"

"Don't get snippy with me, Beau Dixon, just go take care of my future daughter-in-law!"

"Damn it," I ground out when the call ended and turned, already jogging for the door to the restaurant. But when I walked in, I found Savannah in the bar area, surrounded by our friends, head tilted back as she laughed.

I made my way over there, looking for anything in her expression that would hint at what my mom had been talking about, but she looked light and free for the first time in a long time.

The drink in her hand might've had something to do with that.

The corner of my mouth ticked up when I noticed what she was wearing. It was so Savannah—all comfort and sexuality—and I fucking loved it. An unbuttoned, red flannel shirt that I was pretty sure was new over a pair of skintight black pants that she would live in if she could.

"Fucking hell," I muttered when I saw what was beneath the flannel.

"Babe!" she called out when she caught sight of me, reaching for me and pulling me closer to where she was pressed up against a barstool.

"Your shirt," I said against her lips when she reached up to kiss me.

"You like?" she asked excitedly, grabbing at the flannel and inspecting it as if she were looking at it for the first time.

A rumble of assent built in my chest as I slid my hand around her waist, curling my fingers around the thin, black shirt underneath. "This is see-through."

A wicked glint flashed in her honey eyes when she looked at me.

"You're gonna get me in so much trouble," I murmured as I lifted my other hand to trail the tips of my fingers across her jaw.

A giggle rolled up her throat and danced across her lips. "Look good on your floor though, right?"

"Fucking perfect."

"You're not mad?" she asked, voice dropping to a whisper I could barely hear in the bar.

"Savannah, why the hell would I be mad?"

"Because it was impulsive and stupid, and I should've asked you," she rambled quickly, her head lowering to hide whatever emotion had started creeping across her face.

I pressed my thumb under her jaw to stop her and went still when a body crashed into me.

The impact was a trigger I couldn't afford—not then, not ever. Causing a haze of red to creep around the edges of my vision and every muscle to lock tight in preparation.

Anticipation.

"Oh God, sorry," a voice wrapped in laughter said. "Beau, sorry. Shit, sorry."

My gaze slanted to the side in time to see Tanya using my arm to keep herself vertical. Before I could attempt to start unlocking my body to help her, Alex was there, pulling her up and giving me a look like he knew I was struggling.

"You good, man?" At the dip of my chin, he cracked a smile. "Bartender said they were already three drinks in by the time I got here. Want anything?"

"No."

Shock and disbelief billowed from him. "Not even your one drink?"

"Not this time."

He rolled his eyes but nodded. "Fine, fine."

"But we're celebrating!" Tanya whined and lifted her hand to catch the bartender's eye before quickly swinging toward Savannah and me, forcing Alex to move with her to keep her upright. "It's *so* beautiful." Her glassy stare went to me. "Did she tell you how pretty it is? The most beautiful-est in the whole world of princesses and fairies."

"I think I missed something," Alex said as Tanya sagged against his chest. "I thought we were here to celebrate only having one more semester."

"I didn't know there was a reason," I said as I finally succeeded in lifting Savannah's face and felt my world narrow in on that girl when I saw the tears clinging to her cheeks.

"The fuck?" I breathed.

"It really is so pretty," Savannah whimpered before choking on a sob.

"Oh, honey," Tanya said, reaching for her, but Alex held her back.

"Savannah, what's wrong?" I begged, inching her closer to me.

She waved a hand over her body before letting it fall heavily to my chest, her face crumpling with emotion.

"What—" I looked from Alex's shocked expression to Tanya. "Why the fuck did you let her go shopping if she was this upset about it?" Focusing on Savannah again, I lowered my voice to a whisper. "Savannah, it is not a big deal. Babe, you have to know that. I don't care that you spent money. You shouldn't either."

"It isn't this," she said over a strangled sob, her shoulders hitching as she sucked in jagged breaths. "I . . . I found my wedding dress."

"Okay, great, let's go buy it."

"We did," she said, sounding devastated over the fact

when I would've expected something a hell of a lot different. "And it's beautiful and perfect and wrong—everything about our wedding's just . . . wrong, it's wrong."

Everything went cold.

My blood. My heart. My soul.

Twenty-Four

BEAU
TWENTY-TWO YEARS OLD

I tried to breathe, but my chest felt too tight. Too heavy.

"Savannah," I managed to say through the glass in my throat, "can we talk outside?"

"No." She shook her head in wide, wild shakes as she unsteadily got onto the barstool. "No, I'm celebrating—we're celebrating."

"I think we should talk."

"They aren't here," she cried softly as more tears fell.

I glanced to Alex, and he nodded in understanding, pointing the other direction and turning Tanya that way as Savannah continued rambling.

"Everything's perfect, and you're perfect, but it's all wrong because they're not here." She hit her chest with a closed fist. "Madi was supposed to be there with me today."

If I hadn't already gone still, I would've then.

Unable to move from that paralyzing guilt.

"She's supposed to be there *then*. On the day. But she won't because she left me, and she's just gone." Her forehead creased in pain. "Why did she leave me—and Hunter!" she added quickly. "He isn't here. He's your brother and your best friend, Beau. But he's gone too, and he hasn't said if he's coming to our wedding yet. And, so, it's all wrong."

"Savannah, I'm—"

"*And*," she whisper-yelled, "I just realized this morning that I was late. Like, *late-late*."

It felt like a shockwave hit me. Slammed right into me in a mixture of confusion and wonder and denial. "What?"

"Two weeks late."

"I think I'm pregnant," Madison confessed. "Hunter's . . . if I even am."

"If," I bit out. "You're just gonna throw that shit out there when you don't even know?"

"I'm two weeks late . . . more than."

I shook off that night and the gut-wrenching guilt as I studied the woman in front of me, my voice low and harsh as I demanded, "What? Wait, and you're drinking?"

"I'm not." She waved a hand around her. "I started when we were dress shopping, so there's no—I'm not. But I had started thinking that it might be nice. That I might love being pregnant, even if the timing wasn't right. Because it would be us and perfect and then I was wrong about that too, and I couldn't call Madi for any of it. So, I went and got my nails done and went shopping, and I spent money I shouldn't have."

"I don't care about the fucking money, Savannah," I ground out. "But right now, I think we need to leave."

"I don't wanna go," she said, head shaking fiercely as she

wiped at her wet cheeks. "We're celebrating . . ." Her glassy eyes studied the ceiling. "Something. I don't remember what."

"We can celebrate another time," I assured her. "Let's get out of here."

"I wanna stay."

"Savannah—"

"Man, she said she didn't wanna go," a voice said from behind me just as a palm shoved into my shoulder. "Get the hint and leave the girl alone."

In an instant, everything changed. My breaths slowed and deepened. My jaw ached from the pressure I was putting on it as the world around me became saturated in red.

I slowly glanced over my shoulder at the man straightening behind me and puffing out his chest. Each movement and the challenge in his eyes had that sick, dark need in my veins pumping faster.

Raging.

Begging to do something.

I needed to get Savannah out of there—get *us* out of there —before I lost control.

Challenging me wasn't something that should be done . . . ever. That side of me responded to it. Fed off it until I couldn't stop what followed.

But on a day like then? After near-constant reminders of what I'd done to Savannah and my brother. Of how my girl was still breaking because of mine and Madison's fucked-up attempt to cover what we'd done? I was already standing on a dangerous ledge of guilt and loathing that fueled the anger I tried so hard to suppress.

The softest breath, and I was going over.

I curled my fingers against Savannah's waist. Feeling her

there and forcing myself to breathe. To count backward even as the muscles in my back tensed and twitched in preparation as another guy stood and slowly rounded my side.

Caging me in until I was shaking.

"Beau," Savannah breathed, her hand sliding over my chest and then gripping my shirt tightly. "Come on, you're right. Let's go."

The guy behind me took a step closer and raised a hand. "Darlin', you don't have to go—"

"Don't call her that," I seethed, my voice a sharp warning.

"It's fine," Savannah said quickly, words slurring as she stumbled off the barstool and tried tugging me away. "We're fine and we're leaving."

"Darlin', you can't expect us to let you leave with someone you were refusin' just seconds ago."

"I wasn't—that isn't—*no*," she stammered as she struggled to grip my hands. To soothe them.

Because I'd released her the instant he'd called her *darlin'* again.

Fingers curling into fists as tremors rolled through my body.

"Beau, please," she whispered, voice shaking about as badly as I was.

"Think you're tough shit," the first guy continued as I forced my arm around Savannah and told myself to move. To walk away. To get her outside. "Making women cry. Telling them what to do and where they can go. Bet she falls into doorknobs a lot too, huh?"

No sooner had his hand met my shoulder in another shove than I had the collar of his shirt in my fist. Pulling him close enough to watch his eyes flare with fear before a look settled there that I'd seen too many times in my life.

As if I was proving him right.

"Beau," Savannah begged, soft as a whisper as she pressed harder against my side.

I took a breath. Another. And then another. "Touch me again, we're gonna have a fucking problem. Call my girl *darlin'* again, you're gonna wish you'd never set foot in here tonight."

"Beau," she repeated, this time harsher.

"She doesn't have to go anywhere with you." His stare shifted toward her, and my hand tightened. "You don't have to go with him."

"And you need to mind your business because you have no idea what you were eavesdropping on, you idio—" A breath of shock and pain fled from her as she staggered a few steps to the side, her head whipping around to see the second guy trying to pull her from my hold.

The last full thing I remember was moving Savannah behind me as everything went so fucking red.

And then that dark, sickening rage was there, consuming me until it was all I knew.

Crawling through my veins.

Driving every fierce beat of my heart.

Distorting every thought.

Blurs broken up with flashes so bright and vivid that it was disorienting. Like being in the darkest depths of the sea before being shoved back into a reality that moved at a slightly slower pace. Letting me take in everything that was happening for those seconds before time slipped away again.

My hand on the guy's throat who had grabbed Savannah as I pinned him to the floor, blood pouring from his nose.

My ribs aching in protest from the kick that was delivered there.

Slamming the talker into the bar and dodging his fist before delivering a knockout uppercut to his jaw.

I remembered all that.

Being grabbed from behind and throwing the guy overhead, slamming him onto the floor . . . I remembered that too.

And then screaming.

So much screaming and honey eyes directly beneath me. Her small hand gripping my fist that was raised in the air, ready to strike. Her other hand pressed firmly to my harshly pitching chest.

Jagged breaths rushed from me as I studied Savannah's horrified stare and trembling chin, as shame and humiliation and denial ripped through me when I realized our positions.

I wasn't . . .

I wouldn't have . . .

Never.

"Savannah," I forced out, fear coating her name.

"You wouldn't . . ." she breathed, voice nothing more than a whispered tremor. "I couldn't get you—"

A moan sounded beneath her, and she tilted her head toward the sound before turning completely, revealing what I hadn't noticed before.

The man she was lying on.

The man she'd *thrown* herself on.

"*Fuck,*" I muttered when I saw Alex there, only looking him over for a second before I focused on where Savannah was on her hands and knees next to Tanya as they checked him.

I reached for Savannah, but she shifted away to prevent me from touching her.

Fuck.

Her shocked stare flashed my way, conveying everything I needed to know without saying a word.

I hadn't hurt her . . . and she had nothing else to say to me.

Savannah had never looked at me with anything other than understanding until we were alone and could talk about it freely. This also wasn't the first time one of my friends had gotten caught up in my wrath. For her to have that look on her face, it had my shame burning hotter than ever.

"What the hell, Beau, what the hell?" Tanya sobbed as she scooted closer to Alex, cradling his head in her lap.

"I'm fine," he wheezed, then sputtered out a cough as he met my stare. "I shouldn't have tried to stop you. I knew better."

I clenched my teeth tight and struggled under the weight of loathing bearing down on me.

But I stayed there. Frozen. Unable to say a word.

When the familiar red and blue lights bounced around at the edge of my vision, getting brighter and brighter as they pulled closer to the entrance of the restaurant, I sat back on my heels with a heavy sigh and looked to Savannah.

My world.

My everything.

With a stuttered exhale, she glanced my way. Looking all kinds of confused and trying so damn hard to hide something from me.

"Alex," I gritted out, his name scraping up my throat as my stare shifted to him.

He pushed himself up to sitting and waved me off. "I knew better, man."

My mouth parted just as the doors to the restaurant opened. My eyelids slowly shut as I placed my hands on the back of my head. Vacantly listening as the officers spoke and gave orders as the flashes I could remember from the past few minutes replayed in my mind, ending with Savannah beneath me again and again and again.

Jesus Christ.

I stood when the officer pulled on my cuffed hands and finally looked at the destruction around me.

The broken and toppled barstools. The spilled drinks and broken glass on the floor. Chips littering the bar and floor, baskets tossed carelessly around. Friends watching with varying expressions of disappointment and frustration. Strangers looking at me with shock and hints of fear. The guys who had intervened were pressing cloths to their bloodied faces and speaking to an officer.

And Savannah . . . struggling to find the expression she always wore after I lost control. The one that dared anyone to say something to me or her about what happened. Struggling to hold my stare.

Ripping out my fucking heart even though I'd been waiting for and expecting that reaction from Savannah for most of our lives.

I love you.

I love you.

I'm so damn sorry.

Twenty-Five

BEAU
TWENTY-TWO YEARS OLD

"Dixon."

My stare shifted to the irritated-looking deputy standing at the holding cell door, and I slowly stood from the metal bench I'd been on since the night before.

He played with the keys in his hands before folding his arms over his chest, his head moving in faint shakes. "You gotta be about the luckiest son of a bitch I've ever met."

Confusion and curiosity tugged at me, but I remained silent.

Waiting for him to take me to see the judge or get out whatever he felt he needed to say.

"When they brought you in last night," he went on, "I thought this was gonna be the time we got you. Plenty of witnesses. Destruction of property." He sucked in a breath through his teeth and shook his head again as he reached forward to unlock the cell. But once he had it opened, he stepped in front of me and held my stare. "One day, Dixon. One day . . . that luck's gonna run out, and then you're going nowhere. And I, for one, can't fucking wait."

A tic started in my jaw when he stepped even closer. Knowing exactly what he was doing by getting in my face.

Gently pushing.

Challenging.

Waiting for me to respond.

Ten.

Nine.

Eight.

"You're free to go," he drawled irritably. "You know the way."

Once he stepped out of the way, I walked past him, heading down the familiar halls with him on my heels until I was on my way out.

Until I was on my way to her.

Slowly pacing the length of the lobby with her arms wrapped around her waist, her expression cold and warning anyone to try her.

When she saw me coming toward her, she stopped. Shoulders sagging slightly before she quickly straightened her back. Trying to be so strong when she shouldn't have to.

When she should've never had to go through this shit at all—let alone . . . *fuck, how many times has it been now?*

She offered a supportive smile when I neared her. Short. Pained. Fake as fuck and lacking everything that was Savannah.

And it had a tendril of fear snaking through my chest.

"Be seein' y'all soon," the deputy stationed at the front desk said with a laugh.

Instead of firing back at him as she normally would, Savannah's stare fell to the floor before she closed her eyes tightly and turned for the doors. But the tears she hadn't been quick enough to hide rooted me in place for long seconds before I was able to follow.

Each step taking all my strength.

Each breath feeling like it might be my last.

This was different. She was different. And it terrified me.

I sank into the passenger seat of her car, unable to take my eyes off her. Watching every shift and every emotion she was struggling to hide as she took her place in the driver's seat, mumbling indifferently.

"Those guys tried to say you attacked them, unprovoked. But I told the deputies that one guy had been pushing you and the other grabbed me. I don't think they believed me or anything, but they saw it on the restaurant's video. And you hadn't been responsible for any of the damage in the restaurant." She nodded absently. "That was on them. Not you."

"Savannah, I'm sorry."

"I know," she said, the words bursting from her on a stifled cry. Her chin trembled and her face creased with exhaustion and pain as she dropped her hands and the car keys to her lap. "I know you're sorry, Beau. I just—" Her head shook quickly, fiercely before she straightened in the seat and put the keys in the ignition and cranked the engine.

"Savannah—"

"Not now, Beau."

"I tried," I said gravely, unable to let this rest when I could barely breathe. "I tried leaving. I tried getting us out of there. I tried ignoring all of it. But he touched you, and I . . ." I lifted a hand and stared at her helplessly.

"I know," she whispered, head down and eyes once again squeezed tightly shut. "I've always known, Beau."

She had. She'd understood me when no one else had. She'd seen me when no one else had cared to try.

But that suddenly seemed like a burden she could no longer bear.

And I was scrambling.

For words.

For air.

For peace, when that kind of weight on my chest had panic coursing through my veins and easily bleeding into a half-dozen other emotions I couldn't afford to feel right then.

Shaking . . . fucking *trembling* as I fought to suppress what I'd never been able to control.

All of it growing and growing in the weighted silence of the car ride until everything inside me went horribly, unnervingly still when she pulled up in front of my parents' property, not even bothering to put her car in park.

I ground my teeth so hard my jaw ached as I opened the door. "Every last breath, Savannah," I vowed, soft and low, before getting out.

No sooner had I closed the door behind me than I heard hers opening.

"I said your name," she claimed, voice thick and wavering as she stormed around the front of the car. "I *screamed* your name, and you still didn't stop. I tried to get you to see me, and you wouldn't." A sob crept up her throat as tears rolled down her cheeks.

I went to her on instinct.

Reaching for her. Needing to hold her.

And she stepped away.

Felt like she knocked out my knees and froze me in place with that one, small, horribly significant action.

"You wouldn't," she repeated. "Not until I was the one you were going after."

"Savannah, I—" I choked on my apology, my head subtly

moving as I tried to remember those moments she was talking about.

I always stopped for her.

I always heard her.

It'd been that way since the first day.

"I don't . . . I don't remember," I admitted, shame filling me. "Savannah, I'm so fucking sorry, but I would've never hurt you."

Her head snapped back, her dark eyebrows pulling together in a mixture of surprise and confusion. "I know," she said slowly, confidently. "You think I would've thrown myself on top of Alex when you were about to swing if I didn't?"

My hands slowly curled into fists at her reminder. Stomach dropping and fear turning my blood to ice at the image of Savannah beneath me as all that red-hot rage pounded through my veins.

"That was dangerous," I ground out.

"I am not afraid of you," she said just as fiercely. "But I can't do this anymore."

I staggered back a step and then I was falling into an abyss.

Drowning in open air.

Dying . . . this had to be what death felt like. Slow and excruciating, only to be brought back to start from the beginning.

And only a second had passed.

"I love you, Beau," she said through her tears. "I love you more than I will ever be able to explain to anyone."

My head shifted as if trying to block out words I'd expected for years and had dreaded every day of that time because I'd always known she deserved better. My heart beat painfully in protest, twisting and reaching for Savannah in an attempt to keep her.

"But I can't keep watching you take people down, afraid *that* person will be the one who pulls a knife or a gun on you. I can't keep watching you be put in handcuffs, worrying that will be the time you *won't* be getting out after a night or a quick bond. And my heart truly breaks for you because all the assholes in this town have somehow gotten you to believe that you are only your anger, but I know you. I see you, and you are kind and amazing and gentle. And I've spent so long trying to get people to see you the way I do, but God, Beau, *why can't you?*"

My stare flashed to her, studying her determined gaze and wavering chin.

"I want to marry you. I want to have kids with you. I've wanted a life with you since I was a little girl, and nothing about you will ever make me want anything less. But I *cannot* have a life with you if you can't control your anger."

"Savannah—"

"No," she said quickly, cutting off my strangled plea. "No, whatever you're about to say, please don't. Because right now, you can't promise me that you will. And if you tell me you can't without even trying? My heart won't be able to handle that."

"You think I'd throw away my life with you by not even trying? Savannah, I'd destroy the world for you, don't you get that?"

"I don't want you to!" she cried out, gripping at her chest before burying her face in her hands.

I closed the distance between us and curled my fingers

around her wrists, gently pulling her hands away to reveal her tear-streaked face. Each tear that fell and each jagged breath tore at my soul as I struggled not to pull her into my arms when she so clearly wanted to stand on her own.

"I'm sorry."

"I know, but this needs to stop," she said, voice twisting with discomfort. She pulled her hands from my grasp only to curl her fingers around my own. "You get angry? I'll be there to help calm you. Someone pushes you to your limit? Hold that frustration in, and we'll find other ways to get your aggression out. But trust that you *can*, or we're never gonna have a chance."

"We will," I vowed. "I'll keep—"

"Beau, stop," she begged. Her golden eyes met mine, pain swirling within the plea there for me not to ruin this.

Not to destroy *us*.

"It took months of heartbreak and so many tears to come to the realization that I needed to do this for me and for us. And I still continued putting it off because I've been terrified of the possible outcome. So, for me, really think about this before promising anything."

There was nothing to think about.

I would do anything for her, even the impossible.

"And until then?" I asked when she released me and started backing up to her car again.

"What do you mean?"

I clutched at my shattered chest before gesturing to her. "Savannah, I just spent an entire night wondering if we were even getting married anymore."

Shock ripped across her face. "What? Why would you —*what?*"

"When I got to you last night, you started crying because you'd found your wedding dress, and you kept telling me everything about our wedding is wrong."

Savannah's eyelids slowly closed as a mumbled curse slipped free. With a deep, stuttered breath, she looked at me and said, "I miss my best friend. It feels like there's a hole in my life, and whenever I start trying to mend it, something huge happens that I wish I could share with her. But last night was just . . . all that pain fueled by alcohol, and I'm sorry. I'm so sorry for that. Marrying you anywhere, at any time, even with no one around, would be my idea of perfection."

She said the words, and from the emotion weaving through them, I knew she meant them. But that look in her eyes shattered it all.

Like she was afraid we wouldn't make it there . . . because of me.

"I love you, Beau Dixon," she said as she rounded her car. "Know that you can do this. You can absolutely do this."

She got in the car before I could respond, trying to hide the new tears building in her eyes, and drove away, continuing on past her house.

"I got the plantation house for the wedding." I stared vacantly at where her car had been as the news I'd been waiting to voice drifted away with the winter breeze. I let my eyelids close and clenched my jaw as Savannah's words replayed in my mind and had that fear I'd been running from for years catching up with me. "Small. Simple. Sunset. Peonies. *There*." I swallowed past my shame and regret and uncertainly whispered, "It can finally happen."

Turning, I slowly started down the long driveway, mind

reeling from everything Savannah had said that morning and the night before.

Everything that had *happened* the night before.

I dragged a hand over my jaw as I climbed the porch steps, slowing when Cayson eased through the front door, dressed for the garage he worked at.

A knowing smirk tugged at the corner of his mouth. The kind that said my parents were fully aware of where I'd been. Just as he was passing me, though, it fell. Making him look all kinds of hesitant as he turned to continue across the porch backward. "Hey, uh . . ." Lifting one of his hands in surrender and gesturing to himself with the other, he said, "Messenger, yeah?"

It was disturbing.

The way actions and words had such a profound effect on me.

Two words and a fucking gesture had the world slowing and every part of my body tensing. Had a sickening poison creeping through my veins in unsettling anticipation.

At the slow curl of my fingers, Cayson rolled his eyes but went on. "You know that girl Hunter's engaged to?"

I gave a slight nod.

I never could remember her name. I hadn't bothered to try. Until the day Hunter called to say they were getting married, no one in the family had because we'd all known the girl was one thing: Madison's rebound.

"They finally break up?" I asked tightly.

A laugh scraped up Cayson's throat. "Mom would be throwing a party if they had. Anyway, uh, she called because apparently she does that now. Wanted to let you know *they* wouldn't be coming for y'alls wedding."

I worked my jaw a couple times before dipping my head in acceptance.

Cayson looked equally sad for me and ready to flee if I made one move in his direction. "Man, I'm sorry."

"Why?" I asked gruffly. "I don't give a fuck if he never comes back at all." The comment was a lie twisted with truths and fell heavily from my tongue.

I wanted my brother back.

I wanted my best friend the same as Savannah wanted hers.

I wanted *before*.

Because God knew I couldn't handle the aftermath. Couldn't handle looking him in the eye, knowing what I'd done to him. How I'd hurt him. Hurt *them*.

A scoff of disbelief and annoyance burst from Cayson as he turned and left.

I didn't react to it. I couldn't when my mind was so weighed down with everything else.

The second I stepped inside, Mom was there. Looking ten shades of pissed and worried as hell.

"Beau, sweetheart. There's something I need to tell you."

"I already know about Hunter," I murmured as I headed for the stairs.

A saddened noise left her as she hurried to keep up with my steps. "Can we sit in the kitchen and talk?"

I turned at the bottom step, head listing. "Mom, I haven't slept—"

"Kitchen," she snapped, voice slightly frantic as she headed that way.

I stood there for a moment before following after her. Jaw clenching tight when I rounded into the kitchen in time to see her brush at a tear.

The only two women in my life who mattered were crying because of the things I'd done and the way I was. Hadn't known I could hate myself more until that moment.

She turned, storming toward the table with mugs and coffee pot in hand and refusing to look at me. But I saw the tears filling her reddened eyes. Saw the way she was pressing her mouth tightly together to keep from crying.

"Sit," she demanded as she set the mugs and coffee on the table with loud thuds.

I started toward the table, watching as she shakily filled her mug and moved onto the second. "I'm good," I said softly. "I don't want—"

"Sit," she yelled, seconds passing in silence before she continued pouring the coffee.

Once I'd sank to the bench opposite her, she slid a mug toward me and fell into her own chair.

"Thank you," I muttered, curling the hot mug close to watch the steam rise.

For long minutes, neither of us spoke. Considering she'd given up doing anything more than giving me a disappointed shake of her head for years, I wasn't sure what she planned to say then or if she expected me to start pouring out my goddamn heart and apologizing profusely.

Neither would happen.

Not with her.

I had a good mom. The four of us put her through hell— me especially. Still, she rolled with whatever we dealt. She publicly stood up for us and defended us to the death. But there was no denying that she was lost when it came to me. That the possibility of what I would do *next* had worried her since I was a little kid. There was no denying that if someone claimed I did something . . . she absolutely believed it.

Feared it.

Agonized over it.

I'd learned long before Savannah ever came into my life that there was no talking about my anger to her or anyone else. They didn't understand, and they wouldn't hear what I had to say anyway.

"Are you okay?" she asked as she grabbed the pot to pour a second cup for herself.

I lowered my chin. "Not the first time I've spent the night in a holding cell."

She sucked in an exaggerated breath as if trying to gather her strength or peace and said, "With Hunter."

"I don't give a shit if he's there or not."

She slammed down the mug just as she'd begun lifting it, her devastated stare snapping to me. "That is the biggest crock of shit I have ever heard, and how dare you use that language in my kitchen."

A smirk tugged at the corner of my mouth, but I fought it. "Yes, ma'am, I'm sorry."

Her head shook as she studied me. "What happened?"

My amusement faded as the brief glimpses I could remember of the fight flashed through my mind. "I got arrest—"

"Not last night," she said, voice softening. "With *you*. What has happened? These past few years, there's been a change in you. More fighting, more arrests. You're . . ." She glanced away, throat working furiously. "You're so angry. More than ever, Beau, and everyone can see it. *Savannah* can see it."

My jaw twitched at the sound of her name.

"Can't *you*?" Mom nearly begged.

I didn't respond even though I knew she was right—I'd *known*.

And I knew why.

That night with Madison had destroyed everything.

I'd been racked with guilt and fear for those months before deciding to tell Savannah. Before Madison had turned the tables and decided to leave.

Agreeing to that bullshit had been the second biggest mistake of my life.

These years of watching Savannah break over Madison's leaving. The constant reminder that my fiancée wasn't the same because of it—because of me—took its toll. All that anger and guilt building and building and unleashing on anyone who crossed my path.

"Beau, something's gotta change," she said when she realized I wasn't going to answer.

"I'm aware."

"Savannah used to come here or stay at county until they released you, but she's stopped doing that in the last year."

I instinctively glanced toward the entryway at the news, every cell in my body responding. Needing to find Savannah to fix what I'd done.

"Instead, she's been calling to let us know when it happens . . . but the call we received last night was from one of the deputies," she said, her tone at once wary and frustrated. "The only reason we knew she was getting you this morning was because she'd just arrived when your dad called to get information on what was gonna happen to you. And now?" She looked around as if to remind me that Savannah wasn't there. "Do you see what's happening?"

"Yes," I said gruffly.

"You're going to lose her, son."

My eyelids slowly closed and my fingers curled into fists so tight that my scabbed-over knuckles split. I lowered my hands from the table to my lap even though I was sure my mom had already seen them.

I felt weak, like my body was gonna give out beneath me even though I was sitting. Because what my mom was saying was too real of a possibility.

Too damn real.

"I think I already am," I admitted on a strained breath.

I think I have been for two and a half years.

I shoved away from the table, stepping over the bench and stalking away as my mom called after me.

"Beau! Beau, come back here!"

I snatched the first pair of keys I saw near the door and continued outside, never slowing as I hit the fob for what ended up being Sawyer's truck and headed that way. Climbing in and cranking the engine before pulling away from the house.

My stare drifted to the Rileys' house as I passed it, but Savannah's car wasn't there. Or at the plantation house or the dance studio or anywhere else I thought she would've gone.

After making a lap around town, I pulled down the side path of the plantation house and shut Sawyer's truck off.

The action bringing a weird sense of déjà vu from the day before.

But the fear gripping my chest and making it impossible to breathe . . . that was new.

Grabbing my phone, I scrolled through the contacts until I found her name, then called the number there as I had every month for the past two and a half years.

But the familiar, automated alert that the number had

been disconnected could be heard before I'd ever lifted my phone to my ear.

Not that I'd expected any different. At that point, I couldn't even be sure if I'd still been hoping for different. But I'd needed to try one last time.

Ending the call, I opened up the messages and started one to her.

Thumbs tapping quickly and angrily on the screen as I forced myself to let everything go.

You're out living your new life and pretending this shit didn't happen. I'm here still picking up all the pieces of your leaving. Every day I'm reminded of that agreement. Of what we did and what I know and how I destroyed the love of my fucking life. Of how I'm still destroying my life with her because of you. And I can't let that happen.

Fuck you for leaving, Madison. You trapped me in a life of guilt, and I hate you for it. We should've told them that first day. We should've told them that last night instead of agreeing you were gonna go because how the hell am I supposed to tell her now? YEARS LATER.

I would give anything to go back and change what we did, but we can't, and you left. You refused to come back even when we helped Hunter go after you. So, I'm done. I'm done letting this guilt weigh me down and destroy everything important to me.

You ruined my life by leaving Amber. Now? I hope to God you never come back.

I PRESSED SEND, not bothering to wait for when it would tell me the message was undeliverable. I'd just needed to get it out at least once so I could let go. So Savannah and I could move on.

I got out of the truck and stormed through the back of the property, body agitated and mind racing too fast to hold on to any one thought. But Savannah was there—over and over and over again. Looking crushed and disappointed and at a loss.

And I couldn't breathe.

I stopped near the far end of the property where Savannah had always pictured our wedding. One hand pressed to my heaving chest and gripping my hair with the other as everything pushed down on me.

Heavier and heavier.

Triggering a need in me that I hated. That made me sick. That could destroy so much more than I already had.

Muscles twitching.

Rage pounding in my veins until my thundering heart was all I could hear.

"*Fuck!*"

Dropping to a crouch, I dragged my fingers through my hair again and again before gripping at the strands.

Ten. Nine.

"Breathe," I said through clenched teeth.

Eight. Seven.

I sat roughly on the ground and then fell to my back. Looking up at the overcast, winter sky that was tinged with red before closing my eyes.

Six. Five.

"Fucking breathe."

Four. Three.

I forced my fingers from my hair and begged my body to stop trembling. To relax. Begged my chest to move regularly.

Two.

One.

MY EYES OPENED SOMETIME LATER, heavy and searching.

Searching out the night sky that didn't seem right. That didn't match the familiarity of waking up with the body pressed to my side and the intoxicating smell of sugar and vanilla surrounding me.

The combination disorienting me until I remembered coming to the plantation house. Until I realized that Savannah was actually there, asleep on the ground and curled up against my side with a thick blanket covering us both.

"Savannah," I murmured as I twisted to look at her. Lifting my hand, I eased the hood of her sweatshirt back enough to trail my fingers along her jaw, my gaze taking in her relaxed features.

This girl who had been changing my world and stealing my heart since that first day.

"I'm sorry for everything," I whispered, voice thick and rough with emotion. "I . . ." My throat worked as I struggled to voice my greatest shame. Choking over the words when they finally escaped. "I slept with Madison. She left because I wanted to tell you. Everything—all of your pain—is because of me, and I'm so sorry."

The backs of my eyes burned, and my hand trembled against her skin as my chest wrenched open wide.

"I've hurt you in ways I swore I never would. I don't deserve you . . . I never have. But for the rest of our lives, I'm gonna try like hell to be worthy of you," I promised. "No more arrests. No more fighting—nothing. Never again, I swear."

I dropped my head against hers and closed my eyes tight when the tears built, savoring the way her body moved against mine as she burrowed closer and let out a contented sigh in her sleep.

"I love you, Savannah Riley," I said softly. "With every last breath."

Twenty-Six

SAVANNAH

I'd just started gathering everything from the kids' rooms and the room my parents had stayed in to clean them when Emberly and Rae walked into the house the way everyone always did. Announcing themselves much the same way they had a couple days before.

"This house always smells like heaven," Rae moaned.

"If it's those muffins again, I'm stealing them," Emberly added, their voices drifting up the stairs before they started climbing them.

I started coming out of the hall just as they reached the top, both wearing identical, expectant and determined looks on their faces before Rae gestured to Emberly. "This is all her idea, but I won't apologize for it."

"The kids are already gone, yes?" Emberly asked, looking like she was ready to start delivering instructions. Before I had the chance to answer, she looked pointedly at the sheets in my arms. "What needs to be done?"

"Excuse me?"

"Put us to work," she said, nodding quickly like she was in a hurry.

A startled laugh left me. "I'm . . . no. This is nothing. This is what I do, Emberly."

"Right, but we have things to do, and we can't get to them until you're done with all this. So, let's go."

When I just stared at her for too long, Rae released a sigh. "Try to remember who we're dealing with. She got her new place completely fixed up in a week and a half."

Emberly nodded and lifted a brow, her plum-painted lips lifting in a victorious smirk.

"Um . . ." I used the big bundle of sheets in my arms to gesture toward the room just behind me. "This bathroom and the kids' bathroom need to be cleaned—and the kitchen. I'm starting the laundry and then I'll put new bedding on and clean their rooms. I did all the other rooms yesterday."

Emberly let out an amused huff and turned, descending the stairs as she called out, "Bathrooms."

Rae's eyes went wide with panic as she turned to follow. "What if I burn down the kitchen?"

"It's *cleaning*," Emberly yelled back, "not *cooking*."

I stood there for another second, trying to wrap my head around what was happening before trailing after.

———

WHEN RAE and I were finishing putting the laundry away in the linen closet a few hours later, Emberly came in, forehead creased in confusion.

"How do you make this work?"

"What?"

She held up the phone in her hand. "Your speakers. The ones that are always playing music in your kitchen."

"Oh, you have to—" My head jerked back. "Is that my phone?"

Her stare drifted to the side for a moment before sliding back to me. "Possibly. I had to put a new playlist on there."

Rae held up a hand. "Remember who you're dealing with. She's a force."

A stuttered laugh left me because I knew that, I'd just never had it directed at me. "You just—"

"Em?"

I lifted my hands at the sound of Cayson's voice. "What exactly are we doing today?"

Emberly just backed out of the closet, smile all kinds of giddy. "One second."

"Force," Rae repeated as we followed her out, but her tone was pure adoration.

We rounded into the entryway just as Emberly slipped up to Cayson, already pressing up on her toes to steal a kiss.

"How you feeling?" he asked, voice soft as he pulled her closer with one hand while keeping the other outstretched. Grasping a coffee and bag that boasted the Brewed logo. His stare flickered to us as she answered before his head lifted, his brows pulling tight. "Now I really feel like I picked up the wrong order."

Emberly laughed as she pressed another kiss to his mouth before reaching for the drink and bag. "Nope, this is it, and I appreciate it."

"There's three of you," he said slowly when she started backing away.

"Yeah, but this is an emotional intervention," she explained as if it should've been obvious.

"A what?" I asked dully.

The corner of Cayson's lips slowly lifted in a smirk. "Dixie Chicks?"

Emberly lifted a shoulder, her face all wry amusement. "Of course."

"I love you," he said simply, then looked to her sister, his head dipping in a nod. "Rae." His stare shifted to me, his shoulders shaking as he fought a laugh. "Savannah . . . just let it happen."

"Let what happen?" I asked, but he turned to leave, glancing over his shoulder at Emberly one last time as he slipped out the door.

She sighed when she faced us, eyes and smile dreamy.

"This is a *what*?" I asked.

"Right," she said, snapping out of it and pointing toward the kitchen with my phone. "Let's go."

"What is an emotional intervention?" I hissed at Rae as we followed.

"Told you, you need to let your world implode."

"I thought that's what we did the other day on the floor with coffee and muffins."

She snorted. "That's cute."

"Oh!" Emberly said excitedly when music started pouring through my kitchen. "I figured it out. Okay, so . . ." She whirled on me, expression stern but full of sympathy. "These are for you. A caramel macchiato—*decaf*." She pointed at my belly and lifted an eyebrow.

"I can have caffeine."

"Right, but how much have you already had today?" she challenged, then nodded in victory when I couldn't respond because she was right. "And here's a turkey sandwich, some fruit, and wedge fries." She gestured to the food when Rae set out a plate and started transferring everything from the bag onto it. "Eat it all. You're gonna need it."

"Why?" I asked warily.

"Trust me," was all she said as she grabbed the plate and drink, taking them over to my large table. Once I was seated, she sat in the chair next to me and grabbed one of my hands. "No changing the playlist I made for you. No more cleaning. No baking. No doing anything at all but sitting right there."

"What? Why?"

"Trust me," she repeated. "You sit there, and you let them help you."

"Who?"

She pointed up, indicating the voices drifting through the speakers. "Now stop asking questions."

My chest pitched with a huff. "You can't expect me not to when y'all walk in here and demand to be part of my cleaning process and then start giving me orders. *In my home*."

She made a bemused face, whispering to herself, "It's like you don't know me at all," before leaning forward to press a loud kiss to my cheek and then standing. "We love you."

"We absolutely love you," Rae echoed.

I sighed and asked, "When *can* I move?"

Emberly shrugged and looped her arm through Rae's as they turned to leave, calling over her shoulder. "You'll know."

Another burst of air fled from me, my head shaking at the absurdity of it all. Dropping my head into my hand when the door shut, I let out a muffled groan. "This is stupid."

Already, my knees were bouncing. My mind racing with all the things I needed to do—the list was short.

Horribly short.

The list of things I *could* do was much longer, and I knew

it would only continue growing because I could always find something to keep myself busy. To keep myself moving.

But I could do this.

I picked at a piece of fruit, my stare already drifting to the time on the clock as my knee bounced faster.

Forcing out a breath, I nodded resolutely. I could stay in one place for as long as it took to finish the lunch, then I was done with Emberly's ridiculous no-moving exercise.

I WAS BEGINNING to think I hated Emberly.

Then again, I was also starting to think she might be a genius.

I'd moved from the table after finishing off about half the food, despite her demands. But I'd only made it to the couch before moving up to my bathroom a couple hours later. Letting the hot water and steam from the shower soothe my aches and hide my tears as my chest had ripped open. My heart slowly bleeding as the past weeks had tormented and plagued me. Whirling around and around in horrifyingly vivid colors and realizations until I was bare and broken in ways I'd never imagined possible. Until I was curled up in bed in one of Beau's shirts even though the sun was still out. Tracing the angel wings on my wrist with the tip of my ring finger . . . tears having long since run dry and sure I wouldn't be able to shed another.

World sufficiently crumbled, the way everyone had been waiting for.

Mangled heart vainly trying to find a regular rhythm when every thought of Beau made it stutter and falter.

More terrified than before that we couldn't survive this.

Twenty-Seven

BEAU

I took the turn onto the gravel drive a little too fast but was too pissed to care. My anger only grew when I saw all the cars gathered in front of the house. The sight of Cayson's truck adding fuel to the fire even though I'd been told I would find him there—find *Emberly* there.

Skidding to a stop, I yanked my keys out of the ignition and got out of my truck, slamming the door as I went. My steps hard and furious as I stormed up the familiar path to my childhood home, a hell of a lot different than how I'd gone walking up with my kids just two days before.

Crossing the wide porch, I yanked open the storm door and slammed my fist against the solid wood of the front door, calling out, "*Cayson*."

I waited for what felt like minutes but was maybe only a second, my body twitching and trembling with soul-darkening anger before I started reaching for the handle.

But the sound of laughter coming from the barn had me stalking off the porch and in that direction just as my brothers stepped through the large, open doors.

Hunter's expression shifted from surprise to his own form of aggression as soon as he noticed mine. Then he was hurrying to release the little girl in his arms and pushing her toward Madison.

But I wasn't there for them.

"Cayson," I snapped as I continued toward the group. "Where the hell is—" My hands curled into fists as the girl I really wanted to see came bouncing out of the barn, reaching for Cayson and coming to an abrupt stop when she saw me. "What the *fuck*, Emberly?"

My brothers started for me as the girls stayed behind, both wearing identical expressions that plainly said they were preparing to stop me.

"You need to go," Hunter said, voice all a low warning in a tone he knew he shouldn't use with me.

"I'm gonna kill her."

Cayson reared back at the words before launching at me. "Touch her, and I'll kill you."

My eyes rolled as I stopped directly beside them. Letting all that red in my world and poison in my veins consume me.

"Beau, one more step, and I'm letting him go," Hunter ground out, teeth clenched as he tried to hold Cayson back. "You need to leave."

I held out my arms to show I hadn't moved before tossing one in Emberly's direction because this was *Emberly* we were talking about. The girl could scrap with all four of us because she'd been raised with us—but I'd never hurt her in my life, and I wasn't about to start today.

But she'd still pushed too far.

Turning on her, I demanded, "The hell did I do to you?"

Her eyes darted around before landing on Cayson and Hunter, her lips parting as confusion marred her face.

"Emberly."

Her stare shot back to me, her shoulders bunching up. "I don't—I don't know what I did. I tried—I helped—I mean, I thought I helped."

"How the fuck is what you did helping me?" I shouted, causing Emberly to jerk back as Madison rushed Avalee toward the house.

"Enough," Cayson snapped as Hunter said, "That's it, you need to go."

"I haven't moved," I said, turning a cold glare in their direction.

Hunter gave a hard nod. "That can change fast."

"I'm in control," I said, voice low and filled with steel. "Keep him away from me, and it'll stay that way."

"Stop yelling at her," Cayson demanded from where he was now only being held back by a firm grip to his bicep.

I slanted my head. "I'm not promising that. Not after what she did."

"I don't know what I did other than try to help," Emberly cried out from where she stood a dozen feet away.

"Seriously, Beau, she did that for you," Cayson ground out. "For Savannah and you."

I waited.

Counted backward.

Let myself feel all that racing anger and aggression before I asked him, "You knew, and you didn't think to warn me?"

"There was nothing to warn you about," he said with an irritated huff.

I gestured to where Emberly stood but didn't take my eyes off him. "Stephanie Webb was waiting in my office almost completely naked this afternoon. Tell me how that wasn't something to warn me about."

Cayson's eyes widened and his stare shifted to Emberly just as she said, "Oh no."

"Yeah," I coughed out a bitter laugh. "I'm trying to fix my life, and you're doing whatever the fuck you can to make sure I fail in that."

Her head shook quickly. "No. No, I'm not."

"She was in my office *without her clothes on*, Emberly. One of my assistant coaches was with me when I opened my office door. Please tell me how this helps me with my wife right now."

I watched as her face fell before she could cover it with her hands. Her head continuing to move in faint shakes as if she didn't realize it was still moving.

But I just stood there, waiting for her to explain when it felt like the life I was already losing at a rapid pace had truly slipped through my grasp a couple hours before.

When I'd walked in on the vice principal waiting for me in my office . . . stunned wasn't a sufficient enough word. But it'd taken a second before I could move. Before I realized she was actually sitting on the edge of my desk in nothing but her underwear.

Hands resting behind her and chest pushed out to emphasize that she wasn't wearing a bra.

I'd staggered back and shut the door, but my assistant coach, Kevin, was already backing down the hall, head shaking and disappointment dripping from him as he'd said, "Not gettin' into this with you right now, Dixon," no matter how many times I'd tried to explain I didn't know what the hell we'd walked in on.

When I'd attempted to go into my office a few minutes later, she hadn't moved.

I'd stood in my doorway and yelled for her to get dressed and get out.

An hour later, I'd been called into a meeting with her, the principal, and a member of the school board for having inappropriate relations on school property during school hours.

"And considering one of you is married," the principal had said, looking at me with deep disappointment.

"Oh, you haven't heard he and Savannah are getting a divorce?" Stephanie had asked, eager to spill gossip.

"We are not," I'd said softly, voice promising wrath and showing hints of my pain and fear because this bullshit would be town news before I ever got to Savannah, and she already hated me.

The principal made a disapproving humming noise as she'd looked to the board member, letting him take over.

"Stephanie said you told her I'm in the middle of a divorce," I began when Emberly didn't offer anything.

Emberly's head shook wildly. "I didn't."

I put up a hand to stop her. "And because she's eagerly telling people that we've *been* having an affair, and I've been staying at her place, the school board wouldn't even hear my side. They just took her story as truth, and now we've been written up for having sex in my office even though I was never within ten feet of her when she had her clothes off. And if there is another 'occurrence,' we lose our jobs."

Emberly bent, her hands falling to her chest as my brothers hissed curses beside me.

"Which, I don't give a fuck about her. But *me?*" A weighted breath dragged from my chest. "A kid heard me yell at her to get dressed, and that's how it got back around to the principal. I work in a school, Emberly. We didn't just get written up for lewd acts in the workplace—it's also *in a school with kids present*. Do you know what that alone is gonna do to me?"

"Fuck, Beau," Hunter murmured.

"And all because you have to go and tell your goddamn customers that I'm getting a fucking divorce?" I yelled, never losing Emberly's glassy-eyed stare. "But, why not?" A sound that was full of my bitterness and pain left me as I stumbled back a step. "I'm already losing everything else, might as well finish destroying my life, yeah?"

"I didn't," she cried out. "I'm not. She came in to grab lunch—she did. I'd just gotten there, like, *just* walked in. I was still walking to the bar when she caught up to me. She said she'd been hoping to see me because she wanted to ask about my condo, but I told her it wasn't available right now. And she said, 'Oh, I know, I was just wondering if you could tell me why Beau Dixon's been staying there. Seems kinda weird when his wife and kids are in that big house.'"

She lifted her hands before letting them fall to her stomach. "I just looked at her. I didn't know what to say. But Stephanie said, 'I know that's his truck that's been parked out front late nights and early mornings. I saw him getting into it when I was headed into work the other day.' So, I just kinda shrugged and said my condo was always available to family before walking away. That's it. That was the entire conversation. I never said anything about what's been happening or even hinted at a divorce."

"Nothing," I said, voice hard. "Someone asks you about me? You say *nothing*."

"Okay." Her head bounced in a shaky nod. "Beau, I'm

sorry. What can I do? I'll go to someone and tell them she's lying."

"Don't you think you've done enough?"

"That isn't fair," Cayson said from beside me, but I was already turning.

Already heading back to my truck.

Every step felt harder than the last. My body heavier. As if I could feel the gossip and judgment from the town weighing me down because I knew what this would do to my marriage.

And I hadn't even had a part in this shit.

"Beau," Hunter called out when I was nearing my truck, voice close behind.

"Need you to leave me alone."

"Maybe you should just stay," he said. "You don't need to be out there making any decisions with all this shit going on in your head."

A sneering laugh bled from me. "Think you told me to leave about five times."

"Beau." He grabbed my door once I had it opened, positioning himself so I wouldn't be able to shut it. "This is messed up, I don't even know what to say about all this. But we can figure it out. We can figure out what to do."

"There's nothing to do," I ground out. "Don't you get that? I have to go tell Savannah and hope she hasn't already been told by a dozen other people. Hope there's some way she actually believes me when I already know she won't."

His brows pulled close together before he tugged at the bill of his baseball cap, a slow, heavy breath leaving him. "Stay. Wait until you're calm. Let us all think of some way to fix this."

My head shook because he wasn't understanding there wasn't a way to. "Move."

He started stepping away, then rocked back and settled against the door, hesitation pouring from him. "Every time you've shown up this past week, I've thought back to the day Dad's will was read," he said after a moment. "That was the last day we saw each other for nearly ten years. Now every time you leave, I can't help but wonder how many years it's gonna be until I see you the next time."

A grunt of understanding built in my chest. "Yeah, well . . ." I turned my keys over in my hand before reaching forward to put them in the ignition. "You and I are done forever, so I'll probably see you in a few days."

Hunter coughed out one of his rumbling laughs, nodding as he did. "All right." He pushed from the door but didn't move to leave. Instead, that hesitation grew and grew. "Beau, none of us want this for you or Savannah. All of us . . . we'll do anything to help y'all."

My stare fell to the side as that fear I'd been drowning under gripped my throat, making it hard to breathe. "We were already far past help. And now with this?" A miserable sound left me as I finally cranked the engine. My jaw strained as I reminded him, "I'm supposed to be moving out tonight."

He stood there for a moment before nodding. "Yeah. Well, I hope you don't. But if you need anything, we're all here for you. Just maybe don't go charging at any of the girls, saying you're gonna kill them."

A laugh scraped up my throat. "It's Emberly," I said, one of my shoulders lifting as if that explained it. As if that proved I wouldn't have touched her. The girl had been more like a little sister than anything.

"Yeah, and Savannah's always been like family for the rest of us," he said, easily showing the similarities between the two. "What if one of us did that to her?"

"I'd fucking destroy you," I promised softly, my stare searching for my other brother and Emberly, who must've gone inside.

"Exactly." He grabbed my door, his hand tapping the side of it for a second as he thought. "Good luck today, man. I know we talked the other day, but I'm so damn sorry for my part in this. I never wanted this, you have to know that."

"I do," I murmured, and I did.

If I put aside all my grief and anger, I did.

I would've done the exact same thing, if not worse. I'd just needed someone to blame for my world falling apart.

I grabbed the handle of the door and waited for him to step back before shutting it. But just as I was about to put my truck in gear, I stopped and rolled down the window.

Hunter lifted his chin in question from where he stood, waiting.

"There's something I said to Peter Rowe the other day, and it's something that's pissed me off for ten years."

Hunter's chest pitched with his amusement. "Think his brother's pissed you off for a lot longer than ten years."

"Yeah, not Philip," I mumbled, my eyes rolling. "Why didn't you come to mine and Savannah's wedding?"

For long seconds, Hunter just stared at me. When he finally spoke, his voice was a mixture of irritation and impatience. "Are you fucking kidding me?"

"I'm asking, asshole."

A harsh breath left him, his head shaking as he rocked back a step. "Man, why would I have come? You and I had nothing to do with each other before I left for the Army, and then the invitation came all torn up. It was kind of a clue you didn't want me there."

"The fuck?" I whispered, thinking back to that time.

When Hunter just gave me a look like he didn't want to play this game, I gestured to the house. "No. No, Savannah and I sat on the living room floor, putting all the invitations in envelopes before addressing them one night. We didn't do shit to yours."

"Piper brought it to me—" He stared off to the side before a grating laugh left him. "Piper brought it to me that way," he repeated as if that explained everything.

"Who the hell is Piper?"

"My ex," he stated dully. "She hated the idea of this place . . . apparently even just to visit for my brother's wedding." He lifted his hands in a way that said there was nothing he could do, but his expression dripped with remorse. "I didn't know."

"Why would you?"

It's like he'd said: We'd had nothing to do with each other, and that was all on me for pushing him away.

Putting my truck in gear, I glanced back at the house and shrugged. "I'd change it if I could."

"Yeah, I think we'd all change a lot of things if we could." He stepped closer, his voice barely above the rumble of my truck. "But there's no getting those years back. There's no changing what happened. And as much as I wanted to hate y'all for what happened, I can't. Because what if that had been me with someone else? What if it had been Savannah?"

A muscle twitched in my jaw before I roughed over it with my palm and forced the thought from my mind.

"None of us remembers that night, man, and Savannah knows that. She's just struggling with what followed." He rested his hand on my door, expression all worry mixed with encouragement. "Don't let tonight be something else you can't take back."

"She doesn't wanna talk. She doesn't want me there," I said, reminding him of everything we'd talked about the other morning.

He tapped his hand on the door a couple times before backing away. "She just hasn't given y'all a chance to work through it yet. She will."

I offered him a nod before reversing and starting the short drive to my place, wishing I had an ounce of the confidence Hunter had. But I didn't. I hadn't even before the bullshit with the school's vice principal happened.

Now that our kids were on their way to Utah with Savannah's parents, I was honestly terrified for what waited for me inside the walls of what had always been mine and Savannah's haven.

The word *divorce* had already been said so often, even by our daughter. I was afraid my wife was about to make it a reality.

Twenty-Eight

BEAU
TWENTY-TWO YEARS OLD

I sank deeper into the seat of my car and stared vacantly ahead at my parents' house . . . my mom's house, I guessed. The house I'd only moved out of a little over a month before. Just to have my world shatter beneath my feet.

Again.

I clenched my teeth tight against the fresh wave of pain and grief, letting my eyes close when the burning there became too much.

After finally getting everything we'd ever dreamed of, after walking into the plantation house through the front door with the keys in hand, Savannah and I had gotten right to work.

Planning out renovations and where to begin—*the kitchen, Beau. Clearly.* What our timeline would look like and how fast we thought we could get Blossom Bed and Breakfast officially up and running—*do we have to wait for renovations to be completed?* And—*oh! Let's throw a house-warming party!*

Crazy girl.

My *wife*.

I would've said yes to anything she'd asked for. Anything to keep that joy bursting from her. To keep that smile lighting up her face in a way I hadn't seen in so long. To continue walking into whatever room she was in to find her dancing again.

So, a week after we'd moved in, we had the party in the exact spot we'd had our wedding just two months before. Friends and family coming and going until the late hours of the night.

But I'd known . . . I *should've* known.

I'd felt it in the air. Ominous and thick and making me all kinds of anxious for terrible reasons.

I had held tight to Savannah, stare darting around, looking for the threat as I'd forced myself to remain calm. To breathe . . . and found my dad. Looking the same as always and somehow different.

In his stare. In the way he'd smiled or held his drink. I wasn't sure.

"You good, old man?" I'd asked after slipping away from Savannah.

He had offered me a beer as he reached for another, but I'd shaken my head.

"Great party." He'd sighed contentedly, smiling as he did, but something about it was off. Like he was baring his teeth, and yet, he wasn't.

But I could feel it the same as I'd just felt Savannah against my side. It was crawling over my skin and seeping into my blood. My fingers were flexing in a horrible attempt to keep them from curling into fists. That familiar darkness I'd tried outrunning my entire life.

"You good?" I'd repeated, voice lower, rougher.

He'd glanced at me, brows raising. "Oh, you know. That brother of yours." A tsk had left him as he'd shaken his head. "Can't stop getting himself into trouble. Just got back from bailing him out of county again."

"Cayson?"

"'Fraid it's bad this time," he'd said in way of confirming before sighing again. "Don't know what I'm gonna do with that kid."

EARLY THE NEXT MORNING, Savannah's parents had swung by again to let us know they were moving back to Utah. Mr. Riley had a great job opportunity waiting for him, and they wanted to help care for their parents who all had various health issues. They'd been planning the move for a while but had held off for our wedding and to not ruin our excitement over the plantation house.

Despite our early history with them, it'd come as an unwelcome shock to me, and Savannah had been devastated.

In the middle of trying to help them pack and comfort Savannah that evening, I'd gotten a call from my mom. Wondering if we'd seen or heard from Cayson because no one else had since our party. Dad had been grumbling in the background that Cayson was probably just hiding out because of what he'd done, but it wasn't long after that they'd realized he was *gone*.

Mom was a wreck. Dad? He just shut down. Wouldn't talk to anyone about Cayson or what was going on. And then a few nights later, Mom drove out to the orchard when Dad didn't come in or answer any of her calls.

He'd had a stroke and was already gone.

I lifted my phone from the cupholder of my Explorer and

hit the name I'd been repeatedly calling for weeks, my anger and resentment growing with each ring.

When Cayson's voicemail picked up, I wanted to yell at him as I had so many other times on his voicemail. I wanted to hit him even though I'd promised Savannah, and I hadn't taken a swing at anyone or anything in the months since that promise.

"Fuck you, Cayson," I breathed into the phone, my stare finding the house again. "Shoulda been you."

I got out of my car and slowly headed up to the house, wishing I was anywhere else. Wishing I was about to do anything else other than listen to my dad's will being read.

Sawyer was inside, near the front door and lingering by the stairs. Face pale and eyes shadowed with purple from sleepless nights. His head slowly turned to find me there on a delay. "I can't be here," he said sluggishly. "I gotta go."

"We have to be here," I reminded him.

"I can't—I can't." His head shook quickly. "I need to be with her. I don't have time for this," he shouted.

I grabbed the back of his neck and pulled him close, gripping him tight to me as his body wrenched with silent sobs. "Savannah went over to Leighton's when I came here," I said softly. "She's gonna sit with her until you can go back over there. All right?"

His head shook against my chest. "What am I gonna do? I can't—I can't lose her. I have to fix this. How do I fix her?" he cried, the words weak.

The muscles in my jaw strained as I tried to hold it together for him.

As I tried to be there for him when we all knew there was nothing to be done.

The day of Dad's funeral, Sawyer had gone to find out why his lifelong girlfriend hadn't been there. Why she hadn't really been anywhere lately. And had been slammed in the face with what she'd been keeping from everyone behind that crazy mass of hair, a shit ton of clothes, and perfectly crafted lies.

She'd been starving herself for longer than any of us knew, and she was long past the point of saving even though Sawyer was trying so damn hard to do just that. Her organs had already started failing. Each day, she slept longer. Each day, she became weaker.

Watching Leighton die was destroying Sawyer—was wrecking all of us more than we already had been. Watching my youngest brother bear this weight, as if it were all his fault, was tearing me up inside because there was no convincing him otherwise.

I glanced up at the sound of someone coming down the stairs and went still at the sight of Hunter as I had every time I'd seen him in the past weeks.

Expression carefully blank, but there were a hell of a lot of questions and frustrations lingering behind his narrowed stare.

As if he might know something.

As if, during his time in the Army, he'd started hating me the way I'd always expected him to. *Needed* him to.

Except I'd washed my hands of the shit that happened with Madison. I'd needed to in order to move on with my life with Savannah. Looking at Hunter's accusatory stare had that guilt and fear clawing at my chest and ice freezing up my veins all over again.

Had me restless.

Had me worried about what I might do, and I couldn't

afford that type of worry. My life and my marriage were at stake.

Once Hunter had passed us and was headed for the dining room, I released Sawyer and directed him to follow. "I'll get Mom."

He didn't respond, just started walking away, looking haunted and like he might collapse at any moment.

With a heavy sigh, I turned for the kitchen, eyes widening as I took in the endless pots and pans and containers of food.

"Mom," I rumbled as my stare darted over everything to where she was frantically putting containers in a bag. "Mom, you need to stop cooking."

"I have to feed Leighton." She pressed a hand to her chest. "That girl—that poor girl. What are we gonna do if she —" A strangled cry worked past her tightly pressed lips before she hurriedly started filling the bag again.

I grabbed the next container from her, setting it out of her reach. "Mom, you need to slow down. You need to rest." Wasn't sure how she was standing, let alone cooking enough to feed all of Amber. She looked worse off than Sawyer.

"I have to get out of here," she said, words strained. "I can't be—this house." She waved her hands around as tears steadily fell. "I don't wanna be here!"

"Okay, I'll get you out of here."

"He isn't here," she continued on as if I hadn't spoken. "You aren't here. And Cay—" Her jaw trembled violently before her head joined in. After a while, she looked at me, eyes endlessly sad. "Where did I go wrong?"

"What?"

"With Cayson. Where did I go wrong?"

"He's being a selfish asshole, Mom. That isn't on you."

A look passed across her face before it was gone. But I

saw enough to know she thought I was wrong . . . that there was something she wasn't telling me.

"Mom—"

"I can't be here anymore," she said, each word emphasized with her hands trying to encompass the house.

The property.

"Okay," I mumbled. "Want me to tell the lawyer we need to meet somewhere else?"

A trembling breath burst from her as if she'd forgotten all about the will reading. After a few moments, she loosed a pained sigh and left her spot at the counter. Shoulders sagging and body seeming to curve in on itself a little more with each step.

"Let's get this over with and then I'll get you out of here, yeah?"

She nodded weakly as she grabbed my arm, clinging to me like she needed me to keep her standing.

Once we were in the dining room, I sat her in a chair at the head of the table and took a seat beside her. Sparing a quick look at Sawyer's wraithlike expression and Hunter's hardened stare before nodding at the lawyer.

"Let's make this quick," I murmured as I folded my arms over my chest.

A near-silent snort left Hunter. "Have somewhere more important to be?"

"Do you?" I shot back. "Oh, that's right. Sorry, man, I forgot. Anything less than *death* isn't important enough for you."

"The fuck are you talking about?" he ground out, directing all that anger on me before Sawyer snapped, "Shut up!"

Sawyer's chest rose and fell, the movements so big that it

seemed to move his entire body. "The sooner we get this done, the sooner I get back to Leighton."

"This is our dad—"

"I know," Sawyer yelled, cutting Hunter off. "But right now, I'm grieving two people, and one of them is still alive. So, can y'all please shut the fuck up so we can finish this?"

I lifted my hand enough to let the lawyer know he could begin before folding my hand over my chest again.

He cleared his throat as he tapped a large envelope on the table, making sure he met each of us in the eye. "Again, I'm sorry for the loss you've endured, and I'm sorry we're meeting under these circumstances. Not my favorite part of the job." With another tap of the envelope, he opened it up and said, "Thankfully, this won't take long."

Good.

I wasn't sure Sawyer would be able to make it through without losing his mind.

I wasn't sure how long Hunter and I could stay near each other without snapping again.

And Mom . . . she didn't need to be going through that shit.

I listened as the lawyer read off a short note to Mom, apologizing if she was there, for leaving her first. Mom absolutely lost it, but the man continued, reading off that all money and physical possessions were to be left to Mom before turning to us. "To my three sons: Beau, Hunter—"

"Four," Hunter said just as I realized the slip.

The lawyer glanced uncomfortably between the three of us and repeated, "To my three sons: Beau, Hunter, and Sawyer, I leave—"

"The fuck," I muttered as I glanced at Mom in question. Her cries had immediately silenced at the unexpected words, and she was staring straight ahead, looking floored. As if she couldn't understand them either.

A rasping laugh left me as I realized what Dad had done in those days of silence before his death. "Damn, Dad didn't waste any time cutting Cayson out after he skipped town."

"Uh, no," the lawyer said before clearing his throat again and shifting in his seat, still uncomfortable with where this was going. "Your father actually hadn't changed his will since Sawyer here became a teenager."

"What does that mean?" Sawyer asked.

"That Dad hadn't changed anything in over five years," Hunter said just as numbly.

"What does it mean about *Cayson*, idiot," I bit out.

He sent me a cold glare before looking to Mom. The same question in his eyes that had just been swirling through me. "Mom?"

When I looked her way, she was staring at the table. Looking like she was one more piece of news away from going into shock.

Leaning toward her, I said, "We can finish this. You should go rest."

She didn't leave or respond in any way, just continued staring at the table.

I leaned back in my chair and released a sigh when Sawyer asked, "Why would Dad do that?"

"Because he knew something," I answered, remembering the look on Mom's face in the kitchen.

"Like what?"

I glanced Hunter's way at his question before shrugging. "I dunno."

"Then maybe it's a mistake," Sawyer said, tone a mixture of hope and uncertainty.

Hunter and I tried to suppress identical, bitter laughs as the lawyer waved a finger through the air. "No mistakes here. Would you like me to continue?"

"Please," I responded even though continuing felt like walking into an even bigger disaster than we were already in.

Hunter leaned back in his chair as the lawyer went on about leaving it up to us to take care of our family and the town the way Dad had done, and jokingly whispered, "I bet Cays was in a gang."

I rolled my eyes. "Any gang out of Amber would be a joke."

"Stealing goats and shit," he murmured.

The corner of my mouth ticked up. "Idiot."

"As for the matter of the land—including everything on it: The house and barn, any remaining farm animals, the orchard, and the business 'Dixon Farms,'" the lawyer continued, "I leave it all to the son who has always cared about them."

Sawyer and I looked at each other, confusion clouding both our expressions, but Hunter stared straight ahead, eyes wide.

"I can't," I said when no one else spoke, a harsh laugh tumbling free. I lifted my hands in the air. "I fucking can't. Savannah and I *just* moved into the plantation house, and I'm already drowning under everything we have to do to it. Not to mention, I start coaching at the high school next week."

"I'll take it," Sawyer said with a heavy-burdened shrug.

"The fuck you will," I snapped.

"Absolutely not," Mom said, finally speaking again.

"And give up your life?" Hunter bit out. "Your full ride and your career in the NFL that's just waiting for you? No, *I'm* taking it."

"You don't live here," I reminded him.

His cold glare cut back to me. "I'm taking it."

"All that shit he just laid out," I said through gritted teeth, "needs to be taken care of from someone *here*. Again, that can't be you."

"All right." Hunter's head bobbed quickly. "Then let's give it to Cayson—oh, wait." He sat back in his chair, jaw working with his irritation. "I'm taking it."

Silence crept through the dining room for a few moments, thick and ready to explode before the lawyer said, "Okay then, and you are . . . Hunter, correct?"

Hunter gave a jerk of his chin but didn't say anything more.

"Then I have some paperwork for you that I'll get from my car, but that's it for the will." He stood, gathering everything in the envelope and offering us sympathetic smiles as we stood with him. "Thank you for your time. I am truly, very sorry for your loss." With a glance at Hunter, he said, "I'll be back."

I watched until he was out of the dining room before turning on Hunter. "So, what, you're just moving back then?"

"Didn't hear you offer to take it, and someone has to."

"And if I had?" I challenged even though there was no way in hell I could handle the ranch on top of everything else.

His stare drifted to the side and remained there when he said, "The ranch is mine."

"What about the Army?" I said tightly. "What about Kansas and your fucking fiancée who handles all the shit that's apparently not worth your time? Don't you think you should run this past her?"

His stare had snapped back to me, a crease forming between his brows. "What are you talking about?"

A huff escaped me as I started to leave. "Whatever."

He grabbed my shoulder, turning me back around without a care as to what I might do. "The hell is your problem?"

"My problem's that my life is a hell of a lot easier without you in it."

Hurt tore across his face before he masked it. "I've noticed," he muttered. After a moment, he shrugged. "Then I'm not in it."

"Boys," Mom said, voice weighed down with exhaustion and emotion.

"Lost almost everyone else in my life, might as well keep it going," he said bitterly. "Sawyer, you up next?"

"Leave him alone," I ground out.

Confusion and anger flared in Hunter's eyes as he stepped closer, but I kept my fisted hands down at my sides. Forced myself to breathe through the darkness creeping in. Thought about the feel of Savannah in my arms instead of the sick need coating my veins.

"I used to be your best friend. But you've pushed me away for years, then you stand up for *Saw*?" he asked, voice soft. "Fuck you, man. You wanna be done? We're done."

A vicious smirk tugged at my mouth as I forced myself to take a step away. "Enjoy *your* ranch." Turning, I reached for Mom. "Come on, I'll get you out of here."

"She doesn't have to go," Hunter snapped from behind me. When I ignored him, he jerked my arm back from helping Mom up. "Don't be an asshole."

I snatched it from his grasp.

Body twisting.

Fingers clenched tight and muscles tensed in anticipation.

Chest heaving as I stared at him, arm slightly cocked back before I'd managed to lock it all down.

Fuck.

Fuck, fuck, fuck.

I forced each painful breath in and out until my trembling hand was at my side. Until I was turning away from him before I could do something I'd regret for the rest of my life.

"Beau—"

"She doesn't wanna be here," I ground out. "I told her I'd get her out, I'm doing that."

Hunter ignored me, leaning around me to reach for her. "Mom, I don't care what the will said, this is still your home."

I slowly looked over at him, voice low. Lethal. "Was that ever in question?"

He exhaled heavily, nostrils flaring as he met my stare. But before he could say anything else, I led our mom out of the dining room just as the lawyer was coming back in.

"Is there anything you need before we go?" I asked her, watching as Sawyer bolted past us, heading for the kitchen.

"Make sure Sawyer gets the food for Leighton," was all she said as she turned for the front door.

I didn't answer, mostly because I was sure that's what he was doing. I just waited until he came running back out with the bag Mom had been filling up earlier and stopped him with a hand to his shoulder. Searching his eyes that were at once haunted and exhausted as his body jerked anxiously.

"I'm driving you."

"I'm good," he said dismissively.

"You're not."

"I am, and you're keeping me here when I need to be there. So, let me go."

"Saw—"

"Let me the fuck go. I need to get to Leighton."

I let out a slow breath, nodding as I did. Squeezing his shoulder, I mumbled, "Get some rest soon, yeah?"

He made a noncommittal grunt, running past me and out the door as soon as I released him.

I followed after, grabbing my mom's purse as I went. Refusing to look in the direction I could feel Hunter's icy glare coming from. Refusing to take one last look at the house I was afraid I'd never see again.

Once Mom and I were in my car and headed to the plantation house, she eased out a strangled sigh and said, "I don't want to be there."

"I know, Mom."

"I *can't* be there." Her head moved in a mess of shakes and nods. "Hunter can have it. Anyone can have it. I don't want it."

"Mom—"

"I don't," she cried out. After a few seconds, she continued. Voice calmer . . . softer. "It's too big. Too painful."

"What about Sawyer?"

She stared out the window for a while before saying, "I'm not sure he wants to be there anymore either."

"All right." I cleared my throat. "I'll talk to him. We'll figure something out for y'all."

"Thank you," she whispered. "Now, please go make things right with your brother."

I stared at the road, memories flashing. Racing. Threatening to pull me under and destroy what was so perfect in my world.

"Yeah, we'll see," I mumbled, the lie falling from me like poison.

THE PAST FEW weeks played in my mind on repeat as I tore up the old kitchen floor a while later. Movements jerky and agitated as I battled the emotions tied to each hit to my family.

Savannah's parents leaving.

Cayson disappearing.

Dad dying.

Hunter returning.

Leighton wasting away before us.

My family fracturing and falling apart from it all. And there was no fixing it.

Weeks . . . that was all it took for everything to shatter beneath me.

"Beau?"

My head snapped up at my name. My chest wrenched at the pain twisting that voice—*her* voice.

I dropped the scraper and pushed to my feet, already running out of the kitchen before the front door ever shut. Finding Savannah rushing through the entryway and grabbing her up in my arms just as she broke.

Her body jerking with a sob as she curled into me, her voice soft and small as she rambled, "Oh God, oh my God, how is this happening? Beau, she's dying—Leighton's dying."

I stepped back until I hit a wall, then slid down to the floor while keeping her in my arms. "I know," I said, voice tight as I lowered my head to hers.

"She's so tiny, Beau. How did she hide that from everyone? And her parents just don't care or don't get it. Her mom opened the door and told me to keep it down while I was there since they were being forced to work from home now. I wanted to scream at her that, for once, their daughter needed to be more important."

"They've always been assholes," I reminded her gently.

"If they would just look at her, they would see how everything about her is so weak and fragile. She even—" Savannah's head shook against my neck. "She fell asleep in the middle of a sentence," she whispered as if it had terrified her.

I ran one of my hands up and down her shuddering back, trying so damn hard to be strong for my wife when the girl we were talking about had been a constant in my family's lives since she and Sawyer were in preschool.

But there was nothing to say. We had all missed it because Leighton had wanted it that way, had *manipulated* it that way, and now we were too late. And my brother was putting that blame on himself.

"Did Sawyer get there?"

"Yeah," Savannah said through shaky breaths. "He had a huge bag of food, and he looked—God, he looked so confident that today would be the day she kept something down. He's so sure he can reverse what's already been done. It's breaking my heart."

"I know." I passed a kiss across her forehead before letting my head fall back against the wall as I continued that battle. As those flashes came faster and faster.

"I feel so heavy," she mumbled a few minutes later. "My body, my heart . . . everything feels so heavy lately. How are we supposed to get through all this?"

"Together," I said without hesitation.

Her fingers brushed against my cheek, and I turned my head to press my lips to them before climbing to my feet with her secured in my arms.

She didn't protest or reveal her surprise. Just burrowed her head deeper against my neck as I started through the entryway and climbed the stairs, letting me carry her to our bathroom.

Setting her on the edge of the counter, I removed my arms from her slowly. Lingering. Holding and touching her to remind her that I had her. That I was still there.

That I wasn't going anywhere.

"Stay," I mumbled before pulling away and walking over to the tub. Turning on the water and waiting for it to warm up before putting down the stopper to let it fill.

An exhausted hum of appreciation sounded in her throat when I made it back to her, her golden eyes slipping shut as I stepped between her legs to hold her close.

"We'll get through this together," I repeated, lifting my hand to trail my knuckles down her jaw. "Just like we have everything else."

"Okay," she said softly, the corners of her mouth lifting.

Pressing a slow, lingering kiss there, I lifted the shirt off her body and let it fall to the floor before unclasping her bra and helping her off the counter. When I reached for her shorts, she grabbed the bottom of my shirt, but I stopped her.

"This is for you," I explained when her stare met mine, all questions and need and pain.

"Will you stay?" she asked quickly. Eyes searching, pleading.

"Of course."

Once the rest of her clothes were on the floor, I led her into the tub and watched as she slowly sank into the water. Each movement somehow graceful and sensual without her even trying.

Kneeling beside the tub when she rested her arm on the

edge of it to look at me, I dipped my hand into the water to pour it over her arm and shoulder and breasts.

Another one of those appreciative hums sounded, her eyelids fluttering shut. "How did it go with your family?"

My hand paused just above the water before I cupped another handful. "My mom's asleep in one of the guestrooms," I said instead. When Savannah opened her eyes wide with surprise, I explained, "She said she couldn't be there anymore. Too big, too painful. Said a few times on the way here and after we got here that she doesn't wanna live there at all. That she thought it would be best for her and Sawyer if they got out of there." I nodded, swallowing thickly as I tried to block out the image of my mom when I'd found her in the kitchen. "She might change her mind later. She needs to rest. Grieve. She went right into caring for Leighton —same as Sawyer. They're both gonna break if they don't slow down soon."

Savannah nodded as she rested her head on her arm. "And if she decides to move out? What happens to the house?"

I focused on the water pouring out of my hand and over her skin for a moment before saying, "Hunter took it."

"Took . . . what do you mean he took it?"

I heaved a sigh as I leaned forward to turn off the water, then sat back and held her stare. "Dad left the house—every-thing—to one of his sons. Well, Me, Hunter, or Sawyer, because Cayson wasn't listed as one of his sons, and that slight had nothing to do with him leaving."

Savannah's mouth parted in shock, but sadness etched deep within her eyes. "Oh, Beau . . ."

"Whatever, he's brought it on himself."

"Beau," she whispered, her hand reaching out to touch my free one at the pain in my voice.

I was pretty fucking sure I hated my brother.

His leaving after our party started a domino effect that was the cause of my world shattering. I was also pretty damn sure my dad would still be alive if Cayson hadn't left.

But for Dad to have cut him out of his will over five years ago? I wasn't even sure Cayson had gotten his first arrest five years ago, and even those had all been bullshit. If anyone deserved to be cut out, we all knew it was me for what I'd done and put my parents through.

As much as I hated Cayson, as much as I never wanted to see him again for what he'd done to our family, I'd felt bad for him during that reading.

With another weighted exhale, I told Savannah about the rest of the will reading. How everything had blown up between us when the orchard had been up for grabs and how we'd left it, then circled back around to how I'd found Sawyer and my mom when I'd first walked in.

"Maybe they *should* get out of there and let Hunter have it," I said as I watched the water run from between my fingers and over her skin. "Might be too many memories for them to heal the way they need to."

"How are you?" Savannah asked suddenly.

"I'm fine," I responded immediately, stare darting to hers at the unexpected question. "I just wanna take care of you. Help you. And I need to find a way to help my mom and Sawyer before they break from all this, but I'm struggling to figure out how."

"Because you need someone to take care of you too."

I gave her an amused look, the corner of my mouth ticking up. "I'm fine."

"You can't take all this on by yourself, and no one expects you to. Together, right?"

"You and me," I clarified. "My family needs me."

"It goes for them too. Everyone will get through it together. But we all need you to grieve too. *I* need you to let things out. Slowly. Carefully. Otherwise?" Her words hinted at everything she wasn't saying.

I would explode.

Her eyes danced when she reached forward to grip my shirt and pull me closer. "Let me help you with that."

I brushed my mouth across hers. "It's my job to help *you*."

"Together," she reminded me, lips capturing mine as she continued pulling me closer and closer.

A grin tugged at my mouth. "What're you doing, angel?"

"Trying to pull your giant self in."

A rumble of a laugh built in my chest. "Told you, this is for you."

"Okay," she said seriously, only moving back far enough to press her forehead to mine, her grip on my shirt never loosening. "I need my husband to get in this tub and start letting go of some of the pain and anger he's keeping inside."

I opened my eyes to find her studying me, silently begging me. My head subtly moved against hers. "You gonna let me take my shirt off?"

She tugged harder, bringing me closer to the tub, in response.

I reached for the button on my pants, and she quickly shook her head. "No. Get in."

"Savannah—"

"Right now."

I slipped my wallet out of my pocket as I captured her mouth, using the distraction to take off my Converse and socks before she could make another move.

"That's cheating!" she said with a shocked gasp, looking

all kinds of offended as she hauled me closer. Succeeding in pulling me over the tub and nearly getting me inside, but I hurried to grab the sides so I wouldn't fall on her.

Staring at her as I held myself above the water—above *her* —in my shirt and jeans.

"This is what I need," she said resolutely. "This is what you need."

"You're going to pay for this in so many ways," I promised, the rough words raking up my throat.

Heat flared in her eyes and a blush crept up her cheeks as she sank deeper into the water.

I slowly lowered myself in, a gravelly laugh breaking free at the uncomfortable feel of it all. Once I was in, I grabbed my wife and situated us so she was stretched out above me, water sloshing over the tub and onto the tiled floor as we moved. But then I had her in my arms, all bare skin and deep breaths and contended sighs, and I wasn't sure a moment could get much better than that.

"Better?"

Her eyelids shut as she burrowed deeper into my chest. "Mmhm." Placing a hand against my soaked shirt, she said, "Now, tell me how you're really doing."

"Perfect."

She tapped my chest. "Here."

I leaned my head back against the lip of the tub and let my eyes close too as a heavy sigh left me. All my pain freely bleeding as I let myself *feel*. "I'm fucking wrecked."

Twenty-Nine

SAVANNAH

I glanced around the side of the bedroom I was facing, my heavy eyelids blinking slowly as I tried to orient myself when the room was darker than it had been when I'd lain down.

I wasn't even sure when I'd fallen asleep, only that I felt different. Better. All that heavy pain I'd been struggling under no longer seemed to be bearing down on me and filling me. The hurt and their betrayal all lingered in ways that felt manageable for the first time.

The day had left me mentally and emotionally lighter than I'd been in weeks. Yet, somehow, I was still exhausted.

And starving.

Emberly really was a genius.

I sat up, hand searching for my phone and curling around it when I found it near me on the bed. My heart dropping to my stomach when my stare skipped right past the time to the dozens of messages and calls I'd missed.

The previews showing more than enough.

. . .

I JUST CAN'T BELIEVE it . . .
   Who would've ever thought . . .
   How could he think he'd . . .
   I hope you kick his ass to . . .

AS MUCH AS those texts made my stomach clench, I knew they were unavoidable. That *this* was unavoidable. Truthfully, I couldn't believe we'd managed over three weeks in a place where private business was town gossip the instant it happened.

A weighted sigh fell from my lips as I ignored the countless messages to text my mom. My finger paused over the screen when I pulled up her messages, my chest warming and a soft laugh tumbling free when I saw the picture she'd sent not long before of the older kids eating massive bowls of ice cream as Levi tried to snag Wyatt's spoon.

ME: Oh my God, I love it! Hope y'all are having fun. Give my kids big hugs and kisses for me. I'll FaceTime them in the morning.

SETTING my phone face down on the nightstand, I stood and started through the house that somehow felt so big and so empty now that I was really alone—without kids coming back after a few hours at school or a husband coming back after work.

And who knew when he *would*.

He'd said he was moving out that night, but that was before he knew the kids were leaving with my parents. We also hadn't talked about what this week would look like for us with the kids being gone.

But I'd still expected him to show.

Or maybe *hoped* he would while desperately needing him to stay away from me. I wasn't sure. I'd been a mess.

But my world had fallen apart, and I'd vainly tried to keep it from my kids. To have small breakdowns in the moments the older two were at school or they were all asleep. Then to realize another was on the way? Something that should've been celebrated but instead needed to be kept hidden during the most damaging time of my life. Add on a completely booked bed and breakfast just as I let Beau back into our lives, and it was no wonder I'd been such a disaster.

My steps slowed as I neared the bottom of the stairs when I realized the house looked the way it always did at this time of evening—just as the sun was going past the horizon. The lights in the house were on even though the thick-slatted blinds were still open to let in every last bit of natural light.

Except I'd gone upstairs hours before, and the lights had all been off.

And the music had still been playing . . .

I forced myself to walk slowly toward the kitchen when my soul wanted to run and my heart wanted to guard itself against the man waiting somewhere in that house.

But when I stepped through the archway, Beau wasn't there.

My eyes swept the kitchen as I continued through it, falling on his keys and urging my feet faster until I came to an abrupt stop just as I started rounding the corner into the great room.

Soul reaching out faster than my heart could build up walls when I saw him lying in the spot we used to occupy when we were still creating our dreams, long before we ever owned the house. Arms folded tightly over his chest and looking so tense, even in sleep.

My stare pulled to the side when his phone vibrated on the hardwood floor, his screen lighting up with one of his assistant coach's names.

I hurried across the floor, trying to keep my steps silent, and bent to scoop up the phone before tiptoeing back to my spot where the great room bled into the kitchen as I answered, "Hey, Kevin."

Silence filled the call for a moment before he hesitantly asked, "Who is this?"

My brows pulled tightly together as I glanced at the screen of the phone to make sure I'd seen the correct name. "Savannah," I said slowly. "I've known you since I taught your daughters' dance classes."

"Right, of course," he mumbled, clearing his throat.

"Beau fell asleep," I said when he didn't go on, feeling awkward and embarrassed, and not sure why. "But I'll give him a message for you."

"No," he said quickly. "It can wait 'til I see him tomorrow. You have a good night now."

"You su—" I lowered the phone when the background noise of the call abruptly disappeared, trying to figure out what happened and why he'd been acting so strange.

As soon as I started my silent walk back to Beau, I looked up to find those midnight eyes open and locked on me.

"Hi," I said lamely, the word nothing more than a breath. "Your phone was ringing—it was Kevin."

He lifted his chin in acknowledgment, his voice all gravel when he asked, "What'd he say?"

"Nothing. Well, I'm not sure . . . it was weird. He said it could wait until tomorrow."

Beau sat up and dragged a hand through his hair and then roughed a palm over his jaw before resting his forearms on his knees. Every movement slow and very clearly a tell that he was gathering his strength.

"We need to talk," he finally said.

My head nodded, these fast, faint movements. "I know."

His stare lifted to meet mine and his head shifted. The movement was so subtle, but it shouted that I was wrong in that way of his. Everything so big and commanding with the smallest of movements.

"We need to talk," he repeated as he pushed to his feet. "Where do you wanna be?"

Nowhere.

With the way he was looking at me and preparing himself, I had a horrible feeling that my world was about to be ripped apart again. And I'd just managed to get to a point where I felt ready to work through what I already knew. I wasn't sure I could handle something else on top of it all.

"Savannah," he urged gently.

"I don't, um . . ." I shook my head fiercely and forced myself to straighten. To stand tall and strong for at least a little while.

Or at least pretend.

I could go back to my imploded world later.

Turning, I headed for the large kitchen table and sat in my favorite chair, letting those walls build faster and faster as I struggled to hide every pain and fear behind them.

Beau stopped behind one of the chairs, hand on the back of it, and hesitated before pulling it out. "Do you want coffee or anything?"

"No, I'd rather you just say whatever you're clearly afraid to tell me."

He sank into the chair, his breath coming out in a giant rush as he folded his arms only to unfold them. Dragging his hands over his legs and clasping them together as he leaned forward.

Everything so telling and so contradictory.

The way he was working his jaw and the panic in his eyes. His restless movements. It was all anger and fear clashing together, and it had a pit of unease opening up in my stomach as I waited for what I would find out next.

"It's going around town that I'm cheating on you," he said after a moment, something like wrath flashing through his terror. *"Currently."*

"With Madison?" I asked through clenched teeth, unable to relax my body as I waited for the shoe to drop.

He gave another slant of his head. "Stephanie Webb."

It felt like I shut down after that.

I heard Beau explain what happened that afternoon with him, Stephanie, and Kevin, and how it escalated with the school. I heard him describe the scene at Hunter's, and Emberly's side of the story. The nonstop calls and texts he'd been getting. I even vaguely registered it was the cause of all the messages waiting for me when I woke up. But I just couldn't connect to him or what he was saying or anything really because I felt numb.

If it was a delayed reaction to Emberly's no-moving exercise, I didn't appreciate it. If it was a result of my world imploding, I hated it. Or maybe it was just that I really *couldn't* handle any more.

"Savannah." Beau's voice twisted around my name when I

stood and began walking away, but I just held up a hand, needing to get away from there.

To think.

Breathe.

"I need a minute."

I wandered through the house, feeling as if I didn't know where I was going and like I didn't want to be there. Like I needed to get away. But leaving the house when that kind of gossip was spreading through town would only fuel it.

When Beau found me a while later, I was in our bathroom, curled up in the dry tub, still wearing nothing more than his shirt. It hadn't occurred to me until right then that I probably should've put something else on.

And the thought of covering up in front of him at all tore at my chest because I'd never felt exposed in front of Beau before then.

He stopped at the end of our long vanity and leaned up against it so he was facing me. Arms folded loosely over his chest and long legs stretched out in front of him. A picture so familiar that it made me ache.

We'd had so many conversations there, just like that, after a long day once the kids were asleep.

Me, soaking in the tub. Him, sitting beside it or leaning against the counter. Making my heart race and looking like my version of a dream even still, all these years later.

All that unyielding passion hidden behind clenched fists and intense looks. The rough laughs, rare smiles, and flashing dimples that were reserved for me. All wrapped up in the deepest blue eyes and jet-black hair and a toned body that promised comfort and security and threatened the cruelest revenges.

But this was different.

The silence that had followed Beau into the bathroom was filled with pain and regret and unknowns. The unstable connection between us was something we'd never encountered before. From the raw fear in his eyes, he was afraid of making the wrong move.

"Are you?" I finally asked a couple minutes after he joined me. When a crease formed between his brows, I clarified, "Having an affair with Stephanie—"

"Is that a joke?" he asked, words soft and filled with offense. "Savannah, you're my goddamn world. No, I'm not cheating on you."

"Have you?"

"No." His head listed and his jaw strained as if realizing he'd answered too soon. "Other than that one night with Madison—which I can barely remember—no."

I twisted in the tub to better face him, mind racing as I thought back to what Hunter had told me and tried to put it with what Beau was saying. "So, you *did* know it was Madison that night."

"No," he said firmly. "I remember tripping onto the bed *you were in*. I remember struggling to even get to a point where *you and I* were doing anything because we were that wasted. I remember repeatedly blacking out before my body basically gave the fuck out. Then *you* said you were gonna be sick." He gestured off to the side. "The next morning, that was what I remembered: *You* had gotten sick. The only way I figured out it was Madison and not you was because you'd apparently been downstairs the entire night while Madison was upstairs, and she'd been convinced Hunter had come to bed when he hadn't."

My head dipped slowly as his story painted the missing side of Madison's.

And it made my stomach lurch as it filled my head with images of them all over again.

"Even if there'd never been you," he began softly, "I would've never done that to my brother. But you? Fuck, Savannah, I was dying after that. It ruined us."

My stare snapped to his, confusion swirling through me as I pushed past the images clawing at my mind in an attempt to understand what he was saying. "What do you mean?"

"The months after. When you thought I didn't want you, or something."

My eyes widened with surprise and shock. "What?"

"The night of their graduation," he explained, watching me like he was waiting for me to remember. "There was a party at my parents' house. I was up in my room, and you came to find me. You said I'd been different. You thought you weren't my world anymore—thought I didn't want *you*. That I only wanted you to continue taking away my anger."

I blinked slowly as I struggled to remember what he was talking about, a whisper of a memory coming to the surface. "I don't . . ." My head shook. "I don't remember that. I mean, I sort of do. I remember that conversation now that you say it, but at the same time, I don't."

Beau gave me a look like he couldn't figure out how I didn't remember. "I'd been crumpling under what happened that night with Madison, and you knew it even though you didn't know why. I thought—Jesus, Savannah, I thought I was gonna lose you that night, and I just knew I couldn't keep going on like that. I'd gone downstairs to get us something to eat, and Madison was right there. Alone. So, I pulled her into a room and told her that I was gonna tell you what happened."

"And that's when she said she'd leave," I whispered in understanding.

"It's one of the biggest mistakes of my life," he said in agreement nearly a minute later, words soft and full of shame. "I knew it was a mistake when I got back up to the room and saw you." His stare fell to the floor, his head shaking subtly. "When I woke up the next morning, I knew I needed to call her and stop her from leaving. And that's when my mom came charging in."

I sucked in a quick gasp and murmured, "Oh, I do remember that."

"She didn't leave my side the entire morning, making me clean up the house for having you in my room. I missed Madison coming and talking to Hunter, and when I got to my phone, she'd already disconnected that number. But, Savannah, I tried to get her back. For you, for Hunter . . . I *tried*."

My eyes rolled. "Beau, she just came back, so I remember exactly how pissed off you were when she did. I remember how rude you were to her."

"Because she came back *now*," he said roughly. "Thirteen years later, when just her being here threatened us." He gestured to the space between us as if to prove his fears had already become a reality. "But when she first left and reached out to you, I was the one who kept suggesting you should tell Hunter where she was. I was the one who helped him get out there when he ran out of money because I was sure he could bring her back. And when he didn't, I had to go through the terrifying process of getting her new number out of your phone while you were asleep in my arms. But when I called the next day, she'd already disconnected that number too. I still called her every month for two years like she might suddenly answer one day. I tried to bring her back for you," he ground out. "I tried to get all this shit off my chest for so goddamn long."

Memories swirled and clashed with what he was telling me and what I'd learned these past weeks and months.

I didn't remember Beau's part in it, but I didn't doubt it.

Beau had never left my side during that time. Beau had never left my side *ever*.

I watched as he struggled to rein it all in. As his body trembled and a half-dozen emotions ripped across his face.

Even though he seemed to be surrounded in his fear, his shoulders were more at ease than they'd been before. As if finally saying the words had lifted a thirteen-year-old weight.

"Why two years?" I asked, caught on those last few sentences. "Not that I knew you were calling her, but what made you stop after two years?"

"You," he said immediately. "I was still destroying us, just slower than before, and I knew it was because there was so much I was keeping from you. Because I was the reason you'd been a shell of yourself for years." One of his shoulders lifted. "The day you told me I had to stop fighting, I called her and got the same automated message. But I knew if I didn't let go of it all, I was gonna keep dragging us down, so I texted her even though I knew she wouldn't get it. Told her how I was ruining us and that I hated her for leaving and what her leaving did to me. That we should've told y'all back then because there was no way to tell you when years had already passed. That I hoped she never came back." His stare found mine. "But then when I woke up that night in the back and found you asleep beside me, I did tell you. I told you everything because I needed to say it once, even if you didn't hear it."

Oh.

I wondered what would've happened if I'd woken to his confession that night. If we would be here now, married. Or if we'd be living different lives, separate and miserable.

And I realized at the thought that I believed him. Every word.

I'd always known since I was a little girl that Beau would give me the truth, no matter what. And even knowing the secrets and deception he'd kept for so long, I could hear the honesty in his painful admission.

"I've been wondering what else I didn't know—what else you've hidden from me over the years."

"Nothing." The word was nothing less than a vow as it scraped up his throat.

"I've felt so stupid and naïve and wondered how I could've been so blind. Wondered if I knew you at all. But you're explaining it in ways like I'd *known* without knowing what was happening."

"You did," he said, the two words sounding heavy. "Savannah, there were times I thought I was gonna lose you because of what I was doing to us. Like when you got wasted and kept saying everything about our wedding was wrong, and I spent the entire night in a holding cell, wondering if we were even getting married anymore."

"When—*oh*," I mumbled as everything started clicking into place. "Your last fight." I pointed toward the open doorway. "Before the other week."

"Right."

I thought for a while, trying to figure out the best way to describe something I wasn't sure I fully understood.

"I don't remember those times," I finally said. "But at the same time, I remember pieces now that you're telling me. I think it might be in part to how emotionally heavy those nights and mornings were . . . Madison leaving and waiting for you to figure out if you *could* control your anger . . . but I also know that isn't it. Or, not all of it anyway," I added with a little shrug.

"Beau, if you told me I was wrong—that you did want me, that I was still your world—then I believed that. I took a day to process what had been happening and my worries, replaced them with the truths you'd told me, and I let it go," I said, lifting one of my hands before letting it fall because it'd always been as simple as that with him. "I mean, I can hold on to things and keep grudges, you know that. Philip Rowe is a prime example. But not with you.

"The only reason I've remembered or held on to the fact that if you fought again, we would be over, was because it was a stand I made for me and our future and because you continued to make that promise to me throughout our marriage. But I didn't even remember the events leading up to it, only that you'd gotten to a point where I felt like I couldn't stop you anymore. And up until a few minutes ago, I've thought that this"—I gestured between us—"was the first time something had come between us. Which is stupid," I whispered, rolling my eyes as I rambled on. "Of course something would've come between us before now because we've been together forever. People don't have perfect relationships. But I don't linger on the imperfections." I pressed a hand to my chest. "I truly move on from whatever it is, Beau. Always. And maybe that's why I'm so afraid now because I don't know how to do that with what's happened."

His stare unfocused as a surge of fear rocked the already unsteady ground we wavered on. All that pain filling the bathroom until we were drowning in it.

He cleared his throat a while later, his head shifting in the faintest of shakes. "A long time ago, you said you didn't want me to destroy the world for you. But when I saw Hunter standing there, looking like he hated me in a way I'd expected him to for so long, I saw *this* happening," he said meaningfully. "That was the beginning of my world—our world—being destroyed. And I would've done anything . . . fucking *anything* to prevent that from happening. Including break my promises to you."

"Why?" I asked, my tone dipping with the disappointment from that afternoon. "Why, when you knew what it meant? Beau, your anger is something I always felt I understood—the fighting too. But those last years, each fight seemed to fuel what was inside you. Like it was addicting to you."

"It is," he said blatantly, stunning me for a moment.

I blinked quickly as I tried to wrap my head around his admission. "So, what happened the other week will lead to another, and that will lead to another, and that will lead to you in jail and gone from us. That is what I was always trying to prevent for our future."

His head shook as I spoke, and for a moment, he just stood there. Brow furrowed as if he was trying so hard to figure something out. "It is addicting and dark and disgusting," he said, his hands coming up to claw at his chest. "It's like I can feel all that anger getting hotter and hotter and moving through my veins and begging me to do something as it consumes me."

I listened intently as he interwove things he'd told me long ago with new pieces I'd only ever guessed at. Parts of himself that he'd been so horrified by, he'd wanted to escape them. Refused to voice them.

When he didn't go on, I said, "And now you've tasted that again."

"I never stopped," he said honestly.

I pressed back against the tub as his words slammed into me, confusing me and filling me with denial. I would've known if he'd still been losing control.

I would've known if he'd been getting into fights.

"I've never understood all this," he said, pressing harder against his chest. "Not the way you seemed to. I've hated it, and I was afraid of it because I knew what I could do when I lost control. I saw the way the rest of the town and my family and your parents were afraid of me. But the more afraid I was, the easier it was for me to snap. Like my fear of what I could do was directly linked to all that shit inside me. But there's no getting rid of that, and there was no way in hell I was letting my anger be the reason I lost you, so . . ." He shrugged, the action weighed down as a defeated laugh left him.

As if it hadn't changed anything in the end.

"I've never asked how you controlled your anger simply because I knew you *could*," I began softly, head nodding subtly as I thought back to those months leading up to our wedding and after.

After he'd first promised he wouldn't get in another fight, I hadn't brought it up. I'd just believed him and moved past it, the same as everything else.

The corners of my lips tilted up. "You know, the whole *no-lingering* thing. I just wanted to be there for you and help you when I saw you getting to a breaking point, but I didn't see a need in asking how you were controlling it because I trusted you." I met his stare and said, "But with what you're saying . . . I'd like to know."

"I accepted that it was always gonna be part of me and started testing it a lot when I was alone,"—he jerked his chin toward the back of the house—"fixing up the back for our wedding. Letting myself get wrapped up in all that haze and anger until it went away on its own, over and over again until I wasn't afraid of the outcome. Until I wasn't afraid of it at all."

"And is that what you still do?" When he nodded, I asked, "Why didn't you do that with Hunter?"

His head lowered slightly as he folded his arms over his chest again. The corner of his mouth twitched up, but his expression lacked all amusement and looked like he was in pain. "That was—" He hesitated for a moment and then shifted his head enough to meet my stare again. "You know when one of the kids is about to get hurt, and you do anything to prevent it, even if you get hurt in the process?"

My head dipped in a slow nod.

"Hunter was bringing the worst kind of pain for my wife and my kids—this bullshit that could destroy you and our marriage, and I had to stop him. So, I let go." One of his shoulders lifted. "Then again, he was already hitting me, and I was terrified in a way I've never been, so I doubt I would've lasted much longer before I snapped anyway."

"You really did choose to break your promise then," I said sadly.

"I told you, I would've done anything to stop that destruction from happening."

"To stop me from knowing what you'd done."

His dark eyes bored into mine, pleading with me to understand. To forgive him.

I forced my stare away and shifted lower in the dry tub,

trying to get comfortable when that unstable pressure in the room made it impossible to do so.

And with each minute that trudged by in silence, that pressure grew until it was unbearable.

"I don't think you should leave," I said as I hurriedly climbed to my feet. "With the gossip and what happened with Stephanie, I think you staying anywhere else is a bad idea—at least until we know where this is headed."

Beau went still at my last words. His expression carefully blank and his stare on the floor.

"Savannah, what can I do?" he asked once I'd stepped into the bedroom, his voice twisting with worry. "Name it, I'll do it."

I turned, already shrugging. "There's nothing you can do. I don't know how to blame you for something that happened on a night none of us can really remember—but I'm so *hurt* by it," I said, my stomach twisting and heart falling to the floor all over again. "It's like I can't escape this image of you and her now, and it makes me sick knowing you kissed someone else . . . touched her . . . fucked her. *My best friend.*"

His eyelids slowly shut as he ran a hand through his hair and then gripped his neck.

"You should've told me that day. You and Madison should've told us that day." I pressed a hand to my uneasy stomach, my body swaying a little when the world went out of focus for a moment. Swallowing roughly, I continued on, words slow and a little thick at first. "I would've lost my mind and screamed at you and probably left the trip early and ignored you for a few days before working through it with you. And if you had, Madison would've never left. You wouldn't have hidden so much from me for so long or broken your promise to the kids and me. You and I wouldn't be in this position right now, and Stephanie Webb wouldn't be naked in your office and telling the town networking system that y'all are having an affair or that we're getting a divorce," I cried out, my body shaking in a way that was completely out of my control. "So, unless you can go back to that night and stop us all from getting wasted, no, there's nothing you can do."

Beau suddenly pushed from the counter and stepped toward me, his movements seeming hesitant even though alarm rang through his tone. "Savannah?"

"I—" A shuddering breath seemed to rip from deep within me, and I started backward. But my steps felt too slow and my body felt too weak. "I have to—"

Thirty

BEAU

"So, unless you can go back to that night and stop us all from getting wasted, no, there's nothing you can do."

What the fuck does that mean?

Because this can't be the end of us. There was no—

Everything disappeared and was replaced with alarm when I noticed Savannah's hands. The way they were trembling against her stomach before they dropped heavily to her sides.

Her entire body was shaking.

I pushed from my spot at the counter and took slow steps toward her as I looked over her. The way her knees were knocking and her body seemed to be moving in small waves.

When I made it back up to her face, her lips were white.

Fuck. "Savannah?"

She blinked slowly at her name. "I—" Her shoulders jerked with a heaving breath, and I hurried to close the distance between us when she started staggering backward. "I have to—"

Her eyes rolled back and her body went limp just as I reached the doorway.

"*Shit.*" I lurched forward, grabbing one of her arms and pulling her close before she could collapse to the floor. "Savannah," I said through clenched teeth, panic crawling up my throat as I lifted her into my arms. "*Savannah.*"

Within seconds, I was lowering her to our bed and had my phone out. "Come on, angel," I whispered as I tapped on the name and put the call on speaker, then brushed my hand across Savannah's clammy skin and found her slow pulse. "Savannah, I need you to look at me."

I ended the call after the third ring and quickly went to the next name, putting it on speaker the way I'd done before.

He answered after the first ring. "Man, I heard what you did—"

"Shut up, Savannah passed out."

"Shit," Sawyer hissed. "Okay, what's she doing now?"

"Fucking lying here, Saw. She isn't responding to me or looking at me."

"How long has it been?" he demanded.

My head shook quickly as I studied her labored breathing. "I don't know. Not even a minute."

He made a sound like he was struggling with what I should do. "If she doesn't come to, you gotta take her somewhere."

"Where?" I snapped. "The closest place is half an hour away."

"What's going on?" Rae asked in the background, and Sawyer hurried to fill her in.

"You should call Mom, she'll know what to do," he said to me, then spoke away from the phone again. "What? Why are you giving me that look?"

"I already did, she didn't—" Relief barreled through me when Savannah sucked in a stuttered breath, her eyes wide and wild and searching, her hands reaching out like she was trying to stop herself from falling. "Gotta go." I ended the call before grabbing up her hands in mine and waiting until those golden eyes settled on me. "Talk to me. You okay?"

Her head moved in a hesitant nod before shaking rapidly as tears filled her eyes and spilled down her cheeks.

"Tell me what to do," I begged softly as I cradled her face in my hand, brushing my thumb across her cheek. "Wanna go to the emergency room?" My phone vibrated, but I didn't look away from Savannah as she continued shaking her head. "What can I get you? You're scaring the shit outta me."

"I don't . . . I don't know," she said and choked over a sob. "I want to sit up."

"I think you need to stay here for at least a few more minutes." My stare darted over her face that was getting more color by the second. "How are you feeling?"

"I'm fine," she said quickly as she wiped at her cheeks and released a steadying breath.

"Savannah, you passed out for the first time in all the years I've known you. You're not *fine*."

I glanced to the side when my phone vibrated another two times, tapping on the messages and opening up the ones from Sawyer.

And going absolutely fucking still.

SAWYER: *Is she okay?*

Sawyer: *Beau . . . maybe you should take her to get checked . . .*

Sawyer: *Did you know Savannah's pregnant?*

. . .

I STARED at the words for what felt like an eternity before slowly looking back at my wife.

Her eyebrows drew close when she looked up at me before she seemed to sag against the bed. "Whatever's happened now, I can't handle it. Just not—" She sighed. "Please, Beau, let it wait until tomorrow."

"You're pregnant?"

Her eyes widened and her face went void of all emotion for a while before a relenting sigh left her, transforming everything about the way she was holding herself and her expression.

Her head bobbed subtly as she whispered, "Yeah."

"When were you gonna tell me?"

"I don't know," she said honestly. "It never felt like the right time, and I didn't know how with everything going on."

"But you told my brother," I said gravely. "That isn't something you keep from your husband, Savannah."

Anger flared in her eyes. "All things considered, you have no room to say that to me. And I didn't tell your brother. I made a slip in front of Emberly and Rae, and they figured it out. They weren't supposed to say anything to anyone until after I'd told you."

"Well, considering you just passed out, I'm glad someone told me." I reached for her instinctively but forced my hand to stop inches above her body. "Now, tell me what you need. What can I do for you right now?"

"Nothing," she said softly, her gaze drifting to the side.

"Right." I exhaled slowly as I pushed from the bed and started across the room, slowing when I reached the door. "Tell me something," I pleaded as I turned toward her. When she sat up and shifted in my direction, I asked, "How long have you known?"

She wavered for a second before admitting, "About a week and a half."

Before she'd ever called me.

Before she'd given me her rings and said I was losing her.

I worked my jaw, head nodding sharply as I stalked out of the room and headed for the stairs. My long steps eating up the space quickly as I went through the kitchen and grabbed a cup, filling it with water and then turning for the fridge. My eyes narrowing on a container with half a sandwich and some fruit right up front.

I reached for it and popped the lid as I walked over to grab a plate at the same moment Savannah stepped into the kitchen.

"How old is this?"

"It's from this afternoon," she said as I set the plate on one of the islands and began transferring the contents. "You can have it."

"I'm not hungry." I couldn't eat if I tried. It'd been like that a lot lately.

I felt sick from the constant unknown with her. From all the pain and fear. Half the days over the past few weeks, I don't remember from lack of sleep. The others, I'd spent hours in the gym, trying to push myself past the point of being able to feel.

Not that it'd worked.

I pushed the cup and plate toward her as she walked back from placing the empty container in the dishwasher. "Eat before you go to sleep."

"I could've done this."

"I know you could've, but you just passed out and you won't tell me what you need. And until you give me a stack of papers and ask for my signature, you're still my wife. Even after that? That baby's mine. So, let me take care of you."

Her honey eyes searched mine for a long while before her head lowered in the faintest nod. "You're leaving?" she asked when I walked over to grab my keys off the counter, her voice hitching.

Curling my hand around the keys, my shoulders sagged with a heavy sigh. "I'm sure there's no way my heart can break more than it has," I began, voice soft. "But then you tell me I'm losing you and give me your wedding rings. You say things like you think I should stay here until we know where *this* is headed and there's nothing I can do."

I turned to face her, studying the way she was trying so damn hard to control her expression. To mask her pain.

Stepping toward her, I moved slowly until I had her pressed against the island with my hands on either side, giving her every chance to stop me. "Savannah, my heart's been breaking for a long damn time because it was agony knowing what I did to you. But this?" My throat worked fiercely when my eyes began burning. "I would do anything to make up for what I've done, and I will do anything to save *us*. Our marriage . . . our family."

My body shuddered as every part of my being rebelled against the words before they came out. "I know you don't owe me anything, but if you really have no intention of even letting me *try* to fix this, then please just . . . just stop dragging this out. End this."

"I don't want a divorce," she said, her voice dipping in all the wrong ways.

Fear grabbed hold of my throat and slowly tightened its grip. "But?"

"But I don't know how to let you do what you're asking. I told you, I don't know how to get past this."

I didn't know how to survive this agony. I wasn't sure I wanted to.

I pushed away from the counter as the first tears fell and reached for my wedding band, feeling like my soul shattered as soon as my fingers grasped it.

"Oh my God, stop," she cried out, gripping my wrists.

"Savannah." Her name wrenched from the depths of my ruined soul as my eyes shut. "I can't keep wondering if the next time I see you is gonna be the time you decide to tell me we're done. I can't keep wondering why Quinn is repeatedly *informing* me that you and I are getting a divorce. All while you're saying things that confirm we will be."

"I don't . . . I don't want—" Her fingers curled tighter against me. "I've never said anything to Quinn or any of the kids. I've been trying so hard to keep all of this from them. She came up with that on her own, and the only time it was said in front of me, I told her she was wrong because that's the last thing I want, I just . . ."

I looked at her in time to see her face crumple with grief, her body sagging and shuddering as her breaths started coming too fast and too rough.

Her head shook quickly as she released me and slipped out from where I'd had her pinned against the island, her sharp inhales echoing in the kitchen as she quickly walked away.

"Can't get past it," I finished for her, swallowing thickly as I pressed my hands to the counter again and let my head hang between my shoulders.

"Do you know why I can't?" she asked.

I hadn't realized until she spoke that she hadn't made it out of the kitchen. I looked over and found her standing in the archway, holding herself up against it and facing away from me. Back and shoulders still moving in these great heaves as she struggled to catch her breath.

"Because I hurt you," I said softly. "I broke your trust and did exactly what I've promised not to."

Her head moved in a bouncing sort of nod as she turned to look at me, one of her hands resting on her stomach. "That . . . yes, but it's so much more than that. You explained things tonight, and they made sense. Like, of course you'd been trying to bring Madi back—that time now makes more sense because you were absolutely furious when she left. And why wouldn't you try to stop Hunter or fight back? It's *you*. I've always known who you are. I never wanted to change you, Beau, I just wanted a life with you. And the path you'd been going down led to you in prison or fighting the wrong person and ending up dead."

Blurs of fights and hours and nights in holding cells flashed through my mind as she continued.

"But the thing is, I made that decision. I made that choice for us, and you agreed to it. And even though this fight with Hunter makes sense, do I let it go? Because almost all of your fights when we were younger made sense. So, what happens the next time, and the next?"

"There won't be a next time," I said gravely.

"And I believe you because you're saying it," she shouted. "Everything you said tonight, I believed—and that's just it. That's why I'm struggling with this. I have felt so stupid and naïve these past weeks because I believed you when everything happened back *then*." She shrugged, her jaw wavering as she struggled to hold it together. "And I kept telling myself I would never be able to believe you again, but the problem is, I do." A soggy laugh fell from her lips. "And that scares me, and it *hurts*, and I am so afraid of finding out there is more you've hidden from me and lied about. Or that you really are having an affair with Stephanie Webb."

"I'm not," I said on a heaving breath.

"I know. I knew when you told me." Another one of those laughs left her, sounding like it wrecked her. The hand on her stomach lifted to her chest. "I am so afraid of losing you, but I am also afraid of being hurt by you and having my world ripped apart all over again. That's why I can't get past this . . . because I am absolutely terrified to."

I waited to see if she would go on and tried to absorb what she'd said.

I understood . . . I did. And I hated that I'd done this to her. I hated that it left us in the same place.

"What scares you more?"

"I don't know," she said softly. "The things we've both said and the things I've done scare me. But I've made sure I wouldn't have a minute to breathe, let alone think, and when I found out I—" Her eyes shut tightly and she leaned heavily against the wall as both hands gently fell to her stomach. "I already felt like I was losing control on keeping everything together, and then you were here, and I just . . ." One of her shoulders lifted. "I fell apart a little more each day."

I nodded as I pushed from the island, grabbing her plate and water and walking over to the kitchen table. After I had her stuff in front of the seat she liked, I sank into a chair a few away from hers so she'd have space. Stretching out with my feet propped up on one of the other chairs and dragging a hand over my face as all the exhaustion from these weeks wove through me. When I was folding my arms over my chest, she joined me. Moving all kinds of graceful and sensual the way she always had, even when we were in the middle of hell.

"When we were, uh . . . sixteen?" I thought for a second before nodding. "Yeah, sixteen. It was right after the first time we'd snuck in here when you said you wanted to elope. You remember that?"

She made an acknowledging hum around a bite of the sandwich.

"I went to your house when you were at dance and asked your parents for their permission to date you."

Her chewing slowed and her eyebrows pulled together. "What?" she asked around the bite.

"They said, 'no.' Not that I expected anything different and not like we hadn't already been together. But I told them about our dream for this place and your dream wedding. Told them how you wanted to give that up to elope just so they couldn't keep us apart anymore and how I wasn't gonna let that happen. Said that I'd be there, asking for their permission until they gave it to me."

"What'd they say?"

A huff left me. "They were pissed, but I got their permission eventually."

She inhaled softly. "That night the Rowes had you arrested." When I nodded, Savannah asked, "Why are you telling me this?"

My stare shifted from the table to her. "I'm trying to think of absolutely anything I've kept from you throughout our lives."

She studied me for a while, looking torn as hell before offering a subtle nod.

"The house," I said after another minute. "When we got married, I told you I'd gotten permission to buy the house, and I had. But I'd already had it for a while . . . months." At her shock, I explained, "I wanted it to be a gift, and I wasn't buying it without you."

"But *months*?" she asked. "It could've been an early wedding gift."

"You really think a few months would've made a difference?"

She huffed and rolled her eyes. "No, and it was perfect, and you know that," she mumbled before taking another bite.

The corner of my mouth tipped up. "Besides, I got permission the afternoon of my last fight," I said, the low words filled with meaning. "I could barely figure out a good time to tell you we could use the back for our wedding. It wouldn't have been the right time to tell you it was ours."

"No," she agreed after a moment. "I guess you're right." Her stare darted between her plate and me a few times as she picked at a piece of fruit. "What else?"

I shrugged as I thought. "I don't keep things from you," I said, feeling that weight press down on me all over again because what I *had* kept from her was now out in the open and had brought us here. "Other than the Madison shit, the only other things I can think of are what I just told you. Things that were for you—for us."

I eased deeper in the chair and fought the pull of sleep when this moment with her was so necessary.

But being in our home and beside her was the most relaxed I'd been in so long.

"Hunter," I said suddenly. "Hunter and I didn't talk for all that time because, in the beginning, I couldn't stand to see him without wanting to die. Then when he came back, he brought back all that guilt and pain that I'd had to push aside so we could move on with our lives. So, I made sure I didn't see him." I met Savannah's disappointed stare and said, "Made sure he wouldn't wanna see me."

"Beau . . ."

"Yeah."

"Does he know that now?"

I lifted my chin in acknowledgment. "We talked when I took the kids over there this weekend."

"That's good," Savannah mumbled, her stare unfocused as if she was thinking about something else. "And Madi's there?"

"Hunter said she's living with her parents, but she's been there every time I've gone over. But they're engaged, so, I dunno. She'll probably move in soon."

Savannah's eyes widened and snapped to me. "They are?"

"I thought you've been talking to my brothers."

"I have been," she said, the words slow and wounded. After a while, a huff punched from her chest. "They probably knew I didn't want to know. Or wasn't ready." She lifted part of her sandwich and dropped it back to the plate, focusing intently on what she was doing when she asked, "Have you talked to her?"

"Barely," I mumbled. "I went there a couple weekends ago when I was in a bad place. I hadn't heard from you, and I was yelling at Hunter. Madison was standing behind him. I said something to her about how what we'd done hadn't ruined all of us, it'd only ruined you and me. I haven't said anything to her since."

I watched the way Savannah absentmindedly nodded, her eyes filling with tears before one rolled down her cheek.

I let my feet fall to the floor and sat up, leaning forward and reaching across the table even as the next heavy tear ripped through me, slaying me with all that grief.

With what I'd done.

"Savannah." My hands curled into fists as the need to hold her and comfort her overwhelmed me, as her pain mixed with my own and kept me in place. "I'm sorry," I said when her head lifted and glassy eyes met mine. "I'm so fucking sorry. If I could go back and change everything, you have to know that I would."

She blinked quickly and hurried to wipe at her cheeks as if she'd just realized she was crying, her head moving in hard and fast shakes as she pushed back in her chair.

"Savannah—"

"No, it's, um . . . I'm tired." Her hand gestured between us. "We've said so much tonight, and I'm just overwhelmed by everything and whatever happened upstairs earlier. I need to go to sleep."

I dropped my head into my hand, nodding and gripping at my hair. "Yeah. Yeah, all right." I stood from my chair and reached for her dishes, but she grabbed them.

"I've got it, it's fine," she said quickly as she pushed to her feet and moved through the kitchen, dumping what she hadn't eaten and putting everything in the dishwasher.

When she finished closing it, she turned to face me and stopped, wide-eyed, when she found me grabbing my keys off the island. "You're still leaving," she said, fear and hurt wrapping around the words even as she tried to sound unaffected.

I gestured to the ceiling. "We keep the guest rooms locked."

"Right," she said with a relieving breath, but disappointment clouded her expression.

"Unless . . ."

"No." The word burst from her, her golden eyes going wide and darting away, looking anywhere but at me as a blush crept up her neck. "No, of course not."

"Of course not," I murmured, then nodded at her. "I'll get everything taken care of down here. You should go on up."

Her head bobbed quickly, her lips shaping into a forced smile as she turned to go.

I waited until I heard her climbing the steps before going through the downstairs, closing all the blinds and turning off the lights, and then headed up after her. Feeling like I'd slammed into a wall when I automatically turned the way that led toward our side of the house and remembered that wasn't where I'd be sleeping. Rocking back, I headed toward the guest side of the house and found one of the rooms already open. And on one of the chairs, some of my clothes.

And everything about it shredded me.

It was more painful than being kicked out of the house because this was us pretending for everyone else that we were okay. This was handing me hope that things could change, that I could fix this, and then being slammed with the harsh reality that I was still losing my wife.

"Tell me there's no one else. That there's never *been* anyone else." Her voice was a whispered plea, twisted with every pain we'd been surrounded in these weeks.

I looked over my shoulder to see her in the doorway, trying to stand so tall and looking like she was on the verge of shattering.

Turning to face her fully, I swallowed past the knot in my throat as I studied the woman I'd loved for so long. "Never,"

I vowed. "From the day you fell into my life, it has only been you."

A soggy laugh tumbled past her lips. "Tell me I'm not stupid for believing you."

I pressed a hand to my ruined chest and then gestured to her, wishing more than anything I could give her what she was asking. "I can't. That's something you need to decide for yourself when you're ready. But know that I can't handle the guilt of lying to you, of keeping something from you. And the times I have, it's almost destroyed us. You'll know if I am."

She nodded shakily and took a step into the room. "Tell me you won't hurt me again."

The plea was so raw and vulnerable that it nearly brought me to my knees. "Savannah, the last thing I've ever wanted to do was hurt you."

"Tell me."

"I . . ." A defeated breath ripped from my lungs. "I can't promise that. But I will do whatever I can to spare you any kind of pain." I took a step of my own toward her, my voice rough and low as I went on. "I know what I've promised you in the past, but if someone's hitting me, I can't promise I won't hit them back. If y'all are in danger, I can't promise I won't do whatever I have to to keep y'all safe. But I can assure you, I am absolutely in control. You and our kids are everything to me, I wouldn't do something to jeopardize that."

The hushed sound that left her was all understanding and acceptance mixed with the remnants of her sorrow. "Okay."

"Okay?"

Her head bounced softly before quickly shaking. "Why are you still over there?"

I was across the room and pulling her into my arms in the

time it took my wrecked heart to thump out a pained beat. Crushing my mouth to hers in a searing kiss that I felt in my soul.

It was sorrow and pain. Claims and vows and forgiveness.

I knew a kiss would never mean as much.

Thirty-One

BEAU

Lifting Savannah into my arms, I pressed her against the wall and savored the whimper that crept up her throat. The way she arched against me and wrapped her legs around my back in moves that were so familiar but still had such a profound effect on me.

"Fuck, Savannah," I ground out as I moved my mouth to her jaw. Gripping her hips tight in my hands.

Needing to feel her.

Taste her.

Know this was real when, just minutes before, I'd been shattering under the excruciating knowledge that I'd ruined my marriage. Betrayed the girl who had always been my everything in irredeemable ways.

I dragged my teeth across the sensitive skin beneath her ear. "Every last breath."

She trembled against me, weaving her fingers through my hair to lift my face back to hers. "I love you too."

Our next kiss was fire.

All demanding lips and punishing bites as we tried to heal

hurts. As we tried to form the shattered pieces of us back together.

"Need you," I breathed against her lips.

An echo of her pain bled free, her head nodding quickly as she attacked the kiss with renewed fierceness between her claim. "I've always needed you."

Sliding one of my hands up her back, I pulled her away from the wall, keeping her in my arms as I left the room. Moving with quick and confident steps across the house to where we needed to be.

In a space that was solely our own—not somewhere I'd been about to spend my nights without her.

And then I was laying her on our bed and curling my fingers around hers. Slowly removing her hands from where they'd been secured in my hair to pin them to the bed and nipping at her bottom lip as I leaned back. Staring down into golden eyes, all wild with need but looking at me in a way that ripped at my chest.

Like she was afraid I might disappear.

Like she'd been suffering under our separation as badly as I had.

"Together," I said, the word nothing more than a rasp as I grabbed the back of my shirt and pulled it off, letting it fall to the floor. "That's how we're making it through this, yeah?"

"Yeah," she agreed, her tongue darting out to wet her lips as she reached up, letting the tips of her fingers trail over my chest and down my stomach before reaching for the button on my jeans.

Everything about her touch so different from just minutes before. Slower, softer . . . easy. But that wild look in her eyes was closing in on frantic as she lifted up to capture my mouth while pushing my jeans and boxer briefs down.

Sitting back, I slowly dragged my fingers up her body, taking my shirt she'd been wearing higher and higher and following the path with faint kisses along her bare skin. Teasing her breasts and savoring every whispered moan and the way she began moving beneath me—little shifts that said exactly what I was doing to her.

Once the shirt was joining mine on the floor, I leaned over her, letting my lips hover above hers. Every breath causing them to brush and making me ache to close that distance.

To bury myself in her.

To make her mine all over again.

But the parts of me that had always been tied to Savannah knew I had to let her take this at her own speed.

"I need you." She forcibly swallowed. "I need to feel you —I need *this*," she begged, voice slightly desperate as she pushed my pants farther down when her body was asking for something else.

All those slow movements and soft touches.

Grabbing up her hands in mine, I lifted them between us until they were resting on her bare chest. "I'm here."

Her breath caught and her eyes searched mine, fear and sorrow and soul-deep need swirling within them. "I'm sorry," she said, lips trembling. "I'm sorry for kicking you out and keeping you from the kids. I'm sorry for refusing to talk to you—to listen."

"Savannah . . ." I released one of her hands, cradling her cheek when her head began shaking.

"I'm sorry I gave you my rings." She blinked quickly when her eyes filled with tears. "Oh my God, I'm so sorry. Everything I said to you, I just . . ." Her shoulders bunched up, and she looked at me helplessly. "It's like I heard myself saying these things to you, and I couldn't stop even though I was so horrified by them. And I felt like I was dying when you said you were gonna move out, but I didn't know how to tell you not to. That I wanted you home. And every chance to tell you, I pushed you back instead because I got so in my head with everything until it felt like I was drowning. And that . . ."—she nodded fiercely—"that's what terrifies me most—you leaving because I made you go. You not being here because I let you go. Not being able to tell you that I didn't mean any of the things I said—I've just been scared and hurt, and I'm sorry."

I pressed my forehead to hers when a soft cry left her and hushed her gently. "It's fine. Savannah, you're fine. I'm the reason we're in this mess."

Her head moved in slow shakes against mine. "I have missed you every minute of every day," she said, voice wavering with emotion. "Please come home."

"I'm here," I repeated and brought her left hand up to pass my mouth across the angel wings tattooed on her wrist. "Not going anywhere."

She pressed her fingers to my jaw to turn my head toward hers, her stare searching my face when she said, "I need you."

Words she'd already said, but this was different. This was vulnerable and soul-bearing. This was a part of her healing that she'd been waiting for.

Brushing my lips across hers, I pushed from the bed, keeping my eyes on hers as I finished undressing. By the time I was slipping her underwear down her legs, the rise and fall of her chest was coming faster. Sharper.

And then she was bared to me and taking my damn breath away.

My world.

My wife.

I knelt on the bed, taking her in over and over again as I spread her legs. "You're so beautiful," I whispered.

A flush swept up her neck, a secretive smile tugging at her full lips as she reached for me to pull me higher up her body.

I let her move me a little ways before dipping down to pass my mouth across her stomach a couple times and placing a soft kiss there.

By the time I was settled between Savannah's legs, her eyes were bright with adoration and excitement as she curled her fingers around the back of my neck and pulled me closer.

"I love you," I murmured before pressing my mouth to hers.

The kiss slow and claiming. Soft and passionate.

A dance with her I would never get tired of.

Her breath left on a stuttered exhale when I rocked against her, slowly sliding my cock against her over and over and teasing her clit that I was aching to devour before pressing against her entrance.

"Beau, please—*oh God*." Her nails scraped along my neck when I began inching in.

Taking my time and savoring the feel of her. The way she gripped me and shuddered around me. Feeling like the best damn thing every time. Shaking my goddamn soul because I hadn't realized just how empty I'd been without her until that moment. How wrong life had been.

"Jesus Christ, Savannah," I said, throat tight.

"I know," she whispered, brushing her mouth across mine. "I know. I love you."

"I'm sorry." I leaned back enough to study her eyes,

watching as they fluttered shut for a moment as she nodded. "Love you with every last breath."

Her answering whimper when I pulled out and pushed back in filled my head and made my blood buzz. Had chills skating across my skin and had me struggling to find and keep a slow rhythm when that sound was pure sin.

When I was already getting lost in her.

Lost in this heaven I'd thought had been ripped away from me.

I made a lazy trail of kisses down her throat, stopping at the pulse-point and feeling the way her skin vibrated against my lips with each moan and inaudible plea as my thrusts gradually quickened. Hardened. Each rock of my hips just as steady and thorough when I sat back and brought one of my hands to where our bodies were joined.

A tremor moved through her when I skimmed my fingers through her slick folds, her voice breathless and pleading as she reached for me. "Beau."

I dipped my head to press another kiss to her tattoo, never losing sight of her eyes as I brushed my fingers against her clit. Unable to draw it out and tease her. Unable to do anything but give her what she needed right then.

Watching the way her eyelids fluttered shut and her back bowed. The way her lips parted and her hands curled into fists against my bare chest before flattening.

Taking in every sound and movement and expression like it might be my last opportunity.

Savoring the way she responded to my touch, each shudder that worked through her body and the way she clenched tight around my cock when I rolled her clit between my fingers. The way her eyelids popped open and a breathless moan ripped from her as she shattered around me.

"Fucking beautiful," I whispered as I worked her through her orgasm. Her little vibrations pushing me closer to the end when I was already there.

With one last brush against her sensitive bud, I curled back over her and wrapped one of her legs around my hip, angling deeper and deeper as my hips rocked faster. Gritting my teeth in a vain attempt to hold off for a while longer when I was buried in Savannah. When my world was righting again after all the shit we'd been through. Surrounded in sugar and caramel and everything that made up my wife.

I wrapped one of my hands in her hair and pressed my forehead to hers, gripping the comforter tightly as I raced toward the end. "I love you."

A bright smile broke across the pleasure on her face and lit up my world. "I love *you*," she breathed, the claim still teasing my lips as I bent to capture her mouth in a kiss that had me spinning.

Felt like I was drowning in her and so damn high off her kiss, I couldn't think straight.

The room could've gone up in flames around us, and it wouldn't have mattered. Nothing else mattered at that moment other than her body beneath mine and the feel of her around me. Her hands pulling me closer and the way her lips moved against mine in a familiar, intoxicating dance.

I hissed out a curse as all that pleasure tore down my spine and dropped my head to her collarbone as I found my own release inside her. My muscles going tight for long seconds before my body began trembling. From the release . . . from all the adrenaline of the night having faded away . . . from the exhaustion of these past weeks.

Pressing a kiss to the underside of her jaw, I eased out of her and then rolled to the side, bringing her with me.

There were so many things we still needed to talk about. We needed to go back over some of the dozens of things we'd already attempted to that hadn't been resolved.

But right then, I couldn't remember any of them.

There was only her, curling up closer to my chest as I brushed my knuckles across her flat stomach. Staring at me with heavy-lidded eyes, smiling softly, and looking so beautiful, it hurt.

We'd had thousands of moments just like that, I was sure.

But I had no doubt, I would remember that one for the rest of my life.

Thirty-Two

SAVANNAH
TWENTY-FIVE YEARS OLD

My stare danced around the empty bedroom as I exited the bathroom, my head slanting as I listened for any sounds.

Any cries.

But there was nothing.

Grabbing one of Beau's shirts, I slipped it over my head and continued out into the hall since we didn't have any guests at the time, my bare feet padding against the hardwood as I headed for the stairs. But when my gaze automatically swept the most important room in our home as I'd started passing it, I stopped.

Chest warming. Heart reaching. Soul melting into a puddle at my feet.

Because there was my big bear of a husband, cradling our nine-month-old to his bare chest as he slowly rocked back and forth in the darkened room. The soft glow from the nightlight capturing the moment perfectly.

As if he could sense me there, he turned, his dark eyes lingering on me as one of those rare smiles crossed his face.

All dimples and adoration and stealing my heart as if he hadn't done that so many years before.

"She okay?" I asked as I crept into the room.

"She's good," he murmured, his voice all a soft rumble. "Just lost her pacifier for a second."

"Oh, sorry I wasn't there."

"Why?" Keeping one of his hands on Quinn's back to hold her close, he reached out to me with the other, pulling me against him to search my face in the darkened room. "I had her."

"Yeah, but I should've been there." My throat felt all tight like I was going to cry, but that was ridiculous.

She'd lost her pacifier. That's all.

Get a grip. This is so not a big deal.

"I had her," he repeated softly. Lifting his hand to trail his knuckles down my jaw, he followed the path with his eyes. "She's my daughter too. You don't always have to be the one who jumps when she cries."

I sagged against him, gratitude pouring from me as I blinked back the threat of tears. "I know, and I know I'm being ridiculous right now," I mumbled quickly. "Thank you for being there, and thank you for letting me take a bath. I needed that time."

"Let you?" A rough, grating laugh built in his chest. Lifting my head to meet his eyes, he said, "Whatever you need, always." He searched my stare for a while longer before murmuring, "Crazy girl."

"I love you."

"Every breath," he vowed, the words moving through my body and doing crazy things to my heart. Brushing his thumb along my lip, he gestured behind me with a jerk of his chin. "Get in bed. I'll be there soon."

I twisted like I was about to go, then turned back into him. Because that demanding tone of his had always gotten to me too. Waking up my body and sending a rush of heat through me. Making me ache with anticipation. "Or you could come with me now . . ." I said, words slow and hopeful.

From the carnal look that crossed his face, he heard the implication behind the whispered words. After another lingering glance, Beau turned for Quinn's crib and gently eased her down without waking her.

I met him at the side, sliding my hand over his and wondering if I would ever stop being blown away by the amount of love I felt for that little girl.

"Never again," Beau whispered as he turned over his hand to grip mine. "I swear to you, I'll never get in another fight. I'll never throw another punch. I'll never be arrested again."

I looked up at him, my throat going tight all over again at the depth of his oath.

They were the same words he'd said to me the morning we'd woken up on the grounds of this house, long before we owned it, a couple days after his last arrest. The same words he'd repeated to me on our wedding night.

And he'd kept them.

He was still the same Beau I'd always known him to be. Surly and terrifying and quick to anger with everyone who wasn't me—well, and now Quinn. But he'd found a way to keep all that darkness and rage at bay until he calmed or could channel it into something else.

Renovating our house. Exercising. Mind-blowing sex.

I preferred the last.

But I couldn't imagine the strength it took to control what had always been so uncontrollable for him. I couldn't imagine how difficult it was to chain something so wild and fierce.

But I was thankful for it.

Thankful for how much he loved me.

"I know," I whispered, squeezing his hand gently.

His stare shifted to me, all love and wonder before he was standing to his full height and twisting toward me. Pulling me closer as he walked me backward, out of the room, stopping to softly close the door behind us. Then he was backing me down the hall, his hands lightly moving over my body and teasing my curves before finding the hem of his shirt I was wearing.

Fingers trailing over the bare skin of my hips and butt before he bent to curl his large hands around my thighs. And then he was lifting me, my legs wrapping around his hips instinctively as he crushed his mouth to mine.

"What do you want?" he asked against the kiss.

"You."

"Rough or easy?" he quietly demanded.

I wove my fingers through his hair, gripping gently to pull him back so I could look in his midnight eyes. "I just want you."

His movements slowed when he approached the bed. Kneeling on it and effortlessly lowering me until I was laid out beneath him. The muscles in his body stretching and rippling with each measured movement as he dipped down to press his mouth first to my covered breasts and then my throat before meeting my lips where he whispered, "Easy then."

My chest rose and fell roughly when he started a slow path down, lifting my shirt up as he went. His kisses hot and teasing and building me up and up and up.

Fire.

I was on fire.

Heat swirling in my belly as unwavering need for the man above me raced through my veins. And we'd barely begun. But it'd always been that way with us.

A frenzy burning hotter and higher until I was consumed in him. In us.

"*Beau.*" His name tumbled past my lips, all trembling need when he settled his wide shoulders between my thighs.

Hands gripping me. Mouth passing lazily across the inside of my thigh like he had all the time in the world to touch me and tease me.

As if he was enjoying the torture.

His stare lifted to meet mine, a wolfish smirk shaping his lips as if he'd heard my thoughts. And then he was leaning forward to taste me.

Slow.

Gentle.

Easy.

A whimper fell from my lips as my entire body reacted to that touch, to his tongue. To the way he flattened it against me before alternating to hard, fast flicks. Winding me up and drawing out the moment until I was begging him to give me what was just out of reach.

But every time Beau felt me get closer, he'd pull back. Slow and soften his movements. Kiss my clit tenderly as if he wasn't driving me insane in the best possible way.

A shuddering breath fled from me when he pressed two of his fingers inside me, curling them expertly as he set his tongue on my aching bud.

My mouth opened on a silent cry as I shattered against him.

That addictive bliss surging through my body and making me feel weightless for those few seconds before I came crashing back to reality.

A reality that felt more like a dream.

"Beau," I managed to say through my ragged breaths.

My body was trembling. Shuddering.

I gripped weakly at his hair as he continued to devour me like he couldn't get enough.

Worshipping me with his tongue and fingers, pushing me through my orgasm until I tumbled into a second one.

Weightless.

Bliss.

And then he was moving over me and settling between my thighs as he deftly removed his athletic shorts. His long length pressing against my entrance as his mouth made a path up my neck.

"Love you," he whispered against my skin.

"Every breath," I vowed as he pushed inside me, slowly taking me inch by inch. A groan raking up his throat once he was fully seated.

"Fucking heaven." His hand curled around the comforter as he eased out before pushing back in. His hips rolling faster and faster until he found a rhythm that had my breaths coming out in soft whimpers.

Had my eyelids fluttering shut as he loved me so wholly, so effortlessly.

"Open," he softly demanded as his lips brushed across my cheek. His dark eyes all love and adoration and fire when I looked into them. "There you are."

Twisting my fingers into his hair, I brought his mouth to mine. Kissing him until I was dizzy off his lips and tongue and the way he moved inside me.

Dizzy off Beau and everything that made up us.

Pressing up with one hand, he grabbed my leg with the other and curled it around his hip as his thrusts quickened. The muscles in his body tensing as he neared his release. As he gently claimed me. Body. Heart. Soul.

It didn't matter how long we'd been doing this or how we came together. Rough . . . easy . . . every time stripped me bare in the purest of ways. Exposing every vulnerability and shaking me to my core. Flooding me with the breathtaking knowledge that this man was mine. That he had so clearly chosen me from that first day and continued to.

A gritted curse burst from him when he came inside me, his body tightening for long seconds before little tremors began rolling through his arms and back and transferring to me.

He slowly released my leg and lowered himself to rest just above me, our chests moving in unison with our ragged breaths as we watched each other in that moment we always lingered in. The fierce beat of his heart matching mine so perfectly and feeling like a comfort in its familiarity.

"You're everything," he murmured. Capturing my lips in a soft but brief kiss as he eased out of me and rolled us to our sides.

Warmth bloomed in my chest, a lazy smile tugging at the corner of my mouth at his words. At the tone. As if he still couldn't believe we were finally here, after everything we'd been through.

I understood it all too well.

But we'd made it through my parents trying everything to separate us before finally giving Beau their blessing. Through their public wishes for me to be with someone else. We'd made it through cop cars and holding cells. Through the repeated, crushing loss of death and people leaving. Of the separation from Hunter and Cayson . . .

Through it all, we'd gotten our dream. The plantation house was ours—fully restored and more beautiful than I ever could've imagined. Blossom Bed and Breakfast had been up and running for a couple years. And we had our little girl.

Beau's stare danced across my face as I thought, a soft smile lighting his eyes as he did.

"What?"

"I hope Quinn has your freckles."

A shock of a laugh bubbled free. "Why?"

His answer was immediate. "I love them. Have since that first day." When I just looked at him with amused confusion, he asked, "You don't remember?"

"Apparently not." But I snuggled deeper into the pillow and curled closer to him, excitement billowing as I waited to hear his side of it.

He sighed and looked toward the ceiling as he thought. "You asked if I was gonna stay away from you because of your freckles. Said you didn't think they belonged on your face."

Another laugh tumbled past my lips, my shoulders shaking from the force of it. "I still think that," I admitted.

His eyes snapped to me and narrowed in a playful glare. "They're fucking adorable."

I lifted a hand in mock surrender.

"When I told you they weren't gonna make me stay away from you, you said something like my anger wasn't gonna make you stay away from me—like they were the same thing."

"*Oh.*" The word was a soft exhale as the memory tugged at my mind. My chest aching when I remembered sitting by a tree with a mud-covered Beau. "Because they both made us sad." When Beau slanted his head in a nod, I added, "But they're both just parts of us."

Eyes bluer than the ocean searched my face again as he said, "I hope Quinn has them."

"I hope she has your heart."

Beau looked as if I'd said the most horrific thing imaginable. For a while, he watched me as if waiting for something. When I didn't offer anything else, he asked, "Why would you want her to have anything of me?"

That ache in my chest grew and grew for the man I loved. The one who, even after years of controlling that darkness and rage inside him, still couldn't see himself as anything else.

"Well, there are a lot of things to want," I said softly, lifting one of my shoulders in a shrug. "Your eyes. Your dimples and your smile."

"I don't smile."

"You do," I argued as a smile of my own broke across my face. "And, oh man, if you ever showed it to anyone else, it'd be enough to stop people where they are. It still stops me."

"You're different."

I lifted a brow, silently challenging him. When he just dipped his head, letting me have that one, I went on. "But those are just physical. Your inner strength is unmatched. And your heart? Beau, you feel everything so deeply, and it's so beautiful. Why wouldn't I want her to have that?"

Long moments passed in silence as he seemed to consider my words. After a while, he spoke. Voice soft and haunted. "Feeling that much can be damaging. I wouldn't want any of our kids to experience that."

I lifted my hand to his face, brushing my fingers across

the hard set of his brow and jaw as my pain for him flared. "I'm sorry," I whispered. "I hate that it feels that way to you —wait, did you say *kids?*"

"Yeah," he responded unapologetically.

"As in, more than just Quinn?"

Confusion creased his features. "I thought you wanted multiple kids."

"Yeah, but that was before I realized how hard fixing up a mansion would be."

"Already done," he said with an easy shrug.

"Or having *one* baby."

"She's a pretty great baby," he added, amusement dancing in his eyes.

"Or looking like a freaking whale for months."

A wicked grin slowly crossed his face. "Babe, do you have any idea how sexy you are when you're pregnant?"

"But I just got my body back," I cried out . . . only to realize I was actually *crying.*

Beau sat up, looking confused and terrified and so, so lost as he reached for me. "Savannah, what—" His head moved. Just these quick, faint shakes as his eyes searched me. "Why are you crying? We don't have to have any more kids if you don't want," he tried to assure me.

"I don't know, I feel so stupid right now," I said as I struggled to sit up beside him. "I cried in the tub because it felt so good to relax in there—like *so good.* I cried when I added a whole mess of salt instead of sugar to my cake batter today. I can't stop crying, and my—" My hands moved to my breasts. To gesture to them . . .

Because they ached.

Oh God.

A gasp ripped through me as I met Beau's worried stare.

"Oh . . . oh my God." I covered my mouth with my hands, denial weaving through me.

I saw the moment it hit Beau.

His brows lifting in understanding and shock before his gaze fell to my bare stomach. "Are you—" His eyes met mine again before a gravelly laugh broke free as he fell back to the bed, pulling me with him. "Babe," he murmured when a sob wrenched from my chest. "It's gonna be okay. If you are, we'll figure it out."

My head shook wildly against his chest as I tried to speak, choking and stumbling over my words. "No, I—oh my God, I —I'm so excited."

His next laugh was louder, fuller as he tightened his strong arms around me. Passing his mouth across my fore-head, his voice was all love and joy as he whispered, "Crazy girl."

Thirty-Three

BEAU

Leaving Savannah and our bed had never been so difficult.

I must've thought up a dozen different reasons to call in these last few days of school so I could spend every minute wrapped up in her, but I'd known I couldn't. Not only did I have to be there, I knew disappearing in the middle of the bullshit with Stephanie would only fuel the gossip, making things worse for me. And, in turn, for Savannah.

So, I'd pulled myself from where she'd slept and gotten everything in the house ready for when Savannah woke before heading out.

My office had been free of naked women, but the looks that ranged from disgusted glares to fuck-me eyes from every female staff member I'd passed on the way there had me rethinking that whole *needing-to-be-there* shit.

At least when Kevin came in halfway through the day, he'd given me an apologetic look as he'd crossed the room to sit in one of the chairs.

"I wanna say I'm sorry," he began, leaning forward and

clasping his hands. "Shoulda known you wouldn't do something like that to Savannah. Just a little shocking when what I
saw, well . . . when it was right in front of me."

I nodded, my stare dragging to my phone when it went off
for the third time since he'd walked in. "If only the rest of the
town knew that."

"Go on and get that," he said, sitting back in the chair
when another chime sounded from my phone.

Picking it up, I held down the lock button until I could
shut down my phone. "It's been going off since before I even
got home yesterday," I murmured as I dropped the cell to my
desk, feeling relief wash over me at the simple act.

When I'd found my phone that morning, I'd had
hundreds of messages waiting for me.

Hundreds.

People pissed that I would hurt Savannah. Disgusted that
I would cheat on her. Calling me a coward for not responding. Letting me know Savannah deserved better. Others
asking if this thing with Stephanie was serious or just a one-
time thing . . . because they were free.

I'd only glanced at a few before deleting them all, but
more came in. My blood crawled with anger that burned
hotter and darker each time my phone went off.

"Town sure can talk," Kevin mumbled in agreement.

I grunted as I bent back over the summer football training
I'd been working on. "One thing I always hated." I glanced up
when the door opened again, jaw aching something fierce
when one of the math teachers poked her head in, lip caught
between her teeth and eyes all dark with want. "No."

"I was just—"

"Whatever it is, the answer's 'no.' Get out."

"Lunch?" she still asked.

My grip tightened on my pen as I stared at her. "I love my wife," I said slowly, voice dark and cold. "Get the fuck out of my office and away from me."

Kevin tsked when she shut the door, looking confused and put off, then huffed out a sigh. "Looks like you might have a problem."

"It's bullshit," I muttered as my office phone rang. Tapping the line, I let the call go through speaker. "Dixon."

"Mr. Dixon, it's Principal Warin. Am I interrupting anything?"

My stare drifted to Kevin at the principal's all-business tone when she usually treated everyone like family. I swallowed past the knot building in my throat and said, "No, ma'am."

"I need to see you in my office. Immediately, if you could."

"Yes, ma'am. Be right there." Tapping off the call, I hissed out a curse and pushed from my chair.

Kevin stood with me, stepping forward and reaching out to grab the door for me. "It's a shame you've had to go through this," he murmured as I neared him. "I'm sorry again for doubting you—even for a minute. You're a good man."

I hesitated near the door, then dipped my head in thanks. "Appreciate that."

I stalked across the campus, my agitation and worry growing with each step. The darkness in my blood roaring to life with each pair of eyes I met as staff left for lunch and mingled in the halls.

It was like being a kid all over again. People judging and whispering about whatever I'd done or *might've* done. Except this was different.

I hadn't been prepared for *this*.

There had been women who expressed unreciprocated interest throughout the years, but where girls fell over themselves to get to my brothers, I'd never had to deal with that headache.

A few during college and after had been brave enough to flirt, but nearly all had kept it to a suggestive look. One that was paired with as much fear of me as there was interest. And that fear had always kept them back.

Until Stephanie-fucking-Webb.

I rapped my knuckles on the principal's door, hand already reaching for the knob when she called out for me to come in.

"Mr. Dixon," she said, looking and sounding all kinds of stressed out as she gestured to a seat . . . right next to Stephanie. Looking every bit the high school vice principal and not like the woman who'd been waiting for me on my desk the day before. "Thank you for getting here so quickly."

"Ma'am," I muttered as I shut the door behind me and stepped deeper into the office. I cut a cold look Stephanie's way as I sat and stilled when I noticed the man standing in the corner—the same school board member from the day before.

Fucking hell.

"It seems," Principal Warin began, sitting on the corner of her desk, "some of the reprimands given yesterday were too severe while others weren't severe enough."

I went still.

Replaying her words and worrying about the next.

Heart pounding a hard, terrifying beat as that poison stretched through my veins. As that darkness waited, begging to be unleashed.

She cleared her throat, her gaze darting to my side. "Ms. Webb, you may go."

My hand twitched.

Mind fucking racing as I thought of what she might've said.

Once the door shut behind her, the board member moved so he was in my line of sight, and the principal sighed. "You said nothing yesterday, Mr. Dixon," she said questioningly.

"Ma'am?"

She pushed from the desk, hands folded in front of her. "It has been brought to our attention that there might be some fabrications to the allegations against you." She hesitated, brow lifting slowly as if waiting for me to speak. "You were given every opportunity to share your side, but you said nothing."

Irritation escaped me on a breath.

"And you're saying nothing now," she added meaningfully when silence filled the room.

"I'm not sure what you expect me to say, ma'am," I roughed out as all that darkness started receding. "I was brought in here yesterday and *accused* of cheating on my wife and having a recurring affair with someone. Immediately after that, I was told what I was being written up for and warned about my future here. I was never asked my side." I shrugged. "Besides, y'all already had your minds made up. There was nothing to say."

Understanding and shame passed across her face as her head fell to the side.

Of anyone, I knew she understood.

When Savannah and I were in high school, Mrs. Warin had been sure I was beating Savannah or had some kind of twisted relationship with her. When I first got the job as assistant coach, she'd been one of the loudest to rally against me. But over the years, Mrs. Warin and I had come to understand and respect each other.

She'd apologized for past judgments, and I'd been happy when she'd gone from our guidance counselor to our principal, knowing she was what the school needed. So, for her to fall so easily to the side of believing the worst in me again, it had pissed me off.

"I'm sorry," she said softly. "Teachers heard kids talking about it, and then Vice Principal Webb confirmed it and elaborated . . . but you're right. We should've gathered both sides before making accusations and taking action."

When she gestured to the board member, he cleared his throat and said, "I second everything Principal Warin said, and please accept my apologies as well as the rest of the boards'." He waved his hands before putting them back in his pockets. "The penalties and warnings against you have been withdrawn, and Ms. Webb is stepping down as an educator for this district."

Surprise wove through me, but I just waited.

"There were eye-witnesses to yesterday's events in your office," Principal Warin took over. Her eyebrows lifted significantly when she continued. "Among other witnesses elsewhere."

One of my shoulders lifted. "Finding her in my office is the only place there's ever been anything."

"We were informed she'd been trying to gather information on you in town recently, and those claims contradicted the details Ms. Webb gave us yesterday. When confronted, she admitted the story of your 'relationship' was fabricated," Mrs. Warin said. "Taking yesterday's events into consideration, as well as the career- and character-destroying story she told to bring you down with her . . . well." She lifted her hands in a way that said there wasn't much left to do, the corners of her eyes creasing with apology.

Except, I still had nearly all of Amber wanting me to pay for something I hadn't done, or just wanting something I refused to give them.

"Is there anything you'd like to say now that we're listening, Mr. Dixon?" she asked, her words slowing and trailing off when someone began yelling out in the front office.

She took a hesitant step toward the door, and I slanted my head in that direction as my blood began buzzing. Reacting to that voice.

". . . ever had a chance with him? Bitch, he's married. And despite what you deluded yourself into thinking, I know how to keep my man satisfied and keep him from straying to whores like you."

Fuck.

"That's mine," I ground out, pushing from the chair and hurrying for the door with Mrs. Warin behind me.

"It's time you leave," someone shouted back just as we stepped into the hall. "This is incredibly inappropriate behavior for a school."

I looked over at the sound of Savannah's scoffing laugh to see every person in the office watching the encounter with wide eyes and trying to hide their shocked amusement before landing on where my wife was looking down at Stephanie Webb even though she towered over Savannah.

"Says the woman who stripped naked and waited for my husband to find her *in his school office*," Savannah bit out, expression pure challenge and looking ready to throw down.

And, fuck me, it was so damn sexy.

"I got her," I said quickly, holding up a hand when Mrs. Warin began stepping forward.

"Highly inappropriate, Mr. Dixon," she said under her breath, but even she was fighting a smile as she turned back to her office. "We'll be waiting for your return."

"Ma'am," I muttered as I started for my wife.

My world.

The girl who set my goddamn blood on fire.

Thirty-Four

SAVANNAH

I really hadn't planned on going to the school. I'd been driving somewhere else, and the next thing I knew, I made another turn and was continuing on until I was parked in front of the high school and stalking up to the doors.

But in all fairness, I'd been going through absolute hell the past few weeks. My emotions were all over the place from Baby-Number-Four. And even though I'd had every intention of only going to settle things with the other half of why my life had imploded, I needed to take care of the person attempting to ruin it just as Beau and I were fixing it.

When I'd woken that morning, everything had felt surreal.

Too perfect. Too dreamlike.

I'd gotten ready for the day and gone downstairs, finding coffee already brewed and a few peony heads from our garden on the edge of one of the islands beside a note in Beau's masculine scrawl.

. . .

BUT AFTER BREAKFAST and talking with the kids to hear all about the fun they were having, I'd finally started going through my phone. All the calls and texts from people I knew but hardly ever spoke to, asking if I was okay. If I needed anything. Everyone claiming they'd always known Beau would do something like this. Calling him disgusting and worthless. Telling me I should've kicked him to the curb long ago.

And my perfect morning had shattered as my heart broke for that man. Feeling like we were thrown back in high school, where he was constantly under the town's judgmental scrutiny, and I was begging them to see him a certain way.

Except this directly affected my marriage and pissed me off.

Which is why I was pushing through the main doors of the school and turning into the front office, staring down each set of eyes that flashed my way. Challenging them to say one word about Beau or our marriage.

If someone so much as hinted at any number of the things that had been texted to me, I would lose my mind.

"Hey," I snapped when the source of all this ridiculousness crossed into the hall from one of the side rooms.

Anger and a strange sense of satisfaction flooded me when Stephanie Webb turned at the sound, shame and embarrassment flashing across her features before she settled on unease.

"You can't be here without a visitor's pass," she said,

lifting her chin and trying to put as much strength behind her words as her worry allowed.

"You shouldn't shove your fake tits in my husband's face, but here we are."

Her eyes widened and darted everywhere, as if the entire town didn't already know some version of the truth, and landed on me when I stopped a few feet in front of her.

"As much as I love your version of what took place, you really think he wouldn't come home and tell me what actually happened?" I asked, voice edged with steel. "But beyond that, you think you would've ever had a chance with him? Bitch, he's married. And despite what you deluded yourself into thinking, I know how to keep my man satisfied and keep him from straying to whores like you."

Anger and humiliation flared in her eyes as she pointed behind me, her voice rising to match mine. "It's time you leave. This is incredibly inappropriate behavior for a school."

A sharp, disgusted laugh burst from me. "Says the woman who stripped naked and waited for my husband to find her *in his school office*," I ground out, enunciating the last words. "You were trashy in high school and you're trashy now. Next time you try tricking someone into fucking you, make sure he's single . . . or at the very least *interested*."

Beau was suddenly there, pushing past Stephanie and coming for me. The corner of his mouth twitching like he was fighting a smile, eyes like fire and burning with a look that had my heart pounding out a wild beat as my stomach erupted into chaos.

All primal need and blatant hunger.

Without slowing, he curled his arm around me and pulled me against his side, quickly leading me back the way I'd come.

"God damn," he whispered under his breath as we pushed out of the main office and into the hall, turning for the large doors that led outside. "Do you have any idea how badly I want you right now?"

I glanced up at him, taking in the sharp line of his jaw as he clenched it tight, and felt a small smile tug at my lips. "Show me."

A groan rolled up his throat as he stopped us a handful of feet outside, turning to face me while keeping me in his arms. "Tempted," he said tightly. "I gotta finish a meeting in there. I'm also supposed to be at Sawyer's right now, so I'll have to run by there for a second after school's out." His head dipped low, eyes holding mine when he continued, voice all gravel and sex. "But when I get home, I'm fucking you wherever I find you."

A shiver rolled through my body at the words that held a hint of warning. "I'll be waiting."

He pressed a hard kiss to my mouth, his tongue slipping between my lips and giving me the cruelest tease before he pulled away and took a step toward the doors again, mischief lighting his eyes. "As much as I loved it, maybe don't come into the school, yelling and calling people whores . . . especially when they've just been fired."

I inhaled quickly but tried to recover. "Oh no," I said dully. "How sad."

"Right." The word was all disbelief as a whisper of a laugh scraped up his throat. "Go enjoy the rest of your day."

"Hey!" At the questioning lift of his chin, I gestured over my shoulder in the direction of our house. "Thank you for my flowers."

One of his rare smiles flashed, his dimples greeting me

for a moment before he pushed on the door. "Angel," he murmured before disappearing inside.

I turned, heading for my SUV and already feeling infinitely lighter than I had hours before and wondering if I should feel bad for any of the things I'd unloaded on Stephanie Webb before deciding I didn't care.

Not then, at least.

Later, when talk in the town shifted to her, I knew I might. I knew I would go over all the other ways I could've handled it. But as I climbed into my car and started toward my original destination, I kept thinking of all the hate-on-Beau messages I'd been receiving because of what Stephanie had done. What she'd tried to do, happily taking Beau down and dragging our marriage through the streets of Amber even when she hadn't gotten what she wanted.

And I knew if I had to do it all over again, I'd go right back into the school and unleash every pent-up thought.

But as I pulled up to Madison Black's childhood home, there were no pent-up thoughts, and that lighter feeling seemed to be disappearing with every second because I had absolutely no idea how this would go.

I just knew it needed to be done.

With a steadying breath, I turned off my SUV and climbed out. Taking in the two-story house I'd spent so much time in growing up before landing on the window of Madison's old bedroom, mostly hidden behind the large tree that had always been our source of mischief.

Stepping onto the porch, I lifted my hand to knock just as the door was opened, revealing a bouncing Avalee and Madison.

"We—" Madison's words cut off when she saw me there, shock covering her face.

"Wyatt's mommy!" Avalee shouted. "Did you bring my friends, Wyatt and Quinn, with you?"

"Not this time," I said and tried to offer her the biggest smile even though my emotions had gone all over the place when they opened the door. "They're hanging out with their grandparents this week—but next time, okay?"

"Did you hear that, Mommy?" she asked, looking up at Madison. When Madison didn't respond, Avalee looked back at me. "We're going to see my Hunter."

"Oh," I said, stepping back.

"No," Madison said so quickly it stopped me in place. "No, uh . . . later. We'll go see him later." She dropped her bag unceremoniously on the floor and then placed her hands on Avalee's shoulders, turning her back into the house. "Go find Mamaw. Ask if you can help her water the flowers."

I gestured awkwardly between Madison, my car, and where Avalee was already darting away. "I don't wanna stop y'all—"

"It's fine, trust me," she said just as fast, voice pleading. "You wanna come in?" Her face creased in a mixture of regret and hope. "We can sit on the floor and plan out a woman-scorned revenge against me."

Confusion moved through me as I took a hesitant step inside until her words tugged at a memory, forcing a stunned laugh from me.

"I CAN'T BELIEVE you're not screaming over this," I'd said to Madison when she'd explained all about her ex-husband's long-term affair. "Or breaking down—something. I'd be an inconsolable mess, curled up on the floor, planning out a woman-scorned revenge."

. . .

"YEAH," Madison whispered as she shut the door behind me and led the way into the living room. "I imagined you doing exactly that if you ever found out."

"I never did." My head slanted as I amended, "I did end up on the floor a lot . . . just not planning my revenge."

Her smile was all pain when she faced me as we reached the couches. Just as she started to sit, she stopped and asked, "Can I get you anything? Water, coffee . . . whiskey . . ."

An uneasy laugh tumbled from my lips as my hand subconsciously passed across my stomach. My head shook even as the words broke free. "Thirteen years?" One of my shoulders lifted. "You can get thirteen years back for me."

Her glassy stare darted away but snapped back to me and widened when I continued.

"Why did you leave, Madi?" I asked, voice filled with pain and begging to understand. "I hate that it happened at all, and I am absolutely furious for so many reasons. But I am so hurt that all of it led to you being so far removed from my life —from Hunter's life—for *years*. That it ended in so many lies. That it drove Beau to lie to me and keep things from me for so long." I clenched my teeth when my jaw began trembling and gritted out, "If y'all had just told us then, so much of that pain could've been avoided."

Her head shook quickly as she sank to the couch. "I was terrified," she said, looking up at me as tears spilled down her cheeks. "I thought—" Her throat shifted with a forced swallow, her eyes pleading with me to understand. "I know Hunter told you everything, so you already know I thought I was pregnant. Hunter's," she hurried to clarify.

"Right," I acknowledged softly as I sat beside her.

"And even then, Hunter was—gosh, Savannah, he was

everything to me, you know that. I would've found a way to marry him, I didn't care how young we were. But still, pregnant at seventeen was an absolutely terrifying thought. Thinking I was pregnant in the middle of the worst months of my life?" A jagged breath escaped her. "I already felt like I was suffocating, then Beau said he was gonna tell you, and it felt like my world started collapsing. I panicked. I was so sure none of us would survive that, so I did what I thought I had to so at least some of y'all would."

"We would've survived better if you'd stayed."

"I was seventeen," she said softly. "I couldn't see that. I made a mistake, and I'm sorry. I'm sorry that I didn't just let Beau do what he wanted, that I pushed him into lying to you for so much longer. I thought I was protecting everyone. If I could change it all, I would."

I nodded, thoughts drifting as I wondered what our lives would've been like if they *had* told us. If Madison had never left.

How different everything would be then.

"Me too," I mumbled.

"But, Savannah, what's happening between y'all now because of this . . . y'all can't get a divorce. You love him too much to let this be the end."

"I—what? We aren't," I said firmly, surprised that Madison would've listened to town gossip.

She blinked quickly, her stare falling to my hands before searching my face. Her voice uncertain when she said, "Hunter said you gave your wedding ring to Beau . . ."

"Jesus, how many people know?" I asked, groaning out my regret and shame.

"I was with Hunter when Cayson called," she explained,

apology twisting around the words. "He said Beau had texted, asking to buy the condo, or something like that. Hunter and Sawyer met Cayson there to talk to Beau. Hunter filled me in the next day."

My head bobbed subtly before shaking. "It was a mistake —I've been such a mess. Hating that Beau's been gone but not ready for him to come back. Every time he tried talking to me, I either lost it and said the meanest things, or didn't say anything at all when I absolutely needed to speak up."

"I'm sorry," she whispered. "I'm sorry for my part in this."

"I know you are, and I know he is," I breathed, my soul aching as bursts of Beau's agony this past week flashed through my mind. "But I wasn't allowing myself to really deal and come to terms with what happened, so I couldn't see a way of getting past any of it. And I kept pushing and pushing him away while, inside, I was screaming, absolutely terrified I would lose him."

"Tell him this," she urged gently.

"I have." I looked to the side as I thought, a wry smile playing at the corner of my mouth. "In so many words. Somewhere in the middle of talking and crying and yelling and rounds . . ." I mouthed the words *one, two, three,* lifting the respective fingers as I did.

Madison inhaled quickly, expression all surprise and feigned shock. "Savannah!"

A soft laugh rolled up my throat, and for a second, it felt like the old days with her. "We're gonna be great," I said confidently, "it just took me a while. Longer than it maybe should've because I was too afraid to see where we'd end up . . . but we really are fine. And speaking of rings." I reached out for her hand, genuine happiness blooming in my chest as I looked at the diamonds decorating the band on her finger. "Congratulations." I tugged on her hand before releasing it. "I get to say that this time."

Her chest shook with a muted laugh, her eyes studying mine as if searching for any lingering resentment. "You're not mad?"

"At you? God, no. I was shocked when Beau said it and mad that the boys kept it from me until then. But you and Hunter? Madi, that's . . ." I shrugged. "I told you when you came back, that's all I wanted for him and what I want for you, even still."

"Thank you," she said, voice soft and strained. "You have no idea what that means to me—what you being here means."

"Yeah, well, for a while, I kinda thought I'd start screaming when I saw you. So, just so that's out in the open."

"I expected it." Her eyes danced as she leaned against the couch, resting her head in her hand. "Something totally amazing in that Savannah way that can make even the Dixon boys hang their heads in shame."

A laugh burst from my lungs. "Well, I think I got all that out about fifteen minutes ago with Stephanie Webb." My eyes rolled as I said her name.

Madison's eyes and lips popped wide. "Oh my gosh, I heard about the *that*. Poor Beau and poor you. What'd you say to her?"

"Um," I said, voice rising in pitch as I avoided her curious stare. "Some things I probably shouldn't have considering I went after her where Beau works. Which, you know, just so happens to be a school." My tone lowered and quickened as I rambled, "I might've mentioned that she was a whore and never had a chance with him, and the next time she tried to trick someone into fucking her, he should actually be single . . . among other things."

Madison's shoulders bounced with her silent laughter. When she finally caught her breath, she said, "Let the town networking system spread that."

"I'm gonna feel terrible for it later."

She made a face like she didn't believe that. "Eh."

Another laugh left me as I matched her position, relaxing against the back of the couch, facing her. Savoring the feel as the last of the weights left me and were replaced with a deep sense of contentment.

The difference after my afternoon alone in my thoughts had been staggering. But my thoughts and emotions had still been so at war until I'd been faced with finally having it out with Beau.

I knew there were still some things he and I needed to discuss. Clear up. But I felt so at peace after fighting it out with him and the short and simple confrontation with Madison.

"So, what else have I missed, since apparently the Dixon boys like keeping me out of the loop?"

Amusement and affection played on her lips as she thought. "Oh!" she suddenly gasped, leaning forward and tucking her legs up under her. "Oh my gosh, so much has happened."

"Oh my God, are you pregnant too?"

Her head jerked back, a startled look dancing across her face for a moment. "What? No." Leaning forward again, she dropped her voice to a low whisper. "You were so wrong about the whole Hunter-and-Isabel-Estrada thing. And, oh my gosh, the whole *that* with them was . . . friend, it was *whoa*. Raf broke up with the homewrecker not long after getting traded to Dallas, and Avalee's so happy to have her dad here. And he and Hunter are really cool with each other, which makes things so much eas—"

"Wait, wait, wait," I said quickly, holding up a hand as I tried to back through what she'd just said about her ex to the first part. "Hunter and *Isabel?*"

Her eyes widened significantly. "Yeah. So, right before I blurted out everything about that drunken night and the following months to Hunter, I found out he was also in love with Isabel. That they'd been in some kind of extremely long-term, non-relationship relationship before I came back. And I'd ruined that too."

I stared at her for a while, completely dumbfounded. "Why doesn't anyone tell me anything?"

"No one knew," she said with a slow shrug.

Sitting back against the couch, I gestured between us with a finger. "Tell me everything."

———

MADISON'S LAUGHTER slowly faded as she reached for where her phone sat on the table a while later.

"It's *my* Dixon," she murmured with a secretive smile as her finger swiped across the screen.

I gasped and reached for my purse, only to realize I'd left it in the car. Not that it mattered, I was pretty sure I'd left my phone at home when the calls and texts about Beau had gotten to be too much. "Oh God, what time is it?"

She turned her phone so it was facing me. "Someone's looking for you."

. . .

Hunter: Beau called looking for Savannah. She still there?

"I HAVE TO GO," I said, already standing.

Madison's brows pulled tight, but she tried to huff out a tease. "You in trouble?"

A wicked grin slowly crossed my face. "I hope so."

Her mouth fell open and she smacked at me with her phone. "Gross. Gross. I don't wanna know."

"You asked."

"And I regret it! I don't need to know about your thats."

"Speaking of," I said a little too innocently as I headed for the door. "Y'all better be using protection."

"Thanks, Mom," she said dryly.

I turned at the door, failing miserably at fighting my excitement. "Emberly's fourteen weeks, right?"

She squinted her eyes at me, trying to figure out where I was going with this as a hum of acknowledgment sounded in her throat.

"Rae's ten." I let my hand pass over my stomach and added, "Almost seven."

She sucked in a gasp, looking like she was ready to burst from excitement. "Are you serious?"

"You're next, and with those gaps, I'd say you might already be pregnant."

Her expression fell. "I'm gonna need to fit into a wedding dress first."

"Would you be mad?"

"Not even a little bit," she said with a grin. "We're . . ." A sharp exhale left her, and her smile softened. "I'm so lucky,

Savannah. *So* lucky to have him. He loves Avalee, and everything he does is for me *and* her. She's never an afterthought for him. He's also very respectful of the fact that she has a dad even though he already views Avalee as his own. But we very much want kids."

"You . . . want kids with Hunter Dixon . . ." I said sarcastically as I fought a smile. "I never would've known."

She playfully smacked at my arm.

"I'm pretty sure y'all had names picked out for your kids when we were in middle school."

"Okay, but they also changed every year," she reasoned before lifting her shoulder in a little shrug. "But, no, I wouldn't be mad. We're getting started on everything thirteen years late, so we're not trying to put anything off. Just taking some things a little slower for Avalee." She gestured to the side with a jerk of her chin. "Moving in with him. The wedding. But we've been taking her to pick out things for her room at his place a little bit at a time, and we're both gonna stay there this weekend to see how she reacts."

"And a baby takes time," I said thoughtfully.

"Exactly."

"On that note . . ." I gave her a suggestive look and opened the door. "I have a husband waiting for me."

A breath of a laugh left her, but she reached for my hand before I could make it all the way outside, her face falling into something more serious. "Thank you. For coming, for *this*. It means everything."

I squeezed her hand. "I missed you," I said simply as I stepped back, thankful that it felt like the world was finally settling back into place. "See you soon?"

"Please."

I offered her a nod as I turned and hurried to my SUV.

Excitement slowly wound through me and filled my veins as I started up the engine, making the small distance that separated me from Beau and his carnal promises seem so great when I was beyond eager to be there. Making me ache for him long before I ever arrived home.

Thirty-Five

BEAU

I pounded my fist on Sawyer's door, ready to get what I needed and get home.

The last hours of the day had dragged. Taunting me with each minute that crawled by that I was only one minute closer to being home with my wife when I'd mentally never left our bed that morning. That I still had hours and minutes before I could crush her body to mine and show her exactly what she did to me.

Then a handful of minutes before I could leave, I'd gotten an email that everyone needed to be present for a last-minute, all-staff meeting on misconduct.

I'd nearly lost my shit.

"I need Savannah's rings," I said as soon as Sawyer answered the door, already pushing my way inside.

"Where were you earlier?"

"Busy. I told you to bring the rings to the school."

"When?" he asked on an irritated laugh as he finished shutting the door behind me.

"I've been texting you for the last—what the fuck?" I

ground out, my stare narrowing on the vulture who'd shown up a year ago, trying to buy our family's land.

A development company had been sending out someone ever since the year Dad died and Hunter took over, trying to buy up the land and turn it into some retail shit I really didn't care about.

Every year, Savannah and I hosted them at Blossom and joined the entire town in hating every minute they were there. Last year, it'd been the asshole walking across Sawyer's living room, face lighting in recognition when he saw me.

"The fuck?" I repeated, narrowed stare shifting to Sawyer when he placed himself in front of me.

"They're Rae's friends," he said softly, voice low and warning me against reacting the wrong way. "He also helped bring Rae back to me last year."

"Hey," the vulture said, extending his hand. "Beau, right?"

I stared at his hand, forcing myself to count backward.

Trying to remember the conversation I'd overheard him and Rae have in my kitchen, where she'd persuaded him *not* to buy the land. But he was back.

"Yeah," he said with an uneasy laugh as he let his hand fall to his side. "Peaceful visit . . . mostly." Half of his face scrunched up like there wasn't much he could do about that. "Company's sending one of the partners no matter what. I'm the only one who will see that land for what it really is, so I figure it's best if I come."

"But they're just hanging out for a few days," Sawyer added.

"They?"

"My fiancée," the vulture said, pointing over his shoulder. "She's out back with Rae and your mom."

I nodded, still having a hard time trusting the guy. "I need the rings," I said to Sawyer.

"Mom's been freaking out, by the way," he called over his shoulder as he walked away, leaving me with the vulture.

"About?"

"You called her last night when you never call her," he explained, voice fading the farther away he got before slowly getting louder again. "Said she called you back a dozen times, but you never answered, and Savannah wasn't at the house when she went there today. Which, by the way . . ." A broad smile was on his face when he entered the living room again. "Number four. You excited?"

"Hell yeah," I whispered as I held out my hand for the rings I'd forced him to take the night Savannah had given them to me. "You know I am." Dipping my head in thanks, I rocked back a step. "And I need to get back to her."

"Beau Dixon!"

I stilled at that voice and tone, same as it had been my entire life, and looked up, already searching for my mom before she came storming into the living room from Sawyer's kitchen. Hand raised in the air and pointing a finger at me even though she looked relieved.

"I have been *worried*." She sucked in a quick breath and let it out just as fast. "You do not call up your mother in the middle of the night and then ignore every one of her returning calls."

"Yes, ma'am," I muttered, glare dragging Sawyer's way at his hushed laugh.

"Hey!" Rae said when she caught sight of me as she

trailed behind, holding a wriggling puppy in her arms. "How's Savannah feeling?"

My mom looked from her back to me. "What happened to Savannah?"

"When the hell did you get a puppy?" I asked, gesturing to the massive, fluffy beast.

Rae did a little dance, her smile wide as she looked to my brother. "This weekend."

"What happened to Savannah?" Mom demanded.

"She passed out," I answered, trying not to remember the way Savannah had looked when her body went slack right in front of me.

Mom's hand lifted to her chest as she took another couple of steps toward me. "Oh dear. Well, is she okay? What happened?"

"I don't know, she's never done that before."

"What was she doing right before?" a woman I'd never seen before asked as she walked past Rae, looking at me curiously.

"Megan," the vulture explained quickly. "My fiancée. She's a nurse."

"And you're the angry one," she said, lifting her hands in mock excitement. "Yay, we met. Rae kinda gave me a rundown on your wife's situation and what was said over the phone last night, but what was she doing right before?"

I let out a slow sigh as I once again sent a glare my brother's way. "She was standing there."

"Had she been standing for a while?"

"No."

"She needs details, man," Sawyer said.

"She'd been sitting," I ground out. "We were talking, and

she was sitting in the tub. Not taking a bath, just sitting in there without any water."

If Megan thought that was weird, she didn't show it. Just watched me, waiting for the rest.

"She stood up and started walking out of the bathroom, turned to say something else, and her face was drained of color. Lips were chalky. Then her eyes rolled back, and her body went limp."

Megan nodded quickly, taking in the information. "I think she's fine. All the emotional stress the two of you have been going through probably aided it, but from what you're saying, I think her blood pressure just dropped when she stood up."

I nodded, trying to be thankful for the assurance and not focus on the fact that a stranger knew the fucked-up details of my marriage.

"Mention it to her doctor anyway at the next check-up, but if it happens again, I'd call the OB or take her to an urgent care."

"What?" my mom cried out, joy pouring from her. "Oh, my heart with all these grandbabies. And you weren't gonna tell your mother?" she chastised.

"Just found out, Mom." I looked around the room, then dipped my head in gratitude at the nurse before setting a glare on Sawyer as he followed me to the door, my voice a low rumble. "Why's your girlfriend telling people shit they don't need to know?"

A smile flashed across his face, but it was all bared teeth and irritation. "You know by now that it takes a lot for Rae to get personal with people. She talked to Megan because she was worried about Savannah—we both were. Megan did some nurse-interrogation thing to get as many details as possible. I was the one who filled in most the blanks because I know what it's like to feel absolutely helpless when something's wrong with the girl you love," he said meaningfully. "Also,"—his gaze drifted back to where everyone was clustered in the living room, playing with the puppy—"Rae isn't my girlfriend."

My stare snapped to him from where it'd settled on the puppy, confusion pushing through me as I worried for what he'd say next after everything they'd already gone through.

"She's my wife."

I slanted my head, sure I'd heard him wrong. "What?"

A smile pulled at his mouth, slow and unrestrained. "We were falling asleep a couple weeks ago, and she goes, 'If I didn't want a wedding, would you still want to marry me?' Like that's even a factor," he said, eyes rolling even as his joy grew. "Then she asked, 'If I wanted to marry you right now, would you say *yes*?'" He glanced at me. "I've never agreed to something so fast in my life."

"So, you just got married," I said dully, trying to wrap my head around the fact that my youngest brother was married and about to be a dad.

"Couple days later," he confirmed. "Gavin and Faith were there, and that's it. We were gonna tell everyone the next morning at breakfast, but then you showed up, pissed off at everyone. And when Hunter was still outside trying to calm you down, Avalee announced to the rest of us that Hunter and Madison had just gotten engaged, like, the night before." He lifted his hands as if to say there wasn't much they could've done after that, and it was only then I noticed the dark wedding band on his left hand.

Not that I usually noticed that shit anyway, but surely someone would've.

I looked over to the living room, searching out Rae, and saw the diamond flashing on her hand.

"And no one's noticed?"

"Well, no one did at that breakfast. And after that all went down, we decided to hold off telling everyone until things calmed down with y'all. So, we don't wear our rings outside the house anymore . . . for now. But Rae forgot one day, and Mom saw. I thought she was gonna kill me when she realized we'd done everything without telling her."

"Fuck, Savannah might."

"Savannah?" he asked with a huff. "What about Em?"

"Emberly doesn't know?" I asked, amusement building in my chest. "You're screwed."

"Well, if we'd invited her, then we would've had to invite Cayson. If we were inviting Cayson, we might as well have invited all y'all."

My head bobbed in a slow nod. "And you're good with how that went down?"

"Yeah." Genuine happiness poured from him. After a second, he shrugged. "Rae's impulsive and still shuts down when she gets overwhelmed. And there are times when it scares the shit out of me because I like stability and need to know what's going on with the people I love—that they're okay—her most of all. But I know she needs to do things at a different pace. And when she's ready for something, she doesn't ease into it. She dives headfirst in this way that's a perfect mixture of us, and I love it."

I nodded for a while before a huff of disbelief left me. "You're married."

His answering smile was damn near contagious.

Grabbing his shoulder, I pulled him in for a hug. "I'm happy for you, Saw."

"Did you tell him?" Rae asked as she appeared beside us.

"About the puppy?" Sawyer asked. "Babe, he saw her."

Rae smacked him in the stomach and looked pointedly at me, waiting for my reaction.

I just dipped my head as I reached for the door behind me. "Mrs. Dixon."

Excitement burst from her in an instant, her eyes darting back to my brother as she said, "That's my favorite."

Sawyer pulled her close, tone dripping with meaning as he focused on her mouth. "Want me to remind you of my favorite?"

"I'm leaving," I muttered as I opened the door, looking to Rae as I stepped out of it. "Welcome to the family."

My head shook as I hurried down the walkway to my truck, still trying to come to grips with the fact that Sawyer had gotten married. Without telling anyone. Especially Emberly, the girl who had been his best friend since they were getting out of diapers, and who was Rae's sister.

But they'd have to deal with her and Cayson later. They'd have to let Hunter know he'd now missed two weddings.

And I'd have to tell my wife . . . after.

First, I had a hell of a lot of making up to do for making her wait. And even more frustrations and needs that we had to take out on each other.

But by the time I made it home, Savannah's car wasn't there. And when I called her, I followed the ringing of her phone to the kitchen . . . that was empty.

I moved through the house, needing to check even though I knew she wasn't there. But with the way she'd just collapsed the night before, and with her being pregnant, I couldn't stop from searching every room as I pulled up the first of two numbers I thought to try.

"Hey," Hunter answered, sounding confused.

I stopped walking and leaned up against a doorway. "What?"

"What do you mean *what*, you called me."

A harsh breath burst from me. "You answered like you don't know why I would call you."

"I don't think you've ever called me before," he explained dryly.

My eyes rolled. "Just wondering if you've heard from Savannah at all today."

"No, but Mads and Avalee ended up not coming over because Savannah showed up there. She might still be there."

I hesitated before confirming, "Savannah's with Madison?"

"Yeah," he said after a moment as if it had surprised him too. "Considering how long ago that was, I'm guessing it's going well."

I grunted some sort of acknowledgment. "Good," I said as I pushed from the wall.

"Need me to call Mads?"

"No," I said quickly. "Savannah's phone's here, but she isn't, so I was just looking for her."

"All right," he rumbled, sounding unconvinced. "Talk to you later."

I grunted some sort of goodbye as I ended the call and slowly forced my fingers to loosen their tight grip on the phone as fear moved through me, thick and hot, at the possible outcomes of Savannah and Madison talking.

There was nothing Madison could tell Savannah that she didn't already know. But the slightest possibility of sliding backward after the progress we'd made had me anxious. Muscles twitching restlessly and blood thrumming a chaotic beat in my veins as I went back through the house, trying to keep myself busy.

Trying to keep my *mind* busy.

Making a mental checklist of all the things that needed to be done and looking for anything Sawyer might need to fix before people started arriving in a few days for graduation.

But by the time a car door closed out front only a handful of minutes later, I was ready to snap. Needing to see that girl to know I wasn't gonna lose her again when I'd finally gotten her back in my arms.

"Beau?" My name rang through the house before the front door shut, and my eyes slowly closed at the way just the sound of her voice slid over me. Calming me and setting my blood on fire all at once.

"Upstairs," I called out as I finished turning off everything in the guest room I'd been checking, locking the door behind me as I listened to Savannah quickly climbing the steps.

I turned just as she reached the landing, every part of my body instantly reacting to the way she was looking at me. Like she'd been waiting for this and needed me to put an end to her aching. Challenging me, as if she was waiting to see if I'd make good on my earlier words.

"I'm late," she said, breath hitching and golden eyes flaring with heated excitement when I started toward her.

"I noticed."

"I'm home."

A wicked smirk tugged at my mouth as I grabbed the back of my shirt and pulled it over my head. "Noticed that too."

We crashed into each other, mouths fighting for dominance in a passionate kiss and fingers hurrying through every piece of clothing as I walked her backward until we hit a wall. A soft giggle climbing up her throat and getting lost in the kiss and her moans as I tugged her bottom lip between my teeth.

Turning her around, I used my foot to shift her legs wider apart, the head of my cock already pressing against her wet entrance.

A groan of need and appreciation built in my chest when she pushed back against me, her pleas getting lost in her ragged breaths.

I dragged the edges of my teeth down the slope of her neck and nipped at her shoulder, my fingers digging tight into her hips at her responding shudder.

"Savannah—"

"I know," she breathed. "Please fuck me."

She cried out when I took her in one long, hard thrust, the sound intoxicating and making my eyes roll back. My heart racing as I pulled most of the way out to take her again and again before finding my pace. One Savannah matched, her hands pressed to the wall to push back against me, meeting me thrust for thrust.

Until she wasn't.

Until she was leaning back and resting her head on my chest, slowing my movements. "Why are you holding back?"

"You're pregnant."

She turned in my arms and took half a step back to look up at me, a whimper falling from her lips when my body left hers. "And that's stopped us before?"

"You passed out on me last night," I reminded her.

Reclaiming the step she'd taken, she pressed close to me, her stare falling to where my hardened cock was straining against her belly. "I don't break . . . not with you." Wrapping her hands around my length, she started pumping, her grip tightening as she softly demanded, "Don't treat me like I do."

That racing of my heart earlier?

It was unforgiving.

Each beat claiming the woman in front of me was mine. Demanding I take her. Make her scream my name.

I removed her hands and let them fall to her sides before pressing the tips of my fingers to her chest and walking her backward until she hit the wall again. Gliding my hand up her throat, I curled my fingers around her jaw and lifted her head to kiss her.

Slow.

Tormenting.

Claiming.

Making her tremble when I let her lip slowly drag through my teeth.

The corner of my mouth twitched up as I whispered against her lips, "Rough then," before delivering a hard, swift bite there.

She was in my arms and on my cock before her gasp of shock and pain faded away. And then her moans were filling my head, and my name was falling from her lips as I fucked her up against the wall, my hips moving in a harsh, punishing rhythm. She leaned forward, nails digging into my neck as she crushed her mouth to mine.

The kiss fierce and broken by our ragged breaths and her pleas for more.

And I gave myself over to my need for her.

Dragging my mouth across her jaw and down her neck to her breasts. Tormenting her with open-mouthed kisses and sharp, unhurried bites. Gripping her like I could claim her through touch alone. Brand her. Fucking her like I needed her to breathe.

Pushing her higher and higher, her walls clenching

around me until she shattered. Crying out and gripping my shoulders so damn tight, a growl raked up my throat and urged me faster still.

I had my hand around her jaw and my mouth on hers, swallowing her moans and demanding more that she struggled to give around her uneven breaths. Her body vibrating against me and sending little shockwaves through me as I neared my own orgasm.

Every sound and movement she made like a shot of pure, carnal need to my veins. The girl had always been an addiction, one I would never get enough of.

A rumble of warning and absolute fucking ecstasy sounded in my chest when she turned things around, taking my bottom lip between her teeth and biting down hard enough I was sure she drew blood.

My eyes opened to find her watching me, all that earlier heated excitement and challenge burning there.

I crushed my mouth to hers, taking and taking from the kiss even when she tried backing away to catch her breath. My hips losing all sense of rhythm as I began fucking her savagely.

Needing her to feel exactly what she did to me—what she'd always done to me. Needing to bring her to the highs I was already at and knowing I never could because that girl was my world.

A curse fell from my lips, and I stilled when pleasure barreled down my spine, my fingers clenching tighter as I poured my release into her. My world threatening to go red the instant I'd stopped toeing the line and fully given over to the darkness inside me.

But the feel of Savannah's weight and her chest pushing

against mine with each ragged breath grounded me, the same as it always had.

"Every last breath," she whispered.

"And long after I'm gone," I murmured against her collarbone.

A contented hum sounded in her throat but ended abruptly. "I think you're bleeding."

I licked the inside of my lip instinctively even though I'd already tasted the copper. "I know." I lifted my head to press a soft kiss to her lips. "I'll repay you one day."

Amusement tugged at her mouth, her eyes dancing at the thought. "I meant back here," she said, her fingers gliding across my shoulders before she let her head fall back against the wall. Her legs tightened around my waist as she gave me a look that had me hardening inside her. "But you're welcome to repay me now."

"Yes, ma'am," I rumbled as I leaned forward to capture her mouth again.

Just before our lips met, the sound of car doors shutting outside had us going still.

Thirty-Six

BEAU

"That wasn't here," Savannah said softly, voice more of a plea than anything because she knew it was.

"Did you lock the door?"

She gave me a look that was just as confused as it was frustrated. "When do we ever lock the door?"

"Damnit," I groaned as I set Savannah on her feet. "We need to start."

"Everyone has keys anyway," she reasoned as we scrambled to gather our clothes and dress. She slowed from pulling on her pants when the front door opened and listened when their voices echoed from the entryway. "It's Emberly and Cayson. Did you know they were coming?"

I gave her a dry look. "I planned on being buried in you all night. No."

A wicked smirk tugged at the corner of her mouth. "It's still afternoon, we have all night."

"One second," I yelled when Emberly called out for Savannah, then pulled my wife into my arms. "As soon as they leave, we're deadbolting the door, and I'm getting lost in you."

She sucked in a soft breath as heat crept up her neck. "I like that plan."

"Also . . ." I released her to search my pockets, my fingers finally curling around her engagement ring and wedding band. "I was wondering if you'd like these back?"

She sagged against my chest, nodding quickly as she reached for them. "Please."

I helped her put them on, then tipped her head back to steal an unhurried kiss. "Love you."

"So much," she whispered against my lips, then placed her fingers against my jaw to keep me there a second longer. "Thank you."

Amusement rumbled in my chest. "Thank *you*." Slipping my arm around her waist, I stepped back to head for the stairs. "Let's go see what they want."

"Um . . ." She tugged out of my grasp, her face scrunching up adorably. "Tell them I'll be down in a minute."

I watched as she began backing away, my eyebrows drawing close. "They're not here for me."

Her voice dropped even lower as if there'd been a chance of us being heard before. "I'm not gonna be able to talk to them when I have cum dripping out of me."

A sharp laugh left me as I watched her hurry toward our side of the house, then started for the stairs.

When I found Emberly and Cayson in the kitchen, they both stopped talking and turned to watch me.

"We're trying to figure out if we've ever heard you laugh before," Emberly said, eyes narrowing curiously.

"That's nice," I murmured, then settled on the other side

of the island they were standing beside, my stare shifting to Emberly. "Need to talk to you."

Her shoulders sagged a bit. Her tongue darting out to wet her lips as her eyes shifted to Cayson for a second. "I've been trying to help—"

"I know," I said quickly, stopping her from freaking out. "You said something today . . ." I looked at her in question, waiting to hear exactly what it had been.

She studied me for a moment as if gauging my anger, then let out a sigh. "Well, everyone's been talking about this thing with Stephanie as if it's Bible," she said, rolling her eyes. "It was pissing me off. So, whenever I had one of my super gossipy customers or someone who works at the high school or is related to someone who does—well, you know, really just anyone—I casually mentioned how sleazy it was that Stephanie was willing to get you fired just because you wouldn't sleep with her. Which, of course, had them asking questions. So, I told them how she'd basically harassed me at Brewed, revealing that she'd more-or-less been stalking you in the hopes you and Savannah were on the outs. And, Beau and Savannah Dixon being on the outs . . . honestly, that's never gonna happen," she added with a wink. "And how Stephanie had still gone total homewrecker on you at the school, and you'd shut her down."

"Jesus," Cayson said on a hushed laugh, but Emberly looked so damn proud of herself until she focused on me again.

Her expression falling and worry stealing across her features.

"I appreciate it," I said, trying to assure her. "Really. All that shit you said changed everything."

"Really?" she asked, grabbing Cayson's hand and trying to rein in the hope bursting from her.

"Yesterday—" I cleared my throat, my head shaking. "What I did, what I said . . . I shouldn't have done that. You didn't do anything to deserve that."

"Oh my God, are you apologizing to me?"

"No."

She bounced on her toes, her smile wide and blinding. "I think you are!"

My eyes rolled. "Why are y'all here again?"

She leaned into Cayson's side as she grinned up at me. "It's okay, I won't tell anyone."

"Hi, sorry," Savannah said as she hurried into the kitchen, her eyes catching on mine and cheeks burning with heat.

I dipped my head to hide the smirk that tugged at my mouth, but my stare followed her as she moved, all grace and sensuality.

"Hey!" Emberly said excitedly. "We brought y'all food, I almost forgot."

"Again?" Savannah made an admonishing sound. "You're always bringing me something."

Emberly gave her a look as she opened up the large Brewed bag. "This is coming from the woman who is constantly giving to everyone else." She set a two-drink drink carrier on the counter, followed by two food containers, explaining, "This is what I have to give, so let me give it."

"The motion detector hasn't gone off at the condo, so we figured you were here," Cayson said to me as Emberly flattened the bag.

When I glanced his way, he was smiling—all encouragement and happiness for us.

"Oh yeah, he won't be needing that," Savannah said definitively.

Cayson's smile grew. "Glad to hear it."

"Thank you," Savannah said to something Emberly had whispered, head faintly shaking. "I really appreciate this, you're so sweet. But you know I can have caffeine, right?"

"It says not to," Emberly reasoned softly as if Cayson and I weren't intently listening.

"I doubt Rae is following that rule," Savannah said pointedly. "And I'm pretty sure it says you can have a cup . . . or two. But I drank at least a cup a day through my first three pregnancies, and my babies were healthy and perfect."

Emberly's eyes slowly slid my way and widened when she noticed me watching. "Hello."

"I already know she's pregnant." My eyes narrowed on Cayson when he didn't react to the news. "You knew?"

He shrugged.

"Emberly!" Savannah scoffed. "You weren't supposed to say anything."

Emberly's shoulders lifted. "It's so hard not to tell him things. But he didn't tell anyone."

"You should've told me," I said, never releasing him from my glare.

He gave another shrug. "I know when to keep things to myself."

It felt like I took a blow to the chest at his unintentional reminder of what he'd gone through at the hand of our dad. How he'd let everyone think the worst of him instead of revealing the truth for most of his life.

I swallowed roughly just as his expression shifted to excitement, and he looked to Savannah. "Guess what?" At

Savannah's humming response, he looked pointedly at her stomach. "I'm gonna be here this time."

I glanced over in time to see Savannah look from my brother to me, trying so damn hard to control her emotions even as her face crumpled.

I held out an arm and pulled her close when she fell against my chest, a soft sob of joy and everything our baby was doing to her breaking free.

"She's happy," I murmured as I ran my hand up and down her spine.

"I know," Cayson said as he looked to Emberly. "You wanna tell them?"

She bounced on her toes and drummed her hands on the island, looking about ready to explode. "So, I mean, I always love coming here because your house is the absolute best and it smells like a bakery. But we're actually here for a reason." Her bouncing and smile grew as Savannah turned in my arms to face her. "We just found out we're having a girl."

"Oh my God, really?" Savannah gasped as she rushed away from me and over to Emberly, the two talking a mile a minute as Cayson headed my way.

"Girls are the best," I said when he joined my side. "You happy?"

A jagged breath left him as he looked to the ceiling. "So damn happy, man. I cried."

The corner of my mouth lifted as I nodded. "I did too."

"Yeah?" he asked, shocked stare landing on me.

"Every time," I admitted. "When they were born? Fuck." My chest pitched with a muted laugh. "I was a mess."

His own breathless laugh left him as he settled against the counter. "Yeah, that'll be me, no doubt. Y'all gonna find out what you're having this time too?"

"I already know."

He slowly looked over at me, a dent between his eyebrows as he tried to figure out how before he asked, "Did I miss how far along she is?"

I listed my head in response but still said, "With Quinn, Savannah slept almost the entire first few months. I even asked her doctor if Savannah was okay because she was only awake a few hours a day. Then one day, she just popped back up and started running around here like she always had. With the boys?" I tilted my chin to where the girls stood. "Emotions on high. Taking her from one thing to the next faster than I could keep up."

Cayson grunted in affirmation.

"It was weird if we went a day those first few months where she didn't start crying over something random—like not liking the way her keys were placed on her keyring." At Cayson's barking laugh, I mumbled, "I'm serious."

"No, I believe it. I've been around pregnant women before this."

I glanced his way at the cryptic words that hinted at a life I didn't know about, but he didn't explain, so I didn't ask.

We weren't there yet.

"We're having another boy," I said confidently.

When he spoke again, his voice was soft and genuine. "Congratulations, man."

I cleared my throat and looked down, head bobbing quickly. "Yeah, I'm not really all that great at saying that, I guess," I murmured in apology. "Think a part of it is that I'm still trying to wrap my head around everything. It's crazy that my two youngest brothers are gonna be dads. It's crazy that you're *here*."

"In your house or in Amber?" he asked, words a half-assed attempt at a joke.

I gave him a dry look and rolled my eyes when he laughed in response. "Think a bigger part is that—well, probably because I am just an asshole, and I don't always say things that I should to y'all or Mom. But I've always had a hard time talking to y'all the way I can talk to Savannah."

"I get that," he said under his breath, a deprecating laugh creeping from him. "Trust me."

I folded my arms over my chest at the second reminder of what he'd gone through and forced back all the worries and fears that came with it.

"But I'm happy for you," I finally said, voice tight. "Really."

"That means a lot coming from you."

"Coming from you."

God damn if that didn't sting.

But I knew I deserved it and more.

I looked over to where Savannah and Emberly had moved to the table, talking excitedly to each other as they picked at food from the containers. "Was one of those for me?"

"Uh-huh," Cayson hummed, adoration pouring from him.

Amusement tugged at my mouth. "Good. She needs it more than I do."

"We're also going to dinner in an hour."

"She'll eat there too," I said undoubtedly.

He grunted in acknowledgment. "She was getting sick all the time, but she kept saying she felt great. Wanted to keep working all day. Then she was sick a little less and a little less. Next thing I know . . ."—he gestured to the girls—"two dinners." He grinned at me, shrugging. "Whatever she wants, man."

"That's the way it should be," I said in agreement. "So, have y'all told Mom that you're having a girl?"

Cayson's smile turned feral before disappearing altogether. After a while, he tilted his head in denial. "Saw has company, and Emberly wanted to check on Savannah after yesterday, so we came here first. I figured Mom would hear from one of y'all or hear us talking about it at breakfast one weekend. I don't really give a shit how she finds out."

I waited.

Focused on the immediate reaction to his words and demeanor.

Let myself feel it all and let it slowly start fading away before I ever attempted to respond.

"Thought y'all were doing okay." I tried to unclench my teeth when the words came out too hard, too cold, and said, "Saw y'all at Hunter's this weekend."

"I mean, I see her. I talk to her if I have to."

My head moved in a sharp nod as I was dragged back ten years. "Look, I get that I don't know what coming home was like for you. You were pissed at us for not listening, for not believing you—I really get that. Trust me, Cayson." Turning to fully face him, I lowered my voice and said, "We weren't there when all that shit happened to you. But none of us were there when Dad filled Mom's head with a bunch of bullshit about you. And you didn't see her when you *left*."

"Drugs," he said flatly. "She thought I was doing hard drugs. She thought I came back to ask for money or steal it."

"She believed it because we all believed everything Dad said," I said coldly. "After he died, she asked me where she'd gone wrong with you and had this look on her face like there was something she knew about you that devastated her, and I never knew what that was until you came back. But she was a fucking wreck when you left. She and Sawyer moved out of the house because she couldn't stay there anymore with you and Dad not there. And do you know how many times she begged me to go find you? Like I would've gone to find *you*."

His eyes hardened on me.

"I hated you. To me, you ruined all of our lives, and we were fine without you. Sawyer was talking to you, so I knew you were alive." I lifted a shoulder. "That was more than enough for me."

"Thanks," he said tightly.

"Was," I repeated. "I was also wrong, and I'm sorry, Cayson. I'm fucking sorry that I didn't see what Dad was doing, or that you were giving everyone else a version of yourself and hiding *you*. Because, of anyone, *I* should've seen all that," I ground out, regret weaving through my words. "But, Mom? She reacted off what she'd known to be true for at least a decade and guarded herself when you came back, the same as the rest of us did. Then got hit with the truth about Dad, and that shit crushed her. Give her a fucking break. She spent ten years crying to us because you weren't coming home."

Long seconds passed before he weakly nodded. "Yeah." His stare darted all around before settling on me. "Yeah, you're right."

I settled back against the counter and looked over to see Savannah and Emberly watching us as they spoke quietly, Savannah seeming to take in the feel of the room and my mood before smiling softly at me.

"Emberly's gonna be pissed," Cayson said with a huff. "You *actually* apologized to me. Twice."

"Idiot," I mumbled under my breath. "Speaking of

pissed . . ." I glanced over at him. "I already know he has company, I saw them, but y'all should really go see Sawyer."

Suspicion slid across his features. "Why?"

I gave him a look as if he should know better than to expect me to tell him. "You shoulda told me my wife was pregnant."

"And then *I* would've been kicked out of my house," he said blankly.

"Good thing you have a condo."

"Asshole," he muttered, but his mouth was lifting in a grin as he started stepping away. "Hey." He turned back, his smile softening as he looked at me. "I'm glad y'all worked through everything. Really, man, we were all hurting for y'all."

"Me too," I said quietly. "Appreciate your help and the condo. I'll get my stuff out of there tomorrow."

He nodded as he faced the girls. "Em." When she looked at him, he gestured out of the kitchen with his head. "Let's get out of here. We need to swing by Sawyer's real quick."

"Yeah, I dunno how quick it'll be," I said under my breath and bit back a smile when Cayson gave me a questioning look. "Have fun with that one."

"What am I walking into?" he asked, all hesitance.

I just lifted my shoulders.

"Damn it," he hissed as he held out a hand for Emberly.

"I ate your dinner. Sorry, but not really," Emberly said in a rush as she grabbed hold of Cayson's hand and began quickly pulling him away so I wouldn't have the chance to respond.

I just smiled at Savannah as she pressed close to my side and followed them to the door.

Once they'd left, after Savannah and Emberly had said half-a-dozen goodbyes and finished other conversations they'd been having, I locked the door and latched the deadbolt.

"Hey, I thought of something when I saw you and Cayson talking," Savannah began, wrapping her arms around my waist and looking up at me.

I dipped down to pass my mouth across hers, then started leading her toward the stairs. "Yeah?"

"Wait." She pulled me to a stop, eyes wide. "Is that the first time you've really talked to him since he's been back?"

"No. I've seen him a few times these past weeks."

"Oh, well, it was nice to see," she said, a soft smile tugging at her mouth as she started up the stairs. "Anyway, I was thinking . . . you explained last night how you've managed to control everything over the years—how you stopped being afraid of what you might do."

"Right," I said when she looked to me in question.

"But when Cayson came home and exposed everything about your dad, you were terrified in a way I've never seen you." She reached up, gently grasping my shirt. "Beau, you were afraid to be around the kids."

Assent rumbled in my chest as I turned us and started for our room. "That . . . yeah." I scrubbed a hand over my jaw before shrugging, not wanting to voice the thoughts that had haunted me.

"What?"

A heavy breath escaped me after a moment. "When Cayson first explained everything about Dad and said he thought Dad might've been like me as a kid, it scared the shit out of me," I admitted. "The only way I've figured out how to control my anger is to accept and welcome it when it's there. And I kept thinking, what if that's what my dad had done? What if controlling it got to be too much, and he snapped on

Cayson one day, then continued to because he knew he could get away with it? And what if I eventually do that?"

"Beau," she whispered, voice twisting with anguish. "You wouldn't. I know you wouldn't."

"That's how I got past it," I muttered, head nodding absentmindedly. "Because I'd die before hurting one of them."

"You're an amazing dad," she said, eyes searching mine to make sure I was listening.

To make sure I *heard* her.

"Yeah, well, we all thought he was too," I said pointedly.

Her head shook as she grabbed my hand and crawled onto the bed, pulling me with her. "If I'd ever had a second of fear or the slightest hesitation with you, we never would've had kids. And you . . ." She glanced away for a moment, a bright smile creeping across her face. "The kids and I are so beyond lucky to have you."

I fought a smile at the glistening in her eyes and dipped low to place a trail of feather-soft kisses from her lips to her neck, breathing in all that sugar and the faintest hint of cinnamon. "I love you."

"I love *you*."

Brushing my knuckles across her stomach, I asked, "So, what are you thinking for his name?"

"*His*, huh?"

I lifted an eyebrow and looked pointedly at the tears filling her eyes. "Babe."

She glared at me for a moment before understanding fell across her face as she sucked in a slow breath. "Oh . . . oh, that makes sense."

I hummed my agreement and gave up fighting the smile when I said, "And showing up at the school today."

"Okay, but wait . . . that was so not planned, and you know she had it coming."

"I never said she didn't."

"Did she really get fired?" she asked, eyes widening when I dipped my head in response. "What happened, and what does that mean for you?"

I rolled to my side and continued my lazy trail against her stomach. "More or less, we have Emberly to thank . . . and Kevin. All my write-ups were dropped."

"Really?" Relief wrapped around the word and poured from her. "Oh, thank God. I still can't believe any of this happened. I could've punched one of her fake boobs."

A startled laugh burst from me and was echoed by Savannah, all soft and slightly embarrassed.

"I could've. I was so mad," she mumbled, heat creeping up to her cheeks as her golden eyes danced around my face. "Try to get my husband to sleep with her and then say all the things she did and bring the town into it."

"Walking out there and seeing you ready to throw down . . ." A groan built deep in my chest. "Do you know how hard it was to walk you outside and not take you to the nearest empty room and fuck you right then?"

Her next grin was pure sin as she rolled to her knees and pushed me to my back, following me down until she was straddling me. "I know you said all *night*, but—"

"Now," I said firmly, my voice gravel as I pressed her harder against me. "Night starts now."

She reached for my jeans, fingers stilling once she'd gotten the button undone. "Oh! I still love *Kevin*."

"What the fuck?" I demanded, harsh and low.

"For a baby name—for a girl," she clarified as if I should've known what she was talking about.

I dragged a hand over my face, my head shaking quickly. "Savannah, don't ever say another guy's name when you're on top of me. I don't care that we're still dressed."

"It's for a girl," she reasoned.

I lowered my hand and gave her a look. "For the fourth time, we're not naming a baby after Kevin."

"It wouldn't be *after* him. I just love the name."

"Do you know how fucking weird it is every time I see him after we have this conversation? How awkward it would be to say, 'Hey, Kevin. We're naming our baby Kevin . . .'" I lifted my brows, but she just continued to stare at me, not ready to surrender on this one yet. "Besides, I am positive we're having a boy."

"Again, it's not like we'd be naming a baby after him," she repeated. "If I was gonna name our baby after someone, I'd name him after you. Or Hunter or Cayson or Sawyer."

I gripped her hands and forced out a slow breath. "I need you to get off me."

Her eyes widened and a wounded sound left her. "Why?"

"Savannah, you're undoing my pants and naming off my brothers."

"You asked what I was thinking for the name," she said as I gently eased her off me and got off the bed.

"I regret it," I said with a rough laugh. "God, I regret it." I turned to see her sitting on her knees at the side of the bed, eyes slightly narrowed as if I'd asked for it.

My crazy girl.

Closing the distance, I curled my hands around her cheeks and released another slow breath. "The first few months of your pregnancies are always a wild ride. And trust me when I say, I fucking love every single part of you and those rides." I pressed a slow kiss to her mouth and then rested my forehead against hers. "I love you. You are my world. But I need a cold shower now. After that, I'd like to take you on a date."

Her soft inhale was approval enough for me.

"When we come home, as long as you're done naming off other guys, I'm undressing you and burying myself inside you."

"I'm already done naming off people," she assured me.

A smile slowly tugged at my mouth as I pressed another kiss to her lips. "I'm gonna need a minute to recover from that one, angel. Date?"

"Yes please."

"We can talk about all the baby names you want," I promised as I straightened and took a step back just as my phone chimed in my pocket.

Her face scrunched up in indecision. "There are only girl names coming to mind now that you said I'm having a boy."

"Maybe I'm wrong," I said as I grabbed my phone and bit back a curse when I saw the preview of the text.

"You know you're not." Savannah's words came out slow and drawn out as she stood to see what was on my phone. "What's wrong?"

I showed her the screen, not that it would explain anything to her.

SAWYER: *What the fuck man?*

"WHAT'S GOING ON?" Savannah asked as I tapped out a response.

. . .

ME: They needed to know. Hunter needs to know. Y'all will be a hell of a lot happier once everyone does.

LOCKING THE SCREEN, I tossed my phone to the bed and turned to my wife, already preparing for her reaction. "About Sawyer and Rae . . ."

Thirty-Seven

SAVANNAH

A shocked cry escaped me and faded into a soft laugh when large hands molded around my hips and pulled me back into a warm, muscled body a few days later.

Leaning fully into his chest, I let my head roll to the side when Beau started making a line down the side of my neck with his mouth. My eyelids fluttering shut and my hands stilling on the island.

The baked goods forgotten.

"Fuck, you smell good," he growled against my skin before giving a gentle bite.

"Such a bear," I murmured teasingly.

Assent rumbled in his chest and vibrated against my back. "Walking into this kitchen and finding you dancing is one of my favorite things."

I twisted in his arms to look up at him, his dark eyes studying me with so much love, it was staggering. "Really?"

"Yeah." He said the word as if he couldn't understand how I didn't know that. "I know if you're dancing, you're happy. Dancing when you're doing what you love most in the kitchen you dreamed up?" His shoulders lifted as if that explained it all.

The corners of my mouth twitched as awe and love for that man wove through me. "We dreamed up," I corrected.

He gave me a doubting look that was playful and adorable and solely mine. "Two islands and double the size." A smile slowly crept across his face. "That was all you."

"And I was right, wasn't I? I need both of them."

His voice was all easy amusement when he said, "Never said you were wrong, just that the kitchen was all you."

"Well, then, you're welcome," I said as I grabbed a chunk of one of the Danish twists I'd been snacking on and lifted it for him to try.

But then he was slowly taking the pastry from between my fingers while his eyes stayed locked on mine, and I was kind of forgetting everything else and the fact that we had a houseful of guests arriving soon until his eyes widened and appreciation sounded in his throat.

"Babe," he groaned around the bite.

"Right?" I asked and smacked at his hand when he tried to take the rest of mine. "I made them last weekend, and they were gone crazy fast."

He held my hands away and grabbed the last half of the pastry, holding it high up in the air so I couldn't take it back. "You smell like lemon," he said pointedly before taking another bite, silently asking what else I had made.

I pointed over to where I always left the pastries and goodies guests could snack on in pretty dessert displays. "Mini salted caramel Bundt cakes and mini lemon blueberry chiffon cakes . . . and that's mine."

"And it's really fucking good," he murmured, voice all rough and low as he pressed a slow kiss to my lips.

Bringing the twist down to my face, he let me take a bite then backed away until he was out of reach, mouth twitching with a wicked smirk.

"You're so mean."

"Never," he said as he popped the last bit into his mouth, smiling as he chewed when I grabbed another and slid it closer to me.

"This one's mine," I said firmly.

"Yes, ma'am." He ran a hand through his still-slightly-damp hair from his shower, then gripped the edge of the island, muscles rolling and twitching as he held himself up and distracting me completely. "The rooms are ready and the outside's done. What can I help you with?"

I tore my stare from his arms and tried to think, but my thoughts were on him and his body. The way he looked when he held himself above me and how hard he'd made me come that morning before we'd ever left our bed.

"What?" I finally asked, and looked up to see a knowing grin mixing with his heated stare as it searched my face.

"What're you thinking about, Savannah?"

"Nothing," I lied.

A grunt of disbelief sounded in his throat.

When he pushed away from the island, my heart skipped a beat before taking off—all wild and merciless.

When he rounded my side of it, my stomach dipped with heat and anticipation.

When he slipped up behind me again, large hands curling around my hips and gripping the top of my pants, a flash of need rolled down my spine and had chills raising along my skin.

"What were you thinking about?" he asked as he started

pulling my pants over my hips, dragging my underwear as he went.

"You," I said on a breath, my head falling back against his chest. Pushing back against him when I felt him harden beneath his jeans. "This morning."

His fingers gripped my leg for a moment at the reminder before he slowly trailed them back up and dipped them between my thighs.

A shuddering breath tumbled past my lips, and my eyelids fluttered shut . . . just as the front door opened.

"Are you fucking kidding?" Beau ground out and hurried to pull my pants back up from where he'd left them just above my knees.

I struggled to catch my breath when my heart and body were all over the place, then hissed a curse when I realized who was coming our way. "Shit, that's my fault."

Beau's fingers dug into my hips as his forehead dropped to my shoulder. "I'd make them leave if I didn't need him." A groan that was all kinds of frustration sounded from behind me as he moved away, whispering, "Later," as he did.

"Looking forward to it." I met his stare, all carnal need, and prayed I didn't look half as flushed as I felt when Sawyer and Rae entered the kitchen.

"You can't really expect me to let her come over without me, all things considered," Sawyer said with a shrug.

"I only called her for a reason," I said, pointing at Rae. "And I still can't believe y'all got married without telling me. You assholes."

"Which is why she isn't here alone."

"I'm pretty sure I hate both of y'all," I continued even as I grabbed a couple Danish twists for them.

"You have your tools?" Beau asked after he finished

turning the music down, eyes narrowed on Sawyer for the interruption. "I can't get a spigot out back to stop leaking."

Sawyer looked at me as if gauging what I planned to do with Rae before sighing. "Yeah, give me a second."

I slid one of the twists toward Rae, then started setting up some of the others exactly how I wanted them in the display case as she slowly started toward me. "So, how long do you think you'll hate us? Because Emberly said 'forever.'"

A laugh bubbled free. "Of course she did." My head shook slowly as I met her worried stare, a soft smile playing on my lips. "I don't. I am so bummed I didn't get to see that boy get married, but I'm also incredibly excited for y'all. And I get it," I added encouragingly. "Emberly does too."

"This isn't poisoned then?" she asked as she brought the pastry closer to her, a mischievous glint in her eye.

I gestured to Beau with a jerk of my head. "He's still standing."

"Comforting," she said sarcastically, then offered him a playful grin before looking at me. "Are you guys missing the kids? It's so quiet in here."

"Too quiet," Beau added.

"We miss them so much," I said. "We've been FaceTiming them a couple times a day. They're having so much fun, and we're grateful that my parents gave us this time together. We needed it."

Beau grunted in agreement. "But we're ready for them to be home."

"Few more days," I said with a sigh, then gave him an encouraging smile.

"Well, I'm glad the two of you were able to have some time alone," Rae said with a nod. "Not that I know what it's like the other way, but . . . you know."

"You'll know soon," I said, my smile widening in response to the one that stretched across her face.

"That's true—oh!" she gasped. "Before I forget, Nathan said to tell you 'hi.'"

I thought for a moment before asking, "Who?"

"Nathan—" She sighed and cut an expectant look at Beau before clarifying, "The vulture."

"I told her," he said unapologetically.

"Right, no, I knew he visited. I just didn't remember his name," I said quickly. "I think it's nice that he's still volunteering to come when he has no intention of doing anything about the ranch."

She made a humming sound that was pure hesitation, her gaze darting around before falling to where she was picking pieces off the twist.

"Rae . . ."

She put the pieces down and met my stare. "You know your house? Not this one," she amended quickly, "the one you grew up in—next to the Dixons'?"

I quickly glanced to Beau when her tone had unease settling in my stomach. "Yeah?"

"I don't know if you knew, but the people who bought it from your parents have always told that developing company that they would sell their property when Hunter sold his land. I think because they knew Hunter wouldn't, but I'm not sure."

"I didn't know that," I said as my unease grew.

Because if they'd changed their minds and sold, and if that company started building something right next to the Dixon land and orchard, it would already start changing everything about our town.

"Well, Nathan got a call from one of the owners of the

company last night."

"They're selling it?" Beau ground out.

Rae's hands lifted as she hurried to go on. "They called the company first to see what they would offer before putting their house on the market, and Nathan was told to go out there before he left. And he did. This morning."

Beau mumbled a curse as Rae continued.

"But it's *Nathan*, so he told them their property was worthless without the Dixon land and made them a horrifically low offer that he knew they wouldn't accept. But . . ." She released a shaky breath and said, "I want to know if it'd be okay with you if Sawyer and I bought it."

A shocked laugh punched from my lungs. "What?"

"Sawyer keeps saying it isn't a big deal, but that's the house you grew up in, and I don't know how you'd feel about that," she rambled quickly. "I don't know if that's weird or absolutely not okay—I'm not familiar with these things."

"Rae," I said softly and waited until she'd taken another calming breath. "I'd much rather y'all be in that house than anyone else. Especially people who would sell it to a company that would destroy it."

"Are you sure?"

"I'm positive." I gestured off to the side. "I know my parents will say the same. But you didn't need to ask, that hasn't been my house for a long time."

She looked at me helplessly. "Seeing how protective everyone has been with Hunter's house and the land is the first family-attachment experience I've had with a house. I just didn't want to do anything that would upset you."

"You won't, I promise."

"I told you," Sawyer said as he came back into the kitchen, carrying a toolbox. "By the way, we're buying your old house before someone else can," he told me with a cheeky grin. With a kiss to Rae's shoulder, he continued through the kitchen and followed Beau outside.

"So, you're buying a house," I said softly as I placed the clear lid on the display case and then carefully carried it over to the other counter. "In Amber, Texas." Smiling at her once I had the pastries where I wanted them, I added, "And you married a terribly stubborn Dixon."

"I did," she said, joy lighting her expression.

"When you showed up here a year ago, I would've never guessed any of that would be in the future for y'all. But I'm so glad for it—all of it. You're perfect for him and this family, Rae."

The corners of her mouth tipped up shakily, and she looked away, still clearly uncomfortable when anyone mentioned family and her. But it was different than how she'd been a year ago.

Not as haunting.

Not pushing her into fight-or-flight in an instant.

Slowly getting more and more used to the idea of having a family—of letting people love her.

"I have something for you, and I hope it's okay," I said as I hurried to the other side of the kitchen and grabbed the small box I'd stashed away, my tone all understanding and encouragement when I faced her again. "I understand if it isn't."

She straightened and carefully set her features into her impenetrable mask when I set it on the island beside me. "Okay."

"When I was growing up, my mom had this necklace that I loved," I began. "I used to play with it all the time when I was a kid, and I always tried to sneak off with it in the rare times she took it off, as if she wouldn't know it was missing." Sorting through the necklaces I wore, I found the chain I was looking for and pulled out the large locket from beneath my shirt. "On my wedding day, she gave it to me."

"It's beautiful," Rae said, voice still somewhat guarded as she held the oval shape in her hand, looking at the engraved whorls and flowers.

"She told me her mom had given it to her on *her* wedding day, and if I was lucky enough to have a daughter, I could do the same." The corner of my mouth tugged up as I grasped the metal. "And the best part?"

Opening the locket, I carefully turned it over so the three pieces of folded up paper fell into my palm.

"Love notes?" she asked, a hint of a tease weaving through.

"Not exactly." I smoothed out one of the small papers and turned it so it was facing Rae. "This is my mom's."

"His voice," she read aloud, then looked at me in question.

A snort left me as I opened the oldest paper. "My grandma—who, by the way, repeatedly hit my knuckles with a wooden spoon because of the sinful things I'd done with a young and devilishly handsome Beau Dixon—wrote this one."

"His bottom." Rae looked at me, eyes wide and amused, before a laugh escaped her. "What are these?"

"What first attracted us to our husbands," I explained as I opened up mine.

"His—" She paused and then let out a sigh as her stare shifted to mine, smile soft and wistful.

His heart.

"I love that," she whispered.

"Yeah." I echoed her tone as I carefully folded up the

papers and placed them back in the locket. Once it was shut, I reached for the box beside me. "Rae, I know your family was terrible and things with your mom—well . . . I love that you found our family," I said simply.

Her head shifted subtly, all that unease bleeding through.

"I hope over time, we can show you what family is supposed to be like, but I know it won't make up for what you went through. Anyway," I said as I handed her the gift, "I was at the boutique about a month ago, and I saw these— they just started selling them."

Rae lifted the top of the box and stilled when she saw the necklace. The large silver locket that was nearly the same size and shape as mine, with swirls etched into the metal that made them look nearly identical.

"And now that you're my sister too, I wanted to give you this so you could start the tradition in your family, if you wanted."

For long moments, she just stared at the necklace before her head slowly lifted, tears clinging heavily to her eyelashes and slipping down her cheeks.

"I don't . . ." Her head shook slowly as she pressed her lips into a firm line. "Savannah, I don't know what to say."

"You don't have to say anything," I assured her. "If it makes you uncomfortable, you don't even have to take it."

"I want it," she hurried to say. "I want it—thank you. Can I put it on?" The question was all uncertainty as she held the box in front of her like she had no idea what to do with something like that.

"Of course."

I took the box from her when she got the necklace out and watched as awe tugged at her mouth once she had it hanging around her neck and was cradling the locket in her palm.

"Open it," I suggested casually.

Her glassy stare darted to mine before falling back to her hands as she carefully opened the locket. A breathless laugh leaving her when a blank strip of paper fell out.

"Well, Ms. New-York-Times-Bestselling-Author," I said as I stepped away to grab a pen, "what first attracted you to your husband?"

She rolled her eyes as she accepted the pen. "It's nothing as romantic as *his heart*, I'll tell you that." Taking the cap off, she leaned over the island but paused with the tip of the pen to the paper. Her bottom lip caught between her teeth as her stare drifted to the side, a muted laugh shaking her shoulders. "You know, until this moment, I was sure it was his eyes or his dimples," she said as she wrote something down and then handed the pen back to me.

"That family and their dimples," I whispered.

Rae hummed in acknowledgment. "But that wasn't it," she said as she showed me the paper before carefully folding it.

"His *irritability*? Are you serious?"

"I'm so serious," she said as she shut the locket.

"But he was the worst when you first arrived."

"I know." She lifted a shoulder as she leaned up against the island, expression faraway as she seemed to think back. "But I couldn't stop thinking about how infuriating he was, and it made me want to see him again to see what he would do the next time and the next time."

I lifted my hands, then started clearing off the island so I could clean up from all the baking. "Hey, whatever worked for you, I'm just glad it did."

By the time we had everything put away and the counter cleaned, and Rae had stolen another couple of twists to take home with them, the guys were coming back inside.

"Answer's no," Beau said, sounding like he was getting frustrated with having probably repeated himself.

"You're not even gonna let me try it out?"

Beau shot him a hard look as they continued toward the kitchen. "What'd I say?"

"What's going on?" I asked as I folded my arms under my chest, eyes narrowing on the two of them.

Beau gestured to his youngest brother. "He wants to take their new dog with him on jobs—which means *here*."

"No," I said with a scoff. "We don't have animals for a reason. Then there would be fur and a smell—no. And if you want more than one kid, don't try sneaking it past me either."

A ghost of a smile crossed Beau's face as he turned to look at Sawyer. "As I said."

"Good Lord." Rae reached out, grabbing my arm. "He smiles."

I hummed in acknowledgment and sighed. "That was nothing."

"Wow," she mumbled.

"I can hear you," Sawyer said, arms out at his sides and eyes wide. "And I'm never letting you near any of my brothers again."

Rae gave me a knowing smile and then looked back at him, all affection and amusement, but her words were for me. "I do love his unnecessary caveman moments." Touching just beneath her bottom lip, she asked Sawyer, "Is my lipstick smeared?"

I looked at her lipstick-free lips, confusion sweeping through me.

But Sawyer was already stalking through the kitchen and reaching for her with the hand that wasn't holding his tool-box. "We're leaving," he said, voice rough and telling in a way that had me wishing I wasn't present for whatever moment they'd just stepped into. "Now."

Rae smiled victoriously as she let him start pulling her away, hurrying to grab up their pastries and then stopping in front of me as her expression shifted to something raw and slightly vulnerable. "Thank you," she said on a breath. "Thank you so much."

"I'm so happy for you—for both of y'all." I squeezed her arm since her hands were full and said, "Let me know what happens with the house."

Excitement lit in her eyes. "We will. We're going there now."

"After," Sawyer corrected.

"Gross," I said, shoving him away. "You can leave now."

Rae's throaty laugh lingered as they hurried out of the house, calling out goodbyes as they went.

No sooner had the door closed than Beau was pulling me into his arms and lifting me, his mouth on my neck as my surprised giggle filled the kitchen.

Placing me on the edge of the island, he stepped between my legs and ran his hands up my thighs to grip my butt, pulling me as close as possible. "Is it *later*?"

"I sure hope so," I said as I wrapped my arms around his neck and leaned in to press my mouth to his.

When the doorbell sounded through the house, a whimper of frustration rolled up my throat, and Beau's fore-head fell heavily to mine.

"I'm not ready," I mumbled and let my fingers gently trail along his neck.

"We were waiting for them to show," he reminded me even though his tone said that he agreed, that he wished we could have another hour to ourselves.

"I know, and I love it. I just—" I sighed and leaned back, studying all that sexual frustration bleeding from him that only amplified my own.

But that was just how our lives went.

Savoring the very rare moments we were truly alone and trying to steal private moments between Blossom guests and three kids and family stopping by at random. The latter happening more and more often with the fracture between the Dixon family finally healing.

"Later?"

"Looking forward to it," I said, repeating my earlier words.

He pressed a quick kiss to my mouth and helped me down from the island. "Let's live that dream."

Epilogue

SAVANNAH

A whispered moan teased my lips when Beau's large hand gently curved over my swollen stomach and his mouth passed across my neck.

"You need to sit down."

I swatted at his chest dismissively at his umpteenth request. "I will when we eat."

"Savannah." My name was all a rumbled disapproval.

"Bear, I've had three kids, and I practically lived in here with each of them too."

"Not doing *this*," he argued softly, gesturing to where our kitchen was filled with Thanksgiving desserts and dinner prep. The hand on my stomach moved in a slow circle. "Not with *this*."

I let out a breath, trying to be understanding even if he was being unreasonable. Well, my version of unreasonable.

"I let you put the turkey in the oven, and I'll let you take it out," I said as if that had been a great sacrifice for me.

His midnight eyes searched my face, showing exactly how much he wanted to force me to do what he was asking.

I lifted a brow. "Are you gonna finish making all this food?"

A laugh scraped up his throat. "Yes. If you'd just let me."

"Well, I'm not letting you. So . . ." I gave him a look, daring him to make me leave my spot in the kitchen.

"If you're not helping, you're in the way," my mother-in-law said as she came back into the kitchen, shooing at Beau. "Go on and get."

I smiled to assure him I was fine and asked, "Where are the kids?"

"Levi crashed about ten minutes ago. Quinn and Wyatt are watching a movie." He took a few steps back but gestured to me. "Mom, Savannah needs to sit down."

"I'm fine."

"Why?" his mom asked, then looked to me, shrugging. "She's fine. She'll sit if she needs to."

"It's like I've never been pregnant before," I muttered as I went back to prepping the dressing.

"You've never been this pregnant during a major holiday," he said. "Your doctor also said you needed to take it easy."

I pointed at him, sucking in a gasp at the betrayal. "You said you wouldn't say anything, and she also said I was okay to host Thanksgiving."

He gave me a look that was a perfect mixture of adoration and frustration. "Babe, she's never seen you host anything. And she only said *host*. Not bake and cook all day."

"Wait, what'd your doctor say?" his mom asked, turning to look at me. "Is everything okay?"

"Of course," I said just as Beau said, "Mostly."

I stomped my foot and gave him a wide-eyed look. "Beau Dixon, you are in so much trouble right now."

He lifted a brow, the action so subtle but saying so much. He didn't care because he wanted to take care of me.

His mom pointed between us. "All right, someone tell me what's going on with my daughter-in-law and grandbaby."

Beau waited to see if I would explain, and I knew if I didn't say anything, he would.

So, with a sigh, I said, "I sort of—"

"Did," he claimed.

"I *went* into early labor this last weekend. *But*," I hurried to add, "they stopped it, and we're both fine. My doctor said I could still carry to full term."

"But you're supposed to be taking it easy," Beau said firmly.

"And you've been—*Savannah*," my mother-in-law chided. "Go. Get." She gestured to Beau. "Get her on the couch. I can't believe you've let her be in this kitchen all day."

Beau looked at her like she'd missed something important. "I've been in here all day trying to get her out of it, and y'all keep making me leave."

"Well, now *she's* leaving." She grabbed a hand towel and smacked him with it. "How dare you keep these kinds of things from your mother."

He lifted his hands, then let them fall to his sides as he followed me out of the kitchen.

"You are in so much trouble," I repeated once we were in the living room.

"I don't care," he said easily as he helped me onto the couch and then sank to my side, his hand tenderly resting on my stomach. "I know you want to, but you shouldn't be doing all that. You can't, Savannah."

"I feel fine," I said for what had to be the thirtieth time

that day, then gestured to my stomach when the baby hit just below where Beau's hand rested. "We're fine."

Beau's hand shifted lower, his eyes tracking the movement. "He rolling?"

"Yeah, I think that was an elbow." A sound of discomfort rose in my throat before I could try to swallow it back, and Beau's stare snapped to mine.

"You're not fine," he said softly, confidently. "You wanna be because you thrive on these kinds of days. But I see it in your eyes when you think I'm not looking at you, and I hear it in your voice. I heard *that*."

"You don't understand . . ."

"I do. You wanna be running around, taking care of everyone once they get here. And you wanna make sure everything's done and perfect before they do. I know." He placed his other hand on my stomach so he was cradling it. "But right now, I need you to take care of him and take care of yourself."

"Okay, I will sit down for the rest of the night if you just let me finish—"

"No." When my lips parted to keep pleading my case, he said, "My mom's here, she can do it. I'll help."

"Your mom is a really amazing cook, but she doesn't make things the way I do, and I left a bunch of things half-done without telling her what I'd done to them."

Beau stared at me for a long moment before letting out a harsh sigh and pushing to his feet.

Without a word, he stalked across the living room and picked up one of the plush chairs, carrying it over to set it down in front of the large, round table. Seconds later, he was carrying the matching ottoman over to situate it in front of the chair.

"You can tell us what to do from there," he said as he helped me up from the couch, voice low and firm, "but you're not getting back in that kitchen tonight."

"Deal," I said, sure I'd be at the stove sooner rather than later.

I HADN'T EVER GOTTEN BACK into the kitchen, and as soon as people started arriving, I'd been transferred back to the couch.

It felt wrong to sit around while people came into my home. To not get up and greet them and offer them a drink or something to snack on. But, between taking over my kitchen and making sure I didn't move, Beau had made sure I was absolutely catered to while his mom had taken over greeting the rest of the family.

"You went into early labor?" Emberly asked as soon as they arrived, looking like she couldn't figure out if she was more worried or jealous. "I just wanna go into labor." When I looked at her in question, she explained, "Doc told me."

Madison handed me a water and asked her, "How many days past your due date are you?"

"Six," Emberly said with a sigh as she rested her hands on her stomach. "She doesn't wanna come out."

"I went long with Quinn," I offered, trying to comfort her.

"Same with Avalee," Madison added. "She'll come soon."

"I just wanna see my feet." A small laugh left Emberly, but it sounded exhausted. "And sleep. I would like to sleep."

I placed the cup in front of my mouth and swallowed back the laugh that tried to break free.

Emberly didn't need me telling her she wouldn't be

getting much sleep after the baby was born either. I'd always hated when people told me that when I was huge-pregnant and tired.

"When did you have your appointment?" I asked, since it had to have been in the last few days.

"Yesterday afternoon." One of her hands moved tenderly over her stomach. "And *nothing*. She said I'll be good through the weekend, at least. Peeing," she said abruptly. "I'd like to stop peeing every five seconds too."

I looked at Madison when Emberly waddled away to find her losing the fight on covering her smile. "When I had that appointment she's talking about, I had Quinn the next day."

"I had Avalee that night," she added, eyes wide. "My doctor swore I was probably gonna have to be induced after another week. But . . ." She lifted her hands and then patted her barely-there baby bump.

I moved my feet to the floor, my eyes already searching. "I'm pretty sure we're having a baby tonight."

Madison grabbed my shoulder and then pointed at the couch. "Stay there so we don't have *two*."

I huffed a sigh and relaxed against the couch again as I looked around the room until I found Cayson just a handful of feet behind me, talking with his and Emberly and Rae's moms and stepping out of the way when the kids came running through, screaming and being all kinds of wild.

Hunter caught Avalee's shoulders before she could get much farther and said, "Lotta pregnant women. Y'all go run somewhere else, yeah?" As soon as they were off again, he continued toward us. "Y'all need anything?"

"I'm great," Madison said as I asked, "Did Beau send you?"

"Can I not check on my wife?" he asked as he pulled Madison into his arms, feigning offense. But after another second, he admitted, "Yeah."

"I need to get off this couch," I said miserably, then waved Cayson over when I caught his eye.

"You okay? You need anything?" he asked as he hurried over, and my narrowed eyes shifted from him to Hunter.

"He's just worried about you," Madison said, trying to pacify me.

"I know, but I'm not on bed rest yet. And it feels like he's trying to put me on it early."

"Well, if you hadn't spent an entire day in the kitchen, maybe you wouldn't be confined to your *that*."

A smile tugged at my lips despite my desperate need to leave the couch and rush around my house, doing everything myself. "Maybe you should be confined to my *this* with me, and we'll see how long until you go crazy. Anyway!" I shifted my focus back to Cayson, but he was looking around, his brow pinched tight.

"Where's Emberly?"

"Bathroom," Madison and I answered at the same time, then I asked, "Do y'all have her hospital bag?"

Surprise and worry replaced everything in an instant as his head snapped back to me. "In the truck. Why?"

"She's fine," I said quickly. "But she's probably not making it through dinner."

"What do you mean? Why?"

"Take a breath," I said softly and grabbed his hand. "Emberly is fine. Madison and I are just guessing from experience that y'all will be getting ready to have a baby by the end of the night."

"Savannah."

I looked up to see Beau quickly approaching us.

"I would really love to get up." My hopeful smile faded when he handed me his phone. "Who—hey, why aren't y'all here?" I demanded when Sawyer's face filled up the screen.

He scrunched up one side of his face and asked, "Is it cool if we don't come?"

"No, it's absolutely not *cool*. Y'all have to be here."

He pulled the phone farther away, showing off the tiny bundle cradled in his arm. "How about now?"

"Oh my God!" I cried and held the phone out for Madison and his brothers to see. "Oh my God, wait! But it's early—what happened? Is he okay—is *Rae* okay? Where is she? What's his name, and why didn't y'all tell anyone Rae was in labor? Oh my God, Saw, you're a dad."

Sawyer's proud smile beamed over the phone as he waited for me to finish my super-fast ramble. "His name's Griffith. Everyone's great. He's healthy. Rae did fucking amazing."

"Little ears," I chastised halfheartedly.

A low laugh left him. He turned the phone so I could see where Rae was asleep in the hospital bed. "She did great," he said again. "He just decided today was the day he was coming. If he doesn't drop too much weight, he won't need to go to the NICU, and we'll be able to go home in a couple days."

"Oh my God," I said again, my chest warming and feeling too small for my heart. "Sawyer, I can't believe it. I'm so excited for y'all." My stare dragged to the side when Cayson suddenly rushed away and landed on where Beau was talking to my mother-in-law, who looked like she was going to burst from excitement.

"Emberly's water broke," Madison whispered from behind me.

My chest pitched with a huff as I looked up at her. "There might just be two tonight after all."

She squeezed my shoulder, then said louder, "Sawyer, you're pretty and all, but we wanna see that baby again."

Sawyer carefully positioned the phone to show off the sleeping baby in his arm, smile all wonder and unconditional love as he looked down at him.

"Griffith is beautiful," I said softly. "Tell Rae we're so proud of her and happy for y'all."

"I will," he mumbled as he continued watching his son sleep.

"Oh, and if in . . . about half an hour or so, you hear someone cussing you six ways to Sunday between screams of pain, that would be Emberly pissed off that y'all didn't let her know Rae was in labor." I pointed off in the direction Cayson had gone. "Emberly's water just broke."

Excitement and shock covered his face as he looked up. "No shit?"

"Little ears," I reminded him.

"He's sleeping." A smirk tugged at his mouth. "Tell Em to hurry her ass up. We've always said we were separated at birth. It's only right if our kids are born on the same day."

"I'll be sure to tell a woman in labor that," I said dryly and smiled at Beau as he came to sit beside me on the edge of the couch.

He gripped my free hand, his pinky absently tracing the angel wings on my wrist. "Happy for you, man," he said to Sawyer, tone dipping as if he'd already said it before. "Try to sleep. We'll see y'all soon."

Sawyer nodded, his stare already fixated on the bundle in his arm again. "Later."

I sighed and leaned against the back of the couch when Beau ended the call, unable to contain all the happiness filling me. "Can't believe it."

Beau grunted in agreement. "And now Cays . . ." A smile ghosted across his face as his stare flashed up to Hunter. "You ready for that?"

"So ready," Hunter said, smile wide and excitement pouring from him as his fingers trailed over Madison's small bump. "And Avalee's fucking ecstatic."

A soft laugh bubbled past Madison's lips as she imitated her daughter, "Is my sister here yet?"

"Every day," Hunter said in agreement.

"That doesn't change, no matter how many kids you have," I said, looking to Beau when he reached out to tenderly hold my stomach.

"Our day will be here soon."

A contended hum sounded in my throat as I brushed my hand past his. "Hopefully not too soon."

"Let me take care of you, and we'll make it to where we're supposed to." His dark eyes searched mine, pleading.

My eyelids shut for a moment as I reluctantly nodded. "Okay."

"No more trying to sneak into the kitchen?" he confirmed, all amused disbelief. "No more cleaning and fixing things around the house every time you go to the bathroom?"

"I mean, that's a lot to promise."

He dipped in closer to press his forehead to mine. "Savannah . . ."

"Okay, I promise." My claim was nothing more than a breath as his mouth teased mine.

"Thank you," he said on a sigh. With a soft kiss to my lips, he sat back, relief pouring from him. "I love you."

"Every last breath."

The End

Look for more *Brewed* novels from Molly McAdams!
Fix
Whiskey
Glow

Coming soon . . .
From New York Times bestselling author, Molly McAdams, comes a new, captivating series that follows five girls sharing a house in the heart of Hollywood who all have secret lives of their own. From following passions, to loving freely, to working scandalous careers, the Secrets in L.A. series is filled with excitement, romance, and lies.

Acknowledgments

Cory—As always, thank you for being my constant support. Everything I do is possible because of you. I love you!

Molly and Amy—A massive thank you for the never-ending support and encouragement. Your friendships mean the world to me. I don't know what I would do without the two of you.

Molly's Monsters—Y'all are literally the best group on Facebook. Thank you for all your support, encouragement, and the amazing uplifting spirit y'all have created in there.

Samantha, Letitia, & Shannon—Thank you, thank you, thank you for making this book what it is! From the photo to the cover to the edits . . . you're all such rock stars!

Dad & the Coles—Thank you for all the amazing insight into your lives to help make this series what I want it to be. The Coles, I've always loved your gorgeous Plantation House —getting married there was a dream! However, I'm totally obsessed with the transformation into the boutique inn. It's amazing *and* the perfect inspiration for Blossom B&B. Dad, you're pretty much the best ever. Thank you for enduring countless questions as I tried to uncover your produce business and farming expertise so I could make the Dixon's orchard *just* right with little hints of your lifetime achievements. Love you!

About the Author

Molly grew up in California but now lives in the oh-so-amazing state of Texas with her husband, daughter, and fur baby. When she's not diving into the world of her characters, some of her hobbies include hiking, snowboarding, traveling, and long walks on the beach . . . which roughly translates to being a homebody and dishing out movie quotes with her hubby. She has a weakness for crude-humored movies and loves curling up in a fluffy blanket during a thunderstorm . . . or under one in a bathtub if there are tornados. That way she can pretend they aren't really happening.

Made in the USA
Las Vegas, NV
29 April 2023

71307978R10298